THE OAK GROVE CHRONICLES

A Summer Long Remembered

Tate Publishing
& Enterprises

The Oak Grove Chronicles: A Summer Long Remembered

Visit www.tatepublishing.com for more information.

Cover design by Sommer Buss
Interior design by Kristen Polson

Published in the United States of America

ISBN: 1–5988628–4-7
06.09.13

THE OAK GROVE CHRONICLES

Sharon Travers

A Summer Long Remembered

Tate Publishing & *Enterprises*

Dedication

To my husband, Bill, who believed in me. Thank you for your love, patience, and support through these many months of writing.

To my children: Johnny, Laura, Shari, and Jimmy. Thank you for your unfailing love, standing with me through bad times as well as good, and providing me with such wonderful memories without which I could not have created these characters and penned these words. Carry this story in your heart, for it was written for you.

"And now these three remain: faith, hope and love.
But the greatest of these is love." I Corinthians 13:13 (NIV)

Walk With Me to Yesterday

Oak Grove, a small Midwest rural community, is found only in the memory of one blessed with the experience of living in a time long perhaps forgotten. It was a time when no one locked their doors, children were safe to ride bicycles across town, play in the yard after dark, and dream of what tomorrow would bring. A handshake between two men sealed an agreement, and one's word was accepted as truth. Neighbors called to each other across the yard and carried one another's burdens.

Violence was not a part of Oak Grove. There was an innocence and freedom in that small town that is hard to find today. Faith in God was a way of life that sustained us, blessed us, and filled our hearts with love for each other and our Creator.

I am writing these Oak Grove Chronicles for my grandchildren and for you. The stories are fictitious but based on memories that run very close to real experiences. I hope you enjoy them, and perhaps if nothing more, may they jog your memory to a time long ago or give you a glimpse of a time that was very special.

Sharon

Preface

August 25, 1830, seven families stood on a mountain ridge overlooking a valley in the foothills of the Ozark Mountains. They packed their belongings, bid farewell to those who chose to remain, and began a journey none of them would ever forget. Their hearts' desire was a life of peace. Leaving behind the lawlessness that had overtaken their town, this small band of determined people pledged to one another, with God's help, they would find a better place to raise their children. That had been three months ago.

Oliver Madison, lost in thought, stared at the flame in the oil lamp pondering the evening's conversation. He had known it was coming and should have been prepared to give a definite answer, but nagging doubts still plagued him. His friends had hinted at the idea in numerous ways over the last several weeks but never came right out and asked. The weight on his shoulders increased as Oliver watched them gradually assume he would lead them on the journey.

"Time is running out, Brother Madison," Elmer Driscol said, glancing at the others. "We plan to set out in three weeks, and we sure would feel comforted knowing you and Daisy were going with us." Elmer sat back in his chair and looked across the table at Robert Miller.

"I can move the wagons along and choose good campsites," Robert commented, studying his pastor's face. He absentmindedly moved the old worn black Bible back and forth on the table. "We need someone to keep us on the right track through trying times. We need a leader that will keep us grounded and looking to the Lord for guidance."

Louis Seabaugh propped a muscular arm on the table and looked at Oliver. "We figured you would be our best guide being a preacher and all," he commented with a sheepish grin.

"I do not believe I have any more of a direct line to the Lord than you do, Louis," Oliver replied, glancing around the table at his friends. The thought crossed his mind that they looked more like six small boys than grown men. "Give me one more night to pray on it," he implored, wanting release from the doubts that consumed him.

He stood on the porch and watched as they took their leave, noting the relief in their eyes that he wished he shared. Dusk settled on the town as the sun dropped behind the hills, and he gazed down the street knowing it would soon be filled with boisterous laughter that would turn to arguments which would develop into fights. He sighed and retreated inside, wondering on Daisy's thoughts.

That night Oliver found no sleep. He had to be positive, with no shadow of doubt, that leaving was the Lord's will. Responsibility for thirty-nine people, traveling an undetermined length of time and distance to an unknown destination, weighed heavily on his mind. A gunshot sounded in the distance, and Oliver laid his head on the back of the chair and stared at the dark ceiling.

Daisy awakened sometime in the middle of the night and listened to her husband pace the floor in the next room. Rolling on her side, she stared through the window into the starlit sky, and a soft prayer winged its way heavenward. "Please, God, answer him. Let him know Your will and purpose. He loves You so." She sighed deeply at the sound of a chair scraping the floor and knew Oliver was seated at the table with his Bible open in front of him.

Another night she would have marveled at the twinkling diamonds flung across the sky and the full moon's soft glow bathing the hills but not tonight. Her heart was too burdened with the thought of her friends leaving. She wanted so badly to go with them but knew, all too well, it had to be God's will or they would not be happy.

Oliver had struggled with the decision for weeks, and though they had prayed long and frequently together he still remained torn between leaving and staying in Willow Run. Daisy hugged his pillow to her, longing for his nearness, but she knew he would not come to bed until he had his answer. The thought of not seeing her friends again tore at her heart, and a tear slid down her cheek.

Oliver's shoulders slumped and his heart ached for the lost and hopeless souls that had engulfed the town over the last three years. Once a pleasant little place, it now hosted drunkenness and fighting. Shootings and killings were all too common, and fear replaced the peace and safety they had once been accustomed to. Other than their small band of believers, no one had a desire to hear or an inclination to listen to the Word of God.

Much later, Oliver rose from the chair he had occupied for the last two hours and walked to the door. Opening it quietly, he watched dawn slowly break above the treetops. With a heart full of love and gratitude, he lifted his eyes and gloried in the pink streaks of light caressing the sky. He watched his Creator paint the sky in a way no artist would ever capture and was amazed that this same One loved him, listened to him, and answered his feeble cries for help.

Now confident of the path chosen for him, he was comforted with the knowledge that his responsibility was to follow wherever the Lord led. Oliver smiled to himself. God already knew their destination. The doubt, fear, and anxiety that plagued him these last months fled with the night and contentment filled his soul.

Awakening birds filled the air with song, and his thoughts turned to Daisy. She would have accepted whatever decision he made, and Oliver thanked God for her patience and support. He had been aware of the truth in her eyes and knew where her heart lay, but she had not pressured him.

As if on cue, he felt her presence at his side. Turning, he smiled down into her eyes and slipped his arm around her. They both stood quietly and watched the sun rise high above the trees.

Daisy laid her head against his chest and sighed with happiness, feeling his arm tighten around her shoulder. There was no need for words. She saw the answer in his eyes when he looked at her. Joy and anticipation filled her heart as she thought of what lay ahead. They would help one another build homes, establish a community, and worship God together in peace and harmony.

Oliver brushed a curl away from Daisy's face and looked at her tenderly. "There will be some rough times, Daisy," he said softly. "It won't be easy. God does not promise easy." He spoke softly and gazed into her eyes. "But He does bless those who walk with Him and seek His will." His voice was almost a whisper as he spoke. "That's why it took me so long to come to this decision. I had to know it was His will and not mine." He smiled and hugged her. "I confess. I wanted to go as badly as you."

The journey was long and hard. The trip, at times, appeared to be aimless wandering, and frustration was dealt with on a more frequent basis the last few days. Today was different. Excitement in the air arrived with sunrise and floated across the camp. Everyone felt it.

Rebekah Seabaugh lifted her face to the sky and remarked, "I feel the Lord's presence so strongly this morning that I could just shout for joy." Wiping her hands on her apron, she clasped them together with a look of wonderment on her face.

Eva Hunter smiled at her friend. She felt it too and closed her eyes, enjoying the fresh, morning breeze on her cheeks.

Pouring a cup of coffee, Anna Miller grinned at her two friends, sat down on a quilt beneath a tree, and listened to the birds fill the morning air. It wouldn't be long before the day's trek began. She had quickly discovered at the onset of their journey that a few minutes of God's presence each morning strengthened her for the day. Taking a sip of her coffee, she watched her husband saddle his horse and picked up her bible, finding the passage where she had left off yesterday.

Robert Miller awakened this morning with a sense of anticipation, and he was anxious to get the group moving. Settling into his saddle, he glanced at his eight-year-old son, Charles, who tossed his bed role in the back of the wagon. He looked as if he had grown taller overnight. Robert smiled at Justine, three years younger, who was following him around the side of the wagon running a stick along the spokes of the wagon wheels.

Nudging Sam with his heel, he rode to the top of the ridge west of their encampment. The valley that spread out in front of him filled his very soul with a surge of joy. Turning, he shouted and waved his hat for the rest to join him.

James Cook, the nine-year-old son of Isaac and Sarah, yelled at his best friend, Jonathan Hunter. He would race him to the top of the ridge and win. The challenge floated on the morning breeze and captured everyone's attention.

Micah Seabaugh and Jonah Smith pushed their breakfast aside and followed the other two boys.

Speaking to no one in particular, Jacob Smith said, "I think maybe I'll just go take a look at the goings on up there," and he started up the hill.

Louis Seabaugh tossed what was left in his coffee cup, rose from the stump he sat on, and looked at the rest of the men. "Well, let's go."

Children laughed excitedly and called back and forth to one another as they raced ahead of their fathers, wondering what lay over the ridge.

Fannie Driscol, her hands on her plump hips, looked at the women staring after their husbands and children. "Well, are we just going to stand here with our mouths hanging open, or should we go see what all this fuss is about?"

Joyous laughter erupted as the women stopped what they were doing and followed their families up the side of the ridge.

Oliver Madison turned with a smile as he watched Daisy climb the hill. The breeze loosened a dark curl from her bonnet, her cheeks were rosy from the climb, and her eyes sparkled with happiness. He stepped toward her. "Daisy, wait until you see this," he said, pulling her along the last couple of feet.

The scene below was a picture of God's handiwork. The valley was abundant with wild flowers, blackberry bushes, and clear streams of water. Wild honeysuckle and groves of giant oak trees grew everywhere. Three deer stood in the distance and looked at them curiously before bounding off into the trees. A creek, originating high on the mountain somewhere, meandered along the north side of the ridge, flowed lazily down the valley, and made its way around the ridge they presently stood on.

Chirping birds filled the air and a crow called in the distance. The peace was golden, and the group gazed in awe at the scene spread out in front of them. The beauty of the valley and the warmth of the sun on their backs filled each with an awareness of God's presence, and they knew the excitement that had filled their hearts this morning was the nearness of this blessing.

Maxwell Hunter reached for his wife's hand, and they bowed their heads. Each family in turn followed: Isaac and Sarah Cook, Jacob and Faith Smith, Louis and Rebekah Seabaugh, Robert and Anna Miller, Elmer and Fannie Driscol, and Oliver and Daisy Madison. Uniting hands and hearts, they waited on the Lord.

Oliver Madison knew in his soul they had arrived at their destination. He looked up into the eyes of the other six men, questioning their response. A smile broke across each face, and Isaac Cook threw his hat into the air with a shout. It was unanimous. They had come home. They had come to Oak Grove.

Oak Grove Folks
—1946—

Ann Madison (95)
"Miss Mattie"—oldest living resident of Oak Grove—grandparents were among the founding families

Benjamin A. Cook (90)
"Old Ben"—second oldest resident of Oak Grove—grandparents came to Oak Grove with the Seabaugh family. They built and operated the blacksmith shop where Old Ben still lives today.

Jacob W. Cook
Old Ben's nephew (51), wife Liza (49) work and live on the Seabaugh farm

Ben Cook (30)
"Young Ben"—Supervisor at the Oak Grove Timber Company

Mercy Cook (26)
Cook at the Cranston Cafe

Henry Driscol
Mayor of Oak Grove (50), wife Trudy (45)
Have two adopted nieces, Caroline (15) and Elizabeth (10)

Philip Driscol
Mayor Driscol's father (72), wife Lucille (69)

John Walker Family
Sheriff (41), wife Anne (39)—niece of Margaret Miller,
Brenton (12), Preston (10), Josiah (8), Jordan (6), and Garrett (4)

Jim Walker
Fire Chief (36), brother of John Walker, wife Jennifer (35),
Truman (12) and Simon (10)

Robert Miller
Doctor (62), Miss Mattie's nephew, wife Margaret (59)

Alan Miller
Editor, Oak Grove Chronicle (33), wife Lynn (30),
Maggie (8) and Abigail (6)

Michael Madison
President, Oak Grove National Bank (38), wife Ellen (33),
Zachary (6)

William Stanton (29)
Willy's Garage

Melba Maple (27)
Melba's Salon

Mike Daniels Family
Pastor, Oak Grove Baptist Church (38), wife Leah (35),
John (12), Laura (11), Shari (8), and Jimmy (6)

Henry Wilson
Owns Hank's Hardware (49), wife Sally (47) schoolteacher,
Paul (16)

Elijah Seabaugh
Owns farm northwest of town (71), operated Oak Grove's first sawmill with his father, wife Elizabeth (70)

Clifford Charles
Oak Grove dentist (46), wife Teresa (42) schoolteacher,
Jack (15)

Matthew Charles
Works at the Oak Grove Timber Company (34), wife Janet (33)
Terry (14), Carol (8), and Charlotte (6)

Samuel Cranston
Owns Cranston Hotel and Cranston Café (72), wife Abigail (71)

Milly & Molly Cranston
Spinster twins, own The Sweet Shoppe (ages 50)

Paul Smith
works at The Cranston Hotel (68), wife Lottie (66)

Gerald Williams
Oak Grove druggist (42), wife Stella (41)
Peter (15), Patricia (12), and Louise (10)

Pete Williams
Williams Shoe Store (36), wife Annabelle (35) works at the florist
Noelle (10)

Jack Reese
Reese's Market (38), wife Mildred (36)
Karen (15), David (14), Kim (12), and Sandra (9)

Thomas Baker
Proprietor, Baker's Clothier (41), wife Karen (37)

Thomas Driscol
Attorney at Law (50), Mayor Driscol's brother, wife Mary (49)

William Madison
Postmaster (39), wife Hannah (38)

Peter Clark
Pastor, Methodist Church (56), Sarah (53)

Thomas Madison
Co-owner, Oak Grove Timber Co. (50), wife Mary (48)

Robert Seabaugh
Co-owner, Oak Grove Timber Co. (50), wife Lydia (47)

Eli Smith
Works at Oak Grove Timber Co. (30), wife Mary (30) works for the Driscol's, Jake (10) and Carrie (8)

Jeremiah Smith
Works and lives with Miss Mattie (70), wife Hannah (69)

Thomas Cooley
Janitor at Oak Grove Public School (30), wife Alice (29)
Tommy (9) and Betty Jean (7)

The Town of Oak Grove
—1946—

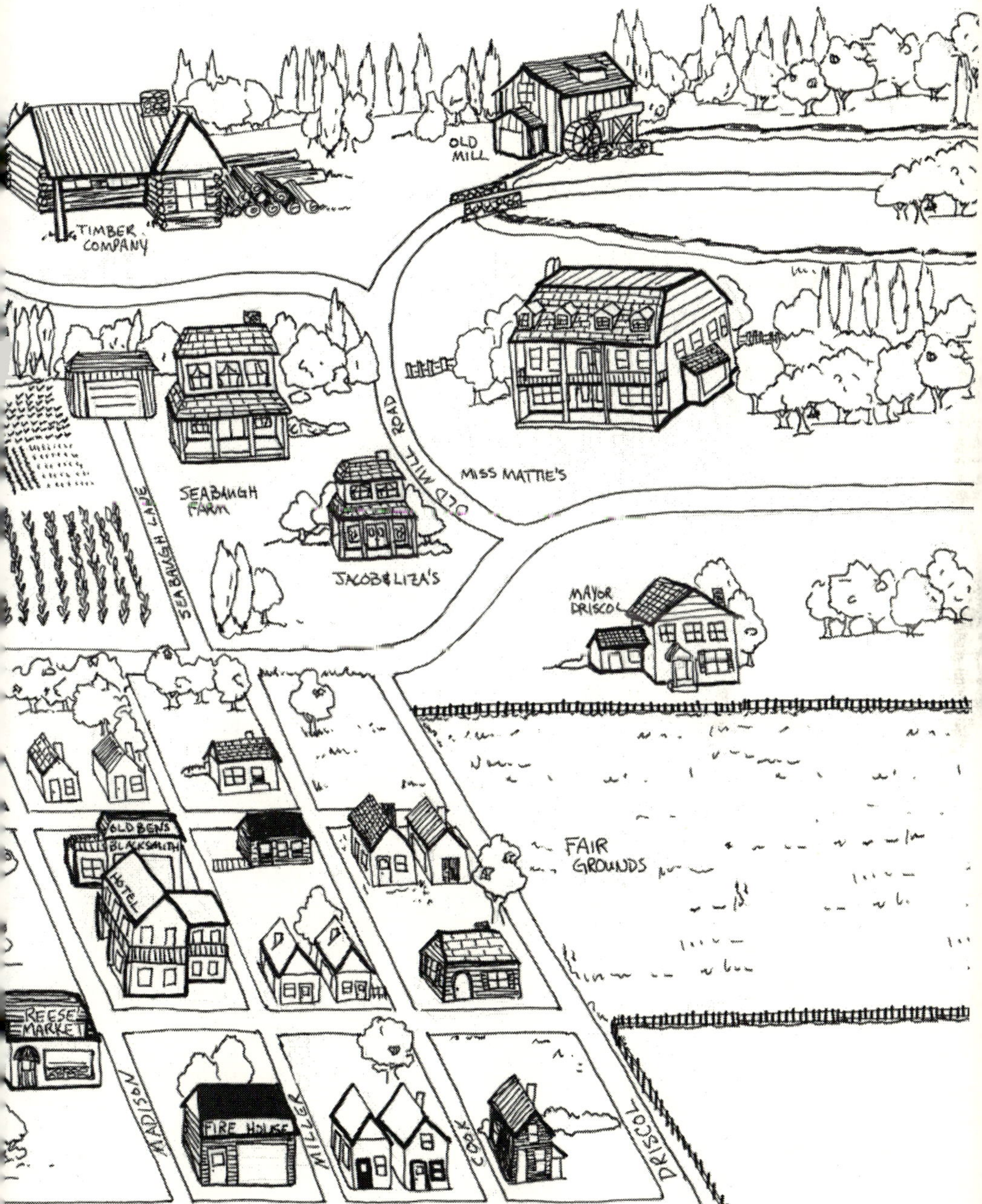
OLD MILL
TIMBER COMPANY
SEABAUGH FARM
SEABAUGH LANE
OLD MILL ROAD
MISS MATTIE'S
JACOB & LIZA'S
MAYOR DRISCOL
FAIR GROUNDS
OLD BEN'S BLACKSMITH
HOTEL
REESE'S MARKET
FIRE HOUSE
MADISON
MILLER
COOK
DRISCOL

Introduction
—June 14, 1946—

It had been one year since President Harry S. Truman broadcast the official end of the war in Europe. The surrender of Nazi Germany, known as VE Day, was cause for great celebration, and everyone prayed for WWII to come to its final close. The United States and allied forces sought peace as they urged Imperial Japan to surrender to the terms of the Potsdam Declaration. Japan's refusal activated plans such as the world had never seen when the United States detonated atomic bombs on Hiroshima and Nagasaki, stunning the world. Finally, the official surrender of Japanese forces was signed September 2, 1945, aboard the Battleship Missouri in Tokyo Bay, bringing World War II to an end.

Thousands of people who returned from the war and those who had loved ones that did not found that their lives resembled a roller coaster. Some hurriedly tried to make up for that which was gone, and others searched for that sense of normalcy they once knew. It was a time to pick up what remained or accept what would never be. Many once again found laughter and hope for the future while others sought glitter and glamour that only superficially covered their broken hearts.

The country watched as the United Nations was formed, Nuremburg trials began, and twenty-eight nations came together forming the World Bank. The news carried the death of General George S. Patton, killed in an automobile accident at the age of 60. Something called a ballpoint pen went on sale at Gimbels' Department Store in New York City, and Paris introduced the bikini to the world.

The sports pages across the country carried news of the organization of the Basketball Association of America. But with the return of players and fans from active duty, baseball was once again America's favorite national pastime. Fans, fortunate enough, flocked to ballparks while the rest of the nation sat around radios waiting for the next home run by Stan Musial, Ted Williams, Yogi Berra, and Enos Slaughter. A young Jackie Robinson signed on with the Montreal Royals, becoming the first African-American to play organized baseball in the 20th century.

Big band music still remained popular. Glenn Miller recordings brought tender memories, Tommy Dorsey and Woody Herman continued to draw crowds wherever they played, and Dizzy Gillespie and Charlie Parker introduced a new form of jazz called bebop. Radio waves carried the voices of Bing Crosby, Frank Sinatra, Doris Day, The Ink Spots, and The Andrew Sisters into homes across America.

John Wayne and Audie Murphy was every man's hero, and every woman fell in love with Cary Grant, Gregory Peck, and Jimmy Stewart. Young girls dressed, talked, and wore their hair like Lauren Bacall, Anne Baxter, Olivia DeHavilland, Rosalind Russell, or Donna Reed, flocking to theaters across the nation when their names appeared on the marquee. Young boys stood in line on Friday nights to watch Roy Rogers, Gene Autry, and Hopalong Cassidy thunder and shoot their way across the screen chasing the infamous band of outlaws dressed in black.

Those who could afford a television tuned in to Yankee Stadium to watch Joe Louis defend his heavy weight title against Billy Conn. The Voice of Firestone and The Gillette Cavalcade of Sports was watched across the country, and Mickey Mouse returned to the screen for the first time since the beginning of World War II.

The sleepy little town of Oak Grove survived The Great War. The folks had cried together, worried together, and rejoiced with one another through those terrible years. Their faith remained strong and secure as their lives continued on an even keel by a force greater than any of them. The love and faith shared in this small town had sustained their parents and grandparents in the past, and now that same faith carried them through the war. Life in this small town was ordinary, slow, peaceful, and satisfying. This lazy little town had overcome insurmountable odds through the years and would continue to do so. Waking up in Oak Grove was waking up to a new day and the wonder of what it would bring.

Chapter I

The Town Square had been the heartbeat of Oak Grove for years. The shops, small and quaint, were built on opposite sides of an area that at one time hosted a meeting hall and house of worship. Today, a fountain surrounded by flowers and shrubs bubbled at one end of the square, and a white bandstand with its red roof occupied the other. Well-groomed honeysuckle bushes bordered the sidewalks and perfumed the air with their fragrance; forever leaving a sentimental memory in the minds of those who, for one reason or another, found themselves leaving Oak Grove. The old bell tower and an American flag stood proudly in the center like a couple of old sentinels, lasting reminders of the early settlers.

The Cranston Hotel's second floor colonnade looked out over the square from the east, and Oak Grove City Hall stood impressively on the west. Shop owners were neighbors and friends who operated their businesses from nine to five, Monday through Saturday.

With the exception of the Cranston Café, the Oak Grove Drug Store was the busiest establishment on the square. Shoppers and townsfolk passed through its doors all day long. Some dropped in for a cherry coke while others purchased toiletry items, medicine, magazines, or any of the numerous items that could be found on its shelves. More often than not, it was a place to hear the latest news or while away a few minutes while one waited for nothing in particular and enjoyed an ice cream soda.

Today found Truman and Brenton Walker sitting side by side on red stools at the soda fountain. Both boys were twelve years old and not only cousins but also best friend as well.

Gerald Williams, hearing the jingle of the door, appeared from the back of the drugstore. "You fellas are a little early again today." He smiled at them and glanced at the Coca-Cola clock on the wall, 3:10. Mr. Williams was a thin man with brown hair, gray eyes, and a friendly smile. He always wore a freshly starched, white apron and a white, soda jerk hat. Taking great pride in his ice cream sundaes, he was always creating new toppings to the surprise and delight of his customers.

"Yes, Sir," answered Truman, "about twenty minutes or so."

Brenton dug in his blue jeans pocket for his money and placed the nickel and dime on the counter. "I guess we'll just sit here and cool off a little." Removing his baseball cap, he wiped his forehead with the back of his hand and placed the Cardinal cap on the stool next to him. The boys, due at The Chronicle at 3:30 to fold newspapers, soon found that chocolate ice cream sundaes fit perfectly into their schedule at least twice a week.

"You'll want your usual then?" Mr. Williams asked as he picked up two sundae glasses, dipped the scoop in water, and filled each glass with two scoops of chocolate ice cream. He liked both young boys. They were well mannered and friendly. Brenton's father was the Sheriff of Oak Grove and Truman's dad was the Fire Chief. Their fathers were brothers, respected, and well liked in the community in spite of the fact they were considered outsiders. They had only lived in Oak Grove ten years. The rest of the folks proudly boasted of roots dating back to 1830 when the town was settled.

The bell hanging from the top of the screen door jingled again, and Truman and Brenton turned as Noelle Williams came through the door. "Hello, Uncle Gerald," she said softly, glancing at the two boys. "I am to pick up a package for Mama."

"Hi, Noelle," Brenton and Truman spoke almost simultaneously.

"Hello," she answered, looking wide-eyed at the chocolate sundaes her uncle sat in front of them. Marshmallow crème and nuts ran over the top and down the sides of the chocolate ice cream, and a big, red cherry sat precariously on top of a dollop of whipped cream.

"Let me get it for you, Noelle." Her uncle wiped his hands on his apron and tugged one of her braids as he walked around the magazine rack to the back of the drug store. Noelle fidgeted with one of the waist-length, brown braids while she stared at the magazines and tried not to look at the boys. They made her uncomfortable. Boys were always so loud, and she could never think of anything to say to them. She wished her friend, Laura, was here. She would be able to think of something to talk about. Laura was not shy at all. She was friendly and laughed a lot just like her daddy, Pastor Mike.

"What have you been doing since school is out?" Truman politely asked her.
Noelle's heart beat rapidly and she continued to fidget with her braid, feeling her cheeks getting warm. She should say something but couldn't think of a thing, so she lowered her brown eyes and stared at the white and black square tile.

Brenton and Truman glanced at each other in the mirror behind the counter. It extended the length of the wall and reflected everything that was going on in the drugstore. Presently, they could see the top of Noelle's head as she stared at the floor. Their eyes conveyed what they were thinking. *How do you talk to girls, especially one as shy as Noelle?* Brenton popped the cherry from his sundae into his mouth. He liked to eat his first. Truman always saved his for last.

"Have you heard the news?" she blurted out, looking up at them with wide brown eyes. Noelle panicked. What on earth made her ask that? She had no news to share with anyone. Why hadn't she asked what they had done all summer or something that made sense? She stared at the blue ribbon she pulled from her braid. Her face felt hot and she wanted to run from the store What will they think of her? Now what was she going to say?

Truman and Brenton both turned, swiveled their stools around, and looked at her curiously. "What news?" Brenton asked as he swallowed the bite of ice cream he just spooned into his mouth.

"Here you are, Noelle. I'll just write this down and your dad can take care of it later." Noelle gave a great sigh of relief, grabbed the package from her uncle's hand, and headed for the door.

Gerald was surprised at his niece's behavior and stared after her with a puzzled expression. "I hope your mama feels better. Tell her hello for me."

"Thank you, Uncle Gerald," she called back, hurrying out the door with the package clutched tightly in both hands.

"Wait, what news?" Brenton called. The jingle of the bell and the slam of the screen door was his only answer.

Mr. Williams turned and looked at the boys. "News? What news?" He glanced from one to the other and then back at the door, wondering what he had missed.

"I don't know." Truman was puzzled as he placed a big spoonful of ice cream in his mouth. "She just asked if we had heard the news, but she did not say what it was." Glancing down, he saw the blue ribbon that matched her dress. He slid off the stool, picked it up, and handed it to her uncle. "Here, she dropped this."

All three stared at the door as though they expected it to give them an answer. Mr. Williams put the ribbon in his pocket and wiped the marble counter top with his rag. He was perplexed with his niece's behavior and wondered what she was talking about. "I haven't heard anything," he mumbled to himself.

The voice of Fred, the weatherman, caught his ear, and he turned to the Philco sitting on the counter behind him. Turning the volume up, he looked through the window across the square and listened for the temperature, wondering how Fred's report would compare with the Coca-Cola thermometer hanging outside the drugstore.

Anne Walker and her youngest son, Garrett, came out of the post office, crossed the street, and stopped to chat with Lucille Hunter and Abigail Driscol. The ladies, as was their habit, sat chatting on one of the benches by the fountain. Gerald watched the three women talk and chuckled when Garrett began swishing the water with his hands. Glancing back at Brenton, he was surprised that he never noticed the strong resemblance between the two before.

"I wonder what she is talking about," Brenton said as he watched Truman take his last bite of ice cream and pop the cherry in his mouth.

Truman pushed his sundae glass back. "It is probably some girl stuff," he answered, "but I don't know why she thought we would be interested."

Brenton looked at his cousin. "She would not have mentioned anything at all unless she was sure that we would want to know. If you ask me, there is more here than meets the eye." Brenton took on his detective-on-a-case attitude. He always seemed to find a mystery in anything out of the ordinary, and he always jumped in headlong to figure it out before anyone else.

Mr. Williams smiled at both boys. "I am sure we will find out sooner or later. Well, good afternoon, Trudy," he said as he watched the plump Mrs. Driscol come through the door, straightening her new hat.

Trudy Driscol owned more hats than any woman in town, not to mention the variety of colors and styles she wore. This one looked like a big bird sat on her head and shed all of its feathers. One long, huge, purple feather hung over the front of her left eye, giving her a comical appearance. She took in a breath and blew out a puff of air in an attempt to remove the feather from her face. Brenton and Truman glanced at each other in the mirror and grinned.

"Oh my goodness, it is warm out there today. It has to be at least 100 degrees. Good afternoon, Gerald. Boys, how are your parents? Tell them hello for me. Gerald, I believe I will have something nice and cool to drink. My, but I am just parched. I do need to cool off. Now, you boys, I sure hope you have my paper on time this afternoon." She momentarily stopped talking and blew the feather out of her face again then checked to see if her slip was showing.

Brenton opened his mouth to assure her they would have her paper on time, but she just continued her nonstop talking. Truman turned away to avoid looking at Brenton. If he didn't, they would both laugh and then they would be in trouble. He watched through the mirror, and every time she moved the long purple feather waved around her head.

"Make sure that drink is the largest you have and plenty of ice too." Trudy threw the request over her shoulder and picked up a Look Magazine from the rack and waved it at him. "I'll take this too. I really must not dawdle too long. I promised to take Caroline over to Edna's this afternoon for a new dress, and I am running behind. You know she will turn fifteen next week. I cannot believe it. She has grown into a young lady so fast." Looking at the ceiling thoughtfully for a moment, she remarked, "I think she would look very nice in a soft green color. It would match her eyes. Don't you think?" She turned to them for an answer but did not wait for a reply and continued to talk. "Now, as for Elizabeth, she doesn't even want to wear a dress. I just do not know what we are going to do with that child. She certainly is not the little lady that Caroline is, but I'm sure that will change in a couple of years."

Truman sighed. How were they going to get out of here without being rude? He could just hear his mother. Mrs Driscol would call her for sure, and then it would be all over town how they had no manners and needed proper discipline. As the Mayor's wife, Mrs. Driscol felt it her duty to report all that went on in Oak Grove.

Mr. Williams smiled at both boys, knowing what they were thinking, and turned to her with a box of assorted chocolates. "Here, Trudy, try a piece of this. It is a fresh batch that Milly brought over from The Sweet Shoppe this morning." He watched her select one of the larger pieces and smiled to himself. "The weather man just said it was ninety-two degrees. I guess the humidity makes it feel much warmer." He placed her usual tall glass of lemonade on a small round table where she had chosen to deposit her packages and purse. Sitting in one of the small chairs at the table, she blew the purple feather out of her face and bit into the chocolate.

Gerald stood with the screen door open, looking at the thermometer. "Fred is pretty good. I've got 92 degrees also." He watched Trudy help herself to another chocolate as he walked back to the soda fountain and glanced at the clock. "Well, boys, it is 3:25. If you want to get Mrs. Driscol's paper to her on time, you better head out to The Chronicle."

"Yes, Sir," Brenton said, almost falling off the stool in his rush to escape. Truman smiled and had an urge to jerk the feather from her hat. "It was nice to see you, Mrs. Driscol. We will have your paper delivered before you get home." He hurried out the door and caught up with Brenton who already made a hasty exit.

"If either of you two boys see Mildred Reese you tell her I'm here at the drugstore," Mrs. Driscol called as the door slammed shut behind him. What Trudy did not know, Mildred did, and between the two they were able to keep track of everything that took place in Oak Grove.

"Man, can she talk or what," Brenton said as he pulled his kickstand up with his toe. "I feel sorry for Mr. Williams. She'll talk his ear off. And that hat; where do you suppose she found that?"

Truman straightened his baseball cap and put his kickstand up. He stood for a moment holding his bicycle trying to look serious, but the grin on his face gave him away.

"What?" Brenton asked, wondering what was going on in his head.

"Well, it is for sure Mrs. Driscol hasn't heard anything, or we would have just heard all about it down to the smallest detail." Truman laughed as a thought struck him. "Hey! If there is any news in town, we are working for the right person." Jumping on his bike, he peddled off down the sidewalk.

Brenton followed Truman down the block to The Chronicle, passing Edna's Dress Shop, The Flower Basket, Oak Grove Bank, Cranston Café, and Ned's Barbershop. He's *right*, Brenton thought. *If anyone knows anything, it would be Mrs. Driscol. She knows everything in town.* Why hadn't he thought of that? He prided himself in the fact that he could usually figure things out first, and Truman just surprised him. Parking their bikes next to the building, they opened the door and walked in. The smell of paper and ink greeted them.

"Right on time, boys." Alan Miller smiled as he dropped a stack of newspapers on the table in front of a window with *THE CHRONICLE* painted on it. He was whistling along with the radio and Perry Como singing something about chasing rainbows. He sat atop his desk and watched as the two boys went to the Frigidaire and helped themselves to a bottle of pop. Their help was working well for him. Brenton was his Cousin Ann's son, and Truman was related by marriage.

The boys, likewise, enjoyed working for Alan. He talked to them like men and had a good sense of humor which made working for him fun. He was tall and muscular and knew all there was to know about sports. He had been a star quarterback in high school and still attended all of the football games. Those stopping by The Chronicle still occasionally looked at the picture hanging on the wall by Alan's desk. The 1931 Oak Grove Football Team did not lose a game that year, and most of the townsfolk could still recall many memorable games and key plays.

Brenton took one-half of the stack of papers and left Truman the other. Both boys occupied stools on either side of the worktable and began folding papers, tucking one side into the other.

"Ice cream good today?" Alan asked. Truman and Brenton looked at each other's face and laughed as they wiped chocolate from their mouths.

"Alan, have you heard the news?" Brenton asked as he looked over at him and folded another paper.

Alan looked curiously at both boys and raised one of his brows. "What news do you have that I don't?" He took two canvas bags from the wall hooks and handed them to Truman.

"Brenton doesn't have any news; he just wishes he did." Truman stuffed some of the folded newspapers in his bag and glanced across the table at his cousin.

The door opened and Pastor Mike walked in with a smile on his face. He was a pleasant man who enjoyed life and displayed an extraordinary love for those around him. His sense of humor endeared him to those who knew him, and the compelling manner with which he carried himself revealed an inner strength that he unashamedly admitted was God's grace in his life.

Brenton looked at him and smiled, thinking he looked different in a pair of khaki trousers and dark blue shirt. He could never get use to seeing him in anything other than the suits he wore on Sunday mornings.

"Well, good afternoon." He smiled, shook Alan's hand, and turned to the boys. "I see you've got these two hard at work." He walked up to Truman and studied his baseball cap. Reaching over, he removed it, looked at it closely, and sat it on top of his head. Walking to a small mirror hanging next to the door, he examined himself in an exaggerated manner, adjusted the too small cap, and turned around. "St. Louis Cardinals; this is a swell cap, Truman. How do I look?" He turned back to the mirror and examined himself again. "I think I need a cap like this. How about letting me keep it?" he asked, walking back to the worktable.

Truman reached for the cap but missed when Pastor Mike stepped back. Looking at the hat, sitting at a crooked angle on his head, Truman began to laugh. "It is much too small for you."

"Do you think so?" He removed it, ran his fingers through his dark hair, examined the cap again, and placed it back on his head. "Maybe if I got a haircut it would fit better."

"I doubt it," Alan laughed. "You would have to shave your head, and that sure wouldn't be a pretty sight." Alan sat on the edge of his desk watching Pastor Mike tease Truman then asked with a serious expression on his face, "Why don't you wear it while you preach?" He smiled fondly at the man. "It would at least get everyone's attention and might even keep some of us awake during your sermons."

Raising one of his brows, he looked at Alan. "Thank you very much for your advice. I'll remember that." He took the cap off and tossed it back to Truman. Taking a seat on one of the stools next to Brenton, Pastor Mike grabbed several newspapers. "I use to be a paper boy myself, a long time ago." The boys watched him flip a paper over and tuck the ends together, surprised at how fast he folded it.

Alan laughed. "I'm glad to know that you were once a paper boy. If I need more help, I'll be sure and give you a call. You do have a bicycle, don't you?" Alan remained seated on the edge of his desk and watched the three fold newspapers. Pastor Mike was one of his favorite people. Actually, everyone in Oak Grove was fond of him, including those who were not church members. "What can I do for you, Pastor?"

Taking his attention away from boys, he looked at Alan curiously. "I just wondered if those posters I needed were ready yet." Mike folded another newspaper and handed it to Brenton. "And yes, as a matter of fact, I do have a bicycle." Scratching his head, he laughed. "Well, sort of; it's in the garage, but Johnny and Jimmy used some of the parts to make a cart, so I am not sure just what I have left in the way of a bicycle."

Alan chuckled, "No, your posters aren't ready yet. I'll have them for you tomorrow." He stood up and headed to the back of the office. "Would you like a Coca-Cola? I am going to have one myself."

"No, thank you. I have to get over to the church for a meeting." He stood up and glanced out the window. "I'll go ahead and take my paper if you boys don't mind." He reached across the table and removed Brenton's ball cap. "Truman is not being very Christlike; not wanting to share his Cardinal cap. How about you, Brenton?" He placed it on his head and looked at both of them. "Does this one fit better?"

"No," they answered at the same time and laughed at the look on his face. He tossed the cap back to Brenton and laughed along with them.

"I have to go. You boys be careful. I'll see you tomorrow, Alan."

"We will. Thanks for helping with the newspapers," Truman answered as he watched Pastor Mike walk out the door. He stuffed the last few papers in his canvas bag and watched Brenton fold the last of his stack, wondering what Noelle had been talking about.

Brenton pulled his bag across the table and proceeded to stuff the papers inside. Alan waved to Pastor Mike through the window and turned back to the boys. "Now what is this about Noelle's news?"

"Well, something is going on. She came into the drugstore while we were there and let the cat out of the bag but would not finish telling us what she was talking about," Brenton replied. He stared at *THE CHRONICLE* written in big red letters on the side of his bag and wondered what was going on.

"She just asked us if we had heard the news," Truman commented, putting the strap of the newspaper bag across his shoulder.

"Well, is that all she said?" Alan asked, looking closely from one to the other. "Noelle is pretty shy, and she doesn't have too much to say."

"Exactly," Brenton commented, picking up his bag. "She knows something we don't." Putting the strap of the canvas bag over his shoulder, he was determined to find out what that something was.

"Hmm," Alan murmured and stroked his chin thoughtfully, "now how did she...?" Catching himself in mid-sentence, he suddenly seemed a little nervous. Truman and Brenton glanced at each other. Something was going on.

Alan slapped his hands together and smiled. "Okay, boys, let's get those papers out." He walked to the window, looked out across the square as though pondering an idea, and then turned and looked at them with a strange expression on his face. "Don't forget to give Abigail her paper, or she'll be mad at you." All three laughed as they thought of Abbie and her latest mission of delivering her own newspaper.

Alan smiled to himself as he thought of his six-year-old daughter. It was a responsibility she had taken upon herself at the beginning of summer and considered no one else in the family quite capable of the task.

"Okay," Truman said, closing the door behind them. Adjusting their newspaper bags, both boys got on their bikes. Riding to the end of the block, they stopped and looked at each other.

"Alan acted funny, didn't he?" Truman glanced at his cousin. "I think you are right, Brent. I believe there is something going on." Bending down, he rolled his pant leg up, not wanting to get it caught in the chain again.

"I told you, didn't I? I told you. I can feel it," Brenton answered with authority and a determined look on his face. "We are going to find out just what all this mystery is about." He glanced back at the Chronicle. "I wonder if anyone else knows anything."

"I don't know." Truman looked at Brenton. "Evidently Alan knows something, so I would think there are others that do too."

"Yeah, you're right there. Keep your eyes and ears open, and maybe we'll hear something." Throwing his leg over the bar of his bike, he pedaled off and called back over his shoulder, "I'll see you tonight."

"You do the same," Truman yelled as he rode off in the opposite direction. The boys argued and mulled over different ideas of who would deliver papers to what streets and finally decided to split the town in half and switch each week. Truman was glad it was his turn to deliver papers on this side of town because he would get finished early. *The Yearling* was playing at The Star tonight, and he wanted to get home in plenty of time to get ready.

Alan stood outside The Chronicle and watched the boys talking at the end of the block. *Now how in the world did the word get out*, he wondered. No one was suppose to tell another soul what was about to happen. This could ruin everything, and they would never hear the end of it. Shaking his head, he went back into The Chronicle, locked the door, and hung up the closed sign.

Truman turned onto Maple Street. *Seven more houses*, he thought to himself. Abigail Miller, the youngest of Alan's daughters, was sitting barefoot on a tree limb, waving. He rode over and waited while she dropped down from the tree. "Hi, Abigail. Here's today's paper; ready for delivery." He handed it to her across the fence. She sat on the tree limb every day waiting for him to bring the newspaper.

"Thanks, Truman. I am going to be a paper boy when I grow up." She smiled up at him with both front teeth missing. "Are you going to see *The Yearling* tonight?" she asked, squinting up at him and shading her eyes from the evening sun with the newspaper.

"I sure am. I think everyone is going." Truman wondered if there was anyone in Oak Grove that was not going tonight.

"Then I guess I'll see you there. Mom said as soon as I got the paper I was supposed to come in for my bath." With another grin, she turned and ran up the sidewalk, her ponytail bouncing as she ran. Opening the front door, she turned and waved.

Truman rode his Western Flyer down the street, tossing the last five papers into the yards. *I guess if I had a little sister, I would want one like Abigail,* he thought. She didn't act like a girl so that wouldn't be too bad.

The smell of fried pork chops greeted him as he rode into the yard and his stomach growled. He was hungry and ready for supper. Simon met him coming out the back door. "Mom said we could go to the movies tonight but we better go early. *The Yearling* is supposed to be really good, and there is going to be a big crowd."

"I heard it was good too. Do you have enough allowance?" Truman questioned his little brother. He had a tendency to spend it as quickly as he got it.

Simon dug in his pocket and pulled out a one-dollar bill. "I have been saving. Willy told me that the movie would be playing here about a month ago and we shouldn't miss it because it is supposed to be the best movie ever made."

Truman was proud of Simon. How he managed to save a whole dollar was beyond him. Of course, he had to admit, if Willy told him something then that settled it.

Simon loved hanging around Willy's Garage watching him work on cars. He was also very impressed that he had returned from the war about a year ago with a Purple Heart. Wondering for days how someone's heart could change colors, he finally asked about it one night at supper. Dad explained that a Purple Heart was a medal given to those injured in battle, and since Willy was shot in the left leg, he was awarded The Purple Heart. He also explained the injury was the reason for Willy's limp. In that instant, Willy became Simon's true hero.

Actually, Willy was everyone's hero in Oak Grove. He was a lot quieter than before the war, but Dad said that a lot of men were like that. "War is a terrible experience," Jim had told Truman when he mentioned it. "We should honor and show respect and gratitude to all who serve to protect our country."

The back screen door opened and Jennifer stuck her head out. "You two get your bikes put away. It is time to eat." She stepped aside as Sport bounded off the porch and ran in circles around both boys. "You should leave a little early tonight. I expect there will be quite a long line at the ticket counter."

Grinning, Simon picked up his bike and walked with Truman to the garage, Sport following at their heels. "Willy said everyone in town will be there tonight." He pushed his bike into the corner by the wheelbarrow and picked up a red rubber ball.

"Hey, Simon, Willy didn't happen to mention anything going on in town did he?" People were always in and out of Willy's Garage, and he usually knew what was going on.

"Sure," Simon answered as he bounced the ball against the wall and watched Truman put his bike in the other corner by the lawn mower. Dropping the ball in the wheelbarrow, he turned and started walking toward the house.

"Wait!" Truman ran to catch up with him. "What's new in town, Simon?" He couldn't believe the luck. His own brother knew what was going on.

"I told you; *The Yearling!* It starts tonight." Exasperated, Simon opened the screen door. "Umm, supper smells good, Mom."

Truman groaned. He should have known. He followed Simon and Sport through the back door. Maybe Brenton found something out or Johnny Daniels. After all, his dad is the preacher. He should know if there was anything happening. He looked at the supper table; fried pork chops and mashed potatoes. Supper was going to be good.

"Come on, you guys, they're going to be here any minute." Brenton impatiently came down the stairs in a rush. He wished they would hurry. He needed to check with Truman before the movie started to see if he heard anything. He walked to the door and looked up the sidewalk at the Daniels' home, but no one was in sight yet. Where were they? Brenton wondered if Noelle would be with them; she usually was, but after her strange behavior today, he didn't know what to expect.

The Star Theater, just four blocks away and across the street from the library, was but a ten-minute walk. Friday nights found the children of Oak Grove making their way to see the latest screen adventure, and tonight's show was one none of them wanted to miss.

Brenton walked back to the foot of the stairs and yelled, "Preston, Joe, will you come on?"

Anne looked around the kitchen door. "Goodness, Brent, you have plenty of time. You don't need to be in such a rush. They'll be down soon. They are just as anxious to see the movie as you are." No sooner were the words out of her mouth, Brenton heard the commotion at the top of the stairs and knew they were coming. Sometimes he thought his mom was magic. Preston, Josiah, and Jordan all appeared at the same time.

"We're ready," Preston said as he double-checked to make sure he had his money. He walked to the door. "Here they come. Bye Mom." He opened the door and stepped out.

"You just wait a minute." Anne called and watched Preston stop and come back in. He knew everything she was going to say. "All of you come here. Do you have your money?" Anne inspected each one of her sons. They were presentable enough. "Now remember, each one of you is responsible for the other, and you all walk together."

"We will, Mom," Brenton assured her. "Preston and I will keep an eye on Jo and Jordan. You don't have to worry."

"They'll be fine, Anne." John looked over the top of his newspaper. "If not, I'll arrest all four of them." He looked at them with a serious expression and watched Jordan roll his eyes. He was a man who enjoyed his sons thoroughly but also thoroughly enjoyed the peace and quiet Friday evenings allowed him and Anne. He grinned slightly and continued reading the sports page.

Johnny knocked on the front door. "Hi Sheriff, Mrs. Walker." He stepped inside ahead of Laura, Shari, and Jimmy. They were all dark headed with brown eyes like their mother with the exception of Laura, who was blonde. She had Pastor Mike's blue eyes, but Anne wondered where her blonde hair came from since Pastor Mike was dark headed also.

Garrett ran across the floor, smiled up at Laura, and handed her a book.

"Garrett, I'll read that to you. Laura is going to the movies." John laid his newspaper on the end table and motioned for his youngest son to come to him. He looked at the eight of them standing by the door. They were all really good kids.

"What are your parents doing tonight?" He smiled at Shari as she brushed Jimmy's hand away. Standing behind her, he flipped her hair back and forth with his hand, waited a couple of seconds, then reached out to irritate her again.

"Will you stop it?" Giving him a dirty look, she only received a mischievous grin and another flip of her hair.

Laura looked at Sheriff Walker with a grin. "Probably the same thing you are. We always get instructions and then sent merrily on our way. I think you all just want to get rid of us."

John looked at Laura and the rest gathered at the door. "Of course, you could all stay home on Friday nights."

"No, let's get out of here," Johnny said, opening the door.

"Let's go. Willy said this was supposed to be the best movie ever made." Jimmy took one last swish of Shari's hair, laughed, and hurriedly followed Preston out the door and jumped from the porch.

"Have a good time," Anne called as she watched them walk through the yard. She reached down and picked up *The Little Engine That Could*, one of Garrett's favorite books. He stood at the door, his hands pressed against the screen, watching the others walk down the sidewalk.

"I want to go too." Garrett looked up at her with a sad look on his face.

"You get to stay with Mommy and Daddy," Anne said as she leaned down and put her arm around him. *He will soon be joining them,* she thought, kissing his chubby little cheek. "Let's get a cookie, and I will read to you."

They had not reached the end of the block when Brenton turned to Laura and asked, "Say, have you talked to Noelle today?" Johnny and Preston looked curiously at him, wondering at his sudden interest in Noelle.

"No, not since Wednesday night at GA's." Laura looked at Brenton and wondered why he would ask about Noelle. "Why? Is something wrong?"

"I don't know. She came in the drugstore this afternoon to pick up a package for her mom and acted sort of strange. Truman and I were just wondering about it."

Brenton glanced at Johnny and Preston and lowered his voice. "I'll explain in a little bit, so just keep walking."

Laura thought for a moment and commented, "I waited for her at the corner tonight, but I guess she is just late." She hoped nothing was wrong. Noelle was her best friend, and they had planned for the last two weeks to see *The Yearling.* She thought a moment more and then turned to the boys. "She was just late and will meet us there. I know she is going. She said she wouldn't miss it for anything." Laura walked along looking down at the sidewalk with a frown on her face, perplexed that Noelle hadn't called her.

Brenton looked at Johnny again. "No one wants to miss this movie tonight. Wait until you hear what Truman and I have to tell you. There is something really strange going on."

The Harding Funeral Parlor, located at the corner of Oak and Elm Street, was the designated meeting place every Friday night for most of the kids in the neighborhood. The stone building sat back among the trees away from the street and was covered on one side with ivy. A long, wide sidewalk led up to large, elaborately carved wooden doors. With its darkened windows, the whole place took on a sinister look as dusk descended and evening shadows spread beneath the trees and enveloped the building like a dark mysterious cloud.

Shari stared at the double doors and darkened windows, deciding that she didn't much care for the place.

Preston looked around. "Don't tell me they are going to be late," he said as he checked his pocket again to make sure he had his money.

Josiah sat down on the step. "Do we have to wait? I want to get popcorn before the show starts. Brenton, you said we should get there early." A concerned look crossed his face. "There's going to be a bunch of people there ahead of us."

Laura looked around, also wondering where the boys were. Truman and Simon were always here before them.

"I don't see why we have to always meet here. This place is creepy." Shari sat on the top step of the sidewalk, glancing over her shoulder at the darkened building. "Whose idea was it to make this a meeting place anyway?"

"There's nothing to be scared about." Laura looked at her younger sister and decided it would be a good idea to change the subject. "Caroline is supposed to have a real nice birthday party Wednesday. I think it will be a lot of fun."

Preston glanced around. He didn't say anything, but with the sun sinking away behind the trees and the street lamps just coming on, he had to agree with Shari that it was a little creepy sitting here in front of the funeral parlor. He often wondered what went on in there when no one was around. Mr. and Mrs. Harding were nice people, but he felt there had to be something strange about a family who lived in a funeral parlor. The front entrance of the Harding home, around the block on Oak Street, looked the same as the rest of the houses with the exception of a large sun porch in the back that connected the house and the funeral parlor.

Suddenly out of nowhere, cries of moaning and groaning filtered through the trees and floated on the evening air. The tall lilac bushes growing along the parking lot shook and bent as though a demon of sorts attempted to free itself. With one mighty shake, two dark shadows burst forth in a tumble, rising up to almost float across the lawn. Moaning eerily with long, misshapen arms, the shadows raced toward the startled group on the sidewalk.

Laura and Shari screamed, and the boys jumped from the sidewalk into the street in a moment of confusion. The dark figures dropped tree branches on the ground, and Truman and Simon ran onto the sidewalk, laughing and moaning again.

"Gotcha!" Truman laughed, looking at the astonishment on everyone's face.

"That was really good," Johnny laughed. "You about scared my socks off."

"I didn't think it was very funny," Laura angrily told him. "You scared the daylights out of Shari and Jordan. Shame on you!" Reaching down, she took the two by the hand and walked off in a huff ahead of the boys, ignoring their laughing and jeering.

"Like we didn't scare you too!" Simon yelled. It had been his idea, and he thought it had been pretty funny.

Laura stopped and turned around. "It would take much more than that to scare me." Turning around, she pulled Shari and Jordan along and giggled. She leaned down and whispered, "It was pretty funny, but don't let Simon know."

By the time they walked the next block, the line of people standing in front of The Star was visible, the lights from the theater lit up the street, and the smell of popcorn filled the air.

"Holy toledo! Everyone in town must be here," Preston yelled as he hurried across the street. "Come on!" He urged the rest of them along, waving his arm for them to hurry. Simon looked both ways and then darted across the street and got in line behind Preston and Ronald Olson. In a matter of minutes, the line had grown longer and circled around the side of the theater. Simon stared at the crowd and wondered if there would be enough seats for everyone. What if they couldn't get in? He looked at the line behind him. Jordan was behind Brenton and Truman who were in deep conversation with Johnny. Laura and Shari were a little farther down the line talking to Noelle.

Elizabeth Driscol waved to Laura and pointed to herself and Kim Reese. "Save us a seat!" She grinned and rolled her eyes back toward her older sister. Laura waved back and laughed.

Caroline Driscol and Karen Reese each carried a pocket book on their arm and were trying to look sophisticated. Dressed in Sunday clothes, both girls had curled their hair and pulled it away from their faces like Betty Grable. Caroline was not wearing socks, and the thought struck Laura that she was probably wearing hose for the first time. Her shoes did have heels on them. Maybe that explained why she was standing so awkwardly.

"I think Peter is probably working tonight." Caroline touched her curls and glanced toward the ticket counter.

Glancing at her friend, Karen wondered what that was supposed to mean. How would she know if Peter were working tonight or not? She acted like they were close friends or something. In fact, he was the topic of Caroline's conversation all of the time lately. All she heard from her was how Peter said this and how Peter did that. Karen had to admit he was cute, but as far as she was concerned, Caroline was going a little nutty over him.

From where she stood she could see Jack behind the ticket window and not Peter, which meant he would be inside. She turned and looked at the line behind them and groaned. Randy and Donnie White were right behind her. Randy was okay, but

Donnie always had something strange in his pocket: frogs, snakes, and snails. One time in the school cafeteria he had shown Mrs. Wilson a dead mouse that he had carried in his pocket all morning, and she almost fainted.

Looking back at the front of the line, Karen smoothed the front of her dress and wiggled her toes, wishing she had worn socks. Her mom wouldn't allow her to wear hose, and now her feet felt clammy and she would much rather have her socks on.

Caroline suddenly whirled around and pinched both of Karen's cheeks and then her own. "That will make our cheeks look rosy. Did it? How do mine look?" she asked, reaching for Karen's cheeks again. Karen stepped back and stared at Caroline who was biting her lips; first the top lip and then the bottom.

"Go ahead," Caroline said encouragingly. "It will make them look red and kissable. Boys like lips that look red or pink."

She's been reading the romance magazines in the drugstore again, Karen thought, continuing to watch Caroline bite her lips. Thinking she looked like a chipmunk more than anything else, Karen decided to pass on that bit of advice. She had never kissed a boy before and wondered if Caroline had. *No,* Karen thought, *she would be bragging about it if she had.*

Simon finally reached the ticket window and handed Jack the dollar from his pocket. He knew he was supposed to get two quarters back. Dad told him when he was changing clothes. Taking his ticket, he dropped one quarter in his pocket and kept the other in his hand for popcorn and candy. Waiting for Brenton to buy his ticket, he stared at the picture in the theater window. *The Yearling* was printed in bold, black letters across the top, and a boy about his age sat on the floor in a barn with a small fawn on his lap.

Preston stood next to him with his ticket in his hand. "I wonder what it would be like to have a deer for a pet?" He looked closely at the picture. "We see them a lot out at Mr. Seabaugh's farm, but they disappear into the woods right away."

Brenton and Johnny joined the jostling crowd slowly making its way to the theater door and paused to look at the picture. "This is going to be such a good movie. Let's go on in and get in line for popcorn," Johnny said, reaching out and grabbing Jimmy by the sleeve. "Come on."

"Hey, where's Truman?" Brenton asked, looking around.

"I'm coming," Truman said, walking toward them. He glanced back at the line and noted Noelle talking to Laura with a frown on her face. *Whatever the news*, Truman thought, *it looks to me like bad news.*

Johnny pushed the heavy glass doors open and groaned. "Gee whiz. The popcorn line is as long as the line outside."

"Give me your money and I'll get the popcorn and candy," Brenton said, looking at Preston, Jo, and Jordan.

Johnny looked at the crowd milling around. "Jim, why don't all of you go find us a seat while Truman, Brent, and I get the popcorn? This place is filling up fast."

"I'll get my own popcorn," Simon said, getting in line behind Truman. Besides, he didn't know if he wanted JuJuBee's or Chuckles.

"Come on." Jimmy led the way down the wide, carpeted hall and entered the first set of double doors on the right. It was darker in here. The lights on the wall were still on, but they would go off in a few minutes. The tiny floor lights, running down the sides of the aisles, didn't help much at all, and Jimmy wondered why they were even there.

"How many seats do we need?" Josiah asked, following Preston who was looking around the crowded theater for empty seats. Josiah glanced at the lights again, wondering how much time was left before they went off. He didn't want to have to sit where the usher's told them.

Preston looked over his shoulder and answered, "We need eight." Stopping about halfway down the aisle, he pointed. "Here. There are four seats in this row and four seats in the next row. You three sit here and save a seat for Simon. I'll sit behind you and save these three for Johnny, Brent, and Truman." He glanced back up the aisle and was glad they had gotten here when they did. The seats were filling up fast. He looked at the clock on the wall and saw there was only about five minutes left before the movie was to begin. Wishing the others would hurry, he glanced around and noticed Laura and Shari sitting with Noelle, Elizabeth, and Kim about three rows to the right.

"Good seats," Truman commented as he sat down and handed Preston his popcorn.

Brenton followed with his hands full. "Here," he said, handing Josiah and Jordan a bag of popcorn and a box of Dots. "Where's Johnny?" Brenton asked Truman.

"He's coming. He was behind me in the popcorn line," Simon said, crawling over Jordan to sit next to Jimmy.

"There's Maggie and Abigail," Jimmy said, looking behind him. "Zachary!" He yelled loud enough to get his attention and waved at all three then sat back and stuffed a handful of popcorn in his mouth. "I wish it would hurry up and start. I can't wait."

Jordan looked at him. "We should have gotten here earlier. We could be sitting on the front row. They're the best seats."

"Just be glad we got a seat," Simon replied, looking around.

Peter Williams escorted Caroline Driscol and Karen Reese down the aisle, shining his flashlight on the floor in front of them. "Here are a couple of seats." He stopped and indicated two empty seats with his flashlight.

"Oh, thank you so much, Peter," Caroline said with a sweet smile. "I could not have found a seat without your help. I am so glad you were here to help us." Smiling again, she lowered her eyes like Scarlet O'Hara in *Gone with the Wind*. Taking her seat, she looked toward the screen and lifted her chin, offering him a glimpse of her profile. Aunt Trudy said it was just like her mother's. She then took on a feigned air of disinterest and tossed her blonde hair over her shoulder.

Karen watched her friend in disbelief and looked at Peter's confused face. "Thank you, Peter," she murmured and sat down, totally convinced that Caroline had lost her mind.

Caroline's eyes followed Peter back up the aisle, and she turned back to Karen. "Doesn't he look handsome in his red jacket and cap?" she asked with wide green eyes and a pleased smile on her face. Karen rolled her eyes to the ceiling and shoved a handful of popcorn in her mouth.

Johnny slipped into the seat next to Truman. "Guess what I just heard?" he whispered excitedly, leaning over so Brenton could hear. "Mr. Madison and Mr. Wilson were behind me at the candy counter, and I heard Mr. Wilson say that the Mayor was determined to keep it a secret until tomorrow."

"Keep what a secret?" Brenton asked, staring at him. "What is tomorrow?" This was getting more mysterious all of the time.

"That's all I could hear. I don't know what they meant." Johnny glanced a few seats to the right and saw Laura and Noelle with their heads close together, talking. "But I bet I know someone who does."

The lights dimmed, the newsreel started, Bugs Bunny made Elmer Fudd mad, and then *The Yearling* hit the screen.

The breakfast tables in Oak Grove Saturday morning found families reliving the movie from the night before. Parents who had gone with their children agreed that it was the best movie they had seen in a long, long time.

Laura sat at the kitchen table with watery eyes as Jimmy, in full detail, told the ending of the movie. "Jody had to really be brave to kill him." He took a bite of his toast and thought he had described the ending pretty accurately.

Shari looked at him with an angry face "I think they could have ended it a different way. I felt sorry for him. I think someone ought to write a letter to whoever made the movie and tell him too."

Leah looked at her four children seated around the breakfast table, reading the emotions in each face. They had talked of nothing else since returning from the movie last night and again this morning. Laura, especially, seemed preoccupied with something. "If you are finished with breakfast, you have your Saturday chores to attend to." Leah knew it was best to get them started early, or it would take all day. Closing the refrigerator door, she glanced at Laura again and wondered what was troubling her.

"Johnny, it is almost 9:30. The rest of the boys should be at the church so you better hurry."

Drinking the last of his orange juice, Johnny took the glass to the kitchen sink. "Okay, I'm going. Do you know where did Dad put the paint?"

Leah looked at her oldest son, now almost as tall as she, and realized he was going to have Mike's height. She could hardly believe he was twelve years old. Where had the years gone? Giving him a quick hug and kiss on the cheek, she smiled at him. "Everything you will need is on the front porch."

"Okay, see you later." He glanced at Laura, wanting to ask about Noelle again but knew it was no use. Laura could talk a mile a minute, but when you wanted her to say something she could clam up and not say a word. Plopping his baseball cap on his head, he grabbed a cookie and headed for the front porch.

Leah unplugged the toaster and glanced at her oldest daughter. "Laura, do you have a minute? I would like to ask you something."

"Okay, Mom." She listened to the bang of the front screen then Johnny's comment. "Gee whiz. How much paint does he think we need?"

Shari and Jimmy put their plates in the sink and headed for the stairs, grumbling on their way up. Saturday morning was the day they cleaned their rooms, and it had to be done before they could do anything else. Laura grinned knowingly. That would take all of ten minutes, and they would be calling down to Mom to check their rooms. She would come back downstairs, set the timer, and they would make a second attempt at cleaning their rooms. *When will they ever learn*? She sat with her chin in her hands and remembered when she cleaned her room in much the same way.

"Is something bothering you?" Leah looked at her, noting the frown on her face and her unusual quietness at breakfast.

"I guess you could say so; although, it doesn't have anything to do with me." Laura wondered how her mom always knew when something was wrong. "Noelle is upset, and I don't know what to tell her." Laura took her plate to the sink and sat back down "It is not really that bad, but you know how Noelle is. She is so sensitive, and I feel sorry for her." Laura watched her mother take a sip of coffee and began telling her about Noelle's remark at the drug store. "The boys are making a big deal out of nothing," Laura said, already feeling better.

Leah sat her coffee down and patted her hand "I am glad you are such a good friend to Noelle. Some people worry over things that you and I would not let bother us. Noelle is a very shy and sensitive young girl." Leah smiled at her daughter and continued, "and we both know how curious boys can be. Why don't you invite Noelle over this afternoon and let your dad talk to her?"

Laura's eyes lit up as she smiled across the table at her mom. "That's what we will do. Dad always knows just what to say or do to make people feel better." She rose from her chair, walked around the table, and gave her mother a hug. "Thanks, Mom."

Johnny made a second trip across the street carrying paint buckets. His Dad asked for volunteers Sunday to paint the cemetery fence so it would look nice for the 4th of July. Several raised their hands, but he chose him, Brenton, Truman, and Larry White because they were older and in the same Sunday school class. "Four of you should be just about right." He had smiled at them and looked very pleased with his choice.

Johnny shoved a gallon of paint to the side and sat down on the church step to wait for the others. Three rabbits studied him as they scampered in and out of the thicket of gooseberry bushes that grew along one side of the churchyard. He wondered what the rabbits thought of him; if, in fact, they thought at all. He sat very still and watched to see if they would come closer until a whistle broke his train of thought, and he looked up to see Larry riding down the street.

"Is everyone late?" Larry asked as he laid his bike in the grass and sat down beside him.

"No, it's just now nine-thirty. They'll be here any minute. Brenton is always on time." He scooted over to make more room for Larry and glanced over at the fence. "How long do you think it will take us to get the job done?"

"Not too long, I hope. We could probably be finished by noon if we really wanted to. The Cardinals are playing the Giants, and I want to get done so I can listen to the game." Larry picked up one of the brushes and felt the bristles. "Did you see *The Yearling*? I didn't see you, but we barely got there on time." He leaned back against one of the white pillars and glanced over at the cemetery, mentally dividing the fence into four sections.

Oak Grove Baptist Church sat nestled in a grove of oak trees at the outer edge of a forest that extended several miles to the west. Seabaugh Creek meandered lazily through the trees and created a safe boundary for young fishermen. No one particularly wanted to cross the creek because of the increased density of the woods beyond. The forest provided a beautiful backdrop for the old, white, wooden church with its gray roof and steeple. It was not unusual, at any time of year, for someone passing through Oak Grove to pull over, grab their Kodak Camera, and take a snapshot of the tranquil setting.

A sidewalk curved across the lawn, guiding one to wide steps leading up onto a covered porch. Red wooden doors were flanked by long windows on both sides that allowed sunlight to stream into the foyer, presenting a warm, welcoming feeling as one entered.

Across the drive, a white picket fence bordered the cemetery at the edge of the forest. Peeling and faded paint on some of the boards produced the task at hand.

"Yes, I think everyone in town was there." Johnny leaned back and thought about last night. All the girls had cried. "It was kind of sad, wasn't it?" Hearing a shout, both looked up to see Brenton and Truman pedaling up the church drive.

"Did you find anything out from Laura?" Truman asked hopefully, as he braked his bike and caught the paintbrush Larry tossed him.

"No. She said Noelle didn't have any news, she didn't either, and that was that." Johnny looked at their disappointed faces and shrugged his shoulders.

Larry looked curiously at the three and asked, "Find anything out about what?"

Brenton sat down on the step, preparing to fill him in on the whole situation, when the sound of an airplane caught their attention. All four boys looked up and watched in amazement as the plane descended, flying low and right toward Oak Grove.

"What does he think he is doing?" Brenton yelled.

The plane went into a dive right over the church, pulled back up into the air, then released leaflets of every color. They floated in the breeze every which way, falling like autumn leaves.

"Let's see what's going on," Johnny yelled, jumping up. Laughing and shouting, they ran into the churchyard, grabbing at the colorful papers falling all around them. Usually someone in a neighboring town was having a sale, an auction, or occasionally announcing a picnic or carnival. Whatever the reason, it always stirred up excitement and curiosity.

Brenton grabbed up a red leaflet from the grass and let out a whoop. All four boys stood in amazement, staring at the leaflet they held in their hands. They couldn't believe it.

"This is it!" Johnny exclaimed. "This is the secret they were keeping until today!"

Truman read his aloud:

HAPPY 15TH BIRTHDAY

CAROLINE DRISCOL

THE AMERICAN CIRCUS COMPANY

Oak Grove Fair Grounds
Friday, June 21
Showtime 7:00 p.m.

Chapter 2

Johnny pushed his empty Wheaties bowl across the table and picked up the Buck Rogers Magic Saturn Code Ring that had fallen out of the freshly opened cereal box. Turning it over, he looked at it curiously and wondered what Jimmy's reaction would be when he saw it. He had talked of nothing else for the last two weeks and checked Reese's Market daily to see if the supply containing the rings had arrived.

Johnny grinned, thinking he ought to tell him there had not been one in it. Tossing it back in the box, he picked up the circus leaflet lying on the table and wondered how his dad could have kept the circus such a secret.

All had been revealed after church yesterday. Pastor Mike walked to the back of the church as usual to give the benediction. He chuckled and told the congregation that confession was good for the soul; therefore, all who wanted to confess their part in bringing the circus to Oak Grove could do so now. Astonishment and laughter filled the church. Wives and children had no idea their husbands and fathers had taken part in the surprise. One watching those coming out the church door would have wondered if there was even a sermon preached that morning with all of the good-natured joking and scolding.

Standing outside, Hank Wilson removed his hat, scratched his head, and said, "When I found out the circus was in Chesterville and was going right by Oak Grove, I thought to myself; now why don't they just stop off here and give us a show?"

Samuel Cranston spoke up, "I couldn't have agreed more. I felt it my duty to bring a little excitement to this town." He looked at his wife, Abigail, and grinned at her astonished face. Turning with a nod of his head and a smile, he looked at his twin daughters, Milly and Molly.

They were identical, and neither had ever married. Besides Mrs. Driscol, they always surprised everyone with the hats they wore. Today they sported simple straw hats with yellow ribbons running around the crown and their names embroidered on the front. They came up with the idea of applying names to their hats, much to everyone's relief, not long after they opened The Sweet Shoppe. It had solved everyone's problem of not knowing who was who and added a little fun for the customers on Fridays when they chose not to wear their hats.

"Why, Sam, you never said a word," Abigail replied. "I wondered where that smug look you've been wearing came from."

Mayor Driscol cleared his throat and said, "When Hank and Sam came to me with their proposal, I felt it my responsibility to follow through and see what could be done." He looked at his adopted niece, Caroline, who would turn fifteen in three days and winked. "The timing could not have been more perfect, and the merchants of our town could not have been more generous with their willingness to contribute in whatever way possible."

Sheriff Walker pointed in the direction of the Methodist Church and laughed. "We are not the only culprits. The Methodists are in on this too," he commented, bringing on a round of good-natured laughter. Oak Grove Methodist Church was no more than two blocks away over on Oak Street where many friends and neighbors attended regularly.

A congenial, dedicated commitment was displayed by members of both congregations when it came to affairs of the community; whether it be something disastrous, the observance of a holiday, or the annual Founder's Day Celebration.

Brenton and Truman's mouths dropped open, and they stared at Alan, leaning against the oak tree with his hands in his pockets grinning at them. "You said you didn't know what was going on," Brenton accused as he walked over to him.

"I don't think so. I believe I said that I did not know what Noelle was talking about." He laughed and tousled Brenton's hair then punched Truman on the arm. "Some detectives you two are. Pastor Mike walked right in The Chronicle and in front of both of you, asked for the posters that he ordered." He laughed and leaned towards them, whispering, "The posters are advertising the circus."

Both boys turned and looked at Johnny. "I didn't know a thing about it." He held both hands up in defense and turned to look for his dad who was talking to Noelle and her mother.

It didn't take long to find out that all the merchants in town had cooperated but decided to keep it a secret in the event that Oak Grove could not be added to the circus' schedule.

Miss Mattie stood in the shade of an oak tree listening to the laughter with a smile on her face. "Oh, Hannah," she said as she turned to the slim black lady standing next to her, "the circus will be fun; will it not?"

Hannah's brown eyes widened in amazement as she turned and answered, "Why Miss Mattie, you mean to tell me at the age of ninety-five you plan on goin' to this circus?"

Hannah's husband, Jeremiah, chuckled. "She best go. Might not be around when the next one comes to town."

"You are right there, Jeremiah." Miss Mattie smiled at him affectionately. "One is never too old to have a little fun." She glanced back at Hannah and grinned. The three had been friends for years. They were like family and had lived with her in the big house on the hill for more than forty years. Mattie did not know what she would have done without them when her husband passed away.

"Come on, Miss Mattie, you better sit yourself down on the bench. Those little ones are gettin' anxious." Jeremiah took her by the arm and assisted her to the wrought iron bench beneath the oak tree. Old Ben had fashioned the bench in his blacksmith shop years ago and placed it there one Saturday afternoon to everyone's surprise.

Miss Mattie was a stately looking lady. She was thin, white headed, and still retained a sparkle in her warm gray eyes. Always demanding truth from those around her, she was also a stickler for good manners and proper behavior. She did have a tendency to give in to the outrageous if the mood struck and occasionally shocked those who were accustomed to her otherwise elegant demeanor. Her heart was as big as the world, and she expressed love generously to those around her as well as strangers. One's social standing made no difference to her, and she was often heard to comment, "The ground is level at the foot of the cross." There was almost a regal bearing about her, and she still stood upright, although now needed the assistance of a cane when walking.

Miss Mattie seated herself on the bench and accepted the red and white square box Hannah handed her. Like a magnet, it drew the younger children to her in a matter of minutes. The habit of giving candy to the children after church began years ago, and it became one of the true joys in her life. Looking at the faces around her now took her back to a time when their parents stood in this same spot eagerly awaiting their candy.

"Miss Mattie, you sure look nice today," Zachary Madison commented as he looked up at her with big blue eyes and then down at the red and white box.

"Young man, are you trying to flirt with me with those pretty blue eyes of yours? Or do you just want what I might have in this box?"

Zachary grinned, sat on the bench next to her, and leaned familiarly against her. Putting her arm around his shoulder, she smiled and hugged him tightly.

"Honest Miss Mattie, I do like the blue flowers on your dress. They match your hat." He glanced up at the blue straw hat on her white head. "But, I like the box too."

Her heart melted at the honesty of the child, and she smiled and raised the lid of the old red and white box. Inside was an assortment that would please anyone: Chuckles, Bit-O-Honeys, Tootsie Rolls, Red-Hots, ValoMilks, Milk Duds, Goo-Goo Clusters, Baby Ruth's, and Snickers.

The same ritual, begun years ago, was still followed as the children formed a circle in front of her. They were all precious to her: the younger of Sheriff Walker's boys; Josiah, Jordan, and Garrett, Zachary Madison, Maggie and Abigail Miller, Shari and Jimmy Daniels, Carrie Cook, Carole and Charlotte Charles, Mike Olson, and Donnie White. Others, too grown up to participate, would occasionally slip by and help themselves to the old red and white box, filling her heart with joy as they grinned sheepishly at her.

Starting with the youngest, each selected a favorite piece of candy, thanked her with a hug or kiss, and skipped off. Miss Mattie sat the box on the bench next to her and looked around. Several women laughed and talked together, and Caroline Driscol and some of the other girls stood at the end of the sidewalk giggling. Their attention was drawn to the parking lot and several boys gathered around an old 1930 Ford belonging to Peter Williams' cousin, Josh. Clumps of men discussed the weather, the hog market, or the price of corn as they stood around waiting for their wives, and several of the smaller children chased each other around the churchyard. Pastor Mike and Leah stood at the bottom of the steps, chatting with the Seabaughs and the Cranstons, and Mildred Reese, rubbing her shoulder, had cornered Dr. Miller with her latest ailment.

They are all my children, she thought as her eyes took in all the familiar faces and varied personalities that were so dear to her. "Thank you, Lord, for giving me such a wonderful and blessed ninety-five years." Knowing her time was drawing near; she sighed, closed her eyes, and listened to the familiar voices.

The breeze caressed her cheeks and hair, and the memory of a wasp getting after Daniel came to her mind. It had flown through the open church window and buzzed around his head a few times. Swatting at it was a mistake, and he finally stood up in the middle of the sermon, scurried up the aisle to the back of the church and out the door, waving his arms. Her beloved Daniel; how she missed him. Opening her eyes, she almost expected to see him standing in front of her and rejoiced that she would see him again soon. But until the Lord called her home, she would continue to enjoy each day to the fullest.

"We are goin' to have to make a trip to Milly and Molly's before next Sunday," Hannah commented, counting the few pieces left in the box. Her stomach growled, and she thought of dinner in the oven. "That fried chicken is goin' to taste mighty good when we get home, Miss Mattie."

Jeremiah drove Miss Mattie's '41 Packard around to the end of the sidewalk. Opening the door, he stood and waited for the two women, knowing it would be a few minutes. There was always a lot of visiting with Miss Mattie. She was special to everyone who knew her. Jeremiah took pride in the fact that he was the only one Miss Mattie allowed to drive her car, and he took the privilege very seriously. The warm breeze rustled the leaves and birds sang in the branches above his head. He stood patiently, not minding the wait, and listened to those talking and laughing with Miss Mattie and Hannah.

Old Ben smiled at him as he walked to the car and reached through the window, laying his Bible on the front seat. Both men stood in companionable silence as they leaned against the car. Old Ben always rode to church with Young Ben and Mercy, but for some reason that none of them could remember he always rode home with Miss Mattie, Hannah, and Jeremiah. Ben readily admitted that he could not remember why, but Miss Mattie said that his coming home with them for Sunday dinner started it. Hannah claimed he took a "fool notion to walk home one spring day," and she told him he didn't have any business walkin' that far as old as he was. Jeremiah stubbornly insisted that it was the year they gave him a ride to show off Miss Mattie's new Ford and insisted the women didn't know what they were talking about. Whatever the reason; it became a habit they all enjoyed and one that no one in Oak Grove thought strange. Old Ben was delivered to his niece's house for Sunday dinner at approximately the same time she and Young Ben arrived home. Those driving by were accustomed to the whole matter and didn't give it a second thought.

Jim and Jennifer Walker slowly assisted Miss Mattie and Hannah to the end of the sidewalk, laughing at something humorous one of them said. "Jeremiah, you take care of these fine young ladies," Jim said as he shook his hand and watched Old Ben help the ladies into the car.

"I'll sure do that, but you know they both can be pretty stubborn." Jeremiah looked at both ladies and then back at Jim with a small smile on his face. He worried about many things and wished he could be more like Hannah or Miss Mattie who never seemed to worry about a thing. Hannah was always telling him that he could worry for all three of them, and he had discovered that was just about the sum of it.

Miss Mattie and Hannah always rode in the back seat, and out of habit, Jeremiah opened the door and double-checked to make sure both were situated and ready to go. Closing the door, he took his place behind the wheel and glanced over to make sure Old Ben was ready. Starting the engine, he waved his hand and drove slowly away.

"What precious people they are." Jennifer hooked her arm through Jim's, and they walked to the car. "It looks like Truman and Simon are ready to go," she laughed as she looked at both boys sitting in the car with their ties removed and their shoes off.

No more than a couple of minutes passed and the parking lot was empty, still, and quiet. Everyone was headed home for Sunday dinner.

Johnny sat at the breakfast table and studied the picture on the calendar hanging on the wall. A man and young boy were sitting on a creek bank fishing; the cork on the line bobbing in the water. Maybe he and Dad could go out to the millpond next week. He would ask him. He glanced at the clock. What was keeping Dad and Jimmy? They walked across the street to the church and were going to be right back, and the three were going to hang circus posters in the square.

Shari, still in her pajamas, wandered down the stairs and into the kitchen. Johnny wondered how she could get her hair so tangled up just sleeping. It looked like a bird's nest every morning. He was glad his hair was short.

Sitting in the chair across from him with a sleepy look on her face, she yawned and commented, "Donnie put a lizard in the piano bench." She looked at him with a matter-of-fact expression. "I guess you better get it out before Miss Myrtle finds it, or she will have one of her spells. I would, but I promised Donnie that I didn't see a thing." She rubbed her eyes, propped her chin in her hands and stared at him. "So, if I didn't see a thing, I don't know it is there."

"We are ready, Johnny. How about you?" Mike stuck his head in the back door and smiled at his oldest son and youngest daughter. Jimmy stood behind him with an armload of posters and was looking proudly at his new decoder ring.

"Okay." He grabbed his ball cap and glanced at his little sister. "Let me run over to the church for just a minute. I have to take care of something."

Mike shook his head and wondered what was going on. He looked affectionately at his youngest daughter as she sat at the table swinging her feet. He closed the door, walked over to her, and retrieved a banana from the fruit bowl. "Good morning, sweetheart. Where's Mama?"

"She's making the bed. Guess what?" she asked, looking up at him with a grin on her face."

"What?" Mike asked as he looked down into her brown eyes and peeled the banana.

A big grin crossed her face. "Mom's making pancakes," she stated, "and I am going to eat lots of them." They usually challenged one another over who could eat the most, and Mike was amazed at how many pancakes one little girl could consume.

He leaned down and kissed her on the forehead. "If I was going to be here for breakfast, I would eat twice as many as you."

"No you wouldn't," Shari giggled. "I would eat three times more than you."

"Oh yeah, smarty pants? Then you would explode and we would have pancakes and syrup all over the kitchen," he remarked, watching her eyes shine with laughter. "Since I won't be here, eat some for me, okay? The boys and I have to go over to the square." He watched her stir a big scoop of Ovaltine in her glass and thought her resemblance to Leah was so strong he could be looking at his wife when she was a little girl.

Shari watched him take a bite of banana. "Dad, Jimmy ate all of the Moon Pics again. I only got one and so did Laura and Johnny." Looking very serious, she lowered her voice and whispered, "Jimmy is sneaky with Moon Pies. I just thought you ought to know." She shook her head and sighed disgustedly, "He is a hog."

Mike smiled down at his youngest daughter and tugged on her ear. "I guess you are right. He is a hog sometime, but he's the only hog we've got. I guess we should love him and be thankful God gave us such a fine, healthy one, don't you?"

Shari rolled her eyes and tried not to grin. "Will you buy two boxes of Moon Pies when you go to Reese's?"

"I tell you what; how about if I buy four boxes You can each put your name on a box and hide it." Mike laughed at the grin on her face and turned to go out the back door. "Tell Mama I'll see her in a little while."

Passing through the foyer of the church, Johnny opened the door of the sanctuary and stood for a minute, enjoying the silence. He knew where everyone usually sat and could almost see them now. A pleasant feeling came over him, and he was glad his dad was the Pastor.

He jumped as a familiar voice yelled in his ear. "What are you doing here?" Laura stood behind him with a mischievous grin on her face.

"You about scared the daylights out of me. I came to free a lizard from the piano bench. What are you doing in here?" He looked at his sister and wondered how she could have slipped up behind him so quietly.

Laura held up a small, white purse. "Noelle left it here yesterday. I am going to her house this morning, and she wanted me to bring it." Laura wondered what made little boys acts so weird and knew before she asked who the culprit was. "Donnie?"

Johnny laughed. "Who else?" They walked over to the piano bench and stood for a moment, staring at it. "Now I know that neither one of us is afraid of a small lizard, but we are going to have to figure out how to catch it so it doesn't run loose and up someone's leg."

Laura giggled as a vision entered her mind of a lizard running loose in the aisles and screaming ladies climbing up onto the pews. She wondered what her dad would do.

Pastor Mike backed his '39 ford out of the driveway and parked in front of the house, wondering what his oldest son was doing and what was taking so long. About that time, the church door opened and he watched Johnny and Laura carry the piano bench down the steps.

"Is Miss Myrtle going to play the piano outside?" Jimmy scooted across the back seat and hung out the window. "She's never done that before."

Mike watched as they sat the bench on the ground and carefully turned it on its side. Laura stepped back as Johnny lifted the lid, and a fairly good sized, black lizard shot free and quickly disappeared. Mike chuckled and watched them carry the bench back up the steps and into the church.

"I guess she's not going to play outside after all." Jimmy sat back in the seat, disappointed. "Miss Myrtle will quit playing all together with lizards in her bench. How do you suppose that lizard got there?" Hanging over the back of the front seat, he looked at Mike curiously. "Do you think she ever will play the piano outside?" he asked, now hanging far enough over the seat that Mike expected him to fall on his head any minute.

He looked at the hopeful expression on Jimmy's face. "I don't know, Son. I am not surprised at anything anymore." The church door slammed, and Johnny and Laura came down the steps, laughing, and crossed the street. Laura stepped on the running board and giggled, "That problem's taken care of." Leaning over, she kissed Mike on the cheek. "Bye, Dad, I'll see you after while."

"Bye, sweetie. You and Noelle have fun." Mike watched her step down and run through the yard to the house then looked at Johnny as he got in the front seat and slammed the door. "Donnie White?" he asked with a grin.

Johnny nodded and glanced in the back. Jimmy sat in the floorboard looking intently at the posters propped up against the back of the seat.

They drove down Spruce Street, made a right on Hunter Avenue, and then a quick left onto Oak Street which brought them right into the town square. Parking in front of the drugstore, Mike looked over his shoulder and grinned at the Moon Pie thief, absorbed with the posters. "Gather them up, Jimmy. Let's go figure out where to put them."

Opening the door, Mike stepped out and glanced around the square. He loved the place. Oak trees provided plenty of shade, and wooden benches surrounded a fountain on the east end. It was a popular place for folks to sit a spell and while away the time. Flowers were well tended, and honeysuckle, growing along the sidewalk, filled the air with sweet fragrance. A small bandstand was located on the west end of the square and the old Bell Tower and flagpole stood in the middle. He wondered how long it had been since anyone rang the bell. It was used for emergencies in days long past, but he could not ever recall hearing it ring. The Bell Tower was part of Oak Grove, and no one could remember it not being there.

"How many posters do we have?" Johnny broke his train of thought as he retrieved two posters Jimmy dropped "Where are we going to hang them?"

"Hey, Dad. Look at Mrs. Driscol's hat!" Jimmy yelled in his favorite outdoor voice as he pointed and stared at the ladies looking out the drugstore window. "She's got feathers all over her head."

"Jimmy, will you come over here." Mike, red-faced and wanting to wring his youngest son's neck, smiled and waved at the ladies. Johnny looked to see who his dad was waving at and caught a glimpse of Mrs. Driscol at the window. He burst into laughter and quickly ducked back into the car, pretending to look for something.

"Johnny, you better knock it off." Mike held Jimmy by the arm. "This is not funny." He bent back into the car to get his hat and looked in the back seat at his oldest son's face.

"Yes it is, Dad. It's really funny." Johnny scrunched down in the back seat and glanced back at the drugstore. "Oh, Dad, here they come," he choked out in panic and buried his face in his hands, laughing.

Mike's face was stern, but he could not hide the laughter in his blue eyes. "Let's just try to act like we have a little bit of decency about ourselves. Now get out and says hello, and, Jimmy, you do not say one word. Do you hear me?" Mike grabbed his hat from the front seat. "Well, good morning, ladies. You are out early." He slammed the car door and maintained a firm grip on Jimmy's arm.

"Oh, yes, we wanted to see the posters. Henry said you would be hanging them up this morning, and since I needed to get some last minute items for Caroline's party, I rode along with him. He is going to meet me at the café for lunch," she commented, nodding her head in the direction of the Cranston Café. The one long, purple feather hung over her eye, and she blew it out of her face and continued her conversation. "You know, Caroline turns fifteen Wednesday. Can you believe that, Pastor Mike? Do you remember when we first brought the girls to Oak Grove? It was ten years ago. I declare; my how time does fly. I just can't believe it, can you? We were just relaxing over a glass of lemonade, hoping to run into you. Weren't we, Mildred?" Mrs. Driscol smiled and nodded at Mildred Reese. Every time she moved her head, the long purple feather waved in all directions.

Not able to move from the grip his dad had on his arm, Jimmy stared in amazement. He had never seen so many feathers or so many colors in one spot in all his life. He recognized a couple of peacock feathers and wanted to ask what kind and how many birds they had to kill to make the hat. Glancing up at his dad's face, Jimmy caught the look he gave him and decided he better keep his mouth shut.

Johnny quickly grabbed the posters from Jimmy, kept one, and handed the rest to his dad. "Here, Dad, you take these and I'll go ahead and put one up in Williams Drugstore." Not daring to look at him for fear of bursting into laughter again, he missed the look of exasperation Mike gave him. Anxious to escape, he made a beeline to the drugstore and stood just inside the screen door, looking back at his dad who held the posters in one hand and clutched Jimmy's arm in a death grip with the other. With a big grin, Johnny laughed and walked over to the soda fountain.

"Hi, Mr. Williams. Do you mind if I put one of these circus posters in the window?"

"My heavens no, I don't mind at all, Johnny. You go right ahead," he answered, laying aside the tea towel he was using to dry Coca-Cola glasses. "It's going to be something having a circus come to town, isn't it?" Mr. Williams leaned across the counter and looked at the poster curiously. "Well, I'll swan; you just put it wherever you think best," he said, still looking at it. "That's the only thing folks are talking about when they come in here."

Johnny walked to the window, carefully moved a Kodak camera, and stood the poster next to a bottle of King's Men cologne. Glancing out the window, he saw his dad showing one of the posters to the ladies.

Mrs. Driscol, looking intently at it, smiled and pointed, said something, lifted her head, and the long purple feather slapped his dad in the face. Johnny laughed and continued to watch. There was no way he could go back out there until they left. Jimmy was staring at Mrs. Driscol like he was in a trance, Dad was scratching the side of his face, and Mildred Reese was straightening Mrs. Driscol's hat. Dad said something, smiled, and guided Jimmy across the street.

The ladies walked back to the drugstore and stood on the sidewalk looking in the window at the poster. Johnny stepped back and bumped into Mr. Williams who was proudly looking over his shoulder.

"Thanks, Mr. Williams," he said, walking to the door. Stepping out, he smiled at the ladies and hurried across the street, knowing his dad was on his way to Willy's Garage.

"Hey, Johnny," Larry White called from the bakery. Johnny waved back and watched him cross the street. His parents owned White's Bakery and made the best donuts he had ever tasted.

"Did you listen to the game yesterday?" Larry asked, handing him a small, white sack. "They beat the Giants 4–1."

Johnny looked inside—donut holes! "Thanks, Larry. Yeah, Dad and I listened to it." He popped one in his mouth and reached for another. "They're playing the Braves today. Say, do you want to see one of the circus posters? Dad just hung that one."

The boys walked over and looked at the bright yellow poster hanging on the side of Willy's Garage. Bold, red lettering advertised The American Circus Co., and a big, blue tent dominated the middle of the poster. On one side, a girl swung from a trapeze, a man on a high wire was on the other, and a variety of animals was displayed at random. The date and show time was painted in a flourish across the bottom.

"Man, I can't hardly wait." Larry looked at him. "This might be the only circus we ever get to see. When do you think it will get here?"

Willy raised his head from beneath the hood of the green Nash he was working on and looked at the two boys staring at the poster. "Pastor Mike said the circus train should get here Wednesday or maybe even Tuesday afternoon." Pulling a rag from his back pocket, he wiped the grease from his hands and looked through the open door.

"Excuse me, boys. I have a customer." He limped passed them, stuffing the rag back into his pocket.

"I have to go, Larry. I'm supposed to be helping Dad hang these posters." Johnny headed toward the street and waved to Mr. Miller who was talking to Willy. "See you, Willy."

"I've got to go too, or Mom will be wondering where I am." Larry fell in step with him as they crossed the street at the post office. "See you later."

"Okay, thanks for the donut holes." Johnny watched him walk down the sidewalk toward the bakery.

The door to the post office opened, and his dad and Jimmy stepped out. "What do you have?" Mike asked, looking at the white sack in his hand.

"Donut holes; compliments of Larry. Have one." Johnny held the sack out and his dad grabbed it from him.

"You are a traitor. Do you know that?" He took one and handed the sack to Jimmy.

"What is a traitor, Dad?" Jimmy asked. He stuffed several donut holes in his mouth and looked at his brother curiously.

Mike took the sack, handed it back to Johnny, and looked at him pointedly. "It is someone who does not stick with you and would rather take the easy way out."

Johnny laughed. "I couldn't help it, Dad. You didn't want me to stand there and laugh in front of them, did you? I didn't want to hurt their feelings."

Mike looked at him in disbelief and shook his head. "No, I wouldn't have wanted you to hurt their feelings."

"Where are we going to hang the rest of these?" he asked and then laughed at the thought of his dad getting slapped in the face with the feather. Raising the sack out of Jimmy's reach, he looked down at him. "Eat what you have in your mouth first. You know what Mom says."

Mike glanced around the square. "I guess we can put one at City Hall and one over at Reese's Market. Alan already has one at The Chronicle."

Saul Smith drove by in his truck, and Mike waved. He looked at his two sons and motioned for them to follow. "Come on, let's finish. Then we'll stop in at the drugstore for a cherry coke."

Johnny looked at his dad like he had lost his mind. "Go back to the drugstore?"

Mike laughed at the expression on his son's face. "They're gone. I saw the ladies going into Baker's Clothing." He glanced down at Jimmy, who was staring up at him, and straightened the baseball cap that sat crooked on his head.

He wiped the sugar from around his mouth on his shirt and asked, "Can I talk now, Dad?"

Forgetting that he had told him not to speak, Mike looked at him in surprise and grinned. "Yes, you can talk now. It's safe; I think."

"Well, I've been thinking. I think Mrs. Driscol's hat is real pretty, and I would rather have a grape Nehi instead of a cherry coke. I also don't think Mom is going to be very happy when she finds out that Johnny is a traitor."

"Doesn't she look pretty?" Shari turned her paper doll around so Maggie and Carole could see. All three girls had new paper dolls and were presently absorbed in dressing them in evening gowns. Maggie, Alan Miller's oldest daughter, and Carol, one of Matthew Charles' daughters, both lived around the block and were spending the afternoon at Shari's house. They sat on a quilt on the front porch with paper dolls spread out around them. A small tea set was shoved to the side and evidence of cookie crumbs was scattered about.

"I wish we had some circus clothes," Maggie commented. "Do you think they make circus paper dolls?" She looked at Shari curiously and then at Carole.

"Mom was at the dime store yesterday. I'll ask her if she saw any." Shari looked up as her dad pulled in the driveway. Jimmy jumped out of the car with a brown grocery bag in his hand and ran up on the porch. "We all have our own box of Moon Pies," he announced proudly, waving the bag around as he jerked the screen open banging it against the wall, and rushed into the house. "Mom," he yelled, "do you know Johnny is a traitor?"

Shari stared after her brother, wondering why Johnny was a traitor, and laid her paper doll down as she watched her dad and Johnny walk through the yard.

"Hello, little ladies," Mike said as he walked up the step, "and what have you three been doing?"

"Hi, Daddy," Shari smiled up at him "We are playing with our new paper dolls."

"You are? How would you like to take a look at this?" Laying an extra circus poster in the middle of the porch, he stepped back and smiled at the squeals of delight. "It's the circus!" Maggie dropped her paper doll and leaned over for a closer look.

Mike smiled at the three little girls lying on their stomachs excitedly looking at the poster and followed Johnny through the front door. "Leah? I think we need to explain a couple of things to Jimmy about gentlemen behavior and women's hats."

Carole jumped up, "Let's play circus! I will swing from the tree and be the lady on the trapeze." Her eyes were bright and shiny as she danced around on the porch.

Shari thought for a moment. "Then I will stand on the back of a white horse and ride around inside the tent. My mom saw a picture of that in a magazine."

Maggie looked at her. "I will be the princess." A dreamy look crossed her face. "I will be the circus princess."

"A circus does not have a princess, Maggie." The voice burst her bubble and all three girls turned to look at Zachary, standing at the bottom step. He held the handle of his Radio Flyer wagon in one hand and an empty soda pop bottle in the other. Several more bottles lay in the wagon along with a tree limb, and a bird's nest placed carefully in the very back of the wagon.

Maggie stood with her hands on her hips and stared at him. "It does too. There is always a princess. You can't have a circus without one."

Zachary stared back at her "Well, you just ask your mom. She'll tell you. She sent me to get you. We are going to Grandma's for supper and she said for you to come now so you could clean up." He sat down on the step and watched her slowly gather her paper dolls. He looked at Shari. "Is Jimmy here?"

"Yes, he's in the house, but I heard Daddy say that he needed a conversation with Mom about ladies' hats." Shari handed Maggie some of the doll clothes. "I guess we can play circus tomorrow."

Maggie held the little blue paper doll box in her hand and looked at Carole and Shari with a smile on her face. "We'll make some costumes. You can come to my house, and we'll look in that old box of clothes Mama has." With that settled, she looked at Zachary. "Okay, I'm ready." Jumping off the steps, she dropped the blue box in the wagon and called back over her shoulder, "See you tomorrow."

"Tell Jimmy hi for me," Zachary said, pulling the wagon along behind him. He looked at Maggie. "Aunt Lynn said we could take these bottles to Reese's Market and get our refund first."

Maggie glanced back at the wagon and counted ten bottles. That would give him twenty cents. He would share; he always did. Now she had to decide what kind of candy she wanted.

"You mean to tell me that there is going to be a real circus here in Oak Grove?" Grandpa Miller asked, looking at his three grandchildren gathered in front of him on the porch. They just finished Grandma's pot roast and were now topping it off with chocolate cake and milk.

"Yes," Zachary said, swallowing a mouthful of cake, "and it might even be here tomorrow. Isn't that right, Dad?"

Michael Madison looked at the excitement in his son's eyes. "It just may. I imagine it will take a couple of days to get the tents up and everything ready." He looked at his father-in-law. "There were no problems at all. Mr. Morton was most cooperative. He said they were passing by Oak Grove and would easily have time for one show."

Robert Miller had been Oak Grove's doctor for the last thirty years. He shared so much joy and pain with his patients that they had become a part of him. Attending a medical meeting last week, he and Margaret decided to take a few extra days to spend with life long friends at the lake. Although he knew of the circus planning, it wasn't until Alan stopped by this morning for coffee that he learned the details.

Abigail put her empty plate on the small, round table at the end of the porch and then perched on the railing. "Grandma, Maggie saw a poster of the circus today. The real circus poster."

"Did you, Maggie?" Grandma Miller turned to her granddaughter with a pleased smile. "And where did you see it?"

Maggie sat on the porch swing between her mother and father and answered excitedly. "Yes, I was playing at Shari's today, and Pastor Mike brought one home and showed it to us. It has a tent and animals and a girl swinging on a swing in the air."

Lynn smoothed her daughter's dark hair and smiled affectionately at her. "That's all she has been talking about since she came home. Actually, I think we are almost as excited as the girls."

Alan looked at his wife and laid his arm along the back of the swing, resting his hand on her shoulder. "I think everyone is going to enjoy the circus. Miss Mattie said Sunday she wouldn't miss it for anything."

Margaret Miller laughed as she thought fondly of her husband's aunt. "Oh, I would expect nothing less from Mattie."

Zachary looked at his mom, sitting in a rocker next to his dad. "Can we go early? I want to see the animals." He glanced at Maggie and then his aunt. "Aunt Lynn, tell Maggie there is not a princess in the circus."

Lynn smiled and glanced at Ellen. Her nephew was all boy and her oldest daughter most definitely all girl. "Well, I told Maggie that I really don't think there will be a princess like she imagines. But, when you see that beautiful girl swinging high in the air, everyone will think she is the queen of the circus."

A very pleased smile spread across Maggie's face as she looked at Zachary and leaned against her mother's side.

"Well, we were both right. I knew there would be no princess," he said.

"Who cares about a princess or a queen. I want to see the lions and tigers." Abigail jumped off the railing and joined Zachary who had moved to the top step of the porch. "In just a few minutes the fireflies will be out." She looked across the yard, hoping to see the first small flashing light.

Robert Miller smiled with contentment as he watched Maggie join Zachary and Abbie on the porch step. The three sat quietly waiting for fireflies that, at any moment, would start flittering here and there across the yard. He thought of how much he loved his grandchildren and glanced at Margaret who was also looking at them tenderly. She looked at him, and they smiled at one another, reading the other's thoughts.

Truman and Simon finished their baths, listened to Captain Midnight, and went up stairs for the night. Jim sat on Truman's bed and Jennifer found a comfortable spot on Simon's. Sport lay in his usual night position on the rug between the beds.

"Do you think the circus might get here tomorrow?" Truman asked hopefully as he looked from his mom to his dad.

Jim leaned back against the wall and yawned. "I don't know. I am not sure when the last performance in Chesterville was. They have to transport all the animals. That should take a while."

"Melba trimmed my hair today, and everyone that came into the shop was excited," Jennifer said, tucking her legs beneath her. "The arrival of the circus train will be quite an event."

"You mean they are going to come in at the depot?" Simon looked with wide eyes at his mother. "I didn't know they would come here on a train."

Jennifer and Jim both laughed. "No. The circus has several trucks that transport animals and equipment," Jennifer answered, looking at Jim questioningly. "I also suppose there are several vehicles that carry the performers, their costumes, and their personal belongings?"

"They have to transport all the tents in something too." Jim sat up as Sport laid his head on his leg, waiting for an ear scratching. "The elephants will walk the whole way, and that will take quite a while. Everyone travels together so they will arrive in town at the same time."

That is why it is called a circus train," Jennifer said.

Truman propped his pillow behind his head. "I want to watch the circus train when it comes into town; but how will we know when it's on its way?" Lying quietly for a minute, he suddenly sat up, an idea popping into his head.

"A bunch of us could get together and put lookouts on the road. We could go out as far as the Seabaugh farm, and we would know when it was coming."

"Boy howdy, that is a swell idea, Truman," Simon exclaimed, sitting up in bed. Sport jumped excitedly on the bed, wagging his tail as though he knew what they were talking about.

Jim watched Truman stare at the ceiling and knew he was already making plans. He stood up and stretched. "That's not a bad idea. I think it would probably work. You will have to get all your friends together early tomorrow and plan it all out." He stared through the window and commented, "Station yourselves at intervals on the road and relay the message into town."

Jennifer laughed. "Are you going to be the captain of this lookout team?" she asked, looking at Jim's grinning face.

Simon yawned. "I wonder how many animals there will be," he murmured to himself.

Jennifer kissed him on the forehead. "I am sure there will be loads of animals. But, for now, you need to get to sleep. You have a busy day tomorrow with all of this organizing you plan to do."

Rising from the bed, she went to Truman for a good night hug. "Sleep tight, don't let the bedbugs bite," she whispered. Walking to the door, she stopped and smiled at them. "Don't forget to thank God for bringing the circus to Oak Grove."

Jim kissed both boys on the head and turned the lamp off. He smiled to himself in the dark. This was going to be fun. Closing the door quietly behind him, he followed Jennifer down the hall.

The same topic of conversation was all over Oak Grove. Terry, Charlotte, and Carole Charles were trying to imagine everything they would see and how many different animals would be in the circus.

Carole rolled over on her bed and related to Terry and Charlotte again what the poster looked like. "There was a big tent, and it had a flag on top. There was also a girl on a swing and a man walking on a rope or something."

Charlotte lay on her side, her head propped on her arm, and asked the same question for the third time. "What kinds of animals? You said there were pictures of animals on the poster."

Carole rolled on her back and looked out the window at the stars in the sky "Let's see, there was an elephant, horses, lions, tigers, monkeys, and, I think, that was all."

Terry listened to her two younger sisters and giggled. "I heard one time that there was a lady in a circus that had a beard that grew down to her belly. I wonder if this one does." She yawned. "I guess we will find out tomorrow." She rolled over, hoping Carole would go to sleep but heard her giggle.

"A lady with a beard, wouldn't that be funny? What if I grew a beard? I won't, will I?" She sat up in bed and stared at Terry with a startled look on her face.

"No, you won't. It is probably a trick of some sort. Now go to sleep." She glanced at Charlotte, relieved that she was finally asleep, and would not be asking about the animals again. Terry thought of what she would get Caroline for her birthday. That might be difficult. She had almost everything. She smiled to herself as she thought of a bottle of cologne that Caroline sampled in Edna's Dress Shop last Saturday. She had removed the stopper, sniffed it, and stated that it smelled *heavenly*. She then proceeded to put a drop of it on her wrist. Maybe that is what I'll get her. After all, she will be fifteen years old.

Noelle lay in her bed wondering what the circus would be like. She felt so happy and excited. She talked to Pastor Mike and told him what happened in the drug store and explained how sorry she was that she made the whole thing up. He just smiled and hugged her.

"God knows just how you feel, Noelle, and He understands what happened. Let's tell Him you're sorry and ask Him to forgive you," he said as he took her small hands in his. They were big and strong just like her daddy's, and he held them while she prayed and told God that she was sorry. Then she didn't feel bad anymore.

Now lying in her bed, she couldn't wait until tomorrow. And if the boys asked her about it again, why . . . she would just tell them the truth.

Chapter 3

Truman jumped out of bed and looked at the clock on the night table, seven o'clock. "Simon, wake up!" He shook his brother's shoulder. "Come on, we have to call the guys."

Simon rolled over and gave him a dirty look. "Leave me alone. I'm still sleepy. Why would we have to call anyone this early?" He yawned and pulled the pillow over his head.

"The circus! We have to get the lookout team together." Truman impatiently pulled a pair of jeans out of the bottom dresser drawer. "Unless you want to sleep through the whole thing."

Simon sat straight up in bed. "I forgot, why didn't you tell me?" He jumped from the bed, ran to the dresser, and pulled a pair of jeans from the bottom drawer. "Grab me a shirt too."

Truman jerked a red and blue striped shirt from the closet and hurriedly grabbed one of Simon's and tossed it to him. "Hurry up. Get your shoes and socks on."

"I sure wish you two would get dressed this quickly on school mornings." Jennifer stood in the doorway watching the boys scramble around the room. "Go ahead and make your beds. I'll have breakfast ready in about ten minutes."

Truman and Simon frowned at each other. This was one more chore that had been added to *the list*. There was no getting around it, so they may as well get it over with. Of all days, this was not a day to poke around, and both boys threw their pillows on the bed and pulled the spreads up over them.

"We need to call the guys right away," Simon said, following him down the hall, carrying his shoes in his hand.

"That's what I told you. We need to call them early." Truman tried to think of the best way to approach his mom about the telephone.

"It's not nine o'clock you know," Simon commented as he sat in the floor tying his shoes. "You know she's not going to let you call anyone."

Truman watched him. "You're probably right, but since it's about the circus, it's worth a try."

"She's not going to let you." Simon stood up and looked at his brother. Lowering his voice he whispered. "This nine o'clock telephone rule is just a bunch of malarkey, if you ask me. What good is having a telephone if you can't use it when you need to?"

"Just let me do the talking, okay?" Truman wondered if his dad was still home or if he was already gone. He might help them talk her into it. He looked at Simon. "Come on."

Simon put a bright smile on his face as he walked into the kitchen, walked up behind his mom, and gave her a big hug. "Breakfast smells good, Mom. You are such a good cook. What are you fixing?" He glanced back at the table and grinned at Truman. It never hurt to start the day off with a compliment, and he was sure they were going to need a little help. Truman pulled his chair out and raised his brows at Simon with a look of disbelief on his face. He wished he would just be quiet.

Jennifer turned with an almost identical look. "Bacon and eggs," she answered, looking strangely at Simon before turning back to the stove. Now what did he think they were having? You couldn't confuse the smell of bacon with any other breakfast food.

She didn't know what they were up to, but without a doubt, it had something to do with the circus. Glancing at the clock, she realized what they had in mind. "Would you put a couple pieces of bread in the toaster please?" Jennifer smiled to herself as she turned the eggs and decided to take advantage of her leverage for the next few minutes.

Truman took a drink of his orange juice, glanced at the clock on the wall, and looked back at Simon as he plugged the toaster into the outlet. Lowering both trays, he placed a piece of bread on each and closed them.

Simon stretched his leg under the table and kicked Truman, motioning for him to say something. Truman sat up straight and cleared his throat. "I think I'll call Brenton and Johnny while you finish frying the eggs," he commented casually as he seriously studied the Taystee Bread wrapper.

Simon held a tablespoon of Ovaltine in midair, surprised at Truman's direct remark, and waited for her answer.

Jennifer glanced up at the kitchen clock then turned and looked at them. "Don't you think they are probably eating breakfast too? You both also have chores this morning, and if I remember correctly, we have a rule about using the telephone. Do you remember what that rule is?"

Truman's heart sank. "Yes, don't use the telephone before nine o'clock unless it is an emergency."

"That's right. It is still pretty early, isn't it?" She walked to the Frigidaire and opened the door.

Simon rolled his eyes and silently mouthed. "Tell her it is about the lookout squad."

Truman shook his head and turned the toast over. It wouldn't make any difference. They might just as well get rid of the phone for all the good it did him.

Jim came through the kitchen door, fastening the last button on his shirt. "What's with all of the long faces this morning?" Retrieving a cup from the cabinet, he reached for the percolator and glanced at Jennifer then the boys. "I thought you two would already be making plans for the lookout squad." He poured a cup of coffee then sat in his chair and looked from one to the other.

Simon glanced up at his mom as she placed a plate of eggs in front of him. "It's not nine o'clock yet. The circus will probably be in town, and we will miss the whole thing." He took a bite of bacon and passed a small piece to Sport who sat next to his chair waiting patiently.

The beagle mysteriously appeared on their front porch one Sunday morning about two years ago. They fed and watered him and waited for someone to claim him, but after several days and many inquiries, his appearance remained a mystery. Jim made the comment one day that the dog was a good sport, considering he was either lost or abandoned, and the name stuck. *Sport* soon found a spot in their hearts, a spot to sleep in the boys' bedroom, and had been a part of the family ever since.

"Oh, I see." Jim watched Jennifer set a bottle of milk on the table and take her seat. Both boys, frowns on their faces and their brows creased, sat quietly. Jim hid a smile behind his coffee cup and looked at his wife. "Well, I suspect the circus performers are probably eating their breakfast right now too. After that, they will have to feed the animals and get all loaded up. Chesterville is a good a forty-five minute drive, wouldn't you say, Jen?"

"Oh yes, at least that long." She put two more pieces of bread in the toaster and smiled at him. "It will take much longer than that with all of the performers, animals, and equipment they have to transport."

Truman sat the Bugs Bunny glass on the table and studied it for a moment. It had originally contained grape jelly but now served as a juice glass. In fact, they had a whole collection of them. He looked up and smiled, "Well then, we have plenty of time, don't we?"

He glanced over at the Frigidaire at the list of today's chores. Mom hung the list early every morning "so there would be no confusion over who is responsible for whatever needs to be done." She explained the whole thing to them that first morning, and said the idea came from Mrs. Daniels who told her it worked really well. It hadn't taken three days for the lousy thing to spread to every kitchen in town. "The List," as it was referred to at school, had trapped just about every kid at Oak Grove Elementary.

Jennifer sipped her coffee and sat her cup in the saucer. "You know, I would hate to miss the circus parade. I know Anne would like to take Garrett too." Lowering the sides of the toaster, she removed the toast and handed it to Jim. "Would you butter these? I'll get the jelly."

Jim sat with the butter knife in his hand and looked out the window. "Suppose we could let everyone in town know, all at the same time, that the circus train is on its way." He looked at all three of them and proceeded to butter a slice of toast. "It would be simple enough."

"How?" Truman and Simon asked in unison.

"Well, the last lookout man could signal someone in the Town Square, and they could ring the bell in the bell tower." Pleased with the idea, he spread butter liberally over the other piece of toast and handed it to Truman.

"But that bell has not rung in the ten years that we've lived here." Jennifer looked at him curiously and wondered what he had in mind. "Do you think it is still in working condition?"

Simon sat his glass of Ovaltine down, sloshing it over the side. "Old Ben! Check with him, Dad. He probably won't let anyone else ring it anyway."

Old Ben, Dad said, had the Wisdom of Solomon and was the second oldest person in Oak Grove. Miss Mattie had him by five years and often referred to him as "the young man at the blacksmith shop."

Their families had journeyed together to settle in Oak Grove "over one hundred years ago." Anyone who ever went to the Founder's Day Celebration knew the history of the early settlers from the re-enactment which portrayed them traveling in wagons, crossing rivers, fighting Indians, and constructing log cabins. The Old Mill on Seabaugh Creek was always started up, and Old Ben was found hammering and banging in the Blacksmith Shop, showing folks how it use to be done.

The bond, born in the early settlers, was shared through the years from one generation to the next and still existed today.

"All right then, let's eat and get moving. Nine o'clock will be here before we know it." Jim took a bite of toast and grinned at all three of them.

Jennifer contentedly watched and listened as they finished breakfast and shared ideas about the circus train. She poured another cup of coffee and wondered if the other mothers were dealing with the same thing this morning.

Jim sat his cup down, rose from his chair, and looked at his watch "I think I'll run on over and see what Old Ben has to say about our idea." Sport followed him to the door and sat patiently while he took the car keys from the peg on the wall. "I'll let you know what he says, but I'm sure he'll think it is a good idea." Opening the door, he let Sport out, the screen slammed behind him, and both boys headed to the sink with their plates.

"Let's get everything done." Truman grabbed the trash and headed out the back door while Simon headed for the living room to gather newspapers. He was not allowed to strike matches when they burned trash, but he could throw the papers in the barrel.

Jennifer glanced at the clock and then at the small mirror in the hall. "Well, let's get moving. I'm not going to miss out on this either."

Jim, needing to fill his gas tank, parked the car at Willy's Garage. It wasn't quite eight o'clock yet, so he knew Willy was still at home. His house was on the left across the street, and The Blacksmith Shop sat directly across from the garage.

Old Ben "got up with the birds," he always said, so Jim knew he would be awake and puttering around. He crossed the street and headed for the shop door that Ben always left unlocked.

Old Ben's residence was connected on the north side with a formal entrance facing Oak Street. A large covered front porch contained several rocking chairs scattered about, a porch swing, and wisteria vines that climbed to the roof on both sides of the steps. Ben customarily spent his evenings in one of the rockers, playing hymns on his accordion. The familiar sound often drew friends and family to his porch and others to their own porch swings.

Jim entered the shop and glanced at the tools and equipment that sat about. They had seen years of use but for the most part sat idle now. Ben still repaired things for the townsfolk, but the blacksmith shop was now mostly a gathering place for the older men and occasionally some of the younger ones in town. The only time anything was really put to a lot of work was on Founder's Day when Ben fired everything up and displayed the skills his father taught him.

Old Ben, as everyone called him, was a gentle man with skin like chocolate and hair as white as snow. He had a ready smile, a white mustache, and warm brown eyes that reflected a wisdom that comes not only with age but a close, personal walk with God. His quiet laugh was accompanied by a twinkle in his eyes when he fondly recalled an incident, told a tale, or quite often found humor in something.

Jim hoped he would age in the same manner Ben had and recalled what he told him one day not too long after they moved to Oak Grove.

"God showed me a long time ago that I could cry or rejoice over somethin' I did not understand. Yes sir, no matter how bad things might grab you, the Lord always turns it into a blessin,' one way or the other."

At the age of ninety, he was amazingly agile and had a mind as sharp as a tack. Standing about five-eleven, his stocky frame bore proof of hard work and healthy living. Occasionally, he smoked a pipe but mostly carried it in the top pocket of his overalls.

Jim glanced to his left as the door to his living quarters opened, and Old Ben walked out. He waved a greeting and smiled. "Good mornin' to you, son. What brings you out so early?" He stood next to an iron gate that he was evidently repairing for someone and gave him a friendly smile.

"I need to ask about the old bell tower and get your opinion on something." Jim watched him move the gate with ease and place it on a long table by the window.

"Well, come on back and enjoy a cup of coffee with me first." He waved his hand, motioning Jim to follow and led the way back into the house.

Jim walked through the door into Old Ben's kitchen. Everything was in place and neat as a pin, probably the result of Mercy's attention. Ben's great niece, she lived across the street and was in and out of his house every day checking on him. Jim pulled out one of the chairs and sat down at the old oak table, breathing in a whiff of honeysuckle that drifted through the open window. The mantel clock in the living room chimed the eight o'clock hour, and he watched Old Ben remove a cloth at one end of the table, revealing a couple of coffee cups, a bowl of sugar, salt and pepper shakers, and a loaf of bread. Glancing around the cheery yellow room, Jim was aware of that sense of peace one feels in a home that has been filled with precious memories and love down through the years. He wondered about all the happy times that was shared in this room and wondered if his own home would one day feel this way to others.

"Well now, what can I do for you?" Old Ben asked, breaking his train of thought as he sat a cup of steaming coffee in front of him and sat down across the table.

Truman and Simon had stood next to the telephone in the kitchen for the last ten minutes, and the hands on the clock finally reached nine o'clock. Truman stood with the receiver to his ear, waiting for Hazel's voice.

"Number please?" the familiar voice on the other end of the line asked. Truman knew she had just rolled her brown leather chair from the desk by the window to the equipment behind her, adding to the groove already worn on the floor. A pencil would be stuck in her red hair, her glasses perched on the end of her nose, and her fingers held the telephone wire in mid-air, waiting to connect him to Brenton's house. He had seen Hazel in action when his first grade class made a visit to Telephone Central.

Telephone Central was nothing more than a small room in Hazel's home that contained the necessary telephone equipment needed to connect everyone together in Oak Grove and elsewhere if need be. Nothing changed from one year to the next as each first grade class made their trip to Hazel's and came home with the same description as the class the year before.

"Hi, Hazel. Would you please get me Brenton's house?" Truman looked at Simon and grinned. No telephone number was needed. Hazel knew all of them like the back of her hand.

"Sure. I guess you boys are excited about the circus. My stars, isn't that something? Here you go." After a couple seconds of silence, Truman waited impatiently as the telephone rang, and Aunt Anne finally answered on the fourth ring.

"Hello," she said, sounding out of breath.

"Hi, Aunt Anne. This is Truman. Is Brenton there?" He watched Simon move from one foot to the other in his excitement as he ate a handful of grapes, and Sport looked curiously up at him from his spot on the floor.

"He sure is. I'll get him for you." He knew she placed the telephone on the table in the hall and wished they had one like it. A seat was attached on one side where you could sit while you talked instead of standing in the kitchen looking at the wall like he was now.

"Hey Truman, what's up?" Brenton spoke into the telephone.

"What do you think about organizing a lookout team for the circus train today? Dad said it would probably get to Oak Grove sometime this afternoon." Truman looked up at the clock. They needed to get moving.

"That's a swell idea," Brenton answered excitedly. Why hadn't he thought of that? "We'll need to get everyone together. Have you talked to anyone else?"

"Not yet, you are the first one I've called. Let's meet on the square. You call Johnny and Larry White. I'll call the Olson's, Jake, and Zachary. Tell them to meet us at 10:00. Oh, and tell Johnny to have Laura gather all of the girls." Truman mentally tried to think of everyone that needed to be notified.

"Girls?" Benton complained. "Do we really need them to come along?" He looked up at the ceiling with a frown on his face. "Gee willikers, Truman, this should be a man's job.

"Do you really think Johnny is going to get out of the house without Laura knowing? She's going to call all of the others, and they will show up anyway. Besides, we might need them for something. Now hurry. I'll see you at 10:00."

He held the button on the cradle and turned to Simon. "Go ahead and get our bikes out of the garage while I make these calls." Removing his finger, Truman held the hand piece to his ear and waited for Hazel again.

Johnny stuck his head around the bedroom door, told Laura what was going on, and said if the girls wanted to help, they better hurry. Laura hurried through the living room and glanced at the clock on the table. It was 9:25. She was going to have to hurry if they were going to get to the square by 10:00.

"Number please," Hazel said as she came on the line again. She could not remember Telephone Central being this busy since the war ended.

"Hazel, could you please connect me with Noelle?" Laura tried to be as pleasant as she could. She felt sorry for poor Hazel, imagining the state of mind she was in. The boys were calling all over town, Miss Myrtle called looking for Dad, and Mr. Reese called to double check a grocery order that her mother phoned in yesterday. Laura knew by now Hazel would know who was going to meet, why, what time, and where. No one in town seemed to mind that she knew all of their secrets. Hazel, also, was aware that every single person in Oak Grove knew she was a well of information. As the official Telephone Central Operator, she had made known from the very beginning that her lips were sealed. "If Alexander Graham Bell came back from the dead," she once said, "I would not reveal one word that may have reached my ears." True to her word, Hazel never repeated anything she heard over the wire.

Laura counted the rings and looked at the exasperated expression on her dad's face when he peeked around the corner for the third time.

"I'll just go over to the church and use the telephone there," he muttered as he walked away.

Mrs. Williams answered on the third ring, "Hello?"

"Good morning, Mrs. Williams. This is Laura. Is Noelle there?"

"Why good morning, Laura. Yes, as a matter of fact she is standing right here."

Laura heard Noelle's footsteps on the floor followed by a bang, causing her to jump and hold the phone away from her ear.

"Laura? I'm sorry. I dropped the telephone," Noelle giggled. Did I break your ear?"

Laura laughed. "No kidding. You almost broke it. Say, the boys have figured out a way to let everyone in town know when the circus train is on its way. We are all supposed to meet at the square by ten o'clock. Can you be there?"

"Oh, that sounds like fun. I will ask Mama but I am sure she won't mind." Noelle glanced at her mother who was sitting in the green chair next to the Philco, listening intently to *Young Doctor Malone.*

"Good, I will call Elizabeth, Carrie, and Kim and Sandy Reese. Would you be able to call Maggie and Carole?" Laura crossed her fingers, hoping she would not get bashful and say she would rather not.

"Alright, I will call them. Ten o'clock on the square at the bandstand?"

"Yes, I'll see you in a little while." Laura stood for a moment with the telephone to her ear pleased with Noelle's willingness. She replaced the hand piece in the cradle then picked it up again.

"Number please," Hazel said in an exasperated voice as she came back on the line. Laura felt truly sorry for her.

Old Ben stood in the top of the bell tower and looked out across the town. He assured Jim Walker the bell was in good working order as they climbed together to the top.

"It takes me a little longer to get up here than it use to, but I enjoy it." Showing Jim the bell, he rubbed his hand across the letters his grandfather had forged into its side: *Oak Grove 1832.*

"When I was a boy, there was just the mercantile, my daddy's blacksmith shop, and the old mill out on Seabaugh Creek." He glanced down and motioned with his hand. "The Baptist church was right here on this same spot until it burned A terrible storm came one spring. Lightnin' struck and burned it to the ground. Some of the men pulled the old bell out, and they later built this bell tower."

Jim looked out across the valley He never fully realized what a beautiful place Oak Grove was. The town lay in a valley surrounded by hills profuse with giant oak and cedar trees. Seabaugh Creek ran along the north side of town, and the lumber mill was partially visible through the trees. The railroad track snaked its way along the edge of town and disappeared into the east woods beyond the old mill. The steeple of the Baptist Church rose among the treetops to the west, and the red roof of the Oak Grove School was visible in the distance.

Jim glanced over, observing a wistful expression cross the old man's face as he continued to talk in a soft, almost reverent voice.

"A few farms were scattered about in the valley. The early settlers totaled seven families to be exact. They farmed and helped one another." Old Ben looked at Jim and leaned against the railing. "Then loggers came and established The Oak Grove Timber Company. They've supplied the surroundin' areas with buildin' material ever since." He rubbed his chin with his hand and continued, "Craftsmen, creatin' beautiful oak furniture followed. Yes, sir, the town grew. Folks moved to Oak Grove and brought new businesses with them." Old Ben was silent for a minute as he stared out across the valley, unconsciously smoothing his mustache with his fingers. He turned to Jim, looked at him with warm, gentle, brown eyes, and spoke in an even quieter voice, "Oak Grove has been home to a lot of good people. This is a special place, and don't you forget it."

Jim touched the old man's arm. "Thank you, Ben. Thank you for bringing me up here."

Old Ben stood with a soft smile on his face and gazed off to the east; lost in his thoughts. Jim patted him on the shoulder and quietly left him to his memories.

Old Ben stared across the valley. Miss Mattie's big house sat atop the ridge overlooking the town where the old homestead originally stood. "You and I, Miss Mattie, have seen a lot." Tears glistened in his eyes and he absent-mindedly touched the bell. "Our days are numbered, my old friend. I don't think either one of us would change a thing, would we?" He stood quietly for a few minutes and then smiled to himself. "Well, now, there is a circus comin' to town and I believe I'll just go; but right now, I've got work to do." Old Ben chuckled to himself and made his way to the steps. He turned and took a last look to the east and smiled. "Miss Mattie, I think this will be a first for both of us."

Ned watched from the window of his barbershop as several children gathered at the bandstand. "Wonder what the youngsters are up to?" he asked, looking back at Hank sitting in the barber chair reading the newspaper. "What do you think they are doing?"

"Probably talking about the circus and waiting for it to get here." He folded the paper and laid it down. "Who would have ever thought a circus would be here in Oak Grove," he commented, leaning to the right so he could see around Ned who appeared to be counting them. "There's quite a few of them, isn't there?" He chuckled and remarked, "I guess I'm looking forward to it too. How about you?"

"By golly, I sure am," Ned replied, walking back to the barber chair. Picking up the barber scissors, he turned Hank's chair around and looked at him in the mirror. "Say, do you recall that year Murphy's Medicine Show rolled through town?"

Hank shook his head. "I declare, that man was nothing more than a shyster. All he wanted was our money. He did a few card tricks, boasted about being able to tell the future, and sold everyone in town a bottle of Murphy's Magic Tonic."

Ned laughed, "You have to admit, the tonic did make you feel better."

"Tonic! He had a stil somewhere and was making his own *tonic*. It was nothing more than corn liquor if you ask me. No wonder it made everyone feel good," Hank replied, shaking his head in exasperation. "I declare, do you reckon he ever got caught?"

"Quit moving your head," Ned said impatiently, glancing at him in the mirror. "Who did he tell they were going to strike it rich?"

"Paul Smith. I forgot about that. He told him there was a fortune waiting for him in the future. I suspect he's long tired of waiting for it."

Ned stopped trimming and glanced at the door as Louis Smith walked in. "Morning, Louis."

"Good morning, fellas." Louis hung his hat on the rack and sat in one of the empty wooden chairs. One of the regulars that hung out at the blacksmith shop, he decided the need of a haircut would have to replace the daily checker game. Philip and James were already arguing over who was cheating who when he left to walk the block and a half to Ned's. "Looks like something's going on over at the bandstand."

"That's what we were just talking about." Hank leaned around again to take another look. "We suspect they are planning something about the circus."

"Dad blame it! You better sit still or you will be walking out of here sideways." Ned placed his hands on Hank's head and held it steady. "When I'm done, you can walk over and find out what they are up to."

By 10:05 most everyone was gathered at the square. Bicycles were parked in a clump in front of the bandstand, several lay in various positions where they were dropped, and two were propped against a tree.

Leaving the Cranston Café, Mike paused by his car and watched Johnny, Jimmy, and several other boys playing catch. He grinned at the laughing comments about getting a better glove when Jake missed the ball Preston threw and had to chase it across the square.

Several girls, including Laura, sat on the wide steps of the bandstand talking animatedly, evidently about the circus. He leaned against the car and watched in amusement.

Shari, Carole, and Maggie were sitting on the railing laughing at Abigail and Carrie who were in the middle of the bandstand. Mike chuckled as he viewed their efforts at tap dancing. Abigail was stomping her feet and waving her arms up and down while Carrie, though not good at it, was doing a much better job.

He watched Charlotte Charles run across the square and stop as Josiah called her name. Handing her a brown paper bag, he said something, retrieved his ball glove from the handlebars of his bike, and ran to join the boys.

Charlotte watched him run across the square then turned and walked to the steps, said something to Laura, and handed her the sack. Pointing to Josiah, she ran up the steps and hopped up on the railing next to Maggie.

Mike shook his head and got in the car He needed to get over to the church and fix a leak from the kitchen faucet. He had noticed it yesterday when he went downstairs to replace a light bulb that Myrtle said was burned out. Turning in front of the Cranston Hotel, he waved at Elizabeth Driscol riding her new bicycle down Oak Street.

She smiled brightly and waved back, pedaling as fast as her legs could go, and Mike prayed she wouldn't run over anyone. He watched as she continued down the street, passing Hanks Hardware, The Sweet Shoppe, and the Dime Store before cutting across the square. Circling the bandstand, she came to a halt in front of the steps.

"Am I late?" Putting her kickstand down, she flopped down on the grass. "I hurried as fast as I could," she said out of breath as she leaned back with her hands behind her.

"No, a few of the others aren't here yet either," Laura answered, dumping a pile of old, torn and stained rags out of the paper bag Charlotte handed her. "I could have brought some of these. We have a lot of them. Mom saves them for dusting and washing windows."

"What are they for?" Elizabeth asked, looking at the old rags.

"Josiah's mom thought we could use them to make signal flags when we see the circus train," Laura said, smiling broadly "Can you believe it? We are going to see a circus."

"I know. I can't hardly believe it either." Elizabeth rooted through the rags, looking at them. "This will be the most fun we have ever had."

Noelle picked one up and examined it. Glancing around, she picked up a stick from the oak tree above and tied two ends of the tea towel to it. "How's that?" she asked with a grin, waving the newly created flag in the air.

Laura looked at the faded red rooster on the worn towel and smiled. "It's a pretty good flag." She grinned again, looking at her two best friends. "This is going to be so much fun. I cannot wait."

"Me either." Noelle twirled the stick around in her hand. "What we are going to do? Did Johnny say?"

Laura watched Preston throw the ball to Simon and shook her head. "No, Johnny just said Truman has a good idea. I wish they would quit playing catch and tell us what we are supposed to do."

The ball rolled across the grass and came to rest at the bottom step. Glancing up, Laura saw the boys walking toward them carrying their ball gloves and looking across the square at Zachary, Mike, and Donnie who were riding toward them.

Johnny walked over and looked at Elizabeth's new bike. "When did you get this?" he asked, walking in a circle around it.

"Uncle Henry bought it for me in Chesterville about three weeks ago," Elizabeth answered, standing up. Red, white, and blue streamers dangled from the handgrips, and she reached out and let them run through her fingers. "My other one was too small, and he saw this one on sale at C&G."

Johnny looked at the shiny red bike with the letters *Schwinn* painted across the center bar. He wished he had a new one. Larry also just got a new Schwinn for his birthday and said his dad bought it at C&G.

"Here comes Larry and Randy," Truman said, hooking his baseball glove over the handlebar of his bike. He walked over and stood next to Johnny. "Pretty swell looking bike, isn't it; even if it is a girl's bike."

"Yeah, but look at Larry's," Johnny answered, watching him ride across the square.

The new black and silver bike gleamed in the sunshine, and there was not a scratch or speck of dust on it anywhere.

Putting the kickstand down, Larry walked over to the bandstand and perched on the railing. Adjusting his ball cap, he watched the boys inspect his new bike. He glanced at Elizabeth's, thinking it was pretty swell too, for a girl.

"So what is the plan?" Josiah asked impatiently, thinking there was something more important than standing around looking at bicycles. "I'm ready. Just tell me what to do."

"Okay." Truman looked around. Pretty much everyone that he could think of was here. "Come over here," he called, walking to the bandstand. He sat on the top step and waited while everyone sat down.

"Well, this is what I was thinking; we are not exactly sure when the circus will get here, so we are going to establish lookout points and relay the message that it's on the way."

"How many and where are the look out points going to be?" Preston asked as he sat on the rail next to Larry and looked around. It sure seemed to him there were too many kids.

"That's what we are going to decide now," Truman answered, looking at Brenton and Johnny and then at the rest seated on the ground. "The plan is simple, and it will work if everyone does what they are told. That is the most important thing. You have to follow orders."

"Good grief! That's all we need is a bunch of boys ordering us around," Elizabeth whispered to Laura.

"What do you think he means by orders?" Josiah asked, looking at Zachary. "What kind of orders?"

"It doesn't make any difference what kind they are. Dad had to follow orders when he was in the Marines, and he said you had to do exactly what you were told; if you liked it or not."

"First, we need a head count so we know how many squads to form." Brenton commented, looking at Truman.

"We might as well do that now. Everyone count off" Truman raised his hand and called out, "One." Everyone followed suit and ended with Carrie Cook as number 24.

"Where are the lookout points going to be?" Jordan asked, knowing he wasn't supposed to ride his bike farther than the square without permission. He didn't want the other guys to think he was a baby, so he hoped his spot would be somewhere close.

"I think we ought to start at the Seabaugh farm," Preston spoke up. "That is all the way out of town at the top of the hill."

Elizabeth waved her hand in the air. "He is right. You can see a long way from the hill and that will give us plenty of time to let Aunt Trudy know. She's busy with Caroline's party and depending on us to tell her when we see the circus as soon as possible."

"We have a plan to let the whole town know all at the same time." Simon sat down next to Truman and straightened his ball cap, feeling important.

"How in the world can we do that?" Maggie asked, staring at Simon, wondering what kind of idea he had. She glanced at Shari who shrugged her shoulders and looked back at the boys.

Truman looked around with a grin on his face. He was anxious to tell them about the bell. "The last squad on the team will be stationed at the Blacksmith Shop. Old Ben has agreed to ring the bell in the square." He watched the looks of astonishment that crossed everyone's face and grinned at Simon when they all started talking at once.

"Boy Howdy! Are you serious?" Jake asked, looking at the boys with wide brown eyes. "Old Ben is going to ring it?"

Ronald Olson looked at Laura. "I can't believe it. I have never heard the bell ring. Have you?" He sat next to her on the grass; but not too close. He didn't want the guys thinking he was sweet on her or anything. He hadn't quite figured out why he liked to be around her. She was pretty, and her blue eyes were the same color as the blue flowers that grew by the front steps of his Grandma's house.

She came with her dad one day to visit Grandma when she broke her arm. They had gone outside to pick flowers as a surprise for her, and he noticed they were the same color as her eyes. Besides that, she could play ball as well as any of the guys. She was always knocking a home run. In fact, if the truth were known, he guessed she was the prettiest girl in Oak Grove.

"No, I have never heard it ring either. I don't think any of us have," Laura answered, looking around. No one seemed to know anyone who had ever heard it ring.

Jake waved his hand in the air. "My Grandma Smith said she heard it ring lots of times. Isn't that so Carrie?" he asked looking at his sister.

"That's right, she sure did. And you can ask Liza too." Carrie replied, looking around. "Any of the older folks can tell you about it ringing at horrible times."

Randy White jumped to his feet. "I heard once that the Baptist Church use to sit right here in the square, and a tornado came one day and picked it up and dropped it where it is now. They rang the bell that day until the clapper fell out."

"It did not! Who told you that?" Jimmy asked, looking at him like he was crazy. "Gee willikers, do you believe everything? Dad has all of the church records in his office, and it's all written down about when and who built the church."

"Good grief," Shari commented, looking at Randy. "Dad said the bell use to be on top of the church a long time ago. So, if the tornado picked up the church and moved it, why did it leave the bell in the square?"

"Well, gee whiz, I was just telling you what I heard," Randy replied, looking at her with a frown on his face. "Next time, I won't tell you if you ask."

"You will too."

"No, I won't."

"Yes, you will."

Truman held his hands up. "Okay, okay. The bell is the same bell that has always been there. Old Ben told Dad this morning. The church burned, and they built the bell tower in its place. It is the same bell because the year 1832 is on the side of it. It is very old."

Abigail looked up at the bell tower with a worried frown crossing her face. "It won't fall down, will it?"

"No, of course not." Jordan looked up at the bell. "Well, I don't think so. Does it still ring?"

Maggie looked at him and rolled her eyes. "Now why would Oak Grove have a bell in a bell tower if it didn't ring?"

"Of course it rings." Truman looked at everyone and continued, "Dad said Old Ben is going to ring it himself. We just have to relay the message to him as soon as we see the circus heading this way. We have to give him enough time to get up in the tower to ring it though."

"Can Old Ben climb up the steps?" Maggie asked, staring at them.

Jake looked at her in exasperation. "Of course he can. I've seen him up there a jillion times."

Truman looked at Laura and Noelle. "Say, if you girls could collect sticks and tie those towels on them, we will start organizing lookout points." He glanced at Brenton and then back at the girls.

"How does this look?" Noelle asked, waving the one she already made.

"It looks swell, Noelle. Make some more just like it," Truman replied, smiling at her.

She was now regarded and treated with new respect by the boys. They were totally impressed that she had been entrusted with the secret of the circus and did not tell a soul. At first, their mistaken assumptions bothered her. She soon realized that the more she tried to convince them otherwise; the more convinced they were that she was a girl true to her word. Laura thought the whole thing funny and laughed about it, so Noelle quit trying to correct the situation.

"Shari, would the rest of you look for more sticks for us?" Laura asked, sorting through the towels and passing them to Noelle, Louise, and Elizabeth.

Shari nodded and looked at the others "Okay, come on. Now they can't be too big or too small," she instructed as they headed off in different directions.

The boys stood in the middle of the bandstand getting instructions. "Jordan, Zachary, and Jimmy; you man the bell tower," Truman said, deciding that would be the best place for them since they were the youngest. "Answer any questions and explain what the bell ringing means, okay?"

Jordan sighed with relief. He liked the spot and wouldn't have to explain anything to anyone since they didn't ask him to go out by the fairground or somewhere else.

Truman glanced across the square beyond the Cranston hotel toward Old Ben's. "Donnie, Mike, and Josiah will be stationed at the Blacksmith Shop. You will be responsible for getting Old Ben to the bell tower." He looked at the three, figuring that would take care of all the younger ones.

Brenton, scribbling on his Big Chief tablet, glanced up at Truman. "How about Randy, Jake, and Ronald out between the Driscol's and the beginning of the Seabaugh farm?"

"That sounds good. Now let's see . . ." Truman looked around to see who was left and realized they had just the right number of boys.

"Say, what about the rest of us?" Larry asked. "Where do you want us?"

Johnny looked at Truman. "We need about two more points, don't we?"

Truman nodded in agreement. "Yes. How about if we have Simon, Preston, and Larry ride out to the other side of the Seabaugh farm; right at Old Mill Road. That leaves you, Brent, and me at the top of the hill by Miss Mattie's. That should take care of it."

Mike Olson swallowed a last bite of cookie and raised his hand, "What are we going to do about lunch and something to drink?"

"Man, this is serious business. Quit thinking about food," Jimmy commented, wishing he had one of the cookies he was eating. If Mike was not eating, he was talking about what he wished he was eating.

"Well, gee whiz, I can't go all afternoon without anything to eat or drink and neither can any of you." He grabbed another cookie from the sack in front of him and took a big bite.

"We can take care of that," Shari replied, looking up at them with a stick in each hand. "Make us the lunch squad. We can use our Radio Flyers and deliver lunches." She looked at Noelle and Laura. "We'll form our own squads."

"That's not a bad idea," Johnny commented, looking at his sister then back to Truman. "What do you think?"

"Sounds good to me," Brenton said, listening to the approval from the rest of the guys "OK, you girls are the lunch detail. We will leave all of that up to you."

Michael Madison, driving passed the town square, noted the crowd that was gathered. Some of the boys, Zachary included, were yelling and waving some sort of homemade flags in the air. Wondering what they were up to, he parked his Oldsmobile in front of the Sheriff's Office and got out. Across the street, Ivy Seabaugh was headed for Dr. Miller's office and Michael returned her wave. Opening the door, he walked into the Sheriff's office.

John Walker was sitting behind his desk looking over some paper work he had put off for the last three days and glanced up as the door opened. "Good morning, Michael." He leaned back in his chair, glad to be reprieved from the work on his desk for a few minutes.

"Morning, John. I came to report a crime." He chuckled as he sat in the chair on the other side of the desk. "It looks like we might have a riot on the town square."

John smiled and shook his head. "Oh they're getting organized. It seems they want to spot the circus train before it gets to Oak Grove." He sat back in his chair and stretched his arms. "They have big plans. Jim came by earlier and said Old Ben has agreed to signal its arrival by ringing the bell."

He recalled how excited the kids were this morning and how his four oldest boys had almost driven him nuts. The idea of waving flags set them to rummaging through an old ragbag Anne kept in the pantry. Preston kept shouting ideas to Brenton, who was trying to make a list of *necessary responsibilities*. Jordan plied him with a bunch of questions about the circus, Josiah spilled his milk, and Garrett was crying because he couldn't go with his brothers. Out of desperation, he decided promptly to go to the café for coffee. He quickly appeased his conscience by promising to take Anne to lunch and made a hasty departure.

Michael sat forward in his chair. "Well, I'm afraid we're going to have to disappoint them somewhat. I've just returned from a meeting in Chesterville and ran into Mr. Morton." He looked at his friend, noting the concern on his face. Michael really liked the Sheriff. He was an exceptionally nice guy, good father, had a great sense of humor, and took his job seriously, using a lot of good, old-fashioned common sense.

"Don't tell me they canceled," John exclaimed with a look of genuine concern on his face. He couldn't even imagine the disappointment that would bring.

"Oh, no. Nothing that drastic. It seems the ringmaster and a couple of the other performers have come down with some sort of stomach ailment. I ran into him at the Chesterville Restaurant and we had a cup of coffee. He said it was nothing to worry about, and they should get here sometime tomorrow." Leaning back in the chair, he folded his arms and shook his head. "The kids are still going to be disappointed."

"You are right about that." John sighed and commented, "They are expecting the circus train this afternoon . . ." He sat thoughtful for a moment and scratched his cheek. "Well, this will give them more time to get organized," he remarked. "It will also heighten the anticipation. I don't know if I can stand that or not."

Michael laughed at him "I guess all of us will live through it. We'll just have to keep the bunch busy." He rose from the chair. "I need to get over to the bank. Do you want me to walk with you to break the bad news?"

"You can walk along if you want," he answered as he pushed the papers aside. "If it turns into a real riot, you are on your own," he commented with a grin as he tossed his pencil on the desk. "I guess we may as well get it over with. I'll just tell them to make their plans for tomorrow." John rose from the chair and then looked at Michael. "Did you want something else?"

"No, I just wanted to let you know about the arrival of the circus. Come on, I'll walk along with you." He watched John grab his hat from the rack and followed him out the door.

"Should we to take our stations now?" Jordan asked Brenton as he picked his bike up and stood next to Zachary and Jimmy. The three six-year-olds comprised the bell tower squad and agreed that this was the most important thing they had ever been responsible for. Zachary was holding his bike, prepared to ride over to the bell tower, when he noticed his dad and the Sheriff walking across the square.

"Hold on just a minute," Sheriff Walker called as they walked around the side of the bandstand. He was amazed at the number of children that had turned out. The boys were gathered in groups of threes, and the girls sat in a circle on the ground with a pile of rags and sticks.

Preston looked curiously at his dad, wondering what was wrong, and then glanced at Brenton who just shrugged his shoulders.

"Hi, Dad," Jordan said. "I'm on the bell tower squad."

"Me too," Zachary yelled, looking at his dad and wondering why he was with the Sheriff.

Johnny looked at Truman. "I wonder what's up."

"I don't know," Truman mumbled, looking at Brenton and then back at the Sheriff.

"Hi, Uncle Michael," Abigail said. She was sitting on the railing, eye level with him, swinging her bare feet back and forth.

Michael reached up and swung her down. "Why don't you sit over there with the rest of the girls? I believe the Sheriff has something to tell you."

John looked at all their faces, hating to disappoint them. "That's right. I want you all to sit down just a minute." He watched as they found seats on the steps and in the grass and waited until all of the chattering stopped.

"You all seem to be getting organized really well. That's good, but Mr. Madison has just come from Chesterville, and I thought I would just walk over and give you an update on the arrival of the circus train." He looked at the faces staring at him and remarked, "Mr. Morton said the circus should get here sometime tomorrow."

Groans of disappointment, mumbling, and sighing was the reaction John expected, and he held his hand up. "Now, listen to me a minute. A couple of the performers are not feeling up to par, and they all need a day of rest. Mr. Morton said they would definitely be here tomorrow." He looked at the disappointment in their faces and continued, "Now this is just one more day; that's all. You won't have to be in such a rush to get ready, and you can even have a couple of practice runs. Then, by tomorrow, you will be set and ready to go."

Michael spoke up. "This will give me time to get those arm bands ready for you." He just remembered a box of 4th of July remnants he had come across in one of the storage closets at the bank a few days ago. A small box of red and blue armbands, signifying the 4th of July softball teams, somehow ended up in the Oak Grove Bank. He suspected Marion stuck them in the closet because she had been one of the team captains two years ago.

"Armbands?" Everyone looked at him with a spark of interest. He glanced at John and was glad he remembered them.

"Well, now what do you think of that? The armbands will make it more official," Sheriff Walker commented. "Some of you might want to let your neighbors know what to expect. Why, there are a lot of things to do before tomorrow."

The Sheriff and Michael listened as the chatter began again, and several ideas started floating around. An argument began over who would wear the red armbands and who would wear the blue. Some of the girls were deciding what to put in the lunches and Jordan and Zachary were waving a couple of the flags, arguing over which was the proper way to handle them. The rest of the boys thought it would be a good idea to ride out and establish their lookout points and then come back and visit with Old Ben.

Sheriff Walker and Michael looked at each other and smiled. "Well, I guess they can handle things here. We may as well leave them to their plans."

Chapter 4

Laura looked at her reflection in the mirror. The light blue dress was one of her favorites. It had short cap sleeves and a rounded neck. The matching sash around her waist was tied in a bow and positioned on the right side of the skirt. Her favorite part was the cut out diamond shapes on the sleeves. She looked at her feet and wished she were old enough to wear more grown-up shoes. Mom said she had to wait until she was thirteen, and then they would talk about it. Her white slip on shoes looked okay she guessed, and her legs tanned from the summer sun almost made her look like she was wearing hose.

The banging of the screen door caught her attention. "Mom, are the sandwiches ready?" Shari yelled from the kitchen. Laura looked at the clock on her bureau, eleven o'clock. That meant the girls were launching their mission. They were supposed to meet at the square, make individual lunches, and deliver them to the lookout points. She thought back over this morning's events and realized she was starting to get more excited about Caroline's party.

She wanted to go along with the rest to see how everything was coming together, but Mom said no. "Your first priority today is Caroline's birthday party. You must always keep your commitments It gives one character and a dependability that others will appreciate, and you will too." She smiled wisely, and Laura knew she was right.

The excitement that surrounded Shari and her brothers this morning was contagious, and she wanted to join them. Jimmy bragged that his squad was more important because the whole town was depending on him to see that Old Ben rang the bell. Johnny informed him that he would be at the top of the hill and would be the first to see the circus train coming into town and without him the bell wouldn't even ring. Shari spoke up and said that if she didn't bring them food and something to drink that they would all have to go home for lunch and probably miss the whole thing.

Dad paused in the doorway with car keys in hand and looked at all of them. "Well, I guess this just proves that each one of you is needed, and it is a team effort. I think it is probably the best team I have seen in a long time." With that said, he walked out the door singing a familiar little song about brothers and sisters loving and helping one another.

Mike had a rich baritone voice and had made up little songs for as long as they could remember. Some of them made no sense at all and caused them to laugh hysterically while others carried a bit of wisdom that always hit home. This morning was one of those times.

Laura came downstairs and watched from the back door as they left. She still wished she were going along. They wore the armbands Marion had found yesterday at the bank and decided that the girls would wear the red and the boys the blue ones. Laura's armband lay on the dresser upstairs.

"Let's wrap Caroline's bracelet," Mom said, holding red tissue paper and white ribbon in her hand. She sat down at the table and patted Laura's hand. "You know, Laura, you are not going to miss anything. The circus train has to come right by the Driscol's house. Everyone at the party will be the first to see its arrival."

"I know. It's just that all the planning was a lot of fun." Laura sat down at the table and they proceeded to wrap Caroline's present.

"After your bath, let's try a new hairstyle," Leah suggested, and that is what they had done.

She looked again at her reflection in the mirror, turning her head from side to side. She did like her new hairstyle and wondered what she would look like with lipstick.

"Mom!" Shari called running upstairs. Poking her head in the door, she stared at Laura with wide brown eyes. "You look really pretty. Your hair is so fancy."

"Thank you." Laura smiled and looked in the mirror. Mom had parted her blonde hair in the middle, combed the sides away from her face, and pulled the back up into a roll. Laura saw the hairstyle on a lady advertising Hoover vacuum cleaners in a Life Magazine one day, and they both liked it.

"Shari?" Leah's voice called from the kitchen. She just returned from Sarah's with a batch of cookies. The Clark's home was situated directly behind the parsonage, and a well-worn path cut through a tall hedgerow, connecting the two pieces of property.

Reverend Clark had been the pastor of the Methodist Church for years. They had no children and more or less adopted the Daniels' children and showered them with attention. The path between the two homes had seen countless footsteps through the years as the two families visited and shared the joy and heartache of those they loved. They laughed over jokes about feuding neighbors and shared all the responsibilities and joy that pastoring a small community brought.

Mrs. Clark, known for her baking, appeared frequently at their back door with something delicious in her hand. Leah had slipped through the hedgerow this morning to pick up the cookies, saving Sarah the trip.

"I'm up here. Have fun, Laura." Shari called as she turned and ran down the steps.

"The sandwiches are in the refrigerator and these cookies are from Mrs. Clark." Leah pulled a grocery bag from the pantry and placed the box of cookies in the bottom. She watched her youngest daughter close the refrigerator door, balancing the stack of sandwiches in one hand. Quickly retrieving them, Leah placed them in the bag with the cookies.

"Now be careful, and don't drop them." Leah looked at her, recalling a loaf of bread she and Jimmy somehow managed to mangle on the way home from Reese's Market one day. They said they dropped it, but it looked more like a truck ran over it. Leah suddenly realized that she never did find out what actually happened to the bread.

I'm going to put this in the basket of my bike, and when I get to Maggie's we are going to put everything in her wagon," Shari replied with such confidence that Leah thought perhaps the sandwiches just might arrive in edible condition. Reaching for the sack, Shari offered her cheek for a kiss then ran out the back door, letting the screen slam behind her.

Midnight, their black cat, raised her head, lazily stretched, and seeing all was well lay back down and closed her eyes. She had long ago become accustomed to all of the commotion and gave no heed to it.

Leah watched Shari ride through the yard and turned to find Laura standing in the kitchen. "Oh, you look so lovely." Her voice was soft, and the awareness that teenage years were not too far away surfaced. She walked to the table and picked up a small box. Leah turned slowly and smiled. "I thought you might enjoy wearing this."

Laura looked at her mother then down at the blue, velvet box. She slowly raised the lid. Inside lay a strand of creamy white pearls.

"These are the pearls Daddy gave you when you got married." Laura's eyes were wide with surprise. Her mother always told her that one day they would be hers, but until then she would be allowed to wear them when she was old enough and only on special occasions.

"Yes, they are. They mean a very great deal to me. I think they would look very nice with your dress and your new hairstyle."

Laura stood very still while her mother put them around her neck and fastened the clasp. She couldn't believe her mother thought her old enough to wear them. "Now let's see." Leah turned her around and smiled. "Oh yes, just perfect."

"Is there a beautiful little girl in this house anywhere ready for a party?" Mike's voice called from the front hall, followed by the slamming of the screen door.

Laura smiled at her mother as she handed her Caroline's birthday present. "Thanks, Mom. I will take very good care of them." Turning, she faced her dad who stood in the doorway. Twirling around in front of him, she showed him her new hairstyle.

Mike's eyes moistened and he smiled at her. "I was planning on driving my little girl to a party, and here I find a beautiful young lady in my kitchen."

"Thanks, Dad. Mom did it." She was not unaware of the tender look that passed between her parents, and it made her feel warm inside.

"You two better go, or you will be late." Leah glanced at her wristwatch and grinned as Mike extended his arm in an exaggerated manner and escorted Laura down the hall. Following them to the door, she smiled to herself and thought her husband would never lose the charm she had first found in him.

She watched as he opened the car door for Laura, her heart filling with tenderness when he turned turn back and looked at her with a wistful expression on his face. "Oh, Lord, what is he going to be like when she has her first date?"

"Did Mom tell you we are supposed to pick up Noelle and Terry?" Laura asked as he backed the car out of the drive.

"She sure did." Mike looked over at his daughter and took note of the pearls. Leah had mentioned last night that she was thinking of allowing her to wear them. Laura was looking out the window, a very pleased look on her face, and her fingers touched the pearls on her neck. Mike smiled. His wife made another very wise decision.

Noelle lived just around the block and usually walked to their house, but today was special, and he volunteered to pick her up and drive the girls to the party. Parking the car, Mike got out and walked up the sidewalk to the small porch. He wore a soft smile on his face and his eyes reflected tenderness as he thought of Noelle and her relief after they prayed together.

"Come in, Pastor Mike," Annabelle Williams greeted with a friendly smile as she held the door for him. "Thank you for driving the girls to Caroline's party." She was a sweet, quiet lady, passing the same personality to Noelle.

"It is my pleasure," Mike commented, stepping into the living room. "How are you today, Annabelle?"

"Just fine, Pastor. Won't you sit down? I'll get the girls." Annabelle smiled and disappeared down the hall.

Mike sat on a green, overstuffed sofa and studied a photograph of Noelle on the table at the end of the sofa. It looked perhaps to be a first grade picture. Her braids were not as long then, and her two front teeth were missing.

"We are ready," Noelle said as she came around the corner of the living room. She smiled shyly when she realized he had been looking at her photograph.

Terry Charles stood next to her. "I walked up to Noelle's so you wouldn't have to make another stop." Blushing slightly, she smoothed the pink dress she wore and crossed the room, retrieving a small daintily wrapped gift from the coffee table. Her thick black hair curled in a style of its own, held in place by a pink ribbon that matched her dress. Terry was suddenly self-conscious and wondered if the pale pink lipstick her mom allowed her to wear was too dark.

"Well, you two look lovely today." Mike smiled fondly at both girls as he rose to greet them. Noelle wore a yellow dress that made her brown eyes look even darker. Her hair was not in braids today, and the long mass hung to her waist held back on the sides with yellow ribbons. Glancing at his watch, he commented, "I guess we better go. We do not want to be late now, do we?" Opening the door, he followed the two girls out the door and assured Annabelle again that it was no problem.

Both girls giggled as Pastor Mike held the car door for them, and he smiled to himself at their excitement.

"Hi, Laura. You look so pretty," Terry said as she scooted across the seat to make room for Noelle.

"Both of you do too," Laura replied with a big smile on her face as she looked at both of them. *We all three look grown up*, she thought as her dad started the engine and they drove down Pine Street. He drove three blocks to the square and slowed the car. All three girls strained to look out the window.

Jimmy, Zachary, and Jordan sat on the ground next to the bell tower with their bicycles lying beside them.

Melba, leaving the drugstore and heading back to the hair salon, stopped on the sidewalk across the street and called to them. She was presently getting the full rundown on their responsibility for getting Old Ben up into the tower to ring the bell.

Jimmy stood and looked up. "Don't worry, Miss Maple. It's twelve steps to the top, but we are going to help Old Ben get up there." He grinned and conspicuously pushed his blue armband up on his sleeve.

Melba smiled at the gesture "My goodness. What is that on your arm?" she asked, crossing the street.

Jordan and Zachary both stood and readjusted their arm bands. "You can only wear one of these if you are on one of the squads," Jordan informed her importantly.

"Ours are blue; the girls have red ones." Zachary looked up at her and waved at Pastor Mike and the girls as they passed by.

"Dad, look. Jimmy is doing his job," Laura said proudly. "He is explaining to Melba what's going on."

"He is, isn't he?" Mike hoped that was what he was doing. He had listened from the living room while Leah explained that sometimes you should not say everything you are thinking and how he should always be sensitive to women and their clothing. How much he understood was anyone's guess, because he kept interrupting her telling her how pretty Mrs. Driscol's hat was.

"Where is the next lookout point?" Mike asked.

Noelle spoke from the back seat, "The blacksmith shop is next and then Caroline and Elizabeth's house.

"There's Donnie, Mike, and Josiah," Terry said as they approached Old Ben's shop. They all three sat on a bench beneath the tree. Mike and Donnie were listening to Old Ben who lifted his arm and waved as they passed, and Josiah was looking through a pair of binoculars toward the fairground.

Trying to focus on Randy, Jake, or Ronald whose lookout point was supposed to be west of the Driscol's, Josiah was having a hard time finding them. He looked farther down the road in the direction of the Seabaugh Farm and finally spotted Jake perched on the top railing of Mr. Seabaugh's fence. He was laughing at Randy who appeared to be acting like a chicken in the middle of the road.

The girls waved at Mike and Donnie as they passed, and Laura looked anxiously ahead as her dad made a right turn onto Spruce which would take them to the Driscols. The big, white house east of the fairground still sat on the same spot as the original homestead. Always well maintained through the years, it was one of the most beautiful homes in Oak Grove. The two-story structure sat on a knoll surrounded by oak trees with a winding lane leading up to the house. Sweet magnolia grew in abundance along the white fencing that bordered both sides of the lane, sending its sweet fragrance drifting across the yard. A wide, covered porch, supported by white columns, wrapped around the front and west end of the house, affording one a clear view of the small pond that nestled among the trees not far from the house.

"Oh, look," Noelle exclaimed as the house came into view. Balloons were tied along the fence leading up the lane, and red, blue, and yellow streamers attached to the pillars on the porch fluttered in the breeze.

Glancing at Laura, Mike could see the anticipation in her eyes and smiled as he stopped the car in front of the house. "Well, here you are, ladies; right on time. Tell Caroline happy birthday for me, will you?"

"I will, Dad" Laura opened the car door. "The party is over at three o'clock." Lifting the red tissue wrapped gift from the seat, Laura glanced at it, hoping Caroline would like the bracelet and stepped out of the car.

"Thank you, Pastor Mike," Noelle and Terry chorused.

"You're welcome." He smiled as he watched the three walk to the porch. A melancholy feeling surfaced as a memory of Laura, about the age of four, came to mind. Leah had taken her to her first birthday party, and he sat in the car and watched them walk to the door. She thought she was so big, carrying the birthday present, and turned about halfway up the sidewalk and waved to him with a bright smile on her face.

Elizabeth appeared at the door and smiled. She held it open for the girls and glanced at the car. "Hi, Pastor Mike," she called.

Mike waved back and grinned to himself as he watched Elizabeth close the door and disappear into the house. She had been a rambunctious little thing all her life, and Mike had no doubt she would remain that way. A longing to see Leah tugged at his heart, and he turned the car around and drove back down the lane.

"Elizabeth, your dress is really pretty," Terry commented as they followed her into the living room. It was a lilac color with small, dark lilacs on the white collar. Laura, Noelle, and Terry smiled at each other, knowing how much Elizabeth hated dressing up.

Karen and Kim Reese had already arrived and were sitting on the sofa talking to Patricia and Louise Williams seated across from them on the window seat.

Laura glanced around the room. A blue and gold, flowered, love seat sat in front of the fireplace, and matching blue wing back chairs sat in front of a large window that overlooked the yard and pond.

A small table covered with pink lace sat in the doorway to the dining room. Caroline's birthday presents had been placed there and Laura added hers. She glanced into the dining room and was surprised at the length of the dining room table. It seemed much too big for the Driscols, but the oak top, polished to a shine, was very beautiful. A glass basket containing a bouquet of fresh cut flowers sat in the center, and a shiny, silver, tea service sat on a sideboard against the far wall.

Laura smiled as she recognized Mary's humming in the kitchen and knew she was probably as busy as a bee.

"Laura, you can sit over here," Elizabeth said, motioning to one of the wing back chairs.

Laura sat down and watched her pull the curtain back and look out. "You should see those boys. They are not paying any attention or watching for any signals. Jake and Randy are chasing each other around in the field. We better not miss the circus parade," she commented with her hands on her hips. A look of frustration on her face, she sat on the arm of her chair and glanced around the room.

"Everyone is here. Caroline should be down in a minute." She leaned close to Laura, raised both eyebrows, and whispered, "She snagged her hose and you would have thought the world just stopped turning on its axis."

The giggling girls looked at one another, suddenly feeling at ease. Elizabeth's outgoing personality, coupled with a boldness to say whatever entered her mind, was appealing and refreshing but at times got her in trouble. Caroline, quite different, thought her younger sister to be something of a rebel and was often exasperated with her actions.

Their mother had died when Elizabeth was born, and their grieving father left one day and never returned. The Driscols, without a second thought, had taken their nieces and raised them as their own. Elizabeth never knew her parents, and Caroline remembered very little. Mrs. Driscol displayed photographs of their mother on the mantel and placed one in each of the girl's room. Determined that Caroline and Elizabeth would know what a wonderful person she had been, Trudy spoke about her freely.

Although the sisters looked nothing alike, their smiles erased any doubts as to their relationship. It was the one characteristic they both inherited from their mother. The captivating smile was evident in her photographs.

Elizabeth's features were more like her father's. She inherited his dark hair, olive skin, and high cheekbones. Her nose turned up a bit on the end, but, as her Aunt Trudy always reminded her, she was petite like her mother. Her blue eyes, fringed by long, dark lashes, were without a doubt her best feature.

Caroline, on the other hand, inherited her mother's blonde hair, green eyes, and perfectly straight nose. Her heart shaped face, accented by a tiny dimple in her chin, was the same as the photograph of her mother. She was tall and slender, evidently inheriting that from her father, although her Aunt Trudy never mentioned it.

The clock in the hall chimed the noon hour, and Elizabeth, sighing impatiently, walked to the staircase and looked up. Whirling around with a big grin on her face, she flew across the room in a very unladylike manner "Here she comes," she whispered excitedly and flopped down in the chair.

They heard Caroline's footstep on the stairs, and then she appeared in the doorway. The Mayor, appearing from somewhere from the back of the house, stood next to the table that contained her birthday presents and looked with surprise and pride at his niece.

Indeed, Caroline looked beautiful. The soft green of her dress drew attention to her eyes, changing their hue to a striking emerald. It had a scooped neckline, no sleeves, and the straight skirt stopped right at the knee. A belt fit tight around her waist, and a corsage of white and yellow rose buds was pinned to her left shoulder. Her shoes, white open toed heels, matched the small purse she held in her hand. Caroline's blonde hair was parted on the side and softly curled in the Bette Davis style, and she even wore red lipstick. The girls looked at her, somewhat in awe, as though they were looking at someone they didn't know.

"Happy birthday, dear," Mayor Driscol said, walking across the room. He stopped and looked at her fondly, kissed her forehead, and glanced at Trudy who stood in the doorway with tears in her eyes, smiling at both of them. He was amazed at the transformation, suddenly aware that Caroline would be cause for worry in the near future. He wasn't sure if he was ready for that just yet.

His train of thought was interrupted by the chattering girls, and being the only male present decided it would be a good idea to retreat to the den.

Simon, Preston, and Larry, stationed at Old Mill Road, were discussing how long they thought it would take the American Circus Company to get to Oak Grove. "We might have to stay here till midnight," Simon said as he watched Preston whittle a stick with his pocketknife.

He was sitting on the ground leaning against a tree with a look of frustration on his face. "How do you suppose he does it?" Preston asked, examining the stick he just carved into another stick.

"How who does what?" Larry asked, turning his attention away from the road and back to Preston and Simon.

"Mr. Seabaugh." Preston threw the stick down. "He can take a piece of wood and his pocket knife and carve anything. I wish I could do that."

Simon plopped down on the grass next to him. "Yeah, you should see the lizard he carved and gave me. He carved a ship from a block of wood and gave it to Truman for his birthday last year. Truman painted it, and you would think he bought it in Chesterville for sure."

"Well, the only thing I am sure about right now," Larry said, climbing on the fence, "is how hungry I am getting. Where's the food detail anyway?" He looked toward town. "Gee whiz, what if we have to stay out here till this evening? Are they supposed to bring us supper too?"

Preston watched him teeter back and forth on the fence, waiting for him to fall off on his head. "I guess they will. They're not going to let us starve to death."

Simon lay on his back looking up the road that led to the old Seabaugh Mill. "I wonder what it is like up there at night." He turned and looked at Preston. "Have you ever been there after dark?"

"Where?" Preston eyes following Simon's gaze. "At the old mill? Not me! No way! Daytime is fine but not after dark."

Larry half-jumped and half fell off the fence and walked over to them. "Do you believe all that stuff people say about that place?" He dropped down on the grass and looked questioningly at them with wide eyes.

"I don't know if I do or not, but one thing is for sure, I am not ready to go up there at midnight and double check." Preston closed his knife and put it in his pocket. "Brenton and Truman helped Mr. Seabaugh last summer for a few days mending fence. They said at night they could hear strange noises coming from the direction of the old mill."

"What kind of noises?" Larry asked, looking up Old Mill Road.

"Well," Simon said, "Truman told me he could hear the mill wheel turning at midnight and a woman screaming."

"That's what Brenton said too." Preston stood and looked toward the top of the hill, wondering if Brenton and the others could see anything yet.

Larry, wide-eyed, stared at Simon and Preston. "Gee willikers. Did Mr. Seabaugh hear it too?"

Simon shrugged his shoulder, "Mr. Seabaugh said that when you live outside of town you hear all sorts of noises, and they can usually be explained. He just told Truman and Brenton not to worry about it." He stood up and looked down the road toward town. "I don't know. As far as I know, they have never gone out there after dark to check on the noises. I am getting hungry too. Where are those girls?"

"Food! How can you think of food at a time like this? Geeminitly, we could all be murdered tonight standing here waiting for the circus." Larry looked anxiously toward the Old Mill Road and vowed that he was going into town as soon as the sun went down.

Preston and Simon both laughed. "You just said that you were hungry. Nothing is going to bother us. The road all the way into town is filled with kids, and a circus train is headed this way."

Preston looked at him and laughed again. He reached for the green canteen strapped to his bicycle and was glad he brought it. The sun overhead was bearing down, and if not for the shade of the tree and the slight breeze, he would have been tempted to run up to the Old Mill and take a dip in the pond. The cool water tasted good, and he glanced at Larry's worried face and grinned.

"Just the same, I hope it gets here before dark." Larry climbed back up on the fence, sat on the top rail, and looked across the road. The breeze, blowing the tops of the cornstalks in a rippling fashion, made him sleepy, and he turned his attention to the cows grazing lazily behind him in the pasture. Simon and Preston both sat with their backs up against a tree reading comic books. Larry looked down the road again and wondered how long they were going to have to wait.

The girls were seated at a table under the oak trees; a clean, crisp, linen tablecloth spread over it, and a white milk glass basket filled with yellow, blue, and pink flowers sat in the center. A small, brightly wrapped gift lay in the middle of each plate, and Laura stared at her name written on the tiny card attached to it.

Caroline sat at the head of the table smiling prettily. She could hardly believe this was her fifteenth birthday. She asked Aunt Trudy to invite boys, but she adamantly refused, saying she could wait until next year. Caroline didn't mind too much, for that had been the answer she expected. All of her close friends were here, and that made her happy. Caroline knew she could be difficult sometime, but she also knew the girls liked her. She suspected they were all a little jealous because she was the oldest girl in their church; except, of course, for the ones that were really a lot older. They were the seventeen-year-olds who graduated and would be off to work or getting married by the end of summer.

There were several others at school, but they did not come to church, and that was where most of Caroline's social life centered. Aunt Trudy asked if she wanted to invite some of the other girls, but after thinking about it, she decided she would rather have just her close friends After all, they might think she invited them just to get presents.

Mrs. Driscol and Mary came from the house carrying pitchers of lemonade. Mary, Mrs. Driscol's best friend, worked for her. She was a thin black woman with lively, expressive brown eyes that she passed on to her children, Carrie and Jake. Mary had arrived at the Driscol's front door one week after they brought the girls to Oak Grove. She gave advice when it was not asked, talked back when Trudy mouthed her frustrations, cleaned house the way she thought it should be cleaned, and was not intimidated by Trudy in the least as most people.

Mary had watched Caroline and Elizabeth grow through the years. Elizabeth and Jake, only four months apart, toddled around together, and Caroline had mothered both of them. By the time Carrie was born two years later, the three were fast friends anxiously waiting for the birth of *their baby*. Mary stood with the pitcher of lemonade in her hand and smiled fondly at Caroline, thinking how the years had flown.

Laura watched as Mrs. Driscol and Mary poured lemonade in fancy blue glasses. Each glass contained an umbrella toothpick with a lemon wedge and a strawberry stuck on the end. She hoped she would not break her glass. Glancing across the table, she watched Noelle very carefully take a sip and knew she was thinking the same.

Terry sat to Caroline's left and Karen on her right. Karen and Terry would both turn fifteen soon also, and Laura wondered if they would always remain good friends.

Glancing across the table at Noelle, she knew they would be friends forever.

"I want all of you to open your gift," Mrs. Driscol said. "This is a special occasion, and I want all of us to remember today. I just can't believe my little Caroline is fifteen. Where did the years go, Mary? It will be Elizabeth next before I know it. Then they will be married and gone. Oh, dear." She wiped her eyes with her handkerchief and sniffled.

Mary patted her arm. "Quit your frettin,' Trudy. Today is supposed to be happy, now hush. Go ahead girls, open your gifts."

Removing the ribbon from the shiny yellow package, Laura glanced at Elizabeth who seemed just as surprised as everyone else. She pulled the wrapping paper away, laid it on the table in front of her, and lifted the lid. Her eyes widened in delight as she gazed down at a delicate, gold bracelet. A small heart dangled from the center of the chain, and Laura lifted it carefully to read the inscription, *special friend.*

"Mrs. Driscol, this is so beautiful. Thank you," she exclaimed, looking at the plump little lady standing with her hands folded in front of her with a sweet smile on her face. Laura was taken aback and tried to figure out what it was that seemed different about Mrs. Driscol today.

"Aren't they pretty?" Noelle asked with shining eyes. "Thank you, Mrs. Driscol." She turned and looked closely at Elizabeth's bracelet. *"Special Sister*. Oh Elizabeth, that is so sweet."

"It is, isn't it?" Elizabeth replied, looking at her Aunt Trudy with a big smile and then at her sister who was grinning at her. She knew instinctively that Caroline selected the bracelets, and a warm feeling came over her as she thought of the inscription on hers.

Mrs. Driscol stood behind Caroline and watched the girls admire them. Pleased with their surprise, she dabbed tears from her eyes. "You are all very welcome. Now, go ahead, put your bracelets on. Oh, Mary, it just doesn't seem possible . . ."

"Trudy!" Mary stated firmly in her ear. "Straighten up, or I may have to send you to the house with Henry," she commented firmly, glancing at the back side of the porch where Mayor Driscol relaxed in one of the wicker chairs.

Louise fastened the clasp on her bracelet and whispered to Laura, "They really are pretty, aren't they? I didn't know we would get a gift."

"I didn't either." Laura touched the strand of pearls on her neck. *I will always remember today*, she thought and looked down at the bracelet on her wrist. "They look so pretty with our dresses, don't they?"

"Yes, they do. What a special day; the party, our bracelets, and the circus . . ." Louise answered with a happy smile.

"Henry, you may as well come all the way out here instead of watchin' from the porch," Mary called to Mr. Driscol. "These girls need a gentleman's company and a little admiration."

Mr. Driscol stepped from the porch and walked slowly through the yard. He stopped at the end of the table with a smile on his face and looked around.

"I was just listening to the chatter and admiring from a distance. Ladies?" He removed his hat and swept it in front of him in a very gentlemanly fashion. Strolling around the table, he smiled and called each girl by name, admiring her bracelet as thought it was different from the one he just looked at.

Laura giggled at Noelle's red face when Mr. Driscol stopped and spoke to her. "Noelle, you have such a beautiful head of hair," he exclaimed, patting her on the head. Noelle's face was crimson, and she stared down at her hands.

Elizabeth glanced up at her uncle, observing his smile and hand resting on Noelle's head. "Why, Uncle Henry, you will make Aunt Trudy jealous."

The girls at the table laughed at the horrified expression on his face as he looked at Mrs. Driscol standing next to Mary with a grin on her face. "Trudy, are you jealous?"

She looked at him threateningly. "Now, Henry Driscol, you know if you ever do anything to make me jealous, I will replace that white hat on your head with a frying pan."

Laura looked at Noelle, and they burst into laughter. She had never seen Mayor Driscol or Mrs. Driscol act in such a way. Mr. Driscol, always so businesslike, was acting like a charming gentleman, and Mrs. Driscol, always so fussy, was being sweet one minute and threatening to use a frying pan on Mr. Driscol the next.

"Well, Mary, let's get lunch," Trudy said, watching her collect the wrapping paper. "I suspect the girls are probably gettin' hungry."

"Are we ready?" Maggie asked the other girls. All seven wore blue jeans, white shirts, and red armbands with the exception of Abigail who added a white sailor cap with an American flag to her attire.

"I think so. We've counted the sack lunches three times," Shari commented, looking at the red wagons. She looked at the others with a big smile "I think we look very official."

"I do too and very patriotic," Carrie commented. "It was a good idea, Shari."

Charlotte tapped her chin with a finger and stared at the wagons. "Let's double check just one more time to make sure each sack is the same." She moved her head back and forth, conscious of her dog-ears brushing her neck. Her cousin, Hillary, came for a visit last week with her hair fixed in dog-ears, and Charlotte liked it so much, that her mom now put her hair in dog-ears every day. She even tied them with red ribbons this morning.

"Gee whiz," Carrie complained, looking at her wagon. "Do we have to?"

"Okay, sandwiches." Abigail called out, looking in the sacks in her wagon. She glanced at the others, "Well come on, we might as well, or she will gripe if we don't."

She waited as the other girls checked their sacks. Receiving a nod from each, she read off the rest of the items. "Chips, cookies, Root Beer, apples, and Snickers."

"Then that's it; no more counting. Let's go," Abigail exclaimed, pushing the band farther up on her arm. Grabbing her sailor cap from the wagon, she plopped it on her head at a crooked angle and started across the square, pulling the wagon behind her.

"Say, are we still going to meet back here to eat lunch?" Sandy asked, walking alongside of Maggie. "I'm already hungry."

"Of course," Maggie replied, turning to look at her sister. "Abbie, don't you eat without us, do you hear? We've got farther to go than you do."

"We'll wait," Abbie called over her shoulder, heading for the bell tower.

Ellen and Michael Madison sat in a booth at the window in the Cranston Café watching the boys at the bell tower.

Ellen, checking to see if any of their tomatoes were ripe, had just come in the back door when the phone rang. "I would love to have lunch with you," she answered smiling. "I'll be ready in ten minutes." She went upstairs, changed into a little blue dress that Michael especially liked, and grabbed her new pair of low heels. She and Lynn, shopping in Chesterville a couple of weeks ago, both bought a pair. She slipped the white, open toed shoes on and buckled the strap around her ankle, wondering if Michael would even notice them. Looking in the dresser mirror, she ran a brush through her blonde hair and freshened her lipstick. Taking one last glance, she rubbed her finger across her bottom lip and smoothed the color across her cheeks. Picking up her pocketbook, she went out to the porch swing to wait for Michael.

They now watched Zachary who appeared to be giving orders to Jimmy and Jordan. Paying him no mind, Jimmy was telling Jordan something and pointing to the top of the tower when Abigail and Charlotte walked up pulling their wagon.

The three boys gathered around Abigail and she told them something, gesturing with her hands. Charlotte, sitting in the wagon, appeared to guard the lunches. Whatever she was saying, it had its effect because the three boys immediately sat on the ground.

Michael chuckled and looked at Ellen "Just like a woman; giving orders and making men follow them." Ellen grinned at him and watched as Zachary sat on the ground and rummaged through his sack.

"Which song would you like to hear?" Michael asked, digging in his pocket for change. Ellen leaned next to him and looked at the remote selector on their table.

"Umm, let's play something fun." She read the song titles and then grinned. "How about Hey! Ba-Ba-Re-Bop; Glenn Miller's version though." Lionel Hampton's rendition was also listed, but she like Glenn Miller best.

Michael dropped the nickel in the slot and sat back. "I like it best too." He smiled at her. "I'm glad you could have lunch with me." *She has the most beautiful blue eyes,* he thought, looking at her. They were fringed with long, dark lashes and their striking color was even more brilliant from the blue dress she wore.

"I'm glad you called. We haven't done this in a while." Laura smiled at him and glanced out the window. Her brother and Lynn just emerged from Hank's Hardware and were crossing the street. "Here comes Alan and Lynn."

Glenn Miller's song filled the café, and they sat back in the booth and watched Alan and Lynn cross to the bell tower and stop to talk with the boys. Lynn shook her head, they both laughed, and then strolled hand in hand across the square.

The buzz from the lunch crowd was friendly and familiar to their ears as Alan open the door and held it for Lynn.

"Hey, Alan, are you going to get on a bicycle and deliver the papers yourself today?" Ned called from the lunch counter. "It looks to me like the circus squad stole your paper boys."

Alan waved his hand and laughed as the heckling started. He was accustomed to it, and the men knew he could give as well as receive. Bantering and joking was just one part of lunch at the busy little place.

The Cranston Café did a lot of business during the noon hour. The atmosphere was warm and jovial with a lot of noise and laughter, and the merchants long ago found that it was more convenient for them to run in for lunch instead of going home. The cost was low, food could not be better anywhere, and socializing was and always had been a big part of Oak Grove.

Red booths sat along the walls of the café, and small square tables, adorned with red and white checked tablecloths, took up space in the center. Matching café curtains hung at the windows, and a Wurlitzer Jukebox sat at one end of the room. The lunch counter with its red stools took up the back wall, and behind the counter one could see Mercy dishing up orders through the open window. The old wood floor, bearing many dents and scrapes, was kept freshly mopped and waxed. Several paintings of Oak Grove's early days hung on the white walls, results of Mayor Cranston's Grandmother. Gifted with an extraordinary talent, her brush had captured several early homesteads, the old Baptist Church with its bell, Seabaugh Mill, The Mercantile, and three wooded landscapes.

Lynn joined Michael and Ellen, waved to Mercy, and slid into the booth. "Have you ordered yet? I'm about to starve." Laying her pocketbook on the seat, she watched Alan walk to the lunch counter to talk with Ned and Hank.

"They will be back on the job tomorrow," Alan told Ned. "Ron agreed to include the newspaper with today's mail so I guess the boys owe him one."

"That's mighty nice of Ron to deliver the papers for the boys," Pete Williams commented.

"It sure is." Alan slapped Nelson White on the back. "That peanut coffee cake Lynne brought home yesterday is gone. You tell Barbara she outdid herself this time."

"Much obliged. I'm glad you liked it," Nelson answered. "I believe it is one of my favorites too."

Barbara and Nelson White, taking advantage of the baking skills Barbara inherited from her French grandmother, decided to go into the bakery business. An opportunity they couldn't pass presented itself a few years ago, and they built and established the bakery, now widely known for its extraordinary French pastries. Folks passed through Oak Grove to visit the bakery, and quite frequently, people from Chesterville and surrounding towns made special trips to sample some of the puffy delicacies.

Alan left the men at the counter and joined Lynn, Michael and Ellen. "Are you two here for the show?" he chuckled, looking out the window in amusement.

"The show is Abigail ordering the boys around." Ellen laughed as she continued to fondly watch her niece.

Lynn laid her menu down, tapping her fingers with the music. "We were watching earlier from The Chronicle. I guess when it comes to food men listen no matter what age they are," she commented, looking sideways at Alan with a grin.

Louise walked up to the table with her pad and pencil in hand. She had worked at the café for years and knew what everyone usually ordered, insisting that she only wrote it down so Mercy would know how many orders to dish up. Her black hair, worn up atop her head and held in place with combs, was covered with a black hair net.

"Afternoon, folks. It's nice, isn't it? I like to see children involved in a project and all of them working together," she commented in her familiar monotone as she stared through the window. Louise was a woman that rarely smiled, never had a whole lot to say, and when she did it was usually curt and blunt. She also was found lacking in personality, but everyone in Oak Grove was use to her ways and paid her no mind. They also knew she had been the sole supporter of her ailing mother for as long as anyone could remember and respected her for it.

"Today's special is chicken stew with dumplings, green beans, pickled beets, salad, rolls, and apple, cherry, or peach cobbler." Louise dully recited the menu, knowing they would all order it. Chicken stew was one of Mercy's specialties, and they often times ran out.

All four look at each other and grinned. "There is no question on my part. That's what I'm having." Michael looked at Ellen. "How about you, hon?"

"I will too." She watched Louise raise an eyebrow and turn to Alan and Lynn. "Are you two going for the special?"

"We sure are, Louise, thank you," Alan answered, watching her. "You know us so well, I would bet you wouldn't even have to come and ask. Isn't that right?" He always tried to drag a few more words out of her but seldom had any luck. Today was no different. She nodded, stuck the pencil in her hair, and walked off.

"Have you seen the Mayor this morning? I need to talk to him about the 4th of July celebration at Miss Mattie's?" Michael asked Alan. He waved at Hank, walking toward the door, and watched Louise clip their order to one of the clothespins in the window behind the counter.

Ellen looked at Michael. "Today is Caroline's birthday party. I'm sure he will be home all day. I understand it was to be a very special celebration for her."

Laura and Noelle glanced across the table at each other and grinned. This was so much fun. She was so glad she came. Although she never considered not coming to the party, she sure was happy to be here.

Mrs. Driscol and Mary rolled a teacart across the soft grass. Fancy silver lids covered platters, concealing that which was beneath. Laura had never seen anything so fancy. Mary placed a large platter at one end of the table while Mrs. Driscol sat two smaller ones at the other. A gentle breeze stirred the leaves and sent the fragrance of honeysuckle across the yard. Ducks quacked their way across the pond, and Laura wondered if they would come up to the table.

Placing her napkin in her lap and realizing she was very hungry, Laura hoped she would not drop anything on her dress or the tablecloth. How embarrassing that would be. She wished she was more relaxed and glanced across the table at Noelle who was absentmindedly rubbing her fingers back and forth on her napkin. Laura smiled to herself, knowing Noelle was just as nervous as she was, and wondered if she was thinking the same thing.

Mrs. Driscol smiled at Caroline. "Mary and I are going to the house now. You girls eat your lunch and enjoy yourself." Lifting the lids, they placed them on the bottom tray of the teacart and put the pitchers of lemonade within easy reach of the table. "Help yourselves; Mary and I will be back in a little while." Laura watched the two women walk across the yard toward the house and wondered what it would feel like to be rich.

The large tray was filled with tiny sandwiches cut in a variety of shapes with small cherry tomatoes and tiny pickles scattered around them. One of the smaller trays contained toasted flat bread cut in circles and topped with a variety of cheeses and sausages. The other tray displayed apple slices, strawberries, orange slices, grapes, cherries, blackberries, and pineapple chunks. Two round, clear, glass bowls that Laura recognized from holiday dinners at church contained potato salad and slaw.

Glancing around the table, she was unsure whether she should serve herself or wait for Caroline to start eating. What was it that Mom told her? "Always watch the hostess and follow her lead?" What if she fell out of her chair backwards, should she do that too? Laura grinned. It was something like that; she should have listened more carefully.

"I'm going to eat. I'm hungry," Elizabeth said, breaking the ice. She helped herself to the cheese tray and passed it to Noelle. Laura sighed and relaxed as she smiled at Elizabeth. She was so honest and easy going. Caroline had a tendency to "put on airs" as she heard someone say one day, but she liked her anyway. She always treated her very nicely and hadn't even told on her and Elizabeth the day she caught them in the church kitchen eating a piece of Mrs. Driscol's orange pudding cake.

Mrs. Driscol baked the three layered orange cake especially for a former pastor who always bragged that it was the best cake he had ever eaten. The church dinner that Sunday was in honor of his fifty years of service in the Lord's ministry, and a large crowd from neighboring churches had turned out.

It was Laura's turn to take their class offering upstairs, and Elizabeth made an excuse to go to the bathroom. They cut through the kitchen to check out the food and wandered around the tables looking hungrily at the fried chicken, casseroles, vegetables, and desserts. Opening the refrigerator, Elizabeth spied her Aunt Trudy's cake. Glancing at Laura with a grin, she said it seemed logical to her that it would be alright to go ahead and eat a piece.

"After all, we brought it and no one is going to miss one slice of cake after it is cut anyway," she said, grabbing a knife and two forks from the drawer. They were in the process of devouring it when Caroline, delivering her class offering, walked through the door and caught them red-handed. She looked at them in surprise, commented that Aunt Trudy was going to kill Elizabeth, walked over to her and ate the bite of cake Elizabeth had on her fork. Handing it back to her, she turned around and walked upstairs. Elizabeth told her the next day that her Aunt Trudy came to the conclusion that Brother Jenkins, not able to wait, had helped himself. As far as Laura knew, they never told her any different.

Laura looked at Caroline sitting at the head of the table. She looked very pretty and so grown up. She even had a boyfriend who her Aunt and Uncle didn't know about. Elizabeth told Laura it was Peter Williams, but she said she doubted if *he* knew about it and confided to her that Caroline vowed he would kiss her before the summer was over. "Have you ever heard of anything so sickening!" Elizabeth exclaimed.

Laura hoped she would be as ladylike as Caroline when she turned fifteen. Glancing at Elizabeth, she tried to imagine her a young lady but could not picture it at all.

Louise passed the tray of cheeses and toasted bread, and Laura helped herself to what she thought was an appropriate serving. She didn't know what she was so worried about. If this is what money did to you, then she was glad her family did not have much. By the time her plate was full, the conversation had turned to the circus.

"I wonder what time the circus will get here?" Kim Reese asked, looking around. "Just think; if it comes to town before the party is over, we will be the first to see it."

"To think that the circus will arrive on my birthday is a present in itself," Caroline commented from the head of the table. "When I saw the leaflets Saturday, I was thrilled." She lowered her eyes and tried to blush. She had practiced blushing since she read about it in a True Romance Magazine one day in the drug store while waiting for Aunt Trudy to finish talking to Mrs. Miller. "I had no idea Uncle Henry was going to surprise me like this."

Elizabeth looked at her sister and rolled her eyes heavenward. Glancing at Laura, she mocked the lowering of her eyes, and they both giggled. Laura loved it when Elizabeth mocked her sister, imitating her actions perfectly. Laura knew she was only joking because, in spite of all of her complaining, Elizabeth loved Caroline. One day, in confidence, she told Laura that when she grew up she wanted to be just like her.

"Isn't this fun?" Noelle whispered across the table to Laura. "Everything tastes so good."

Laura nodded with a mouth full of what she thought was chicken salad and cucumbers. There was something crunchy in it, but she wasn't sure what it was. *Whatever it is*, Laura thought, *I would like to have another one.*

"Next year Aunt Trudy said I could invite boys." Caroline smiled at the girls with a pleased look on her pretty face.

Elizabeth set her glass of lemonade down with a thud and looked at her sister. "What on earth for? That would be a sure fire way to ruin a party."

Caroline looked at her younger sister with an air of mature patience. "One day, Elizabeth, you will understand and feel the same way." She daintily bit into a juicy red strawberry and wiped her mouth delicately with her napkin.

Most of the girls at the table thought much the same as Elizabeth with the exception of Terry and Karen who smiled knowingly at Caroline.

"Would anyone care for another tea sandwich?" Caroline asked, performing her role as perfect hostess. "There is plenty." She passed the tray to her left and let her eyes travel around the table to each of the girls.

Laura returned Caroline's smile and gladly took the tray of small sandwiches. She had not wanted to come right out and ask for another; not with what she still had on her plate. She did not want Caroline to think she was a pig. The vision of a pig sitting on a chair at the table popped into her mind, and she snickered. Noelle glanced at her curiously from across the table, wondering what was so funny. Laura imagined a pig sitting in Noelle's chair and laughed aloud.

"Hey, what is so funny?" Elizabeth asked, looking at Laura. The others turned to stare at her, and the vision of a whole table full of pigs under the oak tree popped into her head. She burst into laughter, not caring what anyone thought, and buried her face in her hands.

Noelle looked at Elizabeth and laughed. "I don't have any idea what she is laughing about." Elizabeth and Noelle looked at one another and then back at Laura. Merriment danced in Elizabeth's eyes and she giggled as she looked back at Noelle's grinning face.

Caroline looked at the three questioningly, and a broad smile spread across her face at the girls' gaiety. Karen's laughter reached her ear and she felt Terry poke her in the rib as she giggled. The truth of the old saying, laughter is contagious, swept across the table like a breeze preceding a spring thunderstorm. Within a few seconds, the whole table was in an uproar.

What in heaven's name is so funny?" Mary asked, standing next to the teacart. She had crossed the yard unnoticed and was amazed at the scene beneath the trees. Every girl at the table was in stitches over something. Caroline held her hands across her stomach, and Elizabeth's face was buried in her hands. Mary smiled to herself. She had been a little concerned about the age difference in some of the girls, but evidently that was a needless thought.

Elizabeth wiped her eyes and looked at her. Opening her mouth, she tried to speak but burst into laughter again. She finally managed to choke out, "We don't know why we are laughing, Mary." The remark only prompted a fresh fit of laughter.

Mary shook her head and chuckled "When you ladies are able to compose yourselves and make it to the back porch, we will have cake and ice cream." Retrieving the trays from the table, she placed them on the teacart and pushed it across the lawn to the house, smiling to herself.

"Boy Howdy, lunch is finally on its way," Johnny yelled, jumping from the tree limb. The boys quickly discovered that the branch was just high enough to allow them to see over the next hill and decided to take turns, switching every fifteen minutes.

Brenton, sitting on the grass with his back against the tree, closed his pocketknife and stood up. "Finally!" He walked to the middle of the road and watched the girls climb the hill.

Sandy and Shari walked on either side of Maggie as she pulled the wagon. Reaching the top, she dropped the wagon handle, took off her shoe, and shook out a small rock. "It is a long way up here." She crossed the road and sat in the shade of the tree, putting her shoe back on. "There's your lunch."

"What did you bring?" Brenton asked, hurriedly grabbing a sack and a bottle of pop from the wagon. "Root Beer; swell. I'm hungry and thirsty." He held the bottle of pop in his hand and looked around. "Oh, no. You didn't forget. . . ."

"It's in the wagon," Maggie commented.

Brenton pushed the sacks aside and grabbed the small metal bottle opener.

Slipping it over the top of the bottle, he caught the edges of the cap, and popped it off.

Shari, watching him take a big swallow, realized she was very thirsty and gazed down the long empty road, wishing the circus wagon would appear from over the hill. In the distance, Miss Mattie's horses grazed in the pasture across the road from the entrance to her farm. The graveled lane led up through the trees, curved around in front of the big white house, then wound its way back down the other side where it joined the lane again. The red roof at the top of the hill was partially visible through the trees, and she knew from the way the house was situated on the hill that Oak Grove was visible from the second story balcony.

"You haven't seen anything yet?" she asked, looking back at the three boys.

"Only Jacob Cook on his tractor," Johnny answered, wiping the perspiration from his forehead with the back of his hand. He grabbed a sack from the wagon and took a big drink of Root Beer. "Aaaah, this tastes good."

"I'm thirsty too." Pushing aside an extra brown sack, Sandy sat down in the wagon. "We should have brought something to drink."

Maggie jumped up and danced across the road. "I think of everything," she announced. "Look in the sack and give me one." She smiled proudly as she watched Sandy pull an Orange Whistle from the sack.

"Hurry up. Throw me the bottle opener when you're done. I'm dying of thirst."

Truman jumped up and looked down the road. The rumble of an engine sounded from over the hill, and for one silent moment they all stood and stared at one another. Thrusting his Root Beer to Maggie, he scrambled up the tree.

"What do you see?" Brenton called, looking from Truman to the top of the hill, straining to see.

Shari's heart beat wildly. They would be the first ones to see it arrive.

Johnny jumped around laughing; "This could be it. Man, I hope it is."

Truman looked down and waved his hand. "Forget it." He jumped off the limb. "It is just one of the log trucks heading back to the woods."

"I was hoping it was the circus train," Shari said disappointedly. She stood quietly for a moment, eyeing up the tree limb. "I think I might climb up there and look around."

Brenton looked at her with a look of exasperation. "No. I'm afraid we can't allow that." Swallowing a bite of his baloney sandwich, he looked at her seriously. "You see, we are responsible for this lookout post, and we wouldn't want you to get hurt and have us answer to the Mayor or the town council."

Shari rolled her eyes. "For crying out loud, I can climb just as well as any of you guys. You get to do everything." She placed her hands on her hips and looked at Brenton with a stubborn look on her face. "If I really wanted to climb that tree I would," she said, "and you couldn't stop me either." Taking a big swallow of her Whistle, she stared at him.

"Come on, Shari." Maggie pulled her arm, looking at the Snicker Bar Johnny was unwrapping. "Let's go. I'm getting hungry."

"Me too, let's go back and eat." Sandy held a handful of wild daisies she had collected on the way up the hill and stuck one in her hair. "I wish we would have brought our lunches with us."

Maggie picked up the black wagon handle. "Me too," she sighed, "but the plans were for all of us to eat together." Pushing her armband back up, she looked at the boys' blue ones. "I'm glad Zachary's dad had these, aren't you?"

"Yeah, it was pretty nice of him. I'm glad he found them." Johnny watched a chicken hawk glide above the pasture across the road and land in one of the trees. The white fence bordering the field was one that Brenton and Truman helped Mr. Seabaugh repair last summer. He was supposed to go along but sprained his ankle jumping off the garage roof, and Dr. Miller said he should stay off of it for a few days.

They spent two nights on the Seabaugh farm and came home with mysterious tales about a woman screaming. "Brent," he said wondering about it, "did you ever find out about those noises at the Old Mill last summer?"

"I don't want to hear anymore." Shari turned the wagon around. She had heard plenty tales about that night and each telling got a little scarier. "Come on, let's go eat lunch with the rest of the girls." Pulling the now empty wagon, the three girls headed down the hill.

"Ninny, Ninny, scaredy cat!" Truman yelled laughingly as they headed down the hill. The only answer he received was no answer.

The girls finally stopped laughing, finished their lunch, and now sat on the porch, watching Caroline unwrap her gifts. She already opened several, including a Philco radio from her aunt and uncle. They plugged it in and much to Caroline's delight The Ink Spots were singing "To Each His Own."

Elizabeth handed her sister the next present, and Laura recognized the red tissue paper and white ribbon. Mom helped her select the gift and assured her that it was perfect for Caroline. She watched her remove the ribbon, hoping she would be pleased with it.

"Well, will you hurry up," Elizabeth said impatiently. "At this rate, we will be here all night. The ice cream will melt and the cake with be as dry as August grass." Noelle pinched Laura's arm and tried not to laugh at the stern look Mary gave her.

Caroline glanced at her sister with a deep sigh and wondered if there would ever be any hope for her. "All right. I am sorry. It is not every day a girl turns fifteen."

Mr. and Mrs. Driscol sat on the swing, and Mary was seated in a white wicker chair. Laura again was struck with the thought that she had never seen this side of Mr. and Mrs. Driscol before.

Dad was right when he said you should not judge people because you don't know what they are really like or what has happened to them, Laura thought. How many times had she heard both of her parents say that?

"Oh, I love it. This is beautiful, Laura," Caroline cried, lifting the pearl bracelet from the box. Of course, the pearls were not real, but they were very pretty. The gold bracelet had three pearls in the center and one tiny pearl hanging at the clasp.

"Thank you so much." She smiled at her happily. "I'm going to wear it right now."

She slipped it around her wrist and fastened the clasp. Extending her arm, she proudly displayed the bracelet and smiled at Laura again.

"She really likes it," Noelle whispered, leaning close.

Elizabeth handed Caroline the last present and sat back down. Relief was evident in her face and she tugged on the collar of her dress.

Uncle Henry watched Elizabeth and smiled. Her spunk had always amused him. By the time she was two years old, she already displayed a determination and will of her own that was so much a part of her personality. Her relentless pursuit of the ducks and geese all over the yard was a chase she refused to give up until they took refuge in the water. Even at that, she needed to be watched closely for fear she would go in the water after them.

"Oh, Terry, you didn't!" Caroline squealed as she unwrapped a small bottle of Chanel No. 5. "Thank you so much." Very carefully she removed the lid and dabbed a little on her wrists. "Thank you, everyone, for everything." She sat back in her chair, pleased with her gifts, her friends, and her party and pondered where to put her radio.

Mrs. Driscol smiled fondly at the girls looking at Caroline's gifts. "Would anyone be interested in cake and ice cream?"

"Beat you again, James," Phillip Driscol said, grinning at James Madison. They sat on each side of an old barrel that years ago collected rainwater but now served as a support for the checkerboard. Both men habitually dropped by the blacksmith shop and today was no exception.

James leaned back in his chair and hooked his thumbs in his suspenders. "You know your luck will not hold out, so don't start getting all puffed up." He smoothed his mustache with his fingers and scratched his head. James was a wiry little man with amazingly clear blue eyes for a man of his years. His thick red hair stuck in all directions as though it had never seen a comb, and the old hat he always wore lay on the floor next to his chair.

Louis Smith, sitting in an old ladder back chair with his feet propped on an old nail keg, shook his head at both men Their daily bantering over the checker game was an ongoing argument Whoever won four out of five was champ for the day and he played the loser. The four had shared a lot of checkers and memories through the years; developing a deep and lasting friendship that spanned times of heartaches and joys, success and failure, and the ups and downs of everyday living.

Louis was seventy-one and felt every year of it. Aches in his joints kept him stiff most of the time, and he marveled that Old Ben was able to get around like he did. Louis's wife, Sarah, was Ben's niece and was also still pretty agile. He figured she would probably be getting around just like Ben if she lived that long. He watched Phillip rummage in the cooler for a soda pop. "Why aren't you at your granddaughter's birthday party? Grab me a root beer will you?"

"Lucille is fixing supper and we'll celebrate tonight," Phillip replied, opening both bottles on the side of the cooler. He took a drink of his Coca-Cola, handed Louis his bottle of pop, and sat down. "I think today was reserved for giggling girls."

Old Ben took the pipe from his mouth. "Remember when we use to get excited about birthdays?" The men silently agreed for a couple of minutes, and Old Ben sat back in his rocker and chuckled. "Remember the year you forgot Sarah's birthday, Louis?"

"I declare, she didn't speak to me for a week." Louis shook his gray head and laughed. "Didn't even fix my supper I had to go over to Hannah's to eat."

Phillip studied one of the beams that ran across the top of the shop then looked at him with a grin on his face. "As I recall, you spent a lot of money on her at Williams Drugstore and the Sweet Shoppe, didn't you?"

"I reckon I did. She always reminds me at least two weeks ahead now." Louis stared at the floor for a minute, thinking about the last few birthdays. "Well, I declare . . . she hasn't said too much about her birthday the last couple of years. I think she's tired of countin' them."

"I guess we have all gotten that way," Old Ben commented as he rocked in his chair. "I thank the Lord everyday for the years He's given me on this earth. If He gives me another one, that's just fine, and if He decides to take me home, that's even better."

The men sat quietly, nodding in agreement, and the clock in Ben's living room chimed two o'clock. There was a quiet closeness in the blacksmith shop, and Louis looked around the walls that still held the tools Ben's family had used for years. He kept them well oiled and in working condition.

Louis chuckled and looked at him. "I wish you could oil my old bones and keep them workin' like you do these tools, Ben."

"Believe me, Louis; if I thought I could, I would." Old Ben smiled and let his eyes roam around the walls.

The tools had seen a lot of work by craftsmen through the years; lasting results were visible all over town. Louis wondered if his life would leave any marks in this world when he was gone. He sure prayed that it would.

He looked at the old black, potbellied stove sitting in the middle of the shop and pondered on its use through the years. Even it had served its purpose, and Ben still used it on cold days to heat the shop and cook a pot of something or other.

James walked to the cooler, helped himself to a Coca-Cola, and checked their supply. Monday mornings they each brought a different brand of pop, relieving Old Ben the expense and insuring there was always plenty on hand.

Ben tapped the tobacco from his pipe and walked to the door. "Guess I better check on the patrol outside."

The boys' excitement was contagious, and he observed the men glancing out the window several times. Frequently, one of them got up and walked outside, looked across the lot of Willy's Garage to the square beyond the Cranston Hotel, and then wandered back in. Ben stuck the pipe in the top pocket of his overalls and smiled to himself as he headed for the door. He had to admit he also was looking forward to the next couple of days.

"You're really going to ring the bell?" Phillip asked, following Ben out the door.

What was it. . . . .about fifteen years ago when you last rang it?" He tried to remember the year but was unsure. "I recollect it was the day a tornado was spotted, but can't recall the exact year."

"I sure am; just as soon as I get the word. We can't disappoint these children." Pulling an old red and white kerchief from his pocket, he wiped the perspiration from his forehead and replaced it. "They are the next generation, Phillip. I don't reckon they should grow up associatin' a ringin' bell with only bad news."

The two men walked around the side of the Blacksmith Shop to Ben's front yard. "Sixteen years ago; the tornado was in the spring of 1930."

Mike, Donnie, and Josiah's lookout point was the tree in Ben's front yard. They had a clear view down Oak Street to the Fairground and were presently sitting on the ground playing Mumbly Peg.

"That doesn't count. You didn't throw it the way I did," Josiah complained, looking at Mike.

"I did so." Mike pulled his pocketknife out of the ground and looked at Donnie. "Didn't I?"

"Nope, Jo held it on his finger and flipped it."

"So did I." Mike looked at both boys. "I did it just like you, Jo."

"You did not."

"Did."

"Did not," Josiah replied, closing his pocketknife as Old Ben and Phillip walked up "We haven't seen or heard anything yet, Ben," Josiah commented importantly, dropping his knife in his pocket.

"Let me check again for you." He walked to the sidewalk, lifted the binoculars hanging around his neck, and looked beyond the Fairground toward the Driscols. He didn't see any of the boys. "I wonder what they're doing," he mumbled.

Old Ben smiled affectionately at the three boys. He differed with the children's parents and their instructions to call him Mr. Cook, saying he had been called Ben "for almost a hundred years" and would rather keep it that way. He often was heard to say Mr. didn't necessarily carry respect, and he had learned years ago respect was reflected in a person's eyes and in the manner with which he treated you.

He patted Mike on the shoulder as he watched Donnie drop his knife in his pocket and run to the sidewalk where Josiah still looked toward the Fairground. The boys came from good homes and often ran in the shop with a message, looked around out of boredom, or just wanted to hang around with him for a few minutes if he was working on something.

"I sure wish we would get the signal," Mike said, glancing at his armband. "Ben, do you see this? You have to be part of the lookout squad to wear one."

Ben tousled the boy's hair and pointed to his blue armband. "Yes, sir. Brenton, Truman, and Johnny dropped by early this mornin.' They explained my responsibility and told me to wear it on my right arm. I put it on and haven't taken it off." He grinned at Phillip as they watched Donnie hurriedly switch his from the left to the right arm.

"I wondered if you had one," Josiah said, walking back into the yard. "Hi, Mr. Driscol."

Phillip smiled down at them and spoke sincerely, "You boys are doing a fine job. Why, everyone in town is waiting and listening for the bell to ring. You make sure you get Old Ben over to the square in plenty of time."

"Yes, Sir. We surely will," Josiah said as he removed the binoculars from around his neck and handed them to Donnie. He was about to choke him to death in his attempt to get them off of him.

"Say, how would one of these taste?" Mr. Williams walked up behind them with three chocolate ice cream cones in his hands.

"Swell! Thanks, Mr. Williams," the boys answered with pleasure, taking the cones from him.

"You're welcome, boys." Mr. Williams wiped his hands on his white apron. "I believe I'll take some over to the bell tower too. How about you old fellas? You'll have to pay for yours though. Free ice cream is for the lookout squads only." He chuckled and checked his watch. "I have to get back. Melba popped in for her afternoon break, and I left her in charge of the store. She may be setting up her salon right at the counter." He straightened his white cap and paused for a moment, watching them enjoy the ice cream. "Say, would one of you boys run down to the bandstand and tell the girls to run up here. I've got one for them too."

"I'll get the message to them," Phillip assured him, as the three walked around the side of the Blacksmith Shop and cut across Willy's lot.

Gerald waved his hand and hurried across the street to the drugstore. Phillip's eyes traveled along the block and around the rest of the square, noting the familiar businesses and shops. The typical coming and going of the townsfolk flowed back and forth, and if not for the fact that a circus was on it way, the day appeared as ordinary as any other. The familiar sights and sounds filled him with contentment, and he glanced toward the bandstand.

The girls sat on the floor, playing Jacks and the boys at the bell tower were on their knees playing marbles. Elijah Seabaugh stopped to talk to them, and Clyde pulled up in front of Melba's Salon, letting Mildred Reese out of the cab. A breeze rustled the leaves overhead, and a whiff of Cranston Café's lunch special reached him. Laughter drifted from the water fountain where Margaret Miller, Sarah Clark, and Abigail Cranston, relaxed on one of the benches. Phillip looked up at the cloudless sky. "It's a beautiful day," he murmured quietly.

Old Ben thought much the same and smiled at him. "The innocence of youth; it's a shame they can't keep it, isn't it?" Old Ben looked tenderly at the children on the square. "May God bless them, Phillip." He turned to his friend and rested his hand on his shoulder. "You go tell the girls to get their ice cream cones and then come on. We'll see how many checker games you can lose."

Terry and Karen sat on either side of Caroline watching Mrs. Driscol light the candles. "I don't believe I have ever seen a cake so pretty," Terry commented as she looked at the white cake edged with pink icing. "Happy Birthday Caroline" was written in pink and surrounded by white, blue, and pink flowers. Tiny, sparkly flakes of colored sugar were scattered across the top.

"Mrs White baked the cake," Noelle commented. "There is no one else in Oak Grove who can bake like she can." The fifteenth candle was finally burning and the girls looked at Caroline.

"Make a wish, dear," Mayor Driscol said, looking at his niece fondly.

Caroline closed her eyes for a moment and smiled as she opened them. She bent down, blew the candles out, and looked around happily when the girls joined Elizabeth singing "Happy Birthday," loudly and off key.

Mary, watching from the kitchen door, suddenly saw Caroline six years old again. Tearing up, she hastily wiped at her eyes and walked into the kitchen for the ice cream. "I've been around Trudy too long. I'm startin' to act just like her," she grumbled, reaching for the ice cream freezer.

Mrs. Driscol sliced into the cake and laid the first piece on a small, delicate, crystal plate next to a matching punch cup. Mary added a scoop of ice cream, handed it to Caroline, and hugged her. Mrs. Driscol and Mary continued their slicing and scooping amid talk and laughter until all were served, and they finally sat down to enjoy their portion of cake and ice cream.

"I hope I don't break this," Noelle whispered, taking a bite of her cake. "I bet they cost a dollar a piece."

Laura looked at her. "Do you think so? They are very delicate looking. Why did you have to say that Noelle? Now one of us will probably drop one for sure." Laura took a bite of cake. "Golly, this is so good. Chocolate is my favorite."

Caroline suddenly jumped from her seat, ran to her new radio, and turned the volume up. Frank Sinatra's voice carried "They Say It's Wonderful" across the porch. "I love this song," she said dreamily and slowly turned in a circle with her arms out to an imaginary dance partner.

"Oh, good grief," Elizabeth muttered and took a big bite of cake.

Louise leaned across and whispered to Laura and Noelle, "I didn't really want to come today, but I am glad I did. Hasn't this been fun?"

Laura glanced at Noelle. She didn't think Louise should have come right out and said she didn't want to come but realized that she too had been more interested in the arrival of the circus than the party. She was glad Mom encouraged her to come. She would not have wanted to miss this party for anything.

Elizabeth sat down next to Noelle. "I guess she'll keep that thing turned up all the time now. I'll probably be deaf by the time I turn fifteen."

Frank Sinatra's last strains faded away and Mrs. Driscol turned the volume down. "We must be able to hear each other speak," she said, looking at Caroline. "Barbara exceeded my expectations for your cake. It was beautiful, wasn't it? I think the only other cake that was as pretty was the one at the Christmas dinner at church two years ago. Do you remember?" Trudy turned to her husband who nodded in agreement. "It had the star and angels on it. She is very good and has quite a talent. And today could not have been a more beautiful day."

Laura and Noelle glanced at each other and then averted their eyes. *Here she goes,* thought Laura. When Mrs. Driscol starts talking, sometime there is no stopping her.

She grinned, thinking of the time her dad drove to Chesterville to bring her home from her sister's house. Mayor Driscol was sick, unable to get out of bed, so Dad told him to "stay put and I'll go get her." He walked in the back door, right at suppertime, with such a look on his face that they all thought something awful happened. He announced that he was positive Mrs. Driscol had been vaccinated with a Victrola needle, and it was only by the grace of God that she didn't ride home with a rag stuffed in her mouth.

She and Johnny started giggling and Mom hurriedly turned to the kitchen sink. Shari stuffed her napkin in her mouth and Jimmy, mocking her, laughed and shoved his napkin in his mouth.

Mom told Dad he shouldn't say things like that in front of the children and to go relax for a few minutes. He looked around the kitchen, shook his head, and walked into the living room, muttering something about peace and quiet.

Elizabeth sprang out of her chair and dropped a hunk of cake on her shoe. "What was that?" She stared out toward the pond. All eyes followed, wondering what she was looking at.

"What's what?" Caroline asked, watching her sister hurry across the porch and turn her new Philco off.

"That! Can't you hear it?" Elizabeth skirted around the porch swing and jumped off the porch, her lilac skirt flying up.

Laura's eyes widened. "Yes, I hear it too. It's the boys! Johnny is blowing his whistle!" she exclaimed. Her hands shook as she sat her plate on the table and looked at the rest who stared at her curiously. As though an explanation was necessary she blurted out, "The circus! The circus is on its way!"

Flying down the steps, she followed Elizabeth around the side of the house, hearing the excited chatter of the other girls as they came to life.

Laura and Elizabeth flew through the yard and were already at the end of the drive, looking at the top of the hill. She could hear Johnny repeatedly blowing his whistle, Randy and Jake were both waving flags frantically in the air, and Ronald was running around in the middle of the road shouting and waving his arms.

Laura stood next to the fence, her heart pounding in her chest. She didn't feel very ladylike and she really didn't care. She turned and looked at the rest of the girls running across the yard in as undignified a manner as she had. She giggled at the sight of Mrs. Driscol scurrying along with three ducks quacking close behind.

Elizabeth stood in the middle of the road looking toward the Seabaugh Farm. She could see Simon and Preston waving their flags madly. Laura joined her and laughed as Elizabeth grabbed and hugged her. "It's coming. The circus is finally coming!" she squealed as they jumped up and down.

Laura looked down the hill toward town and the Blacksmith Shop but did not see anything. Weren't they watching for the signal?

Elizabeth looked at Laura "Who is at the blacksmith shop? Aren't they paying attention?" she cried impatiently.

Noelle ran into the road. "Josiah, Donnie, and Mike. They are the squad at Old Ben's." All three girls stared down the hill, straining to see some activity.

Caroline and the rest of the girls stood in the yard, excitedly looking both ways. Randy and Jake continued to yell and wave their flags as Elizabeth paced back and forth in the road. She turned and with a frustrated look spun around in the road. "Whistle, Laura!" she commanded. She stood with her hand on her hips and a look of total frustration on her face.

Laura looked at her like she was crazy. "Whistle?" she asked. Why would she want her to whistle now? They often times whistled songs while listening to the radio, but now?

"Not regular whistling but the way you do it with two fingers." She motioned for the other girls to get quiet and stared at Laura, waiting.

It finally dawned on Laura what she wanted her to do. Johnny taught her how to produce an ear-splitting whistle that Mom told her many times was not very ladylike. Putting two fingers in her mouth, she took a deep breath and let out a whistle that hurt their ears.

Ronald turned in the road and stared at her with wide eyes. Not only was she the most beautiful girl in the world, but she was talented too. "I bet they could hear that in Chesterville." He continued to look at her in amazement. Maybe one day he would marry her. What kind of boy would not want to marry a girl that could whistle like that?

Randy and Jake continued to wave their flags, and all eyes focused in the direction of the blacksmith shop; nothing but silence.

"Do it again!" Elizabeth commanded. Laura took a deeper breath and blew a second time. They waited again. Nothing!

"Try once more," Elizabeth said, raising a fist in the air. "I better not have to go down there, or they will be sorry."

"They heard you, Laura," Caroline shouted and laughed excitedly, pointing to the white flags waving in the air.

"They see us! They see us!" Jake yelled, waving back at them.

Clapping and cheering stopped and everyone got quiet as they looked back and forth from the hill to town. Old Ben should be ringing the bell any minute.

"I don't think I've ever been so excited," Noelle told Louise. "We will be the first ones to see it. Well, besides the boys at the top of the hill."

It seemed like an eternity as they waited. The bell was not ringing and the hill obscured any sight of the circus train.

Mary stood in the drive alone, looking up. She was anxious to hear the old bell ring. She remembered her grandmother saying many times, "Take heed. When the bell in the square rings, somethin' bad just happened or is goin' to." She often told stories of tornadoes that ripped across the valley, fires that burned barns and homes to the ground, and the year of the earthquake when it rang for help to those trapped and injured. Her most profound memory, she always said, was when the bell signaled the end of World War I. Grandma couldn't keep from crying every time she got to the war. "So many loved ones marched off and never came home."

A year ago World War II had ended, and more young men and women lost their lives. Oak Grove's new fire whistle signaled the end of that Great War. *Now,* she thought, *now Old Ben is goin' to ring out a happy occasion*, and she stood and waited.

Then, in the quiet moment of that summer afternoon, the old bell rang out loud and clear that which everyone was waiting to hear. The American Circus Company was on its way to Oak Grove!

Chapter 5

Old Ben, still holding the rope in his hand, looked toward the east. *One or two more rings should be enough*, he thought. He could not see the circus train but knew it was over the ridge and would soon be in sight. He was half pulled and half pushed to the tower in what he figured was record time. Scratching his white head, he chuckled as he thought about all that transpired in the last ten minutes.

Josiah burst through the door with eyes as round as saucers. "It's coming, Ben! It's finally coming!" he shouted, jumping up and down. Donnie flew in right behind him, crashed into his backside, and bumped into the barrel that held the checkerboard. Checkers flew all over the floor, and Phillip jumped back out of the way, knocking his chair over.

"Come on, Ben, the bell, the bell! You have to ring it!" Josiah attempted to pull Old Ben out of his rocker and fell backward in the floor.

Jack, Willy's black and white border collie, chased Mike into the Blacksmith Shop barking and running in circles. Thinking it to be a game, he ran around the stove and jumped for the tea towel Mike still carried in his hand. Swinging the flag out of Jack's reach, he lost his grip and sent it flying across the shop where it landed smack across James' face.

"I believe it is getting rather dangerous in here," James said in a muffled voice as he peeled the towel from his face and held up the stick that landed in his lap.

Thinking to be in a safe place and out of the way, Louis moved back against the wall that held several old harnesses. Taking a drink of his root beer, he watched Phillip's foiled attempt at gathering the checkers when Jack ran between his legs, knocking him off balance. Louis burst into laughter and put his hand against the wall, entangling it in one of the harnesses. In an attempt to free himself, he pulled it down over his head and managed to spill root beer all down the front of his shirt and trousers.

The boys pulled Ben out of his chair, pushed him out the door, and propelled him across the street, encouraging him to hurry. Jack, confused by the commotion, continued his barking and jumping as he ran in circles around all of them.

Zachary, Jimmy, and Jordan stood at the bell tower transfixed at the sight coming toward them. The boys, jumping and yelling, pulled Old Ben along. James, his red hair sticking in all directions, carried a tea towel in one hand and a stick in the other. Phillip was rubbing his backside and Louis, wearing what looked to be leather straps on his shoulders, was pulling his wet shirt away from his body as he hurried along behind the rest.

The girls at the bandstand instantly knew the time had come. Abigail jumped from the rail and headed to the bell tower, losing her cap halfway across the square. Maggie, Carrie, Charlotte, and Shari jumped up, squealing with excitement, and ran down the steps toward the bell tower.

Shari's heart pounded in her chest with anticipation as she glanced up to the top then back at Old Ben. "Be careful," she called. Maggie gripped her arm and they watched him take the first step. "Gosh, I hope he doesn't fall," Maggie murmured.

What began as a quiet afternoon quickly changed. Ben now stood in the top of the tower, watching the scene unfold below him. Milly and Molly were in front of The Sweet Shoppe in their red and white aprons talking excitedly. Elijah Seabaugh and Hank stepped out of the hardware store, and Samuel and Hannah Cranston came out of the hotel and were standing on the lawn. Lottie appeared on the porch with a feather duster in her hand, and Paul came from the back of the hotel carrying his pruning shears. William Madison looked out the post office window with a grin on his face, and Barbara White stood in front of the bakery wiping her hands on her apron, talking to Margaret Miller. Several from the drugstore and café emptied out onto the sidewalk, laughing and chatting as they looked up at him.

Ben watched Willy walk from the garage, wiping his hands on a rag he pulled from his back pocket. He greeted Jack with a pat on the head, looked up, waved at Ben, and then turned his attention to the other side of the square. Old Ben's eyes followed Willy's gaze where it rested on Melba, standing in front of her beauty shop. Ben grinned and his brown eyes twinkled. Could there be somethin' going on here? Why not? They were both single.

Ben guessed Melba to be in her late twenties. She had green eyes, hair like copper, and a bright friendly smile that would stop a young man like Willy dead in his tracks. As far as Ben knew, she had no family in or around Oak Grove.

Talking to Ned, standing in the door of the barbershop, she laughed as Nelson White pushed Ned aside and stepped out on the sidewalk wearing a barber cape and his face still lathered up. Melba shielded her eyes from the sun then looked up at Ben with a bright smile and waved.

Glancing back at Willy, Ben noticed he had walked closer, and although he was talking to Samuel Cranston, his eyes were still fixed on Melba. *Willy needs someone besides Jack,* Ben mused to himself. *Melba probably has no idea he finds her attractive. By golly, I'll have to do somethin' about that."*

The commotion on the square reached Alan, and he motioned to Lynn, and Ellen. "I believe it's time," he announced, opening the door of The Chronicle. The flag, as though to herald the occasion, waved in the breeze atop the flagpole, and they watched Old Ben reach for the rope.

Ben felt a lump in his throat as his hand closed around the rope. The remembrance of days long past flew fleetingly through his mind, and he pulled. The bell rang out crystal-clear, and he grinned as he spoke to himself, "This old bell still sounds mighty good. Granddaddy would be proud."

Dr. Miller stepped out of his office and looked around the square at the folks gathered and shook his head as he gazed up at the top of the bell tower. He was amazed at the agility the old gentleman still possessed.

"Hey, Doc," John Walker called, emerging from the Sheriff's office with Anne and Garrett.

"Daddy, are the ephelants coming?" Garrett asked as John sat him in the front seat. Anne laughed and hugged him. "Yes, Garrett, the ephelants are on their way." Removing the small comb from the side of her brown curls, she glanced in the mirror, smoothed the side of her hair, and slid the comb back in place, aware that she was almost as excited as Garrett.

"Well, I guess the children are finally getting what they've been waiting for," Dr. Miller commented as John idled his '40 Packard in front of his office. "Afternoon, Anne." Dr. Miller smiled at Garrett, produced a cherry sucker from his shirt pocket and handed it to him.

"Thank you," Garrett answered as he grabbed the sucker in his chubby little hand and handed it to Anne to unwrap.

"Good afternoon, Dr. Miller. Thank you," Anne replied, removing the wrapper from the sucker.

"I guess I better try a little crowd control out at the Fairground." John laughed and put the car in gear. "Talk to you later, Doc."

Alan watched the Sheriff drive down Oak Street and thought about the gang of children that was probably already gathering in the middle of the road. "Why don't you two get in the car," he told Lynn and Ellen. "I'll get the kids and we'll ride out to the Fairground." Crossing to the square, he called to Abigail and Maggie.

"Daddy, the circus is on its way!" Abigail shouted, running toward him. Her sailor cap flew off of her head, and Maggie, right on her heels, swept the cap up and shoved it on her head, almost covering her eyes.

"Can we go to the Fairground?" Maggie asked, looking up at him with eyes as blue as the sky.

"Yes, we'll do that now. Go get in the car while I get Zachary." He looked around for his nephew and spied him climbing the steps of the tower. He was on the fourth step by the time Alan reached him. "Hey, buddy, want to ride out to the Fairground and watch the circus train?"

"Nope. I'm going to ring the bell." He looked at Alan with a determined look on his face and took another step up.

Ben looked down at them and commented, "Zachary, you won't be able to see the tigers up here. You better go with your uncle." He knew that would do the trick. The boys talked of nothing else all morning.

Zachary turned and looked at Alan. "Is Dad going too?" he asked, resting one foot on the next step.

"I sure am, and we better hurry," Michael said, walking up behind Alan. "Are you going to drive out?"

"Yes. Ellen's already in the car. Come on and ride out with us," he offered as Zachary jumped from the second step and ran across the square.

Alan and Michael waved up at Old Ben. "I'd say he's ready for the circus, wouldn't you?"

Through the trees, Ben could see the first truck slowly rolling down the hill. He looked down on the square and noted Sheriff Walker standing with his car door open, trying to get one of his son's attention.

Turning at the sound of his name, Josiah saw him motioning to him. He grabbed Jordan by the sleeve and excitedly pointed at him. Realizing Dad was on the way to the Fairground, they made a beeline to the car.

Phillip, James, and Louis were laughing and talking to Pastor Mike and Leah, relating the chaos in the blacksmith shop, and the folks who stepped out of the café and drugstore headed back inside.

Ben rubbed his fingers across the old bell and smiled wistfully for a moment before he turned to make his way down the steps. "Guess I better go clean the shop."

"Are you making it down okay?" Pastor Mike called as he watched Ben slowly descend the steps.

"I'm all right," Ben replied, reaching the last step. "She sure sounded good, didn't she?" he asked, grinning proudly as he smoothed his mustache.

"You sure are right about that, Ben. That old bell rang out loud and clear." Mike observed the pride in the old man's eyes. "Thank you, Ben."

"Glad to do it, Preacher." Ben looked around, noting several folks headed in his direction, amazed that something so simple could give pleasure to so many people.

"I guess I better take Leah to watch the circus train," Mike commented. "She said she wanted to check on the kids, but I think she might just want to see it herself. Thanks again, Ben." He walked toward his wife who was standing in front of the Dime Store talking to Margaret Miller.

By the time Sheriff Walker reached the Fairground, children were scattered all over the road laughing and talking excitedly as they anxiously waited for a glimpse of the circus train. Jim pulled onto the grass of the parking area right behind him and got out. "Hey, brother, do you need some help?"

The Fairground, enclosed within a white fence, had two large gates, affording access to the front entrance as well as the back. Huge oaks had been cut to clear the area several years ago when Miss Mattie donated the ground to the city. Located just west of the Driscol home, it was used mainly for the annual Easter egg hunt and The Founder's Day celebration.

"Let's get them out of the road," John told him. "Those trucks are going to need all the room they can get. I'll open the gates." He walked to the entrance and raised the wooden bar that held them closed. Swinging the gates wide, he secured them against the sides of the fence and glanced at the empty fairground that would soon be filled with colorful trucks and tents.

Jim walked out into the middle of the crowd. "Okay, everyone, let's move over behind the fence. Come on; clear this road," he called as he took note of several cars arriving from town and circus trucks coming from the opposite direction.

Quickly clearing the road, a pile of bicycles accumulated beneath the oak tree as the kids headed hurriedly for the fence. Music floated gaily from over the hill, gaining everyone's attention, and they strained curiously to see from where it was coming.

Jennifer perched on the hood of their car and motioned Anne to join her. "Come and sit with me," she said. "This is a pretty good seat." She wore a red and white checked dress with a square neck, and her thick, blonde hair was pulled away from her face and held in place with a red ribbon.

She is so pretty, Anne thought as she opened the car door and watched Garrett climb up on the hood of the car. "Oh, this is a good place to sit and watch," Anne replied as she joined her.

"The ephelants are coming, Aunt Jennifer." Garrett looked at her with wide brown eyes and offered her a lick of his sucker. Sitting next to her, his attention was immediately drawn to the first truck entering the gate.

Carrie and Louise gripped the fence as they watched it slowly turn into the Fairground. "American Circus Company." Louise read the big blue letters on the side of the truck while she jumped up and down excitedly.

Carrie's brown eyes were wide with wonder. "The man with the tall black hat and whistle is called the Ringmaster," she stated proudly, pointing to the picture painted on the side of the truck.

How do you know that?" Louise asked, climbing the fence and settling herself on the top rail. "You've never been to a circus before."

A loud horn blasted forth, and both girls giggled as the driver waved. He wore a large black hat with a yellow flower on the front and a red ball stuck on the end of his nose.

Carrie pushed up the red armband she had worn all day and climbed the fence next to Louise. "Because when Papa and I stopped for gas at Willy's the other day he told us that he had seen a circus once, and the ringmaster is the one who stands in the middle of the tent and tells everyone what to do and when to do it."

The lively music floating across the field grew louder as a brightly colored, red wagon drew closer. Several large copper pipes running up the side of the wagon produced the happy melody, and the driver appeared to be thoroughly enjoying himself.

"A calliope!" Anne exclaimed. She watched in amusement as Garrett waved his arms in time with the music.

Another truck pulled into the fairgrounds followed by another and then another. They all bore American Circus Company on the side. Pictures of animals and beautiful girls were colorfully painted on both sides of the trucks.

"Can we stand by the fence?" Maggie asked, jumping from the car. Abigail and Zachary tumbled out behind her, excitement on their faces as they strained to see where the music was coming from. They watched with wide eyes as the colorful trucks slowly made their way through the gate. "Me too, Mom," Zachary yelled, jumping up and down.

"Just stay on this side of the fence," Lynn instructed and watched as they raced off to join the rest.

"Oh, my gosh!" Josiah exclaimed. "Will you look at that?" Four enormous elephants lumbered through the gate, their heavy weight shaking the ground. A girl in a green costume rode atop the lead elephant, waving both arms as she smiled at the crowd gathered. The huge animal raised its trunk in the air and sent forth a loud call that completely cleared the whole top rail of the fence.

"Man, they are huge," Mike said, looking through the rails. "How would you like to ride one of those?"

"Not me" Josiah exclaimed. "I'll stick to Miss Mattie's horses. And you wouldn't ride one either, Mike."

"If a girl can ride an elephant, I can. I'm not scared!" he boasted, and then backed up as another of the huge animals stepped a little too close to the fence.

"Horses. Oh, look at the white horse," Maggie exclaimed, staring in awe. "They are beautiful." Her eyes roamed down the lane to the rest of the trucks and she wondered which truck the princess was in.

Zachary stood with his mouth dropped open. A large, brightly painted red wagon contained three lions prowling behind heavy bars. "I didn't think they were that big." He gulped and thought of what his dad told him about a man who actually stuck his head in a lion's mouth. "The man is crazy," he mumbled as he stared at the cage.

"What man?" Abigail asked, looking around for a crazy man in one of the wagons. She glanced back at Zachary and wondered what he was talking about.

"The man who stuck his head in the lion's mouth," Zachary answered as he watched the lion cage pass.

"I didn't see any man in that wagon with the lions." Abigail looked over the fence at the next truck. Her sailor cap had slipped sideways and a streak of dirt was smudged across her right cheek.

A picture of colorful clowns with red noses was painted on the side of the next wagon. The driver waved and Shari giggled, "Look, Carrie, he is wearing a red ball on his nose like the picture on the truck." The clown stuck a large blue horn out the window, honked at the children, then smiled when they scrambled for the candy he tossed toward the fence.

Jordan poked Jimmy on the arm as he plopped a piece of Dubble Bubble in his mouth and threw the wrapper on the ground. "Monkeys, Jimmy, look."

"Look at all of them!" Jimmy replied, watching them swing from one bar to the next. Unwrapping a sucker, he tried to count them but found it impossible the way they were swinging and jumping around "Gosh, how many are there?" The chimps chattered noisily and stared at the crowd gathered along the fence.

"Boy howdy! Here they come!" Zachary yelled as another wagon entered the gate bearing four striped tigers. One prowled around inside the cage and produced a loud roar just as the wagon passed in front of them, causing everyone to back away from the fence.

Several more trucks entered the gate and resembled houses on wheels "The circus people must live in those," Donnie said, looking at Josiah. "I thought they lived in tents."

"I bet just the important ones stay in the trucks, the others probably sleep in tents," he answered. "We ought to join a circus. Wouldn't that be fun?"

"Mom probably wouldn't let me," Josiah answered, "but it would be fun."

The last two trucks entered the gate. They were larger than the others were, and Jordan wondered what was in them. He watched his dad and Uncle Jim close the gates as he climbed to the top of the fence and then gazed around in amazement at all of the trucks and wagons parked everywhere.

Applause filled the air as the lookout squads rode their bicycles into the parking lot. The boys, wearing big grins, acknowledged the cheering and immediately headed to the fence. "We followed the circus all the way in," Brenton said. "I couldn't believe it when we finally saw it coming over the hill."

Preston, Simon, and Larry joined them at the fence. "I kept waiting to hear you blow that whistle," Simon said to Johnny. "Then when you did, I could hardly believe it."

"I am glad we had these flags. They worked really well." Preston lifted the one he still held and started waving it. "I thought my arm was going to break from waving it so much." He laughed and looked at Larry, "I'm glad the circus train got here before dark. We didn't want the ghost from the Old Mill to get us."

"I'm not afraid of any ghost," Larry said, glaring at him. "I'm not afraid of anything."

Randy, Jake, and Ronald walked over. "Randy fell backwards off the fence when you started blowing your whistle," Jake told Johnny and laughed as he looked at Randy. "We could hear you loud and clear."

The boys perched on the top rail of the fence and watched the activity in the Fairground while they laughed and relived the moment they had first seen the circus train.

"That bell is something, isn't it?" Truman exclaimed. "We could hear it all the way out on top of the hill. Old Ben didn't have any trouble getting to the bell tower did he?"

"No, not at all," Donnie answered and glanced at Mike. "Everything went as smooth as clock work." He straightened his ball cap and thought about the chaos that erupted in the blacksmith shop. He supposed that they should help Old Ben clean the place up.

For the next several minutes they watched in wonder as the trucks parked in certain areas and workers began unloading trucks.

Johnny sat on the top rail of the fence, completely absorbed with all of the activity, when he felt a touch his arm. He looked around to see his dad, standing eye level behind him.

"Isn't this something, Dad?" Johnny exclaimed. His brown eyes, so full of life, were just like Leah's.

Mike smiled at the resemblance and answered, "It sure is, Son. You boys pulled it off. You did a good job letting the town know it was coming." He smiled at several who had turned at the sound of his voice. "Thank you; all of you."

"You're welcome, Pastor Mike." Brenton answered from his perch next to Johnny. Mike was well liked by all the boys. None of them ever found him too busy that he couldn't talk to them, and he occasionally fished with them out at Old Mill Creek.

"John, do you have your watch on?" he asked, knowing they would not want to go home yet.

"Sure, why?" Johnny asked as he held his wrist up. "I have three forty-five."

"Good. Round up Shari and Jimmy at four-thirty and head for home." Pastor Mike put his arm on Leah's shoulder. "Your mother has dinner in the oven, and by the time we eat and clean up it will be time for church."

Leah looked at her oldest son, sitting on the fence looking down at her. *How did he grow up so fast?* she asked herself and had an impulse to hug him. Using better judgment, she thought it best to wait until later and only remarked, "We are going to pick up Laura from the Driscol's. Now don't forget, four thirty."

"Okay. We'll be there, Mom." He grinned and turned back to watch the activity in the Fairground.

Mike noted the look on Leah's face as she watched their oldest son and knew what she was thinking. He experienced somewhat the same thing this afternoon with Laura. "Come on, hon. let's go get the girls." He squeezed her hand and steered her toward the car.

The back porch of the Driscol home was once again full of chattering, laughing girls as they talked about the circus train and enjoyed another piece of cake. Mrs. Driscol, flustered with all the excitement, took a seat in one of the wicker chairs and was fanning her flushed face with her handkerchief.

"Oh dear, I didn't realize those wild beasts would come so close to my home. Did you see them, Mary?" She wiped the perspiration from her forehead. "What if one should escape? We live right here not far from the Fairground. Now Henry is gone into town to talk to the owner, and we are here alone. Oh, dear. We could be eaten alive. I don't like this situation; not at all. It frightens me. It truly does."

"I'll go get Uncle Henry's shotgun and drop a couple of shells in it, Aunt Trudy. Then we'll be ready," Elizabeth stated with a determined look on her face. Putting the last bite of cake in her mouth, she rose from her chair and started across the porch.

"Lord, have mercy!" Mary cried, jumping from her chair and hurrying to the back door. She firmly planted herself in front of the door with her hands on hips and stared at Elizabeth. "You just listen to me, young lady No one is goin' after a shotgun. So you just sit yourself back down right now!"

Looking across the porch at Trudy, she shook her finger "And Trudy, I don't want to hear another word about wild animals escapin,'" she exclaimed, thoroughly exasperated, as she looked from Elizabeth to Trudy. "Didn't you see those heavy cages they were in? Land sakes, what do you think they are for, decoration?"

Laura and Noelle looked at each other in total disbelief. The idea of Elizabeth with a shotgun put more fear into them than if all of the lions ran across the back porch this very minute.

"Good afternoon, ladies," Pastor Mike spoke from the bottom step. "What is this about a shotgun?" He looked with amusement at the porch full of girls and wondered whose idea that had been. He glanced at Elizabeth's frowning face and knew without asking.

"Come on up and have a piece of cake, Pastor Mike." Mary shook her head and sighed. "No one is gettin' a shotgun as long as I'm around. There was a little discussion about animals escapin' from their cages. Someone had a fool notion to load the shotgun to protect us all." She gave Elizabeth another look of total disbelief and shook her head again.

Mike chuckled at the expression on her face. "No, thank you, Mary. Leah has supper ready." He looked at Trudy sitting in a wicker chair, fanning herself with her handkerchief. She was staring at Elizabeth with something akin to a look of shock on her face.

Trying his hardest not to laugh, Mike cleared his throat, scratched his chin, and stared at the pond. He turned back and looked fondly at the plump little lady who was so flustered. "You have nothing to worry about, Trudy. The bars on those cages are strong. The animals cannot get out. I saw them up close myself."

"Oh, I'm so glad to hear that, Pastor." She put her hand over her heart, looked at him with a timid smile and then sighed as she glanced back at Elizabeth, wondering what in heaven's name they were going to do with her.

"Are you sure?" She wiped her forehead with the hankie and looked at him questioningly. "They are so big and wild. Elephants walked right down the road in front of my house. Who would have ever thought . . . ?"

Taking a drink of her lemonade, she looked out at the pond. "I will never get that sight out of my mind." Setting the glass on the table she looked at him again. "Henry left in a terrible rush to make sure the circus owner, Mr. Whatever his name is, would get settled in the hotel. The girls were all excited, and. . . . oh, Mary, I do believe all the ice cream has melted," she commented, staring down into the ice cream freezer next to her chair.

Mike resisted the urge to run around the corner of the house and laugh. Instead, he walked up on the porch and placed his hand gently on her shoulder. "I am positive you have nothing to worry about, Trudy." Leaning down, he whispered in her ear, "I understand the lions and tigers look wild, but they are really as tame as kittens."

"You don't say. Well, I declare." She looked up at him with such relief in her eyes that Mike felt sorry for her. She smiled and sat up straighter in her chair. "Well then,

Mary, you needn't worry so. You just relax and don't fret about it anymore." Turning, she looked at Mike and shook her head with an expression of "I tried to tell her."

Mary looked with astonishment at her and then glanced at Pastor Mike. She raised her eyes heavenward and retorted, "Well, I never. . . ." Bending down, she grabbed the ice cream freezer from the floor, marched across the porch, jerked the screen open, and let it slam behind her.

Mike put his hand to his mouth, concealing a grin, as Trudy stared at the back door. "Well, now what do you suppose has gotten into Mary? Are you sure you wouldn't care for a piece of cake, Pastor?"

"No, really. Thank you. We always eat a little early on Wednesday nights. I've just come for the girls." He glanced at Laura and noted the amusement in her eyes. He quickly looked away and turned his attention to the rest of the girls. "Do any of you need a ride? I would be happy to take you home."

"I am spending the night so I will not be going home," Terry answered. "But thank you for bringing me."

Laura rose from her seat and set her plate on the table. "Happy birthday, Caroline. Thank you for inviting me." She turned to Mrs. Driscol. "Thank you, Mrs. Driscol, for the bracelet. It is very pretty, and I really enjoyed the party."

Noelle followed close behind Laura. "Yes, thank you very much, Mrs. Driscol."

"Oh, my dear girls, you are so welcome. Thank you for coming." She smiled sweetly at both girls then wiggled her fingers. "I do believe my hand is going to be sore from cranking that ice cream freezer. I wonder where Mary put the liniment. Mary?"

"Thank you for the birthday presents," Caroline said genuinely as she walked to the edge of the porch with them.

"Happy Birthday, Caroline." Mike looked at her and waved to the other girls as he followed Laura and Noelle down the steps and around the side of the house to the car.

"How was the party?" Leah asked the girls as they got in the back seat.

Laura grabbed the rope along the back of the front seat and pulled herself up so she could see her mother. "Oh, Mom, we had so much fun. We ate and laughed. Mr. and Mrs. Driscol are really very funny people. And we were the first to see the circus train." Laura held her arm out. "And look at the gift Mrs. Driscol gave us."

"Well, wasn't that nice? That is very pretty." Leah looked at both girls' happy faces as they sat back in the seat.

"Yes, and there was a table full of pigs." Noelle giggled as she looked at Laura who finally confided to her what had been so funny.

"And Elizabeth and Mary got into it over a shotgun." Laura looked at the astonishment on her mother's face and started laughing.

"They got into it over what?" Leah asked, wondering what kind of party she had allowed her daughter to attend. "Pigs and shot guns!" She turned all the way around in the front seat and looked at Laura and Noelle.

Mike started laughing. "I don't know anything about the pigs, but as far as the shotgun goes, it was nothing." He shook his head as he backed out of the driveway. His blue eyes were full of laughter as he looked at the confused look on his wife's face. "I've got a feeling this summer is going to be one that we won't soon forget."

Chapter 6

Mike parked his car in front of Old Ben's house. Opening the door, he stepped out and glanced at the front porch. A welcoming sight, snowball bushes laden down with large white blossoms grew at each end of the porch, and wisteria vines climbed the front pillars on each side of the steps. A porch swing swayed slightly on the west end of the porch while three old rockers sat facing the lawn on the east end. From the street, the house looked like a normal two-story residence, and unless one went around to the back of the home at 624 Oak Street you would never know it was part of the blacksmith shop.

He glanced at his watch, seven thirty. Ben and Willy would be in the kitchen enjoying their coffee. As he walked toward the house, a squirrel ran up the oak tree, stopped, and peered at him from the back side of the tree. Quickly turning, he disappeared then reappeared a little farther up the tree as he scampered out on a limb. Mike stood on the sidewalk for a moment watching the squirrel stare curiously at him and breathed in the morning air, mingled with the smell of freshly brewed coffee. Birds sang cheerily, and he waved at Melvin passing by in his milk truck. Other than Sunday, Thursday was Mike's favorite day of the week, and he set it aside to visit his congregation at leisure, starting the day early at Old Ben's.

Willy had come over one morning about a year ago at Ben's insistence when he saw him sitting across the street on his front step alone. At first he had been very quiet, almost withdrawn, but with each passing Thursday he slowly came out of his shell and now sat with ease while the three enjoyed coffee together.

"Good morning, Pastor Mike," Mercy said cheerfully as she came out the front door with Jack at her heels. He immediately bounded from the porch and ran barking around the tree, anxious to get at the squirrel sitting at its lofty height.

"Good morning, Mercy." He smiled as he glanced at the tea towel she held in her hand and wondered what surprise she had brought over this week.

"Cinnamon rolls," she said, reading his thoughts. "I suggest you yell for one or Uncle Ben and Willy will have them gone before you get in there." She laughed and folded the towel, tucking one end in her apron.

"I would hate to start the morning off with a fight, but I would for one of your cinnamon rolls," Mike commented, smiling at the sweet young woman. "You do work magic in the kitchen, Mercy. How are you? I missed you Sunday."

"I sure missed being there too, Pastor Mike. Grandma Hope is down in her back again, and I was looking after her. You know how she is. She insists on doing everything herself, even when she shouldn't." Mercy shook her head with a sigh and ran her finger across one of the yellow flowers on her white apron.

"I hate to hear that. Leah and I will drop by and check on her later today," Mike assured her. "We'll see if we can't get some of the ladies to corral her until she feels better."

"Thank you. Grandpa is no help. She won't listen to him." Mercy laughed and shook her head again. "She insisted that they sit out on the porch swing to hear the bell ring yesterday, as though she wouldn't hear it from inside. Somehow, between the two of them, they made it from the bedroom to the front porch. She is a handful. Well, I must go. I need to get down to the café," Mercy said, making her way down the front steps.

"Take care, Mercy. Thank you for the cinnamon rolls." Mike watched her fondly as she walked down the sidewalk humming to herself.

Mercy was Old Ben's great-niece and lived just across the street. Her grandparents lived only three houses away, and with her brother Ben's home right next door, it was convenient for her to check in on all of them daily. Ben didn't take much looking after and was the one who usually checked on her.

As children, she and Ben had grown up on the Seabaugh Farm where their folks still lived today, but on graduating from high school, they both moved to town. Ben, four years older than Mercy, went to work at the Oak Grove Timber Company. Saving his money, he purchased two small homes close to the Blacksmith Shop; living in one and renting the other to Mercy. Everyone in the family worried about her, wanting her to marry and have a family of her own. But Mercy was content with her work at the Cranston Café, taking care of her small home, and looking after her family. "The Lord will provide a husband and children all in His good time," she always replied, believing it with all her heart.

"There better be one left for me, or you two have had it!" Mike called as the delicious aroma of cinnamon rolls greeted him at the front door.

"Don't worry. There is plenty," Old Ben called from the kitchen. Mike hung his hat on the hall tree behind the door. The familiar ticking of the old clock on the mantel reached his ears, and he suddenly realized that sound would always remind him of Ben. A staircase directly across from the front door led to the second floor. Passing through the dining room on the right, he entered the kitchen to find Willy sitting at the table enjoying one of the cinnamon rolls. Old Ben, with percolator in hand, turned from the stove and poured a steaming cup of the rich flavored brew. "Mornin,' Preacher. Sit down and drink your coffee." He refilled his cup and sat the percolator back on the stove.

"Umm, they do smell good," Mike said as he pulled one of the oak chairs back and sat across from Willy.

"They are good. Mercy, I am afraid, is beginning to spoil us," Willy commented, taking another big bite. He pushed the plate closer to Mike. "But I don't mind in the least."

Mike helped himself to one of the rich, warm, glaze covered rolls. He bit into it, finding it filled with raisins and nuts. "Oh, this is good," he said, closing his eyes as though he had seen a vision of heaven. He suddenly looked at Ben and asked, "When is Mercy's birthday?"

Old Ben stared at the sugar bowl and thought a moment. "It is in August, but I will have to check my Bible for the exact date. Why?"

"I thought the three of us ought to get her a gift. She bakes us something every week." Mike took a drink of his coffee and looked from Willy to Ben.

"She sure is thoughtful," Willy said. "That's a good idea. It will be a lucky man that gets her for a wife." He wondered why she had never married and guessed her to be about twenty-four. She was just as nice and thoughtful as anyone could be.

"You are right there." Ben agreed with Willy. "I just hope she doesn't get the idea she has to spend the rest of her life lookin' after me and her folks. Everyone needs someone to share their life with." Old Ben glanced at Willy for some reaction of any kind.

"I am thankful the Lord brought me and Leah together. I don't know what I would do without her." Mike paused a moment and commented softly, "She is my other half and my best friend as well as my wife." He stared into his coffee, thinking of Leah and how she loved him unconditionally.

"Carrie and I had the same kind of marriage." Ben looked out the kitchen window at the bird feeder they had hung together in the tree so long ago. "She's been gone seven years now. I can't wait to see her again."

Willy took another sip of coffee and squirmed in his chair, not knowing what to say. "Well, I guess you just have to wait until the right person comes along," he commented without much conviction. He rose from his chair and limped to the stove to refill his cup.

Mike watched Willy thoughtfully. He was close to six feet tall, and his hair was dark and had a bit of curl to it. His muscles were well toned, and except for his limp he appeared to be in excellent physical condition. His eyes, a dark blue, too often reflected pain and anger, causing Mike a great deal of concern. Willy never opened up to anyone, and much of his life was a mystery to the folks who knew him.

He appeared in Oak Grove at the age of fourteen, a rebellious teenager that his frail mother could no longer handle. His Uncle William wrote his sister, telling her to send Willy to them for the summer. Immediately taking an interest in the garage, he eagerly watched his uncle work on cars. Willy had not lived in Oak Grove more than a few weeks when news came that his mother passed away. Strangely, he did not show any emotion over her death and immersed himself in learning all he could about auto repair. He reluctantly finished high school at his uncle's insistence and filled with mistrust, did not seek out or gain many friends. The winter following his graduation brought the death of William's wife, which left the two of them alone to fend for themselves.

Willy, for the first time in his life, felt responsible for someone other than himself. His Uncle William, at a loss over his companion for so many years, didn't seem to know how to cope, and Willy took on the role of caretaker. Using what his uncle taught him about auto repair, he gradually took over more and more of the business, finding himself doing most of the work and Uncle William now the one watching. They puttered around in the yard and Willy even tried his hand at cooking, but that only resulted in the two eating most of their meals at the café. The bond between the two grew solid and each found solace in the other's company.

December 7, 1941 shocked the world. Japanese forces attacking Pearl Harbor had been more than Willy and the rest of the nation could take as they tried to comprehend what had happened. A sleeping giant awakened as thousands of young men and women rose with a fighting spirit and Oak Grove, as well as the rest of the country, proudly and tearfully watched as they marched away to answer the call to duty, leaving family and friends behind.

Willy left Oak Grove to enlist in the Marine Corps, leaving his Uncle William, as well as everyone else in the country, to live a day-to-day existence waiting for some word of their loved one. More than two years later, February 2, 1944, Willy was severely wounded fighting in the Marshall Islands and sent home to recuperate. The loss of his leg seemed most probable, but he refused to consider it and with a strong will and determination to keep his limb spent agonizing months in therapy and pain.

"I'm not doing this for myself. I'm doing it for all those guys that will never come home. Why me? Why did they die and I didn't?" he yelled in anger at Mike one day in the middle of his therapy session. He grimaced in pain and continued as perspiration poured from him. "I will not give up. I lived and they didn't. I will not sit back and give up," he stated angrily, stressing each word slowly and furiously, his blue eyes full of hatred and bitterness. Mike watched the anger boil in him as he ranted about the injustice of it all, and no matter what Mike said or how he tried to reach him, nothing worked. Willy retreated into himself even more than before. A year later the leg had miraculously healed, leaving him with nothing more than a slight limp. Shortly thereafter, his Uncle William passed away leaving Willy alone with the house, the garage, and Pastor Mike with a great burden on his heart for this young man he had come to love.

"Don't you?" Ben asked, jolting Mike out of his thoughts as he stared at him curiously.

"What? I am sorry. My mind just wandered off for a few minutes." He looked at Ben and wondered what his question had been.

"Melba. She seems like a nice girl. Don't you think so?" Ben asked. "She is a pretty little thing, and she's just as friendly as can be."

Mike glanced at Willy's red face and realized something was going on. "She sure is," Mike answered, noticing the twinkle in Ben's eyes as he continued to stare at him over the rim of his coffee cup. That he wanted him to continue talking was evident, and Mike fixed his attention on Old Ben as he continued the conversation, deliberately ignoring Willy. "She is a very thoughtful girl and has a great personality." Mike feigned innocence of what was going on and continued, "She is one of those rare young women that you can be comfortable with, and she has a beautiful singing voice." Mike glanced at Willy, soaking up every word, then stopped speaking and sat deep in thought for a minute.

Looking directly into Willy's eyes, he spoke quietly but firmly. "She's a girl of strong faith. There's no doubt in my mind she would make the right man very happy."

"Well, now, there you go, Willy. Why don't you call on her sometime?" Ben asked as though the thought just this minute popped into his head.

Willy shifted in his chair and sat his cup on the table. "Oh, I don't think so," he answered, staring at the Frigidaire as though it was fascinating and in need of admiration.

"Well, certain women appeal to some men and some don't," Mike replied, examining his fingernails. "If you don't find her attractive, then that's okay."

"I think she's beautiful!" The words tumbled out of Willy's mouth before he thought, and he looked with embarrassment at his two friends. Self-consciously, he picked up his coffee, took another drink, and stared out the window.

Old Ben and Mike smiled at one other. This was going to take some work. "Why don't you invite her to the circus tomorrow night?" Old Ben suggested, stretching his legs out in front of him as he hooked his thumb in his suspenders and looked at Willy.

Willy looked across the table at him like he was crazy. "She doesn't even know me. I can't just walk up and say, you might have seen me around; would you like to go to the circus? She would think I was an idiot."

Mike leaned back in his chair. "Of course she knows who you are. She sees you all of the time. This is what you need to do." He leaned toward Willy and unconsciously used his fingers as he made his point as though he was preaching a sermon. "Get to know her, you should frequent some of the places you know she'll be, show some interest in her, and for heaven sakes get out of the house a little more and quit being such a hermit."

He paused and looked at Willy, wanting to tell him that if he came to church he could see her every Sunday, but he would wait for the Lord's timing on that. They had gone over that subject several times already. From their conversations in the past, Mike knew Willy was going to take a lot of prayer and a lot of patience and was also beginning to wonder if perhaps the Lord might have to use an on the road to Damascus experience with him like He did with Saul.

"I don't know. She probably wouldn't be interested," Willy commented nervously, tapping his spoon on the table.

Ben sat forward in his chair. "Son, you don't know much about women. They like attention. The kind that lets them know you think they are special." Ben shook his head and smoothed his mustache. "I don't think she gets any of that sort of attention from all of us old fogeys she's always talkin' to. That can't be much of a thrill for a pretty young thing like Melba. You are a right handsome young man. She would enjoy your company."

Leaning closer, he looked Willy square in the eye. "Women want a man to take charge and be their protector. Just step up to the plate and get in the game." He sat back in his chair with a pleased look on his face and looked at Mike who was mulling over the idea of whether he had reached the age of being called an old fogey or not.

He caught Old Ben's eye and picked up on the conversation. "That's right." Mike chimed in. "Melba has a lot of friends, but as far as I know, not a male companion. Maybe that's all you two could be, companions!" He nodded at Ben. This was going pretty well.

"Why sure. That would be harmless enough," Ben commented, "and, by cracky, she's a whole lot prettier than Jack. Yesterday she came out on the square while I was ringin' the bell. That red hair of hers was shinin' as pretty as a red sunset."

The clock in the living room struck eight o'clock, and Willy gave a sigh of relief. "It is time for me to open the garage." He rose from the chair and took his cup to the sink. "The Cardinals are playing the Braves tonight," he commented rinsing the cup out, relieved to end the conversation about Melba.

"We'll see you at the circus tomorrow evenin' I guess?" Ben persisted. He knew Mercy would be going which meant Melba would probably be with her.

"Yes, I plan on going. Simon and the boys gave me the whole run down on the circus train when it came in yesterday." Willy turned and looked at the two men, knowing they both cared for him, and smiled. "I'll see you there." Opening the screen door that led into the blacksmith shop, he limped out the door with Jack following at his heels.

Old Ben and Mike looked at each other. "Well, what do you think?" Ben asked.

Mike looked at his old friend. "You are something. How do you know they would even be interested in each other?"

Mike took his cup to the sink and gazed through the window, thinking what a wonderful thing it would be if the two fell in love. Willy needed someone and so did Melba. He shook his head and sighed. Melba was a young woman of strong faith, and Willy had no interest in the things of God at all. That would pose a big problem or perhaps a blessing. Maybe she could reach Willy where he had failed.

Turning from the sink, he looked at the twinkle in Ben's eye and the grin on his face. Shaking his head, he smiled back at him. "I must get going, Ben." He wondered what his old friend was thinking or, worse yet, what he was planning.

Old Ben sat back in his chair with his legs stretched out in front of him, both thumbs hooked in his suspenders, and a sly smile on his face. "I observed a whole lot yesterday from the top of the bell tower. And I know Willy is definitely interested in Melba."

Mike stood next to his chair and laid his hand on Ben's shoulder. "That would be wonderful, but we might just want the Lord to work this out. Maybe we said too much. Willy's never come into the fold yet. That's my concern."

Ben looked up into his pastor's blue eyes "Sometimes God uses our help, Preacher."

Mike laughed and slapped Ben on the back. "You are right, Ben; that He does." Smiling at the old man with affection, he rested his hand on his shoulder for a moment. "I pray for Willy daily, and my heart aches for him. I know in my heart he will come.

It is just a matter of time." Mike sighed as he looked at his old friend. "I often times want to hurry the Lord along, I guess."

Old Ben looked at his young pastor with great love in his eyes. "We'll just keep plantin' and waterin' and let the Lord reap the harvest when He is ready. Let's just keep on trustin' in His grace."

"That's our peace, Ben. What would we do without our trust?" The mantel clock chimed the quarter hour, and Mike sighed, not wanting to end these moments of fellowship. "I must go. I need to get Leah. We are going to check on Miss Mattie and Grandma Hope." He walked back into the living room.

Ben followed Mike to the door wondering what ailed his sister-in-law. "What's the matter with Hope?"

"I understand she is down in her back again. Leah will organize the ladies to see about her; if she'll let them." He laughed as he thought of the feisty little lady. "We are also gong to run out to the Seabaugh's. They weren't at church Sunday either. I hope Elizabeth hasn't had a setback."

"Tell them hello for me. I'll drop by and check on Hope." Ben worried about his sister-in-law. She could be so stubborn sometimes. Watching Mike take his hat from the hall tree and place it on his head, he chuckled, "Today will seem rather dull in the shop compared to yesterday."

Mike opened the front door and looked at Old Ben. "Thank you Ben. Thank you for ringing the bell. It will be something the children will always remember."

"They need to remember special times. That keeps us goin' when the bridge washes out. If we keep the good times in our heart, we can take them out on a bad day and thank God for sendin' them our way."

Ben pulled his pipe out of the top pocket of his overalls and looked at it almost lovingly. "Carrie saved her money and bought this for my birthday one year. I don't ever use it much anymore, but I like to carry it with me. I think of that day every time I take it out of my pocket."

Mike smiled at his friend. "Memories," he commented as he listened again to the ticking of the clock. "We are making memories every day for someone aren't we, Ben? Most of the time we don't even know it."

"We sure are." Ben studied his pastor's face and placed his hand on his shoulder. "Sure am glad you came to Oak Grove."

"I am too, Ben. I am too" He paused a moment then reached up and patted the hand that still rested on his shoulder. "Have a good day, Ben." Pastor Mike smiled at the old man and then turned and walked down the sidewalk to his car.

"You may not go out to the fairground until all of your chores are done," Anne stated firmly, looking at her five sons seated at the breakfast table "Your father left extra early to check things out. He said he would call later and let us know what is going on out there." She knew she sounded overly firm, but she also knew from past experience that if she didn't get the upper hand first, the boys could manage to talk her into almost anything.

"But, Mom, maybe they need some help or directions," Brenton commented.

Preston rolled his eyes and gave him a look of total disbelief that he would even make such a ridiculous comment.

Anne turned around, a pan of biscuits in her hand, and raised an eyebrow. "Do you really think the circus needs your help?"

Brenton propped his chin in his hands. "I guess not," he answered. "Today is Thursday, isn't it?" he asked in exasperation, looking at Preston. That meant they had to mow the lawn. Well, at least they had two push mowers. He always mowed the backyard and one side of the house, and Preston mowed the front and other side. He actually didn't mind mowing the grass and discovered that if he mowed different designs, it seemed to go faster. Brenton actually prided himself on how quickly he could get the job done. For some reason that he couldn't explain, he liked the feel of the wooden handle, worn smooth from use, and the clicking sound of the mower blades.

Preston, on the other hand, thought he was crazy and approached the whole chore of mowing grass as something that had to be done. He stopped frequently, found more interest in a scurrying lizard, an overly large ant hill, and paused to talk to any and all passing by on the sidewalk.

Anne sat down, extended both hands to her sides and waited while the boys joined hands. Bowing her head, she prayed, "Thank you, Lord, for the night's rest, for this morning's beauty, and bless this food for the nourishment of our bodies."

Preston, also realizing this was mowing, day silently gave thanks that Dad recently had Old Ben sharpen the mower blades.

"I am sure there will be plenty to see all day," Anne commented as she passed the biscuits and buttered one for Garrett. "Just get everything done, and when your father calls, you will be ready." She knew they were excited and supposed the other mothers in Oak Grove were dealing with the same thing.

"I can't wait," Josiah spoke up. "Did you see how huge those elephants were? Mike Olson said they pick people up with their trunks. Do you think they do?"

"The ephelants." Garrett's eyes widened as he looked at her. "I want to ride one of them. Can I, Mom?" he asked with a hopeful expression and ran his finger through the jelly on his biscuit.

"Oh, I don't think they allow that," Anne answered, watching the look of disappointment cross his face.

"No. They aren't going to let anyone ride the elephants." Josiah looked at his little brother and then back to his mother. "But then again, maybe they will."

"They are not going to let anyone climb on an *ephelant* and ride." Preston said stressing the word. "This is a circus. We go there to watch someone else do that. Besides you would be too scared."

"I would not," Garrett replied. He sat his glass of milk on the table and stared at Preston. "I would not be at all scared to ride an *ephelant,*" he answered, also stressing the word.

Jordan looked around the table. "What about the big horses? Do you think we can ride them?"

"They will not allow anyone to ride anything," Anne remarked, exasperated. "Just think of all the amazing things we are going to see. What kind of tricks and acts do you think we will see?" She threw out the question hoping to redirect their train of thought. The idea of her sons on the back of an elephant somehow didn't seem too far-fetched. She would have to keep a close eye on them.

"Why do I need a haircut today?" Jimmy asked as he watched Leah rummage through her handbag.

"Because you hair is about to grow over your ears, and you are beginning to look like, well, I don't know what you are beginning to look like, but it is time for a haircut." Leah looked at her youngest son and smoothed his hair down with her hand. "Johnny will be taking you to Ned's after lunch, and then you may ride out to the Fairground and check on things out there."

Laura, still in her pajamas, walked into the living room and sat on the sofa. "You need a haircut," she said, watching her mother's attempt to smooth Jimmy's dark hair down. "Is it okay to ride out to the Fairground after lunch, Mom?"

Unconsciously, Jimmy touched the back of his hair and gave his sister a dirty look. Why did girls have to notice stuff like that? He sure didn't. Besides, who wanted to sit in Ned's today with a circus in town?

Leah smiled at her and glanced out the window at the sound of Mike pulling into the drive. She turned back to Laura and answered, "Yes. The list of chores is on the refrigerator, there is a casserole that just needs to be heated for lunch, and the boys need to get their haircuts. I have already talked to Johnny and Shari, so they have their instructions."

Mike walked through the front door, hugged his wife, and planted a kiss on her lips. "Good morning, wife," he said, grinning down at her.

Leah looked up at her husband, wondering what he was about. Enjoying his attention, she linked her arm through his and returned his smile. She always looked forward to Thursdays and the opportunity to accompany him on his visits. They often shared times of relaxation, checked on those needing special attention, looked in on the sick, and usually enjoyed lunch with Miss Mattie.

Shari walked down the stairs and into the living room with Midnight in her arms. "Johnny said we couldn't leave for the Fairground until he did," she said with a frown on her face. She sat cross-legged on the sofa next to Laura and stroked Midnight's back. "They have to get haircuts. I don't want to sit in Ned's with all the old men."

Leah smiled at her. "While the boys get their haircuts, you and Laura can do the dishes and fold the towels on the line. You won't even have to go to Ned's, and it's not very nice the way you called them *old men*," Leah commented, looking at her. "You must be a little more respectful, I think."

Shari looked at her with a confused look and leaned her head back against the couch. "But they are all men, they are all old, and they talk about old stuff."

Mike, knowing this could turn into a long explanation, spoke up, "If you all continue sitting here talking about haircuts, you are going to miss the elephants raising the tents." He looked at the three and grinned. "I guess you probably ought to ride out as soon as you can and finish your chores and get haircuts later. Don't you think, Mom?"

Shari jumped, spilling Midnight on the floor, and followed Laura and Jimmy as they raced for the stairs.

"Johnny! " Jimmy yelled, "Dad said we are supposed to go out to the Fairground now. The elephants are working!"

Leah looked at Mike with her mouth dropped open and tried to ignore the amusement in his blue eyes. "I just finished this minute giving instructions for the day, and you walk in and throw everything to the wind," she scolded in a firm voice. Hiding the smile that crossed her face, she turned away and picked up her handbag from the coffee table.

Mike's voice sounded close to her ear, "It's not everyday a circus comes to Oak Grove." Realizing he had followed her across the room, she turned and found herself in a big hug. "Next time you try to hide a smile, don't stand in front of the mirror," he laughed.

Leah glanced at the mirror in the hall and smiled. He laughed again and kissed her on the forehead "The chores will be here when they get back."

"I can just imagine what this place would look like if I left you in charge around here all day," Leah remarked as she stepped away and walked out the door, the sound of his laughter ringing in her ears.

Mike walked to the bottom of the stairs and called, "Laura, Johnny! We are going to Grandma Smith's, out to the Seabaugh farm, and then to Miss Mattie's for lunch. If you need us for anything, have Hazel ring us at one of those places."

"Okay, Dad," Johnny's muffled voice answered as he came to the top of the stairs. Slipping a shirt over his head, he smiled down at him. "Thanks."

"Oh, a little bit of advice. I expect you should be home around two o'clock." Mike went through the time element in his head and continued, "We should be back about three o'clock. It would probably be a good idea if you were all here and had your chores done."

"Yeah, okay Dad," Johnny answered as he plopped his baseball cap on his head. "Cardinals are playing the braves tonight Do you want to . . . ?" His train of thought immediately gone, he tore down the steps in front of Laura and raced through the living room into the hall. "I need to call Noelle first. It won't take long," Laura pleaded, "please?"

Mike listened to the scuffling and giggling in the hall and shook his head. "Sure, let's pop some corn and listen to the ball game," he commented to the empty living room. Glancing through the window, he saw Leah sitting in the car talking to Ron, the mailman and figured they may as well be on their way.

"You all have fun and be careful," he called to everyone and no one in particular.

A strange sound from the staircase reached his ears, and he watched with a perplexed look on his face as a Slinky came into view sliding end over end down the steps, finally coming to a stop at the bottom. Midnight, sitting next to his feet, stared at it for a minute then looked up at him. "We'll be back around three o'clock," Mike told the cat, and with a shake of his head, opened the door and walked down the steps.

"I just need a little bit of a trim, Melba," Sally Wilson said as she sat down in the chair. Sally was Oak Grove's third grade teacher, and her husband, Hank, owned the hardware store. "My hair was fine yesterday and this morning I feel like it has grown an inch over night."

Melba laughed, her green eyes shining, as she twirled the chair around and ran her fingers through Sally's hair. "It does that sometime doesn't it? How much do you want me to take off?"

"Actually, if you could just shape it up like, well, you know." Sally looked in the mirror at Melba with a questioning look in her eye.

Melba stared at her for a moment, wondering what she was getting at. Sally had worn her hair the same way for years, much to her dismay. "No, I do not know. You will have to tell me" She looked at her curiously and asked, "Do you want me to cut it short?"

"Oh, heaven's no. Hank would drop dead on the spot," she exclaimed, her eyes traveling to a magazine lying on the chair she had occupied.

Melba walked over and picked it up, looking at the picture of Bette Davis on the cover. Glancing at Sally she asked, "Would you like it trimmed like this and parted on the side?"

Sally's cheek's turned pink. "You don't think I am too old? I wouldn't want people laughing at me or anything."

Melba shook her head. "Sally, no. You are not too old. In fact, this style would suit the shape of your face nicely, and no one is going to laugh at you in Oak Grove, and you know it." She lowered the back of the seat, tested the temperature of the water with her fingers, and laid Sally's head back in the bowl.

The shop door flew open with a bang, and Trudy Driscol blew in like a gust of wind. "I just never thought I would live to see this day," she cried, wringing her hands. "It is awful, just awful. What kind of impression is this going to leave on the young people of our town? Oh, dear! I am just beside myself; just beside myself." Flopping down in one of the chairs, she fanned herself with her handkerchief. Grabbing the huge green straw hat with its orange flower attached to the front, she threw it on in the floor. "The world is just going to the devil. I can feel it. I just don't believe it, and here I am trying to raise Caroline and Elizabeth to be proper young ladies. The devil has a hand in this as sure as anything."

Melba and Sally both stared at her like she had taken leave of her senses. "What in the world is wrong, Trudy?" Melba asked as she dried her hands and sat in the chair next to her. "What is the matter?"

Sally returned from the back of the shop with a glass of water and handed it to her "Tell us what has happened?" she asked in alarm and sat in the chair on the other side of Trudy.

"It is that, that circus!" she blurted out. "Have you been out to the Fairground? They are naked! All of them naked, I tell you. What in heaven's name are we going to do?" Her face was as red as a beet. Sitting up straight in the chair, she slapped her hand on her leg. "Well, I know what I am going to do. I am headed straight for Pastor Mike and Reverend Clark. They have to do something about this!" she remarked furiously, pointing her finger at Melba. She sat back in a huff and glared at her reflection in the mirror. With a sigh, she touched the back of her hair and looked at Melba "If you would hurry and get my hair shampooed and set first, I would be much obliged. It really is a mess after Caroline's party; what with the circus train, the melted ice cream, and Elizabeth's idea of using a shotgun."

Melba and Sally looked at one another wondering what in the world had gone on yesterday. Trying not to laugh, Melba looked at her. "Now, Trudy, I can't believe the people in the circus were stark naked without a stitch of clothing on. Now, were they?" she asked as she leaned over and looked at her, raising one of her brows.

"Well, they might as well be. Their arms and legs are bare," she retorted angrily, looking at Sally. "And the front of their costumes reveal much too much of their bosom. It is just unseemly," she exclaimed, crossing her legs and folding her arms across her chest.

"Trudy, I am sure they do not dress like that all of the time. They were wearing their costumes," Melba said, glancing at Sally for support. "That is part of the circus atmosphere. They were probably practicing, weren't they?"

"Well, I for one do not think we should even have a circus in Oak Grove," she stubbornly insisted and continued with her tirade. "It is worse than that musical Henry and I saw last summer in Chesterville."

Sally raised her eyes and looked at her. "I remember you saying how much you enjoyed that movie, Trudy. Let's see, *The Dolly Sisters,* wasn't it, with Betty Grable?" Sally continued, although Trudy refused to look at her. "In fact, you said we should all go see it if we had the opportunity. You made that remark right here in Melba's salon."

"Well, that was different," Trudy snapped. "Those people were not really there. It was a just movie."

Realizing how upset she was, Melba tried to reason with her. "Trudy, why don't you think of the circus as the same thing? You went to the theater and saw a film with actors playing parts." She spoke slowly and softly to gain her attention. "Now, if you went to New York, you could see the same show but on stage. They would have the same costumes as those in the movie, but it would be a live show and they would be dancing right there in front of you."

Melba glanced at Sally who nodded for her to continue. "If we took a movie camera to the circus and filmed it, we could go home and watch it on the wall. It would be the same thing. Don't you see?"

Trudy sat back in the chair and looked at her two friends. Plucking her hat angrily from her head had left her hair standing on end, and she fanned her flushed face with her hankie again and stared at the ceiling for a moment. Glancing at Melba, she plucked a piece of lint from her dress and spoke in a somewhat more subdued tone, "Well, I guess that does make some sort of sense. But, it just shocked me to ride by and see those women running around our Fairground like they owned the place. You know, I have heard of young girls running away and joining the circus."

Sally looked at her in astonishment. "Now, Trudy, you and Henry have done an excellent job raising those two girls, and I know for a fact that neither one would run off and join a circus." She shook her head and scolded her. "How could you think such a thing?"

Sally returned to the shampoo bowl, sat down, and laid her head back. "You really ought to be ashamed, Trudy."

"I have to agree with Sally," Melba commented as she turned the water back on and proceeded to shampoo Sally's hair. "You have done too good of a job with the girls to worry about something like that.

"I certainly hope so," Trudy said with a guilty look on her face. She sighed and retrieved her hat from the floor. Straightening, the orange flower, she asked, "Are you two going to the circus tomorrow evening?"

Melba glanced over her shoulder. "Trudy, I wouldn't miss it for the world. It is going to be so exciting. If I didn't own this shop, I would consider joining the circus myself." She looked at Trudy's surprised face, flipped water at her, and grinned.

"Oh, Melba, you wouldn't dare," she laughed. Laying the hat on the chair, she gave both a timid smile. "Thank you, both of you, for calming me down. It was just a shock to my delicate nature when Henry and I drove by this morning and saw them dressed that way. I guess they probably were practicing. Why, Henry noticed before I did, and he even slowed the car to get a better look." Her voice trailed off and a look of surprise crossed her face. "Well!" She furrowed her brows and stared at the floor for a minute. "Just wait until I get home," she muttered to herself and glanced out the window. Her attention was immediately drawn to Margaret Miller, crossing the square, with an Edna's Dress Shop bag in her hand. "I wonder what she bought."

Sally coughed and began to laugh silently. Melba glared at her, grabbed a small towel from the shelf, and clamped it over her mouth.

Mike parked his car in front of Solomon Smith's house. "No. Other than that, Mercy said she is okay." Mike was telling Leah about Grandma Hope on the drive over. "She said the biggest problem was keeping her in bed. Every time she throws her back out she gets more stubborn, and Solomon can't do a thing with her."

Leah laughed, "I guess we better call in some of the ladies to entertain her then."

She thought of the feisty little lady inside and smiled as they walked up on the porch. Grandma Hope was probably one of the most stubborn people Leah had ever met, but her sweetness mingled with her feisty, stubborn personality made you love her.

"Mornin, Pastor, Miss Leah." Solomon grinned at both of them and held the screen door wide. "Saw you drive up. I sure am glad you dropped by." He stepped back as they came in the door with a look of relief on his face. "I don't know what I'm goin to do with her She won't listen to me at all."

A familiar voice called from down the hall, "Solomon? Do we have company?"

Leah watched the thin black man shuffle slowly to the hall. "I better go help her out here before she tries it herself."

"Oh, no. Don't you dare. We will go back and visit with her in her room." Leah made a beeline down the hall. "Miss Hope, are you decent that I may come in?" she called from just outside the door.

"Yes, dear, come right in and sit down." The little lady removed her spectacles and smiled brightly as Leah walked through the door. Grandma Hope was propped up in a big four-poster bed with her Bible lying beside her. The shades were raised and sunlight streamed through the window.

"Have a seat right there, dear." She motioned to a small green and white flowered settee next to the window. A breeze rustled the sheers at the window and sent the fragrance of a fresh cut bouquet of flowers across the room.

"Aren't they pretty?" Grandma Hope asked, looking at the spray of flowers spilling out over the top of a green, cut glass vase "Solomon went out just this mornin' and picked them for me."

"Indeed, they are beautiful." Leah smiled at the frail little woman lying in the bed. Warm, merry, eyes set in a face full of wrinkles looked up at her and smiled. Her hair, white as snow, was worn in a bun, and she squeezed Leah's hand in hers.

"Now, tell me. How did you hurt your back this time?" Leah asked as she settled comfortably in the soft cushions.

"Solomon knocked over a whole glass of milk and tried to clean it up himself," she said, shaking her head. "You know what a man is like in the kitchen. That's why the Lord made us the cooks." She chuckled and rubbed her fingers across the quilt. Well," she sighed, "I tried to move the kitchen table so I could mop up the mess."

"Miss Hope, you shouldn't try to move a table." Leah looked at her in dismay. She couldn't believe she had attempted to move the heavy oak table.

"I told her to wait until I got back from Reese's Market," Solomon commented. He and Mike stood in the doorway watching her. "Do you think she would listen? She never pays any attention to a word I say. She never has." He shook his gray head in exasperation then smiled at her. "I think she does it on purpose so I will spoil her."

Leah was aware of the affection beneath the bantering. Their love and devotion to one another was clearly evident when they looked at each other.

"Come in, Pastor. Sit here on the side of the bed," she said, patting a spot next to her. Mike crossed the room and sat down. Taking her hand in both of his, he patted it and smiled.

"Grandma, what are we going to do with you?" He studied her with a concerned look on his face. "I miss you when I look out from the pulpit and don't see you." Mike spoke gently as the thought occurred to him that the day would come when she would not be there anymore.

Her remarks on his sermons bothered him at first, but he soon realized that her wisdom and knowledge of scripture was a valuable tool. She generally always had something good to say, but on occasion would make a remark that set him to thinking. Through the years, he had come to realize she was an accurate gauge to measure his preaching. "Your commentary on my sermons is very helpful to me."

"You are going to take it easy for the next few days," Leah commented firmly as she leaned toward her. "Now, you are dealing with me, not Solomon." She held her hands up in protest as Grandma Hope opened her mouth to object. "You are not to worry about a thing. This is what our ladies group lives for. Our whole purpose is to help each other." Leah looked at her pleasantly and asked, "Would you not come to help me if I was sick or threw my back out of place?" The question was asked so sweetly that Mike was impressed.

It was in moments like these that he wondered just how often Leah maneuvered him around that he was not even aware of. He watched her completely take control of the situation and work out all of the necessary details. In a matter of minutes she had mealtime planned, laundry and cleaning accounted for, and assigned Grandma Hope the task of crocheting doilies to sell at the Founder's Day Celebration. She then sat back comfortably and graciously accepted a glass of iced tea from Solomon who was looking at her with an obvious look of gratitude.

Now that Hope would have something to keep her busy while confined to bed, Solomon felt like half the battle was over. With everything settled, the conversation turned to the events of yesterday.

"I tell you, dear, when I heard Old Ben ring that bell yesterday it brought a tear to my eye," Hope said, looking at Solomon. "We've heard it durin' some bad times, haven't we?"

"Yes, Hope, we sure have. That old bell has hung up there in the square for a lot of years warnin' us of one sort of disaster or another." Solomon rubbed his chin and looked at Mike "I remember it ringin' when the school house caught fire and almost burnt to the ground, and if my mind serves me right, back in '83 when a tornado hit and trapped the Stanton's in the rubble of their home." He shook his gray head and smiled. "I declare, it sure was good to hear it ring for a happy occasion. Yes, sir, it surely was." He smiled at Leah. "I guess a lot of you folks have never heard it ring."

"You are right about that, Solomon," Mike answered. "We've been here ten years, and yesterday was the first time we heard it ring." Mike laughed aloud. "It stirred up quite an excitement in town and almost made a shambles out of the Blacksmith Shop. But I'll let Old Ben tell you about that. He said he was going to walk over after while."

Grandma Hope laid her head back against the pillow and commented quietly, "I hope he brings his accordion with him." She yawned and closed her eyes. "I would enjoy a couple of hymns."

Solomon smoothed her hair away from her forehead tenderly as he spoke softly, "I gave her some pain medicine right before you got here. Doc Miller said it would probably make her sleepy."

Mike nodded at Leah. "Let's allow her to get some rest then," he said and held Grandma Hope's small hand in his, praying for God's healing hand to touch her back.

"Hey, Willy! Have you seen the circus yet?" Simon yelled as he and Preston ran into the garage. "It is really something!"

Willy was whistling along with a lady singing something about Buttermilk Sky, and to Preston's way of thinking the radio was much too loud.

Willy looked at the excitement on the two boys' faces and smiled. "Not yet, but I will tomorrow night." He continued whistling as he bent back over the engine of the car.

"How can you wait that long? You should see how big the elephants are." Preston glanced over Willy's shoulder. "What are you doing?"

"I think Mr. White probably needs some new points and plugs," he answered absentmindedly as he continued to look around under the hood.

"Can we get a root beer?" Simon asked, already heading for the soda cooler. Stepping on his shoestring, he made a quick hop and caught his balance. Jack, ever curious as to what was going on, got up from his resting place by the door, walked over to Simon, laid down next to him, and began nipping at the shoestring.

"Grab me one too," Simon called to Preston who was already at the cooler. "Jack, quit," he laughed and pushed him away. The border collie wagged his tail and nipped at the string again.

Willy rose from the hood of the car and looked at both boys. Preston was opening a bottle of pop on the side of the cooler, and Simon was fighting with Jack over his shoestring. "Don't forget where the broom is," he reminded them. Pulling an old rag from the back pocket of his overalls, he wiped his hands and grinned as Jack continued to nip and play with Simon's shoestring.

Willy had grown accustomed to the boys hanging around the garage. They asked a million questions on a myriad of topics to which he usually didn't have the answers. Their curiosity ranged from why cars couldn't run on coffee instead of gasoline to why it wasn't possible to lay on a cloud without falling to the earth. They wondered where bugs went at night and where fireflies went during the day, why oil didn't mix with water, and how Hazel could plug a wire into a hole and talk to anyone in Oak Grove. Baseball was popular, girls were not, and they had spent one whole afternoon trying to figure how the idea came about to bake a cookie. They finally decided someone either left something out of the cake they were baking, or it had dropped on the floor and smashed. That conversation, somehow, led to who first thought to wring a chicken's neck, pluck its feathers, and fry it up for supper. Willy refused to choose a side when they argued over whose opinion was right and found their wild guesses amusing. More often then not, they seemed content to just sit around and watch him work on cars. Willy suspected he was an easy take for a soda pop. Nevertheless, he soon realized that he enjoyed their company, and he missed the endless chattering when September rolled around and they went back to school.

The chore of sweeping the floor and emptying trash developed one day at the beginning of summer when Jim Walker and Simon pulled in for gas. Simon helped himself to a Coca- Cola, and Jim made him pay for it. Although Willy said he didn't mind, Jim was firm about it. The next day they struck a bargain which amounted to the boys sweeping the floor and emptying trash in exchange for a soda pop.

Willy especially enjoyed listening to the baseball game and soon realized that he looked forward to their visits. Before Uncle William passed away, they had always listened to the games together and it felt good to have someone around again.

Simon looked under the hood and watched Willy. "You know everything there is to know about cars, don't you?" he asked in awe.

"Here." Preston handed him his root beer. "I'll sweep. You empty trash."

Simon pulled an empty soda case across the floor and stood on it. "Do you think I will ever be able to learn all of this stuff?" he asked, standing on the soda case. He watched Willy disconnect a wire and asked, "How did you learn all of this stuff?"

Willy was silent for a moment and then answered abruptly, "My uncle." He made no further comment and continued what he was doing with a frown on his face. Simon straightened and looked at him. What had he done to make Willy mad? He sounded crabby all of a sudden.

"Say, are you mad at me, Willy?" he asked.

Willy paused and stared at the engine for a moment. He sighed and looked at the confused expression on Simon's face.

"No, of course not, Simon. You are one of my best buddies. I would never get mad at you." Willy straightened up and patted him on the shoulder. Realizing he had been a little sharp with his answer, he felt bad and absentmindedly stared out the window, unaware of the sad expression on his face.

Uncle William had taught him everything he knew about auto repair, and Willy still missed him a great deal. He and Aunt Lydia took him in when no one else wanted him, and Uncle William had been the only person in his whole life who ever truly loved him.

He insisted on Willy finishing high school, used a firm hand when it came to his behavior, took time to talk with him, and tried to teach him the important things in life. Love was hard for Willy to accept, but Uncle William persisted; telling him how much he loved him and how much God loved him. Willy could not grasp the idea of God loving him and occasionally wondered on it but found it easier to dismiss the idea than to worry about such a matter.

It had been over a year since Uncle William died, and Willy found that he was okay with his life and figured it was about as good as it would ever be. Loneliness plagued him, but he figured that was better than letting himself get hurt again. He grew up knowing he could not depend on anyone, and with Uncle William's death, that idea reinforced itself in his mind.

"I swept the floor, Willy." Preston said, jolting him out of his thoughts. He stood the broom in the corner and spied Mr. White coming towards the open garage door. "Here comes Mr. White," he announced. "Hi, what is Randy doing?"

"He rode out to the fairground to watch the circus setting up. I thought you boys would be out there," he said, bending down to scratch Jack's ears.

Nelson White was a short man with a bit of a paunch due, no doubt, from the pastries his wife prepared at the bakery. The combination of his rosy cheeks, a round, chubby face, merry brown eyes, and curly, brown hair gave him an almost boyish look. He was a pleasant man who was never known to get in a rush about anything.

He continued scratching Jack's ears and glanced up at the boys. "Oh, I just left Hank's. He said they are using the elephants to raise the tents." He walked to the soda cooler and helped himself to a Coca-Cola. Dropping a nickel into a mason jar that Willy placed on top of the cooler, he walked over and asked, "Did you find out what the problem is?"

"Come on, Simon, empty the trash," Preston said as he grabbed the soda case and placed it back by the cooler. "Let's go watch."

Simon grabbed the trashcan. "Put my bottle away while I do this, will you?" He carried the can outside to a bigger barrel, dumped the trash, and ran back into the garage. "Okay, let's go," he yelled, shoving the trash can back into the corner.

"Bye, Willy. See you later." Simon waved and picked up his bicycle. Preston was already pedaling around the side of the garage.

Leah stood arm in arm with Liza Smith beneath an oak tree by the car. "Now don't you worry about your mother at all. I'll have someone there tomorrow morning." Leah squeezed her arm reassuringly.

"Mercy did not say a word about Mama being down in her back. I just talked to her yesterday mornin,' and she didn't even mention it." Liza sighed. "I guess she didn't want to worry me."

"No, I suppose not." Leah watched Mike and Mr. Seabaugh as they stood on the porch talking. "I think you would feel much better if you went to check on her yourself though. How about if I come out tomorrow and sit with Elizabeth while you run into town?"

"Oh, I wouldn't want to be a bother," Liza remarked with a worried frown on her face.

"You are most certainly not a bother. Besides, it will give me the chance to visit with Elizabeth that I missed today," Leah assured her as Mike and Elijah walked across the yard.

"I am sorry Mrs. Daniels," Elijah apologized as he removed his old, tattered cap. "Elizabeth was just so tired this morning. She is going to be sorry she missed your visit."

Leah smiled up at him. He was a tall, broad shouldered man with a face tanned and weathered from days spent in the fields. He was perhaps one of the gentlest men Leah had ever met.

"You just tell her that I will see her tomorrow. Liza needs to check on her mother so I'll have Mike drive me out here, and Liza can ride into town with him. We will both enjoy it."

"That should work out just fine." Elijah smiled at Liza. "Jacob and I have to go to the depot tomorrow to pick up a piece of equipment. You can ride back with us if that is agreeable."

Jacob and Liza had lived and worked on his farm for thirty years. Their house was right across the drive under a stand of oaks. Jacob helped in the fields, and Liza kept Elizabeth company and cared for her when she was sick.

Dear Elizabeth, Elijah thought, looking toward the house. She had been sickly most of their married life.

"Well then Eli, I guess we will see you tomorrow." Pastor Mike shook the firm hand of his friend.

Elijah Seabaugh's clear gray eyes looked directly into Mike's blue ones. "I love you, Preacher." He spoke the words with affection and stepped back. "Tell Old Ben he better quit running across the square like a young kid. I heard all about it. You can also tell him we heard the bell ringing all the way out here."

"I'll do that," Mike chuckled as he rested his hand on the man's shoulder. "I love you and Elizabeth too." He opened the door for Leah, walked around the car, and got in on the other side.

Elijah put the old hat back on his head and waved as they drove down the lane.

Leah admired the well-kept fences surrounding the fields and pastures. "Wouldn't it be nice to live on a farm?" she asked.

"Umm, I guess so," Mike murmured.

Leah, wondering at his unusual quietness, turned to look at him. He had a strong chin and gentle mouth that always wore a smile. His eyes, compelling when you looked into them, were blue and varied in color with his changing emotions. On the very rare occasions when he became angry, they turned a dark steely blue. Mike's eyes revealed more of his thoughts and feelings than his words, and he never considered that to be the source Leah used to so easily determine and understand his moods.

"Thank you, Leah," he commented and glanced at her, a look of tenderness in his eyes. "Thank you for being the wife God gave me." His voice was soft but strong. Taking her hand, he glanced at her again. "You help me more than you know. I love you."

Taken by surprise, Leah was overcome with a sudden shyness that reminded her of their early courtship days so long ago.

She had spent two weeks with her cousin, Carole, one summer and met Mike at an ice cream social at church. She thought him very handsome with his black curly hair and blue eyes. He was much taller than she was, and Leah found herself immediately drawn to him. He was the center of attention, full of life, and well liked by the guys as well as the girls; especially the girls.

Leah soon realized that when Mike set his mind on something there was no swaying him in another direction. Discovering herself to be the object of his attention, she was thrilled and a bit overwhelmed at his persistence. He was two years older than she, had dated several girls, and to her way of thinking, very self-assured.

Leah, on the other hand, had never had a real romance. Growing up with four brothers made her relationships with the boys she knew very relaxed and comfortable. Mike's attention was totally new and different from anything she had ever known.

Mike, likewise, was attracted to this petite, dark-eyed girl with the long black curls. He was captivated when she looked up at him and smiled. Dimples appeared in both cheeks and her dark eyes sparkled. Right then and there, he determined she was the cutest thing he had ever seen. Her sincerity, frankness, and confidence were like a breath of fresh air to him.

The girls he knew played games with their feelings, pretended one thing and then another, and left him in a quandary as to what was going on in their heads. He found Leah fascinating and readily took advantage of the relationship with his best friend, Gene, who was dating Carole at the time. The four were inseparable, and by the end of two weeks Mike was totally charmed and doing everything he could to win Leah's affection. Determined to stay in contact when she returned home, they corresponded back and forth the rest of the summer with Mike managing to see her every couple of weeks.

September found him heading to college and Leah entering her junior year of high school. Holidays and breaks became anticipated visits for both, and Mike was soon driving back and forth to Sheridan at every opportunity. Much to Leah's delight, he quickly gained her parent's approval and affection.

At the request of his pastor, Mike spent the following summer as a counselor at a youth camp and in the fall went back to college. Leah happily entered her senior year and was devastated when November rolled around, and she received her last letter from him. Much to her astonishment, he wrote that he was in love with her but had to "come to terms with many things and hoped she would understand."

Leah—confused, hurt, and angry—vowed to forget him, and with her new availability became the most sought after girl in the senior class. In spite of her popularity, she still held his last letter to her heart and prayed to understand what was happening to them.

At her graduation, much to her amazement, she walked across the stage to receive her diploma and saw him sitting with her parents. To this day, she still could not remember receiving her diploma or walking back to her seat. All she could remember was the pounding of her heart and how she was going to give him a piece of her mind.

He later explained that he stopped writing because he needed to take a long serious look at his life and some very needful soul searching. Aware of God's hand moving in his heart, he found himself compelled to study His word. His amazement of the transforming power within its pages consumed him with a desire to learn as much as he could. The strong calling he felt could not be denied, and he sought to know God's plan and what it meant for him, as well as for her, if she was to be a part of it.

"There is no doubt in my mind," he told her as he looked into her eyes that night as they sat on her parent's front porch swing. "God has called me to preach His word, and that is what I am going to do." He spoke with such confidence that Leah had no doubt in her mind as to his commitment. He looked into eyes for a long moment, and then spoke softly, "I love you, and I know He has chosen you to be my wife."

Leah stared at him in disbelief; not knowing whether to laugh or cry. She had prayed so hard and waited for what seemed like an eternity to know what was going on. Dumfounded, she did not know what to say. This was the moment she dreamed of, and now, she didn't know what to do. Leah stood up then sat back down on the swing and burst into tears.

Mike sat next to her, removed a handkerchief from his pocket, and handed it to her. "I don't think marriage to me will be all that bad," he commented and grinned as he lifted her chin to look in her eyes. "You might just as well say yes. I already asked your father and he agrees that it is a good idea." She had thrown her arms around his neck and burst into tears again. They were married one year later.

Leah's cheeks felt warm, and a deep love filled her heart. "I love you, Mike. I find great joy as your wife and in this ministry that God has called us." She touched his arm and scooted closer to him. "I am so thankful that God has given us this life together." Smiling at her, he turned up the lane to Miss Mattie's house.

"Right on time," Jeremiah called from the enormous front porch that extended around the right side of the house. A second-story balcony ran in the same manner as the porch, providing shade and comfort in the summer and protection from rain in the spring. The upstairs bedrooms each opened onto the balcony, providing cool breezes during hot summer evenings. Sturdy, solid oak railings offered protection on both levels. Every window bore black shutters and was adorned with lace curtains. Clematis vines climbed up the sides of the porch, and ferns were scattered about on the balcony. The huge porch with its white wicker furniture overlooked the valley and Oak Grove.

"Come in," Hannah called from the door. "Miss Mattie is out back pickin' fresh flowers for the table."

Leah walked up the steps and hugged her. "Hello Hannah." She glanced to the left over Hannah's shoulder. "Oh, the horses are in the near pasture," she exclaimed. "They are so beautiful."

Miss Mattie owned several thoroughbreds that were presently grazing in the pasture east of the house. Two brown mares hung their heads over the fence looking at them. "That's Ginger and Peaches," Hannah said, looking at them. "They are Miss Mattie's special pets."

"They are Miss Mattie's spoiled pets," Jeremiah corrected her. "They are waitin' for apples or sugar." He looked at Mike and shook his gray head. "She spoils them somethin' fierce."

Both mares continued to patiently watch the small group on the porch. "Go on," Jeremiah called to them. "You've already had your treat today."

Leah laughed as the two mares turned and appeared to reluctantly walk away. Jeremiah held the door and followed Hannah, Leah, and Pastor Mike into the house.

Miss Mattie called from somewhere in the house. The tapping of her cane and footsteps brought her into the large foyer. "There you two are," she said smiling graciously as she extended her hand to Leah who hugged her. "Pastor, you have a very lovely wife. Do you know that?" She stood back and looked at Leah, then turned and smiled at Mike, raising one of her brows as she waited his reply.

"Yes, indeed. I am well aware of that fact," Mike assured her and winked at Leah. She did look very pretty today. Her dark brown eyes and hair looked even darker with the pink dress she wore, and he watched in admiration as she turned and smiled at Miss Mattie, dimples appearing in each cheek. Mike loved Leah's smile. She had totally captured his attention that first time she turned and smiled at him, and he thought pleasantly of the effect her smile still had on him. Glancing down, her head just reaching his shoulder, he caught a slight scent of the familiar, sweet fragrance of her hair and wondered what he would ever do without her.

"And you, my dear, are well aware that you have a very handsome husband?" Miss Mattie asked, looking back at Leah with a broad smile on her face.

"He is the most handsome man in the world," Leah replied, smiling up at him, aware of the tender look in his eye. She turned back to Miss Mattie, laughed, and linked her arm through hers. "Miss Mattie, what are you up to?" she asked as they followed Hannah down the hall toward the back of the house.

"I am not up to anything, dear ones. I always say we should remember to thank God for the wonderful way He blesses us." She stopped and turned back to Pastor Mike. "But bless my soul, I can see you two do not need reminding. It is evident in your faces." She grinned and sighed, "How refreshing. Well, enough of an old lady's ramblings. Hannah has prepared an excellent lunch and we need to be enjoying it."

"Brenton!" Josiah yelled as he burst through the back door and slammed the screen up against the house. Jumping from the back porch, he ran through the yard and grabbed him by the shirt. "Brenton!"

Brenton stopped mowing and looked at the excitement on his brother's face. "What?" he asked and watched Jordan leap from the porch and head in their direction.

"Dad just called. He'll be here in fifteen minutes," he shouted, jumping up and down. "We can go to the Fairground. You better hurry with the grass."

Jordan made a quick turn and called over his shoulder, "I'll go tell Preston."

Brenton looked at the back yard. He didn't have that much left to mow. Determined to get the job done before Dad got home, he pushed the mower rapidly through the yard wondering if Preston was about finished. He also needed to call Truman and let him know he was ready to go to the Fairground.

Anne and Garrett came from the basement carrying a basket of bed sheets. Sitting the clothesbasket on the ground, she waved to Teresa Charles who was checking her tomato vines. Taking the clothes pins Garrett handed her, she hung one of the sheets and realized it was about to drag on the ground.

"Garrett, can you help me raise this clothes line?" she asked and watched while he grabbed one of the clothes line poles. Determined, it took three attempts, but he finally caught the line in the notch, pushed the pole up, and grinned proudly at her. Grabbing a handful of clothespins out of the bag, he stood patiently waiting.

Anne noted Brenton furiously mowing grass back by the fence and smiled. *Jo must have told him John called,* she thought to herself. She hurriedly hung the other sheets and glanced at her watch. "Come along, Garrett. Daddy will be here soon to take us out to the Fairground."

"Will we see the ephelant?" Garrett asked. The excitement on his face and the shine of his brown eyes tugged at her heart, but before she could hug him, he was headed across the yard as fast as his chubby little legs could carry him.

Truman sat at the soda fountain wondering where Brenton was. They left the Fairground around lunch, and he had not seen him since.

Mr. Williams appeared from the back of the store carrying a box of napkins. "Hello, Truman. What can I get you today?" he asked, placing the box on the counter. "Have you been out to the Fairground?"

"I was out there earlier today. You should see the elephants work They can move anything," Truman replied. The bell over the door jingled and he turned, but it was only Hank from the hardware store. "Hi, Mr. Wilson," Truman said as Hank sat down at the counter.

"Hi, young man," Hank answered with a nod of his head. "How about a cherry coke, Gerald?" he asked, sliding a nickel across the counter. "Give Truman one too." He placed another nickel on the counter and looked at him. "Say, did I hear you talking about the elephants?"

"Boy howdy, you should have seen them. I didn't know elephants could work like they do. They move all kinds of equipment and poles around." Truman grabbed a handful of napkins from the box and filled one side of a black napkin holder, flipped it over, and stuffed the other side full.

Gerald placed cherry cokes in front of Hank and Truman and then gathered the rest of the napkin holders. "I would have liked to have seen it myself," Gerald replied, filling one of the napkin holders.

The bell jingled again and Ron walked through the door. "Afternoon, fellas," he commented, wiping his forehead with his handkerchief. "It sure is warm out there.

That looks good. I believe I'll have a cherry coke too," he said, dropping his brown, leather, mail pouch on the floor.

"Thanks for delivering the paper for us yesterday," Truman told him as he filled another napkin holder.

"It was no problem. I was glad to do it." He slid the mail across the counter. "Here you go, Gerald."

The screen door opened, and Melba entered with a bright smile on her face. "Hi, guys," she said cheerily and slid onto the stool next to Truman. "What's everyone up to today; besides checking out the circus?"

All three men smiled at her. "Not much," Hank commented.

"The usual mail delivery," Ron said, taking a drink of his cherry coke.

Melba looked at Truman, glanced at his Cardinal cap, and put her arm across his shoulder. "Are you going to listen to the game tonight?" She tilted her head sideways and leaned toward him with a friendly smile.

Truman sat stock-still and stared at her red lips. The smile moved up into her sparkling green eyes, and he decided, in that instant, that she had the prettiest eyes he had ever seen. They were the same color as one of the cat's eye marbles he had in his coffee can at home.

Melba arched an eyebrow and waited for a reply, his loss for words surprising her. He and the rest of the boys at church were always friendly and gabbing about something.

Her eyelashes are really long, Truman thought to himself. A sudden hard pounding in his chest made it difficult to breathe and his face felt flushed.

"Another root beer float?" Gerald asked her.

With a toss of her head, she turned to answer, and Truman stared with fascination at the way her red hair curled on the ends. "Of course. I believe I am addicted to them, and I am going to get fat if I don't stop these afternoon breaks," she said laughingly and reached in her pocket. "I will grow out of my clothes and have to buy new ones."

Her voice was soft, and her laugh pleasant. Truman thought of all the times he listened to her sing in church. "Her voice is as clear as a bell." Who said that? He remembered someone making that remark after she sang a solo one Sunday.

"I need to take it with me though. Mrs. Cranston is due any minute and I have to get back." Turning back to Truman, she asked, "Well, are you?"

"Huh?" Truman looked at a couple of freckles on her nose and was aware of a jittery feeling in his stomach. He wiped the palms of his hands on his jeans and suddenly felt sick. He sure hoped he was not coming down with something.

"The ball game; the Cards are playing the Braves. Are you going to listen to it?" Melba asked, wondering what in the world was the matter with him. Noticing his red face, the realization struck her that she was the cause of his nervousness. Patting his hand reassuringly, she scooted back on her stool and smiled at the thought of how precious he looked.

"Oh, yeah. I'm going to listen to it. Are you?" Truman answered, wondering if his ears were as red as they felt. Why in the world did his ears feel warm?

"Here you go, Melba" Gerald sat the float on the counter. He had been watching Truman's reaction to her friendly, casual manner and was amused at the way she unconsciously charmed him. Gerald turned away to hide his knowing smile and glanced through the mirror at him again. Too many years spent behind this counter had taught him to recognize that look on many a young boy's face. The first awareness of a pretty girl and her charm had a way of sneaking up and slamming a young man right off his feet. He grinned and glanced at Truman's red face.

"Thank you, Gerald. I'll see you, Ron." Melba slid off the stool and leaned toward Truman. "Say, I bet we beat them by six runs." She waved at Gerald and Ron and headed for the door.

Truman sat in a daze listening to the jingle of the bell, aware of a soft fragrance of something nice lingering in the air. Glancing in the mirror, he looked at his image, sat up a little straighter, and wondered how old Melba was.

Brenton hurried through the door and took the stool Melba just vacated. "Sorry I am late, but I had to go home and finish mowing the lawn." He looked at Truman. "What is the matter with you? Your face is all red."

"Is it? I don't know," Truman answered in a confused tone. He looked in the mirror at his red face, and for a reason he didn't understand, was embarrassed. Truman felt like something private just happened, or he had a secret that he didn't want to share and was totally puzzled about the whole matter.

Ron pushed his empty soda glass back, stood up, and slung the mailbag over his shoulder "Have you been out to the Fairground?"

"Yes, you should see all of the tents they raised. I don't know what they are all for, but I can't wait to find out." Brenton watched as he adjusted the mailbag and put his cap on. "Thanks for taking care of the newspapers for us, Ron."

"Sure, no problem. I'll see you tomorrow, Gerald," he said, readjusting his mailbag. He glanced at Truman, looked at Gerald with a knowing grin, and headed for the door.

"Your face sure is red. You better stay out of the sun." Brenton stared at Truman and then looked at himself in the mirror. He was okay. Looking at Truman's arms, he commented, "Only your face got any sun, and it's as red as a beet."

"Don't worry about my face," Truman retorted. He was irritated and wished Brenton would mind his own business. He suddenly felt all out of sorts and glanced at the clock. "I'm going to *The Chronicle*. It's three-twenty." He spun around on the stool and slid off. "See you, Mr. Williams."

"Well, what's eating his craw?" Brenton commented, staring after Truman. He slid off the stool and looked at Mr. Williams curiously. With a shrug of his shoulders, he rolled his eyes, and followed him out the door.

"I'll see you fellows," Gerald called, waving them off with a handful of napkins. He shook his head and chuckled to himself. "Well, there's another one down for the count."

Chapter 7

Zachary stood at the front door watching and waiting for his Dad to get home. He wore a pair of navy blue shorts, a blue and white checked shirt and his newest pair of Keds. His hair was combed and parted on the side, and he was ready to go.

"When is Dad going to be here?" He took another look out the door then walked over to the sofa where Ellen was sewing a button on his shirt.

"He said he would be here at four o'clock, so I would think any minute." She glanced at the clock on the table and bit the thread. "All he has to do is change his shirt. Are you getting hungry?" She put the thread and needle back in the small, wooden sewing basket and stood up, closing the lid.

Zachary nodded, watching her fold the shirt and lay it across the sofa. "Can I have a cookie?"

"May I have a cookie; and yes, you may. It is probably going to be a while before we eat." Ellen walked to the hall closet and placed the sewing basket on the top shelf next to a record album containing several new 78's.

She and Michael had purchased a new record player for their anniversary last year with the idea of spending nice quiet evenings together. How long had it been? Pondering on it for a moment, she realized it had been more than a month ago that they bought *Surrender* by Perry Como. They had not even listened to it yet, and Ellen decided right then and there that one night next week they would do that very thing.

Following Zachary into the kitchen, she took a bottle of milk from the refrigerator and removed the small round cap. She was going to have to tell Melvin to leave two quarts of milk tomorrow. *Michael is working entirely too much*, she thought. Pouring a tall glass, she placed it on the table for Zachary, and replaced the milk in the refrigerator. She sat down, and glanced at the grocery list she had started this morning. Picking up the pencil, she added Ovaltine. Zachary was drinking twice as much as usual, trying to save enough seals for a Captain Midnight Decoder Ring, which explained the need for more milk lately. They were almost out of shampoo, and she added Halo to the list. The popular Halo jingle from the radio ran through her mind, and she wondered if it had glorified her hair like it was supposed to. Adding Old Dutch Cleanser and Ipana Toothpaste, she pushed the list away as Zachary placed the big red apple cookie jar on the table in front of her.

Maggie and Abigail had one just like it. Grandma brought them back when they went on vacation to the state of Washington. It was really far away; that much he knew for sure. Grandpa pointed it out to him on a map of the United States. Oak Grove was in the middle of the map, and Washington was all the way across the map by the ocean. Placing three cookies on the table, he replaced the green lid and returned the cookie jar to the counter.

"Zachary, I see your roller skates on the porch." Ellen looked at him with a frown and pointed to the skates lying in front of the screen door. "Go put them away before someone falls over them."

Skating up and down the block in front of the house was something he enjoyed, but why he chose to remove his skates at the back porch Ellen didn't understand. He would skate up the front walk, follow it around the side of the house, and sit on the back step to remove them.

Leaving the skates at the bottom of the steps once too often proved the end of Michael's patience and he took them away, not allowing him to skate for a week. Unfortunately, the risk of tripping over them at the bottom step became a risk of tripping over them at the back door.

"If you leave them there again, I am going to put your skates away for two weeks this time." She watched him hold a cookie between his teeth and grab his skates. "Where is your skate key?"

Zachary took the cookie out of his mouth. "It's in the pocket of my jeans," he said with a guilty look on his face. He knew he was supposed to put the key in the cigar box on his bureau, but he forgot and left it in his pocket again. Mom always found it when she sorted the laundry.

"Go get it." Ellen gave him a threatening look and grabbed a wooden spoon. She smiled at the sound of his giggling as he ran down the hall. "And put it where it belongs," she called after him.

Zachary rummaged through the clothes hamper at the end of the hall and dug the skate key from the pocket of his jeans. His cigar box, containing several items of questionable worth, sat on his bureau. Lifting the lid, he tossed the key in with his collected treasures: a rabbit's foot, his lucky penny, a skeleton key, and his Tom Mix pocket knife. It also contained three cat's eye marbles, a chunk of fool's gold, Chinese handcuffs, a roll of caps, a lock that he didn't have the combination for, and a broken watch. He admired the contents for a moment then let the lid drop at the sound of a horn in the driveway. Dad was home.

The screen door slammed, and Michael called out, "Is anyone ready to go to the circus?"

"Yes!" Zachary shouted, running into the living room. "Hurry, Dad, change your shirt so we can go."

"We sure are," Ellen said, walking into the living room. She wore a light green pair of slacks with a matching green and white blouse. A white belt fit snugly around her waist, and she wore a pair of white flats. Her blonde hair, pulled away from her face, was held in place by a white ribbon tied in a bow, and Michael thought she looked quite fetching.

"Thanks for sewing my button, Hon." He kissed her on the nose and looked at her with a pleased smile. "You look awfully pretty this evening."

Ellen returned his smile and watched him change shirts. "Thank you. Were you busy today?"

"Yes, we were. Every person who came into the bank today talked about the circus tonight. It seems everyone in town is going."

"Well, I guess so. I cannot imagine anyone not wanting to be there." Ellen watched him button his shirt and tuck it into his trousers. The light blue shirt made him look quite handsome and was one of her favorites.

"Let me wash my hands and comb my hair real quick." He walked down the hall and called over his shoulder. "Do you know what we need to do?"

Ellen followed and stood in the doorway watching him comb his hair. "No. What do we need to do?" she asked.

Michael washed his hands and accepted the towel she handed him. Drying his hands, he looked at her for a minute and smiled. "Today, I was thinking that I would enjoy spending a nice relaxing evening listening to some of those new records we bought. We haven't done that in a long time."

Ellen laughed. "I was just thinking that very same thing a few minutes ago." She watched as he hung the towel on the hook; pleased with the thought of the two of them enjoying one another's company.

He hugged her. "I guess great minds work together."

The car horn sounded, and they both laughed. "I guess Zachary is ready to go to the circus."

"Come on, we better hurry," he said laughingly and propelled her toward the front door. "Zachary is going to drive off and leaves us without a ride."

Maggie and Abigail, gripping the rope handle along the back of the front seat, bounced up and down giggling and chattering with excitement. Each wore a yellow sundress with white butterflies embroidered on the skirt. Straps crisscrossed in the back, crossed over the shoulder, and buttoned in the front Abbie, insisting on wearing the sailor cap that was part of her lunch mission attire, had it perched at a crooked angle on her head.

"Are we supposed to pick up my parents?" Alan asked Lynn. Printing the paper for early delivery was a task that kept him busier than usual, and he couldn't remember what they decided.

"No, they said to go ahead and they would see us there." Lynn turned to the two girls and looked at the excitement in their eyes. "You two, please sit back in the seat and stop bouncing. Watch out the window. We will be there shortly." Turning around, she smiled to herself. She couldn't fault the girls; she was excited also.

"But I can't wait," Maggie exclaimed. "I want to see all of the beautiful girls. Mom, can you make me a circus costume?"

Lynn smiled and wondered how long they would play circus after tonight. "Yes, I will. You can help me." She thought of the box of old clothes and pieces of fabric that she had saved through the years, and a piece of blue satin came to mind. She could not recall when or what she used it for, but it would be a perfect piece for a costume.

"Will you make Abigail one too?" she asked, looking at her sister. Maggie's dark blue eyes, fringed with long black lashes, was the first thing everyone noticed about her. With her round face and engaging smile, she was everyone's sweetheart in a matter of minutes. Her thick, dark hair with its hint of curl was parted on the side tonight and held in place by a yellow, white, and green flowered barrette.

"I don't want a girly dress," Abigail commented. "I want a costume like the man on the side of the truck with the tall hat and whistle." The girls did not look anything alike. Abigail's hair was light brown, and her eyes, dark as coal, always reflected a bit of mischief. Her face was thinner than Maggie's, but she also had a winsome smile and a friendly personality that people found delightful.

She looked seriously at her mom and informed her, "I already have a whistle. All I need is the hat and coat."

Alan laughed, "We should have known Abbie would want to be the ringmaster." He looked at Lynn and shook his head. Maggie was all girl, and Abigail was a full-fledged tomboy.

"We will see what we can do about both of your costumes," Lynn promised.

Sheriff Walker parked his car in the first parking space at the Fairground. Garrett sat on Anne's lap with Jordan between him and Anne. Brenton, Preston, and Josiah were in the back seat straining to see what was going on.

"Will you look?" Josiah scooted up and looked out the front window. He pointed to a row of red tents. "What are all the tents for?"

Opening the door, John stepped out with the boys spilling out after him. Looking down into Josiah's excited face, he answered, "That row of tents is the midway. There are all kinds of games to play and sideshows to see."

Josiah and Jordan stared with round eyes across the field. "What about the big tent, Dad? Is that where the circus will be?" Jordan asked, pointing to a big blue tent with a yellow and white striped top. An American Flag stirring in the breeze, beckoned folks to an entrance presently prohibited by lowered tent flaps.

"Yes, they call it the big top," he answered, walking to the other side of the car. He noticed several cars arriving and motioned for the boys to step back. "Stand over by the fence out of the way." Music drifted from the midway and the smell of popcorn and hot-dogs filled the air.

He helped Anne out of the car and took Garrett by the hand. "I need to talk to the boys," he said, indicating three teenage boys standing next to one of the oak trees. "I'll be right back."

Paul Wilson, Jack Murphy, and Peter Williams watched the Sheriff walk toward them, wondering if there were any special instructions. They had directed parking for the Easter egg hunt and the Founder's Day Celebration for the last two years and were not surprised when he asked for their assistance again.

"There's Truman and Simon," Jordan yelled, watching Uncle Jim pull his car into the parking spot next to theirs. Jennifer waved at Anne. Stepping out of the car, she laughed and looked around. "Just think about it; seven little boys and a circus. Is this America or what?"

"It sure is. I guess the boys are as excited as mine?" Anne asked, watching Truman and Simon jump from the car and run to the fence, joining the others.

Reaching into the back seat, Jim retrieved three red vests and slammed the door. "I'll be right back," he told Jennifer and headed toward his brother who was talking to the three teenagers.

"Jim almost forgot the boys' vests," Jennifer said, looking at Anne. "We had to turn around and go back. Truman and Simon were so afraid they were going to miss something." She looked toward the midway and laughed, "I kind of felt the same, but here we are. Let's go get in line before it gets too long."

"Hey, Mom is headed for the ticket booth," Brenton announced. "Come on."

"We are going to be the first ones in the Fairground," Josiah yelled, jumping and punching the air with his fist.

"Come on, Dad," Preston called impatiently, motioning with one hand and holding Jordan back with the other.

"Okay, let's get the tickets." Jim looked at the excited bunch of boys and grinned at his brother as they stepped up to the ticket booth.

"How many?" the strange looking woman asked in a raspy voice. Simon stared at her with wide eyes. A red bandanna was tied around her black hair, and she wore a bright, multi-colored dress. Several strands of beads hung around her neck, and big gold hoops hung from her ears.

"Four, please," Jim answered, handing her the money.

Simon continued to stare in awe. She had the rosiest cheeks he had ever seen, and her mouth was painted a bright red. Something blue was painted on her eyelids, and she wore several bracelets on her wrists. He looked in amazement at her hands when she handed his dad the tickets. Her long fingernails were painted red, and she wore a ring on each finger. Simon's hand rested on the counter, and without warning she reached out, patted it, and gave him a broad smile. "You have fun, young man," she said with such kindness in her eyes that Simon instantly took a liking to this strangely dressed woman.

Music played loudly, and men called attention to their games. "Five chances for twenty-five cents," a man yelled from one of the red tents. "Come on, win a teddy bear for the little lady," he called to Jim. He wore a white T-shirt that had American Circus Company written on the front. A round, straw hat sat on his head, and he chewed on a cigar hanging from his mouth when he wasn't calling attention to his game. Balloons filled the back wall of the tent, and he held several darts in his hand. "How about you, young man?" he called to Preston.

"Maybe later," Jim told the man, placing his hand on his nephew's shoulder. "Let's check out some of the other tents first, okay?" he said, glancing down at Preston.

"Look at all the people." Brenton caught up with Truman and looked behind them. "Everyone must have decided to come at the same time."

"How about you fellas?" A man called in a loud, friendly voice from the tent across the way. He was fat and wore the same shirt as the other man, but this one had a jolly face and grinned at them while he tossed a baseball in the air. "Just knock over three bowling pins, and you get one of these prizes." He pointed to several large stuffed animals on a shelf behind him. "Five balls for one dollar."

Jordan felt the money in his pocket and thought Uncle Jim had a pretty good idea. He was going to wait and see what was here before he started spending his money.

Farther down the midway, Maggie and Abigail jumped up and down, clapping their hands. An old man dressed in a black suit coat and a pair of patched trousers stood in front of them. An old, brown, tattered hat sat on his gray head, and a pair of spectacles slid halfway down his nose. A monkey was dancing to a lively tune the old gentleman cranked from a box hanging around his neck. Wearing a blue vest and cap, the small animal danced with enthusiasm until he stopped cranking the handle. In one quick leap, he jumped onto his shoulder and clapped his hands.

Lynn, Alan, and the girls, along with several others, had gathered in amusement to watch. Jumping down, the monkey approached Abigail and looked at her curiously. Bending down to pet his head, she was startled when he reached up and grabbed her sailor cap.

"Hey, that's my hat," Abbie objected then giggled when he handed her his red cap. Uncertain as to what she should do, she stared at him a moment and then placed his cap on her head.

"Skipper, you give that little lady her hat back," the Organ Grinder said.

Skipper ran in a circle around the old gentleman then jumped onto his shoulder again.

"You look just like him," Lynn laughed, looking down at Abbie. "All you need is a tail."

"Skipper, I said, give that hat back to the young lady." Turning his head, he looked at the monkey on his shoulder and gave him a stern look. Jumping to the ground, Skipper made his way to Abigail, sat down in front of her, and handed her the sailor hat.

Maggie poked her sister with an elbow. "Give him his hat back." Removing the small red cap from her sister's head, she handed it to him.

Placing the cap on his head, he looked up at Lynn, took her hand, and started dancing.

Alan looked at the expression on his wife's face and burst into laughter. The monkey was a show in himself. The old man smiled while he watched the crowd enjoy his little friend, and after a few more of the chimp's antics, removed his hat and set it on top of the organ. Alan reached into his pocket, retrieved some coins, and dropped them into the old, tattered hat. Expressing his thanks with a nod of his head, the old gentleman turned and made his way farther down the midway, cranking the lively tune while Skipper danced along in front.

A few more tents along the midway found Shari, standing in line to see the bearded lady and watching Carole hurry toward her. "Have you seen the bearded lady yet?" she asked.

"Yes, Mom and Dad took us in earlier." Carole leaned closer to her and whispered. "Guess what else is in there?" she asked mysteriously.

"What?" Shari looked at her friend with wide eyes, wondering what else was behind the tent flap.

"A mermaid lady," Carole stated importantly. "A real mermaid lady. She has a tail, real long blonde hair, and everything."

"No," Shari said. "Laura told me mermaids were just pretend." She looked at her sister who was waving her arm, trying to get Noelle's attention. "Is she ever going to be surprised. See, she doesn't know everything," Shari commented, turning back to Carole. "I am not going to tell her. She will just see for herself."

"The mermaid is pretty, too. I have to go. Daddy is going to try to win us a stuffed animal," she said excitedly and ran off to catch up with her family.

Shari was astonished; a real mermaid lady. She couldn't wait to see what she looked like, and she couldn't wait to see the look on Laura's face.

Moving up in line, Laura wondered why in the world a woman would want to have a beard. She glanced around, looking for Elizabeth but did not see her. Maybe they were still in the long line at the entrance. Johnny already found Brenton and Truman, Jimmy took off with Jake in a rush to see the biggest snake in the world, and Shari and Dad wanted to see the bearded lady, so here they were. She wondered if Noelle or Elizabeth had been in to see her yet. Glancing back at Shari, she wondered why she was staring at her with a mysterious grin on her face. "What are you grinning about?" she asked.

"Nothing," Shari answered.

"Come on, girls," Leah said as the tent flap was pulled back and it was their turn to enter.

Two tents away, Zachary stood stock still with his mouth dropped open. A huge snake was wrapped around the neck of the man inside and was crawling down the front of his chest.

Ellen turned away, not able to watch, and Michael was laughing at her. "Come on, hon; just think of it as a beautiful necklace. I'll get you one," he teased.

"Will you just be quiet. I can't even think about it." Ellen turned around. "How long do we have to stay here?" She could see Zachary out of the corner of her eye, and he was transfixed, his eyes as big as saucers, and he was not moving a muscle. With a shudder, she looked away and saw Pastor Mike, Leah, and the girls laughing as they exited the bearded lady tent. She would just stand here and not think about what was going on behind her.

Zachary's voice sounded loud and clear. "He sure is the fattest snake I ever saw." Feeling lightheaded and a little ridiculous, Ellen glanced down the midway and concentrated on Eli and Mary Cook buying cotton candy. Ellen waved when they turned and began walking in her direction. She took a deep breath and sighed with relief when Mary waved back.

Eli smiled as they approached and joined Michael and the boys. He was a tall, quiet, pleasant man devoted to his family. Possessing a dry sense of humor, he surprised many people with his wit since he was not a man of many words. After one got to know him, he was found to be wise beyond his years, and a man that many of his co-workers at The Timber Company sought for advice.

Eli treated Mary like a jewel and spent a lot of his free time with Carrie and Jake.

"Would you look at that?" Jake exclaimed. He was a smaller image of his father but possessed Mary's outgoing personality. "Dad, that snake is wrapped completely around the body of that man." His voice grew louder, "Man, Zachary, look how fat that snake is. Isn't that something?"

Mary, taking one look at Ellen's face, knew something needed to be done. "Ellen and I are goin' to walk over and get a bottle of pop." She reached for her hand and laughed, "I don't like them either, but I don't think I have ever turned green over one."

"Thank you, Mary." Ellen took a deep breath. "Men and boys; how can they stand some of the things they do?" She felt much relieved as they walked away toward the Coca-Cola wagon. "I thought I was going to literally get sick," Ellen commented, taking a deep breath as she stood in line with Mary.

"Everyone is having a good time, aren't they?" Mary pointed down the midway to one of the tents where Mercy and Melba were throwing baseballs and laughing.

"Hey, Mom," Zachary called, running over to her. "The man let me pet the snake. I really did. I touched it," he exclaimed. "Jake and Jimmy did too. They are really not that bad." His eyes were full of excitement as he continued, "You should have seen me. Dad said you wouldn't want to cause you are delicate. Why are you delicate?" he asked, looking up at her. "Mary, are you delicate?"

"Gee willikers, no. Mom chops their heads off with a hoe all the time," Jake loudly boasted.

Ellen looked at Mary in surprise and then felt Michael's arms around her shoulder. He grinned and hugged her. "Are you okay, hon?"

"You better take her over and win her a nice prize real quick if you don't want to find yourself in a whole lot of trouble," Mary laughed.

"I think that is pretty sound advice." Michael took Ellen by the arm. "Come on, Zachary. Let's see if we can find Grandma and Grandpa. I'll see you later, Eli. Thanks, Mary." He steered Ellen away, leaving Eli and Mary both grinning and wondering how anyone could be so afraid of snakes.

Caroline Driscol was chattering Elizabeth's ear off. "I just know Peter saved that parking place for me. It was so close to the entrance," she commented, turning to look Elizabeth in the eye. "Did you notice that?"

Elizabeth glanced at her sister. There had been an empty parking space but she couldn't imagine that Peter actually saved it for Caroline. Uncle Henry, perhaps, being the Mayor and all, but not just for Caroline. Of course, there was no way one could convince her of that. Elizabeth sighed and looked at the crowd of people, trying to spot Laura or Noelle. If she had to wander around with Caroline all night listening to her talk about Peter, she might just run off and join the circus like Aunt Trudy had preached against for the last hour.

"Caroline." Karen Reese came up from behind them. "I've been looking for you. Look what I won throwing darts." She held up a Kewpie Doll with fat, rosy cheeks and red lips. "Have you ever seen anything like it?" she asked and halted as she glanced at Mrs. Driscol's hat. It was yellow with a large brim turned up on one side with miniature pieces of fruit holding it in place. A large, blue ribbon, tied in a bow, circled the crown with small clusters of grapes dangling from the ends.

Karen stood for a moment holding the Kewpie Doll, at a loss for words. She knew she shouldn't stare at Mrs. Driscols's hat, but she couldn't seem to help it. "The hat, I mean, the doll is cute. Don't you think?" she asked, handing it to Caroline. The doll had short, wavy, black hair and wore a red bathing suit with little red shoes. "Come on, there are a lot of games and prizes to win," she said, much to Elizabeth's relief.

Uncle Henry smiled at the girls. "Go on, have fun. Just meet us at the big top at six forty-five." He gave Elizabeth a firm look. "That goes for you too." The words were barely out of his mouth, and she was headed down the midway.

"Oh, Henry, I don't know if that is such a wise idea," Trudy said with a worried look on her face. "There are strangers in this crowd tonight, and the girls could get in with wrong company. I don't think you realize just what kind of danger they could be in." She pulled a hankie from her purse and dabbed her forehead, watching Elizabeth disappear down the midway. "Heaven only knows what she might do."

"Now, Trudy, all of these people are our neighbors, and both girls are going to be in good company." He patted her arm reassuringly and looked around. "We are right here in our very own Fairground." He turned to her and scolded, "Mary is right. You worry way too much."

Trudy gave him an exasperated look. *Mary doesn't know how to worry*, she thought, straightening her hat.

"Good evening, Mayor, Mrs. Driscol," Samuel Cranston greeted, walking up behind them with his wife, Abigail, on his arm.

"Good evening to you, Sam, Abigail." Thank goodness Trudy would have someone to talk with and might not worry about the girls so much.

"It is quite an evening, isn't it? You did a fine job getting the circus here, Mayor." Sam patted him on the back. "Nothing quite like a circus is there?" They stood quietly for a moment, watching familiar faces pass by.

"You are quite right, Samuel," Trudy suddenly spoke up. "There is nothing quite like a circus. We are so fortunate that Henry was able to arrange it. You mark my words, no one will forget this night."

Henry raised a brow and looked in surprise at his wife, standing there with a proud look on her face, and thought she was the most confusing woman he ever met. She had complained about the circus for the last two days, and now she was pleased about it.

He watched her expression change from pride to concern as she glanced around, and he knew she was already looking for a glimpse of the girls.

Straightening her hat, she looked at Abigail. "You should really drop by Edna's. She just received a new stock of hats. I purchased this one just today. Have you ever seen anything quite like it?" she asked, turning her head sideways.

"No, Trudy, I don't believe I have ever seen anything quite like it," Abigail Cranston answered, looking at it closely. Hearing her husband clear his throat, she refused to look at him and tried to think of a way to change the subject.

Much to Abigail's relief, Trudy spied Dr. and Mrs. Miller several tents away, talking to Old Ben, Young Ben, and Willy. "Abigail, I see Margaret. Come along, let's go chat with her," she said, pulling her along. Trudy, deciding the credit for the circus was totally her husband's due, greeted everyone they passed with a proud smile, inclining her head to display her hat which she though was most becoming.

"Everyone in Oak Grove is here, aren't they? A person should have the chance to see a circus at least once in his or her lifetime," Trudy rambled on, pulling Abigail along behind her. "I do hope everything goes well tonight. Goodness, it is warm. I really must tell Margaret about a dress I saw in Edna's the other day. I thought of her as soon as I saw it. Have you been in there recently? There was a lovely blue suit that would look marvelous on you; and a hat that would match it perfectly."

Sheriff and Jim Walker, across the midway, were involved in a duel throwing baseballs at bowling pins. "Come on, you can do better than that," Jim laughed as his brother threw the last ball and missed. He managed to knock two over but missed the other three.

"I'm not spending any more money. You see what you can do," he challenged his brother. "You haven't won anything either."

The fat, jolly man placed five balls in front of Jim before he had his money out of his wallet. Picking up the first ball, Jim looked at it for a moment and then threw it.

"Come on, you can do better than that," John mocked when he missed.

Jim grinned as a pin fell over on the second throw.

"Come on, Dad. Get the rest of them," Simon yelled, running up behind him. Spying a green and black lizard on the shelf with several other stuffed animals, Simon hoped his dad would win it for him. Lizards were his favorite.

Jim threw the third ball and knocked another pin over. "Come on," Simon yelled, moving from one foot to the other as he watched him pick up the next ball.

Jim looked closely at the pin, threw the ball, and slapped his hand on the counter when he missed it. He glanced at John curiously.

"Come on, little brother," John said, getting a little irritated. He knew something was not exactly right, but couldn't put a finger on just what it was.

Jim, knowing the pins were set at angles causing one's judgment to be a little off, studied them for a couple of minutes then threw the last ball. Barely scraping the pin, it teetered back and forth.

"Fall! Fall! You crazy pin," Simon shouted, beating the counter with his hand. The pin wobbled and then set upright. "Dad, you almost did it. How about one more time?" he asked.

"Nope, let's go try something else," Jim said, taking Jennifer's arm and watching Simon run off down the midway. "What do you think?" he asked looking at John. "I know the pins are angled, but there has to be something else wrong." He looked back with a puzzled expression on his face and shook his head.

"I know. We've thrown too many baseballs not to be able to knock three out of five over," John said, stopping in front of the hot dog stand. "I'm hungry. How about you, Anne?"

"That sounds good. I am hungry too, and I know Garrett is," she replied looking down at him. His eyes were glued to a clown walking toward them with a handful of balloons. "Garrett, would you like a balloon?" she asked bending down. His eyes grew wide with wonder as the clown approached. "What color balloon would you like?" Anne asked.

"Red. I want a red one," he answered, staring at the balloons waving in the air. The clown stopped, leaned down, and looked at Garrett with a big smile. His white painted face, with red mouth, and huge, black eyebrows, was lively and animated. A big red ball stuck on the end of his nose, and he wore a curly, orange wig. His costume was a variety of bright colors complimented by long, floppy, red shoes.

Garrett stared at the clown and backed up closer to Anne. He was not quite sure what to make of this strange looking person. The red balloon waving in the air caught his attention, and he reached out to accept it from the clown.

"Thank you, ma'am," the clown said as she dropped a nickel in his white-gloved hand. He smiled and patted Garrett on the shoulder. "I will see you in the big tent after while." Garrett watched him wander off down the midway, the rest of the balloons waving in the air.

"Let's tie that balloon around your wrist so it doesn't fly away." Anne knelt beside him and tied it loosely on his wrist. "Did you like the clown?" she asked.

He looked at the balloon and then back at the clown. "He was funny looking, but he was nice."

"Why is it that hot dogs taste so much better somewhere other than at home?" Jennifer asked as she passed two of them to Anne.

"I don't know, but they do taste better, don't they?" she answered, handing Garrett his. "I love the circus music, don't you?" she asked as calliope music drifted across the night air above the mixture of laughter and excited chatter.

"Who would have ever thought a circus would be here in Oak Grove," Jennifer commented. They strolled down the midway. The flag, high on the big top, waved in the evening breeze. "What time is it? We don't want to miss any of the show."

Anne glanced at her wristwatch. "We have plenty of time. It is just now six-fifteen," she said, smiling a greeting at Old Ben.

Ben smiled back and waved at Garrett. "There's the preacher," he commented to Ben and Willy. "Let's go say hello." He made his way slowly to a tent where small, glass bowls were grouped together on a table, and Leah was in the process of throwing small, round, plastic balls at them.

"Hello, Ben." Mike smiled, "I see you made it." He shook the old man's hand and turned to the other two. "Evening, Ben, Willy. Leah is determined to win one of these vases, and I think I am probably going to go broke." He looked at the determined set to her jaw and grinned at the three men.

Throwing the last ball, Leah turned and smiled at them. "Good evening. This is harder than it looks. I give up," she said with a sigh and looked at Mike. "I guess you will have to win one for me."

"Well, that puts the pressure on you, doesn't it?" Young Ben chuckled, looking at Mike. His family had tagged him *Young Ben* when he was very small, and it stuck through the years. If his Uncle Ben was anywhere close, the young boy was at his heels, and the two had been inseparable.

"Give it another try, Mrs. Daniels. You can do it," Willy urged, smiling at her. She had a warmth about her that made him comfortable. He didn't feel that way about other women and certainly had not felt that way about his own mother. Willy realized his habit of judging women by his mother's standards was unfair, but he couldn't seem to change his way of thinking. Aunt Lydia had been sweet and kind but passed away and left him feeling abandoned once more.

Laughter and shouts erupted from one of the tents a little farther down the midway. "Willy, let's walk down and see what's going on," Ben said "We'll be back in a few minutes, Uncle Ben. Have a good evening Pastor Mike, Leah."

"Don't worry about me," Old Ben remarked, waving his arm for the two to go ahead. "I'm goin' to make my way down to the big top and find a good seat."

Willy noted Simon and Preston standing at one of the tents, watching and laughing at whatever was going on. A fairly large crowd had gathered and was finding something extremely funny.

"What in the world is going on?" Willy asked as they walked closer.

"For crying out loud," Ben laughed. "It is Mercy and Melba." Drawing closer, they stood behind Preston and Simon and watched. Determined to win a stuffed animal, the girls were attempting to knock the bowling pins over. How long they had been at it, Willy didn't know, but it appeared the jolly man working the game had turned their failure into a sideshow. The Organ Grinder stood at one end of the counter, and his chimp sat on a shelf above the bowling pins. Melba took aim, threw the ball, and the chimp caught it and tossed it back. Laughter erupted from the crowd, and Mercy stepped up to take a turn. The monkey, again, caught the ball and tossed it back, but she missed the catch and got tickled.

Willy watched Melba's face as she laughed at Mercy. Her green eyes were bright and full of laughter and the smile on her face was beautiful. Her nose had a little tilt to it, and her red hair hung loose and free; the curls spilling over her forehead and the length of it down her back and over her shoulder. She buried her face in her hands as she laughed, and Willy noted the shine of her hair. Raising her head, she looked across the top of the crowd straight into his eyes. Flashing him a brilliant smile, she waved at the two of them, and Willy felt as if his heart stopped beating in his chest.

"No more," Mercy said, laughing as she stepped away from the counter. "I've spent all I'm going to. I'm just no good at this."

"Me either," Melba giggled. The chimp, jumping to the counter, shook her hand then ran along the counter and perched on the Organ Grinder's shoulder.

"Hold on there, ladies," the jolly man called above the laughter. "Here you go." He handed each a stuffed monkey. "You've both been good sports."

"Why, thank you," Melba replied, smiling at him. Taking the stuffed animal, she hugged it to her and stepped away from the tent.

Mercy followed, her eyes full of merriment. "Aren't they cute?" she asked, looking at Melba. Both girls looked at one another and burst into laughter again.

"How about it folks? Anyone else like to try?" he called out in a loud voice. "Five balls for one dollar. Come on; show these two ladies how it's done." He looked at Willy and Ben.

Willy held his hand up, indicating his refusal, and noticed Mercy and Melba walking toward them.

"I never heard of anyone getting a prize for losing," Ben remarked as he laughed at the two girls. "How long were you there?"

"Long enough to know the Cardinals would never show any interest in us," Melba answered, laughing and hugging the stuffed monkey to her. She glanced up at Willy and was astonished. *Why, he's handsome*, she thought to herself. Any time she had ever seen Willy he was covered in dirt and grease, had on stained coveralls, and always wore an old dirty baseball cap. She looked in surprise at his dark, curly hair, and was even more surprised when she looked into his eyes. Why had she never noticed his eyes before? They were dark blue with a hint of gray around the edges and fringed with black lashes that were much too long for a man. Melba could not imagine why she never noticed his eyes before.

"Hey, Willy," Simon called as he and Preston ran up to him. "Come down here and look at this huge snake." He pulled on his hand. "Come on, Ben."

"It is the biggest thing you ever saw," Simon exclaimed, turning to Mercy and Melba. "Come on, you've got to see this," he said, looking from one to the other.

Willy looked at the uncertainty in Melba's face and smiled when she looked up at him. He watched as Simon tried to talk the two girls into going along and took the opportunity to observe Melba up close.

A few freckles were sprinkled across her nose, and even as a man Willy could tell that her hair had a natural curl to it. He was taken back by an impulse to reach out and touch the thick auburn curls hanging loosely down her back, and he was puzzled as to where that desire came from.

"Not for me," Mercy said. "You guys go ahead. I think Melba and I are going to get a Coke," she said, looking in both directions for the Coca-Cola wagon.

Melba hid her disappointment. She would have liked to talk to Willy a little. "You all go look at it. I'm going with Mercy to get something to drink," she remarked, knowing there was nothing to do but go with Mercy or appear rude.

"Come on, Willy, you have to see this thing," Simon begged, excitedly pulling on his arm.

"Are they coming?" Jake asked as he ran up to join them. "Hurry, Ben. You've go to see this." The three boys ran off in a flurry of excitement, stopping once to see if Willy and Ben were following.

"I guess we better go take a look," Willy said. "I don't think they will let us alone until we do." He glanced down at Melba. *The top of her head barely comes to my shoulder*, Willy thought to himself. He looked at her slight figure and was amazed at how small she was.

"All right; let's go. Come on, Willy." Ben glanced down the midway in the direction the boys disappeared.

Melba looked up and realized Willy was watching her. "Maybe we will see you later," she commented, feeling somewhat pleased. He nodded his head, a hint of a smile crossed his lips, and he gave her a look that she didn't quite understand. Her eyes followed the tall figure as he and Ben headed in the direction the boys had taken.

For the first time since he had known him, Willy wanted to choke Simon.

"Truman, did you see the snake?" Simon yelled, running past his brother.

Truman watched him, hoping he wouldn't run into someone, and followed Brenton and Johnny to the next tent where they found Laura, Noelle, and Elizabeth throwing plastic rings at soda bottles.

"Did you win anything?" Johnny asked over his sister's shoulder.

"No," Laura said. "I can't get one single ring around the bottles. It looks easy, but it's not, and I'm out of money," she said disappointedly, as she looked at the Kewpie Dolls lined on the shelf at the back of the tent.

"I'll win one for you," Elizabeth commented, laying her money on the counter. She picked up the plastic rings the man laid in front of her and looked at him. *He is old, but he looks nice enough,* Elizabeth thought to herself. Aunt Trudy told her not to trust anyone she did not know tonight.

"Hey, mister!" she called as he moved away. "Do these rings even fit around those bottles?" Twirling the rings around her finger, she looked him straight in the eye and waited for his answer.

Amused by her spunk, the man chuckled and placed a plastic ring around the neck of one of the bottles. "They fit. Just don't throw so hard," he commented and stepped away from the table again.

"Thank you," Elizabeth replied. "I was just checking." Taking her time, she took aim, tossed the first ring and missed the whole table.

"Not so hard, Elizabeth," Truman said. "What in the world are you throwing at?"

Elizabeth glared at him and tossed another that stood upright between two bottles.

"Just kind of toss it gently into the air," Truman said in a nicer tone. He wasn't about to get Elizabeth riled up over a doll. He had seen her in action before and knew she could hold her own against anyone. Reaching into his pocket, he laid fifty cents on the counter.

Brenton leaned close to his shoulder. "What are you going to do with a Kewpie Doll?" he asked laughing.

"It's not the prize that is important, Brent. It is the skill that counts." He watched Elizabeth throw the rest of her rings, with no success, and looked at the disappointment on her face.

What would I do with a silly looking doll, he thought to himself. *It would just be my luck to win one.*

Elizabeth stomped her foot. "I can't do it," she complained. "Go ahead, Truman, see if you can." She stepped back and looked at Laura. "It's harder than it looks. Why do you want one of the silly looking things anyway?"

"I think they are cute," Laura answered, "and it would be a good souvenir from the circus."

The first ring Truman tossed bounced across several bottles and landed between two of them. Tossing the second ring higher into the air, he watched it settle over one of the bottles at the back of the table.

The man shook his head as the third ring hung precariously off the side. "Sorry, it has to land *around* the bottle," he explained.

"How many of these do I have to get?" Truman asked.

"You have to get three out of five," the man answered with an encouraging smile. "Come on, you can do it." Jingling the rings in his hand, he decided the one called Brenton would be the next to give it a try.

Truman tossed the fourth ring higher in the air and it landed around one of the bottles in the middle of the table.

"Come on, Truman," Laura cried patting him on the back. "You can do it," she said, holding her hands tightly together.

"Take your time," Johnny said, coaching him from the side. "Try it nice and slow."

Truman waited, for what Laura thought to be an eternity, and then tossed the ring. It bounced across two bottles and came to rest around the neck of one of the bottles in the last row.

"You did it!" Laura squealed. "You really did it. You've won a Kewpie Doll," she exclaimed, looking at the dolls on the shelf.

"Where are you going to put your Kewpie Doll, Truman?" Johnny snickered and slapped him on the back. "You lucky thing, you got just what you wanted."

"You could always hang it on your bike," Brenton laughed, "or put in on your bureau."

"Well son, it looks like you've won yourself one of these dolls. Which one would you like?" The tall, thin man behind the counter grinned in amusement at the teasing.

"Let her have it." Truman pointed to Laura. "She's the one who wants it. I guess I am the only one with enough skill to win her one." He looked at Johnny and Brenton with a grin and walked away.

"Well, little lady, which one would you like?" the man asked.

Laura pointed to one on the top shelf that was identical to the one Karen had. "Isn't it cute?" Laura asked Elizabeth and Noelle as he handed it to her. She turned to thank Truman but discovered the boys were already a couple of tents down the midway.

Band music suddenly exploded into the air. Everyone turned in the direction of the big top. "It must be seven o'clock." Noelle squeezed Laura's arm. "The circus is getting ready to start." She spun around excitedly, her long braids flying in the air. "Come on, let's hurry," she exclaimed excitedly and grabbed Elizabeth's arm, pulling her along.

"Wait, get your ticket ready," Elizabeth said, bending down to pull her ticket from inside her sock. "You won't lose it if you keep it here." She giggled as she looked up at Laura. "Caroline hates when I do this but she used to do it herself. She would never admit to it though."

Pastor Mike and Leah stood at the entrance to the tent. They had walked Old Ben down to the big top when Leah realized it was six forty-five so Ben would not have to rush.

"I haven't rushed in years," he chuckled. "Well, except for yesterday, and I haven't quite figured out yet how I got to the bell tower. It seems I remember walkin,' bein' pushed, pulled, and maybe even carried." He laughed as he recalled the excitement.

Reverend and Mrs. Clark joined them and were laughing at the tale of Ben's adventure and the chaos in the Blacksmith Shop.

Music poured from inside the tent, and suddenly the wide entrance flaps were drawn back and tied securely. Mrs. Clark smiled. "It seems we timed this just right," she said in her quiet, soft voice.

"It sure does." Pastor Mike followed Old Ben and handed his and Leah's tickets to one of the young boys at the entrance. "I guess we'll get first choice of seats," he said, taking Leah's arm.

"I don't think we will." Leah looked at Mike and then glanced back inside the tent.

Mike's eyes followed Leah's gaze, and he burst into laughter. Sitting in a prime spot, about halfway up, was Miss Mattie, Hannah, and Jeremiah.

"Come on," Miss Mattie called and waved at them. "I saved a seat for all of you." She laughed and indicated the rest of the seats under the big top.

Pastor Mike helped Leah and then carefully watched Ben as they made their way up to where they were sitting.

"How did you ever get in here?" Mrs. Clark asked as she leaned over and patted Miss Mattie on the hand.

Mike chuckled to himself. She never ceased to amaze him. Ninety-five years old and she got the jump on the whole town. How she managed to get in was a mystery. He leaned close to Leah and listened to her explanation.

"I told Jeremiah to drive us around to the back gate," she commented, "and just simply told the young man who came to investigate that I was the oldest living person in Oak Grove, and I owned the property the big top was sitting on. He started to object but I just explained that I was too old to walk all the way down the midway, and I was determined to see the big show." She smiled and with a twinkle in her eye, continued,

"When he said he would check with his manager, I just asked if he was also going to check with his manager about sharing this fresh, warm, strawberry pie that Hannah just baked?" Miss Mattie chuckled. "He said perhaps it would be all right. We could just go on in and choose to sit anywhere we wanted."

Mike threw his head back and laughed. She was probably the most determined person he had ever met in his life.

"A pie will get them every time," Hannah said seriously as she leaned across Miss Mattie with her tidbit of information. "I guarantee it; it will do the trick every time."

Jeremiah shook his head. "I declare, I just knew they were goin' to call Sheriff Walker and we would all be hauled off to jail," he commented with an exasperated look. "Pastor Mike, I'm gettin' too old for this tomfoolery business. You're gonna have to talk to both of them. They won't listen to me at all." He looked imploringly at Reverend Clark. "And it wouldn't hurt none if you had a talk with them too."

Mike looked at the old black man and smiled. "I promise, Jeremiah, I'll bail you out if the three of you ever do get thrown in jail. He glanced at Miss Mattie and Hannah and shook his head. He looked at Leah's laughing face as she studied the three, and Mike suddenly felt a great pity for Jeremiah.

"Poor man," Leah whispered. "I bet they keep him on pins and needles," she said, looking at Mike. The music was lively, and she smiled as she noticed Reverend Clark tapping his toe.

"This place if filling up rapidly," he commented loudly over the music. Leah nodded in agreement and looked around for the four faces that belonged to her. Down on the second row, Jimmy sat with Preston, Jake, and Ronald Olson. Laura was to the left about five rows up with Noelle, Louise, and Elizabeth, and Shari was sitting with Maggie, Carrie, and Carole two rows in front of her and Mike. She searched the crowd but did not see Johnny. With a bit of concern, her eyes swept the bleachers a second time, and she finally saw the top of his head as he followed Brenton, Truman, and Larry White through the entrance.

The circus band began another song, and Leah smiled, feeling like a young girl. Mike glanced at her. "Are you having fun?" he asked as he took her hand in his.

"Yes, this was such a good idea," she answered, smiling up at him. "The children will always remember this night," she said as she leaned closer to him, catching a slight familiar scent of his Old Spice cologne. A sudden thought struck her, and she asked, "Mike, the children, when it's over. . . ."

"I told them to meet us right outside the entrance and not to go anywhere else," he said as he grinned and squeezed her hand. Suddenly the lights went down and a drum roll began.

Laura and Noelle grabbed hands in the dark and giggled excitedly. A spotlight fell on a tall man standing alone in the center of the ring. He wore a bright, red, long tailed coat, white pants tucked into high shiny black boots, and a black vest over a white shirt and red bow tie. A tall black top hat sat on his head, and a whistle hung around his neck. He held a long black stick in his right hand, and raised both arms into the air. Lifting the whistle to his lips, he blew one long, piercing blast. The applause died down, and in the quiet of the tent, the Ringmaster spoke in a deep, loud voice; slowly, emphasizing each word.

"Ladies and gentlemen! Children of all ages! Welcome, to the greatest show on earth!"

Chapter 8

Music split the air and a deafening roar of cheering and applause filled the big top as tent flaps were pulled back and the Grand Entry began.

Outlandishly dressed clowns in a brightly painted yellow car led the procession as a kaleidoscope of wonders followed close behind. Beautiful white horses with heads and hooves raised high pranced by, and an acrobatic troupe bearing one another on their shoulders walked nimbly along while others turned flips or walked on their hands. A group of chimps rode tricycles precariously back and forth as the circus band continued its wild, happy music.

Young girls in shiny, glittering costumes of every color imaginable waved and smiled, and jugglers tossed and caught various objects with ease as they proceeded around the ring. Teams of men and women dressed in matching costumes waved as they walked side by side, laughing and jostling one another.

It was all very exciting and enthralling as young and old stared in fascination. Eyes, wide with wonder, watched in awe as the grand entry of circus performers continued in front of them. Smiles of delight shone on each face, toes tapped to the beat of the music, hands clapped and waved, and excited voices chattered to those sitting next to them.

An exclamation rose when red and yellow circus wagons appeared bearing lions and tigers; their trainers, carrying whips and looking fearless, walked alongside. Mixed in among everything, clowns with white, happy painted faces appeared in various places, darting back and forth towards the audience, evoking joy and laughter as they threw long streams of colored paper into the crowd.

Enormous elephants appeared and slowly lumbered along taking everyone's breath away with their sheer size and power. The young girls atop the huge animals waved with both hands, at ease and unafraid.

Then it was over, seemingly before it even began, as the entourage disappeared through the tent flaps from where they had come. The music slowly died away and the spotlight, shining around the tent, finally came to rest in the center of the ring.

The Ringmaster stood very still with his hands in the air and blew the whistle he held in his mouth. With a broad smile on his face, he spoke in that deep, loud voice, "Thank you, Citizens of Oak Grove, for your wonderful reception of the American Circus Company. You have been most kind. . . ."

Interrupted by a flurry of commotion, several clowns dressed in colorful baggy costumes ran into the ring chasing and beating one another with several questionable items. One carried a rubber chicken, another held a broom, one carried a mop and bucket, and another toted a long water gun.

Mike watched in amusement and chuckled when one grabbed a bucket of water and chased the others. Turning slowly, the clown walked from the ring toward the audience, swinging his bucket back and forth. Large painted eyes searched the crowd, and a huge grin crossed his face as he gave it a swing and emptied the contents onto the unsuspecting victim.

Hysterical laughter broke out as everyone stared at Trudy Driscol. She sat wide-eyed, mouth gaping, and covered in confetti. The clowns could not have picked a better target. Looking down at her lap, she stared at the multitude of tiny, white pieces of paper and burst into laughter.

Miss Mattie, wiping tears from her eyes, was instantly absorbed in the equestrian act that followed. The powerful, white horses were beautifully groomed with black plumes on their heads. "They are magnificent!" she exclaimed as they pranced around the ring, stood on their hind legs, and followed every command given.

A young man grabbed one of the horse's manes and threw himself up on its back. Circling the ring, he slowly stood to his feet, balancing himself. When they reached center ring, the young man turned a back flip and horse and rider made another turn around the ring, acknowledging the applause. Much to everyone's delight the horses lined up, bowed their magnificent heads, and the equestrian act was over.

"Why, this one act alone was worth coming tonight," Miss Mattie remarked, clapping enthusiastically. "If I would have thought it was going to be this enjoyable, I would have had you bake two pies for that poor young man," she told Hannah.

"And now, ladies and gentleman, I take special pride in presenting American Circus Company's next act," The Ringmaster called out in his deep voice. "One that will keep you on the edge of your seat. The world famous, one and only master of the high wire; The Great Sebastian Anderson!"

Lynn gripped Alan's arm. "Oh, this is going to make me a nervous wreck," she said anxiously as the spotlight fell on a man perched on a platform high above the tent floor. Holding a long bar in his hands, he stepped gingerly out onto the wire, inching his way slowly across the expanse below, finally reaching the other side. The applause was deafening and he held one arm in the air, then bowed to the audience.

Alan felt Lynn's grip tighten as the Great Sebastian stepped onto the wire again; this time without the bar. Proceeding cautiously to the middle, he came to a standstill. The silence inside the tent was thick and everyone craned their neck as they stared toward the top of the tent. What in heaven's name was he going to do? Several seconds passed, then suddenly he jumped, turned in midair, and rapidly made his way back to the platform, bringing forth a mixture of applause, whistling, and shouting.

"I can't stand this," Lynn said, glancing at Ellen who sat as though she was in a trance.

The spotlight fell on a young girl standing in the middle of the ring. As the band began a lively tune, she grabbed the end of a rope that hung suspended from the platform above. Twisting her body in time with the music, she maneuvered her way up the rope with amazing speed. Applause followed one final twist of her body, and she stood on the platform alongside the man. Holding hands, they extended their arms in the air and waved to those below.

Ellen turned to Lynn and sighed, "I wish they would hurry and get done. This is driving me crazy."

"I do too," Lynn answered, taking a deep breath. "I am so afraid one of them will fall."

Gasps and murmurs filled the big top as drums began a nerve-wracking beat, and the girl climbed atop the man's shoulder. "I can't watch. I cannot watch this," Lynn said, putting one hand over her eyes.

Alan, at this point, was totally convinced there was no circulation left in his arm and knew if the lights were up it would be completely blue. "Come on, Lynn. You don't want to miss this. Watch," he said as the man stepped out on the wire with the girl on his shoulders.

"No, I can't," she said, her hand still covering her eyes.

Slowly and cautiously, the man stepped out onto the high wire. The young girl, both arms out to her sides, sat perfectly still. Very slowly, he inched his way across the wire.

Alan mentally encouraged the man to continue. *You can make it*, he thought to himself and realized that he had been holding his breath. He had to admit that this really was pretty nerve racking. A few more steps and the man reached the halfway point. Glancing at Michael, Alan shook his head, indicating he wished they would soon hurry and get to the other side. His eyes traveled to his sister's face, and he grinned. Ellen, not moving a muscle, looked like she was made of stone. Turning his attention back to the high wire, Alan saw that the Great Sebastian had only a few more steps to go. In just a matter of seconds he reached the other side, and the crowd in the big top stood to their feet cheering, whistling, and clapping their hands.

"How can he do that?" Brenton shouted above the noise. "How does he keep his balance?"

Johnny stuck both fingers in his mouth, produced an ear-piercing whistle, and continued to clap and yell, "I do not know."

When the applause died down an acrobat team entered the center ring and performed all manner of maneuvers and balancing acts. Zachary watched with big blue eyes when a man jumped from the shoulders of his partner onto the end of a board, propelling a young girl through the air and onto the shoulders of another. They ended the act as a human pyramid, standing atop one anther's shoulders.

Clowns took to the floor again. One was dressed like a baby, wore a bonnet, and rode in a baby carriage. Crawling out of the carriage when the "mother" turned her back to fix her hose, he ran into the crowd and sat on Laura's lap.

Mike and Leah laughed at their daughter's red face as she stared at the clown, not knowing what to do. Elizabeth and Noelle laughed uncontrollably when he sucked his thumb and laid his head on her shoulder.

Patting Laura on the head, the clown stood up, smiled broadly, and leaned into the next row to plant a kiss on Samuel Cranston's cheek. Smiling at the uproar of laughter, he waved and ran back to the carriage.

The spotlight then swung to a large cage in the center ring where four large tigers sat on wooden stools. Ominous looking, their eyes followed the man who carried a whip in his hand. Suddenly the largest cat swung his massive head and growled ferociously as the trainer walked passed him.

"Oh man, what if one gets out?" Jake said, looking at Jimmy with big eyes.

Jimmy stared at the tigers and mumbled none too confidently, "They won't get out." The higher seats now suddenly didn't seem too bad, if by chance, one of the wild tigers did happen to escape.

The trainer gave a command, and at the loud crack of his whip one of the tigers jumped to the floor, rolled over, and leaped back onto the stool. The next command resulted in one of the cats sitting on his hind legs. Producing a loud roar, he tried to grab the whip out of the trainer's hand, but with another crack of his whip, the man circled the growling tiger and smacked him on the back. At the next command, all four tigers sat up on their hindquarters.

The largest cat jumped down and circled the trainer slowly, creeping along in a crouched manner, looking as though at any moment to spring on his prey. With a sudden leap, he placed both front paws on the trainer's chest and licked his face, producing a great sigh of relief from the crowd.

With each crack of the whip, the tigers followed the trainer's command until all four came to rest on the stools.

"What in the world is he going to do now?" Jake asked curiously, as he leaned forward. The trainer attached a large ring to a hook suspended from the top of the cage, struck a match, and stepped back as fire encircled the ring.

The murmuring that swept through the crowd as the trainer approached the largest tiger turned to silence as he stared into the animal's eyes. After a long moment, he stepped back and cracked his whip. With a growl, the tiger lunged from the stool, ran across the cage, and leapt through the ring of fire.

Applause filled the big top, the tiger returned to his stool, and the trainer bowed to the crowd. Waving both arms, he made his exit as circus music filled the tent, the lights came up, and everyone stood to their feet, clapping and cheering.

Mike stood along with Old Ben, Jeremiah, and Reverend Clark. "Well I must say, Pastor Mike, this has been a most enjoyable performance thus far," Reverend Clark commented, looking at him with a pleased grin.

"It sure has," Mike answered, glancing around at the familiar faces. His eyes came to rest on Johnny buying a bag of peanuts and Jimmy who appeared to be trying to borrow money from him. He watched his oldest son check his pocket, shake his head, then turn and scan the crowd. Catching Mike's eye, he waved, said something to Jimmy, and pointed in his direction.

"Here comes our youngest son," he told Leah. "I think maybe his well has run dry." He watched Jimmy weave his way in and out of the people as he made his way up the bleachers.

"Hi, Mom, Dad. Isn't this swell?" he asked, looking up at both of them with big brown eyes. "Say, could I have a dime for peanuts?" he asked. "I spent all of my money, and I'm really hungry."

Mike looked down at his son's grinning face and reached in his pocket. "We can't have you attend a circus and not have peanuts now, can we?" he asked. "You haven't had any yet?"

"I did, but Jake bought them," he explained, "and now we need some more. Really, you see, we each only had half a bag and that wasn't very many. Besides, I think I ate more than Jake and I feel bad about it," Jimmy said, looking up at him with one eye squinted.

"I guess you probably do need some more then," Mike answered, having no doubt in his mind that Jimmy ate most of them. "I wouldn't want you to feel bad about Jake either," he commented, looking down at the grin on Jimmy's face. "I suppose the only fair thing would be for you to buy Jake a bag also." Mike handed him two dimes and smiled at the grin that spread across his face.

"Thanks, Dad." Scurrying down the bleachers, he waved to Jake, standing in line around the peanut vendor.

Leah, a tender smile on her face, watched Jimmy hurriedly make his way back toward Jake. "Do you see the girls?" she asked as she linked her arm through Mike's and let her eyes search the crowd of folks milling about as they laughed and talked with one another.

"Shari is right down there with Carole and Carrie," Mike indicated with a nod of his head. The three were counting money, and seemingly satisfied, Carrie stood, waved at the young man selling cotton candy, then hurriedly scrambled down to purchase it.

Leah smiled as she watched Carrie return with the sweet sticky stuff and sit down between Shari and Carole. The three proceeded to tear pieces of cotton candy from the paper cone and stuff it in their mouths, licking their fingers.

Leah glanced around at the smiling, laughing faces around her. "Mike, look." she whispered, touching his arm. "Look down there behind Laura."

Mike followed her gaze and saw Caroline Driscol smile prettily at Peter Williams sitting next to her. Mike looked down at Leah and grinned, "Trudy will be beside herself."

Glancing over the top of Leah's head, Mike caught Old Ben staring at him with a grin on his face. Following his nod, he looked to the left and saw Mercy, Melba, Ben, and Willy sitting together. Mike looked back at Old Ben and both men smiled.

"Yes, sir, this sure is a fine evening," Old Ben remarked to Miss Mattie as he sat back down, feeling very pleased.

The lights went down, and the Ringmaster once again stood in the center ring and blew his whistle. "Ladies and gentleman, this next act is one of American Circus Company's most popular acts. One, I guarantee, that you will not soon forget," he said, holding the long, black stick in his right hand. "I proudly introduce to you the hilarious, American Circus Company Chimps!"

Several chimps, waving and blowing kisses, entered the spotlight in the back of a red cart. The small, brown pony pulling them stopped, and one of the chimps jumped out, sat on a small blue stool, and clapped his hands. He wore a small red jacket, a red and blue cap, and blue jeans.

A man appeared pushing a small red tricycle and the chimp immediately jumped up and climbed on the seat. Giving him a shove, the man stepped back and allowed him to pedal around the ring. Stopping in front of the cart, he grinned at the audience, climbed off, and clapped his hands.

One of the other chimps jumped out of the cart, ran to the tricycle, and tried to climb on. Shoved off onto the floor, a wrestling match ensued between the two and amid the commotion, another of the chimps took advantage of the situation. Jumping from the cart, he pedaled away, honking the horn.

The trainer finally managed to get all three chimps back into the little red cart, restoring a little bit of order, and sat up a small trapeze on the floor. For the next several minutes they entertained the crowd with hilarious antics and supposedly acrobatic tricks.

One of the chimps, sporting a green hat, scampered to the edge of the ring and sat down, refusing to move. The trainer walked over and commanded him to get back in the cart, but the chimp just shook his head, tipped his hat to the crowd, and grinned. A second command gained a like response and, exasperated, the trainer leaned over and shook his finger, reprimanding the chimp. The small animal smiled at the crowd, then turned back to the trainer and kissed him smack on the mouth. Wiping his face with a big, red and blue handkerchief, he firmly sent the chimp back to the cart.

Another approached from behind and handed him a pair of roller skates. Squatting down, the trainer fastened the skates then stood back and motioned for the chimp to proceed. He merely sat on the floor and waved at the crowd. He prodded him to skate, but again the chimp refused and continued to wave at the crowd. Rolling his eyes, the trainer shook his head and stooped to remove the skates. The small animal grabbed the hat from the man's head, jumped up, and skated in circles around him.

Grabbing him by the arm, the trainer sat him down and proceeded to remove the skates. Meandering over to the crowd, the chimp paused and looked around. To everyone's amusement, he began climbing from one row to the next, coming to a halt in front of Melba. Pursing his lips, he waited for a kiss.

"I don't think so," Melba said laughingly, as she patted his head and suddenly found herself with a lap full of fur when the monkey made himself comfortable and helped himself to her peanuts.

She looked at Mercy in confusion. "What am I suppose to do with him?" The chimp, his lips still pursed, suddenly grinned, and grabbed the bag of peanuts from her hand. Jumping from her lap, he scampered down the rows of seats and returned to the cart, passing the bag of peanuts to the other chimps.

A rich, deep laugh reached Melba's ears, and she realized it was Willy. Glancing behind her, she looked up into his laughing blue eyes. A matter of just a few seconds passed as they looked at one another, but Melba was conscious of an unexpected current passing between them, and she became momentarily flustered. Turning her attention back to the center ring, she wondered why the sound of his laughter had touched her the way it had and was totally baffled by her feelings.

She absentmindedly watched the pony pull the cart full of chimps away, and allowed herself to enjoy the pleasant feeling that had come over her. The spotlight swinging high in the air caught her attention and she looked up to the top of the tent.

Two trapeze artists stood on a platform, and for the next few minutes a young man and woman swung back and forth. Swinging alone or with the man on the same trapeze, the crowd was entranced as they watched them, high in the air. Another man appeared and swung out on a trapeze, landing on the opposite platform. The band began a carefree melody and the young girl swung out alone, spun around, and was caught easily by the man who now swung by his legs. The music continued the slow, relaxing tune, and the young girl seemed to almost float in the air as she was flipped, caught, and swung again. The men flipped her first by her hands and then her legs; over and over, back and forth from one trapeze to the next.

Maggie watched in awe. "She is so beautiful," she said more to herself than Carrie or Carole. Her shiny, green costume sparkled in the spotlight, her dark hair was pulled back and tied with green ribbons, and a diamond necklace glittered around her neck. Maggie knew she had found her princess. Her adoration of the young girl, flying high in the air, suddenly turned to horror when a sudden turn found no one there to catch her.

"Oh, no!" Maggie cried out, throwing her hands up to her face.

Everyone gasped in alarm as she fell, then sighed with relief when she landed in a net, bounced a couple of times, and jumped to the floor to wave cheerfully to the crowd, a bright smile on her face. Following closely behind, the two men joined her on the floor and the three joined hands, raised their arms in the air, and bowed to the applause of the audience.

They disappeared in the darkness as the spotlight swung away and over to an empty animal cage. A young man followed by two big lions ran into the ring. Carrying a whip, he immediately took control, and the lions jumped on the stools to await their commands. Impatiently, one lion jumped from his stool, circled the trainer, and growled. Picking up a chair, he held it in front of the lion that growled again and swung one of his paws. The trainer cracked his whip, and the lion jumped back onto his stool.

Zachary and Abigail sat next to each other watching the lions with wide eyes. "That lion looks awful mean," Abbie said with a worried frown on her face.

"You just have to know how to handle them," Zachary answered, not taking his eyes off the lion. "If I was in there, I would. . . ."

The lion roared loudly, causing many people to cringe. "Well, I guess I'm glad I'm not in there," he said, looking at her in surprise.

Following the trainer's commands, the lions sat up, changed stools, and jumped over barrels. Shaking their heavy manes and growling at him when he stepped too close, they were settled down with a loud crack of his whip.

Then something unbelievable happened. One of the lions jumped onto a stool in the middle of the cage and stared menacingly at the trainer. Drums began a slow, nerve-racking rhythm as the trainer walked slowly toward him. Stopping in front of the lion, they stared at each other for a long, silent moment. Then reaching up, he pried open the lion's mouth and, much to the amazement of everyone under the big top, stuck his head in the its mouth.

"Did you see that?" Zachary shouted. "That was what I was telling you about. He actually put his head in the lion's mouth."

"He must really be a crazy man," Abigail said as she watched the trainer turn and wave to the crowd before he disappeared through the tent flaps.

"And now for our last act. The one I know all of you have been waiting for," The Ringmaster shouted, "The American Circus Company Elephants."

The applause was deafening as the huge animals entered the ring A beautiful girl in a white sparkly costume rode atop the lead elephant as they walked around the ring. Returning to the center, the young girl slid down the elephant's trunk and stood directly in front of the huge animal. Turning, she motioned with her hand and gave a command for the elephants to turn in a circle. Running between them, she gave another command, and each elephant sat with his front feet in the air.

"How can they do that as big as they are?" Laura asked, turning to Noelle.

The circus band struck up a lively song, and to the delight of the crowd, the elephants swung their trunks back and forth in time to the music. At the end of the act, the young girl walked in front of the lead elephant. Sitting on the elephant's long trunk, he lifted her high into the air, and she slid off onto his neck. At the applause, she rode away leading the rest of the animals around the big top. As they approached the right side of the arena, the circus band struck up the same music they performed for the Grand Entry. The elephants made the turn at the far end of the ring, and the rest of the circus performers appeared, taking one last trip around the tent; The Grand Finale.

Clowns in their cars were followed by beautiful white horses, and everyone under the big top stood to their feet, knowing this was something they would always remember. Next, the man and woman from the high wire act paraded by, followed by the acrobats. Then the trainer and one of his tigers passed, followed by the jugglers.

Melba, Mercy, Ben, and Willy laughed as the chimps came by in their cart, and Melba found herself listening again to the sound of Willy's voice; the same stirring of emotion touching her as before.

The two men and the girl from the trapeze act came next, followed by the huge lion and his trainer. Then one more pass with the elephants and they were gone.

The spotlight fell once more on the Ringmaster in the center of the ring with his arms held in the air. Blowing loudly on his whistle, he waited for the crowd to get quiet. In his deep booming voice, he again spoke slowly as he emphasized his words, "Ladies and Gentlemen! Children of all ages! You have just seen the greatest show on earth!" Amid the deafening applause, he held the black stick into the air and strode from the ring.

One could barely hear themselves talk amid all of the applause and cheering. The lights came up and everyone stood to their feet, disappointed that it was all over.

"Oh, that was so much fun." Leah said, her eyes bright and shiny, as she looked up at Mike.

Looking down into her face, he thought how young and pretty she looked. On impulse, he reached over and touched her cheek. "It was wasn't it?" Glancing beyond her, he watched Miss Mattie gathering her purse. "I need to help Miss Mattie," he said, stepping in front of her. "I don't want her to fall."

"Here, Peter, you make sure Sarah doesn't fall. I'll help Miss Mattie." Mike took the elderly lady's hand and put his arm under her elbow. "Come on, Miss Mattie, it will do Leah good to get a little jealous for a change," he said as he helped her to her feet.

"I know better than that," she chuckled as she looked at him. "You have been thinking of strawberry pie since I mentioned it to you earlier this evening. Now tell the truth."

Mike laughed. "I have to admit, that does sound pretty good," he said as they carefully made their way down the bleachers. Leah managed to get Old Ben by the arm, and Jeremiah and Hannah followed close behind.

Young Ben and Willy waited for Ben at the entrance. "That was some performance, don't you think?" Young Ben commented to Pastor Mike. "How did you all get such choice seats?" he asked, looking curiously at the group.

Mike laughed, "You will have to ask Miss Mattie how she managed that." He glanced around at the crowd exiting the tent and noted Willy standing over by the side of the tent watching Melba as she talked with Mercy and Mrs. Clark.

Waving goodbye, Mercy turned and took her uncle's arm. "Come on, Uncle Ben. I need a gentleman to walk me to the car."

"I thought you and Melba had it in your mind to walk," he commented, smiling at his niece.

"We did walk up here, but I think Melba and I are going to ride home with you and Ben," she said as she slowly guided him toward the midway and the parking lot.

"I am going to make sure Jeremiah gets Miss Mattie and Hannah to the car," Mike said, turning to Leah. "I'll be right back, hon."

"Well, Willy, it was a nice evening, wasn't it?" Leah asked, walking over to him.

"Yes ma'am, it sure was," he commented and noticed the joy in her face and the smile that appeared when she caught sight of her children. It troubled Willy for some reason, and he turned away. He watched the other folks pass by as he waited on Ben who was talking to Eli. He was glad he came tonight. It was an entertaining evening, and he had gotten to talk to Melba. Unconsciously, he found himself searching the crowd for her.

Willy watched Pastor Mike return and walk toward his wife, aware of the love and affection between them. He observed the way she smiled and linked her arm through his, and Willy watched them make their way up the midway with their children, laughing and talking excitedly to one another.

A sigh he was unaware of escaped, and he followed Mercy and Old Ben, who were walking just a few feet ahead of him. Young Ben caught up to them, said something, and the three laughed. Willy walked slowly, watching familiar faces meet up with family members; all of them animated and happy. An unexpected sadness washed over

Willy, bringing with it a great crush of loneliness that consumed him in one split second.

Melba, talking to Jennifer and Jim Walker, realized she lost track of Mercy "I better go or Ben and Mercy might make me walk home," she said laughingly and waved as she walked away.

Scanning the crowd for Mercy's whereabouts, she turned just in time to catch the pain and loneliness etched in Willy's handsome face. It tore at her heart, and the revelation took her back to when she first came to Oak Grove. Her life was in shambles at that time, and she had not known anyone. It was a terrible, lonely time for her. Thank God, how her life had changed since then. As far as she knew, Willy had no one; no family at all.

An overwhelming desire to comfort him came over her, and she took a couple of steps in his direction. What happened next was unclear. Willy heard a gasp and saw Melba slipping sideways. Instinctively reaching for her outstretched arm, he grabbed her around the waist, preventing her fall.

"Are you all right?" he asked with concern. He looked down into her green eyes, very conscious of how small she was.

"Yes, I think I just twisted my foot," she said, wincing a little. She glanced up at him with an embarrassed smile. "I don't know what happened." She gingerly tried to put her weight on her foot. "Oh, my. I don't know about this."

"Here, let me help you." Taking her elbow with one hand, he slid his other arm around her back to support her. Bearing most of her weight, he leaned down and asked, "Are you able to walk with my help?"

Acutely aware of the softness of her hair brushing against his cheek and the sweet fragrance that drifted up to him, he steadied her. Conflicting emotions held Willy in its grip. He wished she would say she was fine and walk away, and at the same time he didn't want her to move at all and unconsciously tightened his grip around her waist.

A strong suspicion that he was about to pick her up and carry her entered Melba's mind and she quickly assured him, with a little help, she would be able to make it to the car.

I just rudely walked away from Willy, Leah thought regretfully and turned around to look for him. He was standing close to one of the tents talking with someone and Leah supposed she could apologize tomorrow. The crowd thinned out a bit, and she saw that he was leaning down speaking to Melba with a concerned look on his face. One arm supported her around the waist, and Melba had a grip on the other. A worried expression crossed Leah's face, and she touched Mike's arm. "Mike, something is wrong with Melba," she said worriedly.

Mike looked at the two hanging onto each other, wondering what in the world happened. "I'll see what's wrong. I'll be right back." Concern was evident in his face as he approached "What happened?" he asked, assessing the situation in one glance.

Melba smiled up at Willy then turned to Mike. Looking him straight in the eye, she raised one of her brows and commented, "I'm all right, Pastor Mike; I just turned my foot. Really, Willy is helping me to the car" She stared at him with a look on her face that Mike took as a message to get lost.

Mike coughed, and put his hand over his mouth, concealing a grin. "If you are sure?"

"Oh, yes. I'm quite sure," she replied, staring at him.

"I'll get her to the car," Willy stated firmly. You go ahead with your family." Mike felt as though he was just given an order and realized Willy was not about to let anyone take charge of the opportunity that just fell in his lap.

Mike noted Willy's grip on Melba's arm and observed the smile she generously bestowed on him. Unable to resist the urge to antagonize both of them, he said, "Nonsense. I can drive the car right here next to the fence and you won't have to walk so far." Trying to keep a straight face he continued, "It would be no problem at all, let me. . . . ."

"No, really, Pastor Mike, it doesn't hurt so bad that I can't walk," Melba said sweetly. The tone of her voice masked the look of exasperation in her eye as she stared at him, perfectly aware of what he was doing.

"Alright, if you are both sure you don't need my help, I'll go. Willy you take care of her. Leah and I will check on you tomorrow, Melba." He walked a few feet away and laughed as he shook his head. *Poor Willy*, he thought and caught up to Leah with a smile on his face and amusement in his blue eyes.

"What is the matter with her?" Leah asked amid the chatter of the children. "And what is so funny?"

Mike smiled as he took Leah's arm and watched the confusion cross her face. "Nothing," he whispered, "absolutely nothing." He grinned and remarked, "Melba is just fine. Although, I don't think Willy has a chance in the world. I would say he's caught something."

Chapter 9

Mike awakened, opened his eyes, and swung his legs off the side of the bed. Reaching for an old pair of jeans draped on the back of the chair, he slipped them on and pulled a T-shirt over his head. Running his fingers through his dark hair, he watched Leah roll to his side of the bed and hug his pillow.

The glow of the street lamp filtering through the tree just outside the window lent faint light to the room and cast shadows on the wall. A tender expression crossed Mike's face as he watched Leah sleep. That one small instinctive habit of reaching for his pillow when he arose, always evoked tenderness within him that he could not explain even after all these years. Leaning down, he brushed a kiss on her cheek, quietly slipped out the door, and made his way down the stairs.

Opening the door, Mike stepped out onto the porch and took a deep breath. Fragrant honeysuckle floated in the air and the dark sky displayed a full array of twinkling stars. Mike stood still for a moment, savoring the peace and tranquility that hung lightly on the tip of night's fingers, knowing that in a short time it would glide softly and gently away with the dawn. Walking down the steps and across the yard, he stopped and turned back to gaze at his home. A soft smile touched his lips as the image of his family sleeping peacefully entered his mind. Crossing the street, he walked through the churchyard, up the wide steps, and opened the unlocked door. Stepping into the dark vestibule, he turned left and walked the familiar hallway, following it to the right where it led to his office.

Opening the door, the dim outline of his desk and chair were barely visible in front of the large window. Walking slowly across the room, Mike quietly gazed through the glass into the dark shadows of the forest beyond. He stood and waited, welcoming the familiar yearning deep in his soul. Darkness released its hold as night slipped away, and the promise of a new day gently took its place. The dark gray above the trees drifted into purple and then faded into a lighter shade of rose, waking everything in its path. The dawning of a new day never ceased to amaze Mike, and his eyes moistened as he once again realized the depth of his Father's love. Ever humbled that Almighty God would draw him every morning to share this miracle, he marveled as streaks of mauve painted the sky then ever so slowly changed to soft amber. A wisp of pink cloud floated lazily above the treetops and wafted slowly on its way. Then gently, almost caressingly, tints of yellow spread across the sky as the tip of the sun peeked over the trees, rose slowly, and finally burst into a brilliant ball of fire. Praise and gratitude filled Mike's heart at the miracle of another day presented to him.

His heart overflowed with love as he gazed through the window, transfixed at the sight. Turning reluctantly away, he walked to his chair and sat down next to his desk. Resting his elbows on his knees, his hands folded, and his head bowed, Mike thanked God for the miracle he had just witnessed and waited longingly for that still, small voice he knew would touch his heart. Singing birds announced God's creation, and his heart filled with love for the One who had given him life and love and salvation. He lifted up Grandma Hope and Elizabeth Seabaugh that their health might be restored. His heart ached for Willy's loneliness and his search for that which he did not know. *Draw him to You, Father,* Mike prayed. His heart almost burst to overflowing with love for Leah and their children as he gave thanks for them. The Black family, out on the ridge, came into his heart, and he asked for wisdom to meet their needs. Mike covered his face with his hands and sat quietly, patiently waiting. Then slowly, gently, his heart welcomed that which he longed for. Joy and peace flowed into his heart and soul, washing over him like a gentle breeze. Assurance took root, chasing away the doubts that nagged him about Sunday's sermon. He did not understand the why of this particular message, but he knew God placed it on his heart and thanked Him for His wisdom and timing. Peace and strength flooded his soul, and he acknowledged his Father's guidance.

Assurance filled his heart and soul, and Mike stood to his feet and walked back to the window A deer at the edge of the forest raised its head and stared at him for a moment before bounding off. *What an awesome sight,* Mike thought, and he turned and walked out of his office, closing the door behind him. He made his way down the hall, out the side door, and around the back of the church.

Feeling the strength in his body as well as his soul, he headed into the woods. Fresh dew on the ground and the smell of cedar greeted him as he walked quietly through the trees, enjoying the peace and beauty that surrounded him. Walking a short distance, he leaned against a tall oak and watched small animals move about in the trees. Almost blending in with the forest he stood still, listening and watching to see if the deer would return.

Observing two squirrels chase each other back and forth around the side of a tree, he was suddenly aware of someone running through the woods. Instantly alert, he looked around but saw no one. Curious, he walked farther back into the woods where he thought they had headed and stood quietly, looking in all directions. There was no evidence of another's presence; now or recently. Not moving, he listened carefully but heard nothing else out of the ordinary. He walked farther back into the woods and finally stopped. Beyond this point, brush and briars thickened, and the forest became so dense that he seldom went any further. An uneasiness crept over him, and he headed back to the church. Emerging from the woods, he stopped and looked around again but saw no one Who would be out this early, and why hadn't they made themselves known? His eyes roamed over to the cemetery, and he looked at the freshly painted fence gleaming white in the early morning sun Nothing seemed to be amiss there.

The boys did a good job. I need to bring it to everyone's attention, Mike reminded himself. Again, he wondered who would be out and about this early in the morning.

Entering the church by the side door, he crossed the hall to the sanctuary. It was quiet and peaceful, and he walked back down the hall to check his office. Nothing was out of order. Walking back to the vestibule, he noticed the bulletins Myrtle had mimeographed for tomorrow lying on the table neatly folded. Shrugging his shoulders, he walked outside and crossed the street to the house, knowing Leah was up by now and would have coffee ready.

"Good morning," she said cheerily with two cups of coffee in her hands as he came in the back door. Still in her pink robe and her dark hair brushed back away from her face, Mike thought she looked as fresh as the new day. These few moments together, before the children awakened and the day took on its hectic schedule, was a habit they both treasured and looked forward to each morning. Setting his coffee in front of him, she leaned down and kissed his cheek.

"Good morning, Hon," he said, patting the hand she rested on his shoulder. Absentmindedly, he took a drink of coffee, sat the cup on the table, and stared into it; his mind once again back in the woods.

Leah looked at her husband. She knew him too well. His eyes alerted her that something was on his mind when he came through the door. "What is it? What's wrong?" she questioned, looking across the table at him.

A faint smile crossed his lips as he looked at her. *She can read me like a book,* Mike thought to himself. *She always could.* A puzzled look crossed his face, and he glanced through the back screen and watched Midnight prance through the yard.

"I was back in the forest this morning and heard someone running; close to where I was standing." He immediately wished he had not mentioned it when he saw the worry in her brown eyes.

"An animal most likely," he commented offhandedly, hoping it would ease her mind.

Leah glanced at the door. Midnight was at the screen making her presence known. "Are you sure, Mike?" she asked, walking to the door to let her in.

"Yes, it's nothing to worry about," he assured her as she came to stand before him. Midnight sat next to her feet looking up at him as though she also waited for an answer. He smiled and pulled Leah down on his lap. "It was just an animal, that's all."

She lay her head against his and sighed. "I wish you wouldn't wander around in the woods alone all of the time. Anything could happen."

"Nothing is going to happen." Looking into her dark eyes, he smiled at her. "Anyway, I hear squirrel crime is down from previous years." He laughed as she smacked him on the arm and walked to the refrigerator. Midnight, running back and forth between her feet, arched her back and rubbed against her legs, impatiently complaining that her milk bowl was empty. Catching a glimpse of the milk bottle, she made a beeline for the back porch and sat at the door waiting. Leah opened the screen, poured the milk, and returned to the table. Propping her chin in her hands, she studied her husband, waiting for the next comment or excuse he would offer to ease her mind.

"If I were to guess, I would say it was probably a coyote or maybe a fox." He liberally spread strawberry preserves on his toast and glanced across the table, aware that she was not buying it. "Good preserves," he offered as he took another bite.

Leah sighed and took a sip of her coffee. Setting the cup down, she spread some of the preserves on her toast, though not nearly as liberally as Mike, and wondered who or what he had heard this morning.

Caroline Driscol strolled down the stairs and into the kitchen still in her blue and white striped pajamas. "Good morning, Aunt Trudy," she said cheerily as she walked to the table and poured herself a glass of orange juice.

"Good morning, dear," Trudy replied, surprised at her niece's unusual good humor. Caroline was one who always woke up on the wrong side of the bed. "You are up rather early," Trudy commented, looking curiously at her niece. "I thought you would sleep in. It was rather late when we went to bed."

Too excited to go to sleep right away, they came home, changed into their bedclothes, and sat on the back porch, laughing and talking about the circus.

"I just wasn't tired," Caroline commented as she reached over and picked confetti from her aunt's hair. "You should have seen the look on your face," Caroline laughed.

She gazed absentmindedly through the screen for a bit and then dreamily walked out onto the back porch. A small smile played about her lips as Peter's face came to her mind. *He was so charming last night,* she thought to herself. A warm feeling came over her as she remembered him holding her hand when they exited the big top.

The ducks were already on the pond, and Caroline watched them swim around quacking and bobbing their heads up and down in the water. She sighed contentedly and sat in one of the wicker chairs sipping her orange juice.

Trudy poured water into the percolator and wondered curiously about Caroline's pleasant mood. Whatever the reason, she was pleased and smiled to herself as she measured the coffee and placed it in the pot. Turning the burner on, she sat the coffeepot on the stove and decided that since it was such a beautiful morning, they would have breakfast on the porch.

"Say, Aunt Trudy, have you seen my bracelet?" Caroline asked, peering through the back screen.

"Which bracelet?" her aunt asked, placing a skillet on the stove. She bent down, adjusted the burner, and turned around with a questioning look on her face.

"My new bracelet; the one Laura gave me for my birthday," she said sounding anxious. "I left it out here last night in the fruit bowl and it is gone. Did you bring it in last night?"

"No, Caroline, I didn't," Trudy replied, walking out onto the back porch. "Are you sure you didn't bring it in when you went to bed?"

"No, Aunt Trudy. I am positive," Caroline replied as she moved the fruit bowl and picked up one of the circus programs that Elizabeth left lying. "I put it here in the empty fruit bowl because I didn't want to drop it in the dark."

Trudy looked on the table then bent down and checked the floor. "Well, I declare. I wonder what could have come of it." They both stared at the empty fruit bowl as though the bracelet would suddenly reappear.

"Good morning," Henry said, stepping out onto the porch with a glass of orange juice in his hand. He stretched and took a deep breath of the morning air. "What a beautiful morning. It looks like I'm going to have to mow the grass today." He looked out across the yard for a moment then, puzzled by the silence, glanced across the porch Caroline and Trudy were staring at the fruit bowl like they had ever seen it before.

"Henry, did you pick up Caroline's bracelet last night?" Trudy asked, looking at her husband.

"No, I didn't see her bracelet. Why?" he asked, looking from one to the other.

Tears filled Caroline's eyes. "I left it right here in the fruit bowl last night, and it is gone this morning," she stated angrily as she walked across the porch and jerked the screen door open. Running through the kitchen and up the stairs, she headed for Elizabeth's room.

"Elizabeth!" she called, running into her bedroom. "Elizabeth, wake up!" she yelled, shaking her.

"What? What's wrong?" Elizabeth asked, sitting up with alarm in her eyes. "Is the house on fire?"

"No, of course not," Caroline replied angrily. "Do you smell any smoke?"

"Then leave me alone. I'm tired," she commented with a yawn and rolled back on her side.

Caroline grabbed her sister's arm. "Elizabeth, did you see my bracelet?" she questioned, grabbing the pillow she had placed over her head. Throwing it on the floor, she crawled across the bed and searched the top of the night table. "It is gone. I can't find it." She rummaged through the items on the table then slid off the other side of the bed.

Elizabeth sat up and watched her frantically look around the room and was totally shocked when she sat down in the rocker and burst into tears.

Springing from the bed, Elizabeth grabbed her sister by the shoulder. "Good grief, Caroline. You put it in the fruit bowl on the porch last night. Don't you remember?" She stood next to the rocker with her arm around her then bent down and looked into her face. "I saw you put it there," she assured her.

"I know, but it is not there this morning." Caroline looked up at Elizabeth with tears running down her cheeks. Springing from the rocker, she brushed passed Elizabeth, knocked her off balance, and sent her backward onto the bed. Elizabeth rolled to the other side and flew across the hall to Caroline's room. Standing in the doorway, she watched her sister check the floor, the night table, and the top of her bureau.

"Look under the bed," Elizabeth said as she glanced around the room and watched Caroline poke her head under the springs.

"It is not here!" Caroline cried, sitting in the middle of the floor.

Elizabeth ran downstairs, scurried through the dining room and into the kitchen. Stomping through the kitchen and out the back door, she shoved the screen open and into Uncle Henry's back, dumping orange juice down the front of his shirt.

"Sorry," she mumbled without looking at him and walked across the porch to the table. She stared down into the empty fruit bowl. "Where in the world is it?" she asked, looking at her aunt and uncle.

Caroline came through the door and crossed the porch to the table. Staring at the fruit bowl for a long moment, she looked up at Elizabeth. "We've been robbed," both girls spoke simultaneously.

Caroline looked at her uncle with tears in her eyes. "Someone stole my bracelet."

"Sheriff, my store was vandalized last night," Jack Reese's voice sounded agitated over the phone. "Can you come over and take a look?"

"Of course, I'll be right there," John replied. "Don't touch anything." Perplexed, he placed the phone in the cradle then picked it up again.

"Number, please," came Hazel's familiar voice.

"Hazel, ring my brother for me, will you?" he asked, wondering what was going on. This was starting out as a very strange day.

The telephone rang twice and Jim answered. "Hello," he said, standing at the back door with a cup of coffee in his hand, watching Sport chase a cat through the yard.

"Can you ride with me out to the Driscol's and to Reese's Market? I'm afraid someone's been up to some mischief last night."

"What's happened?" Jim asked, sitting his coffee cup on the counter.

"Jack just called and said the store was vandalized. About ten minutes prior to that, Henry called and said they were robbed."

"You must be kidding. A robbery here in Oak Grove?" Jim asked in total disbelief.

"I'm afraid so. I don't know as yet what exactly happened, but they both sounded pretty upset. I'll be over in about ten minutes, or do you want to meet me at the office?"

"No, come on by and I'll ride out with you. I'm up and ready to go," he replied, placing the hand piece back on the cradle. He stared at the tire swing hanging in the tree with a frown on his face. This was peculiar.

Sport barked and Jim pushed the screen open, letting him in, and continued to stare out into the backyard. Nothing like this had ever happened that he could remember—enforcing curfews, getting after some of the young folks when needed, and the occasional complaint about Cooley when he went on one of his binges, but even that hadn't happened in a long time. No real crime had ever been committed that he remembered.

His brother moved to Oak Grove just a few months before they did. Anne's aunt informed John that Oak Grove was in need of a new sheriff, and the town council wondered if perhaps he would be interested. John and Ann, visiting many times in the past, had come to love the small town and found the idea appealing. With the proposed generous salary and the large house, vacated by the previous sheriff, John felt he couldn't let the opportunity pass.

Not more than six months later, the deputy's wife became ill and they moved back East. The need for a deputy and fire chief for the new firehouse prompted John to call Jim and see if he would be interested in the City Council's proposal to fill both positions. Truman was two at the time, their apartment too small, and the idea of an increase in salary compelled Jim to look into the offer.

Taking a couple of extra days, they spent a long weekend with John and Anne; that was all it took. They both fell in love with the town and the people immediately.

A cup of coffee in each hand, Jim walked upstairs to their bedroom. "Here you go," Jim said, handing Jennifer her coffee. She listened with a frown as he related the news to her.

"That's very strange," she said, sitting in a chair by the window. "Did they break into the Driscol's home?"

"I don't know," he answered. "I guess we'll find out when we get there." Jim changed his shirt and ran a comb through his dark hair. Looking through the mirror at her, he shook his head and laid the comb down. "I can't imagine what's going on," he said, turning to face her. "Come on, John said he would be here in about ten minutes. Let's go wait on the porch." Taking a sip of coffee, he watched Jennifer step into her slippers then they headed down the stairs, both curious as to what was going on.

Jennifer watched a rabbit hop across the yard and a slight breeze touched her cheeks, carrying the fragrance of the roses along the porch. "It is so peaceful. I just can't imagine anyone doing anything like this." She picked up Simon's ball glove, walked to the porch swing, and sat next to Jim. It was unthinkable. Everyone in town knew each other. "Who in Oak Grove would want to cause trouble?"

"It might not be as bad as it sounds," Jim answered. "John said Jack and the Mayor were both pretty agitated when they called." Setting his coffee cup on the porch rail, he shook his head in pity for Henry as he thought about Mrs. Driscol's state of mind. "Here comes John now. I probably won't be gone too long," he said as he rose from the swing and walked across the porch and down the steps.

John pulled up and waved, "Morning, Jen."

"Good morning, John." She waved back and watched Jim walk to the other side of the car.

Simon opened the screen door and walked out rubbing his eyes. "Where are Dad and Uncle John going?" he asked, watching them drive away.

Sport, following him out, flopped down at the top step and watched a rabbit hop across the yard. His eyes followed in bored curiosity for a minute and too lazy to give chase, laid his head on his paws and closed his eyes.

"They had to run over to the square," Jennifer answered, brushing his hair away from his face. "They won't be gone long. Did you sleep well?"

Giving the swing a push with his toe, Simon picked up his ball glove and slipped his hand in it. He glanced up at Jennifer and grinned. "Yeah, I dreamed I was a lion tamer and the lions slept in my room on the floor." He punched a fist in the pocket of his glove and looked at Sport. He didn't even come close to anything fierce.

"I need a refill on my coffee." Standing up, she walked to the door and turned back to look at him. "What would you like for breakfast?" she asked, lifting the milk out of the milk box.

"I'm really not very hungry," he said as he laid the glove on the swing and picked up the Marvel Comic book Truman left outside.

"I guess not. With all that you ate last night, you shouldn't be hungry for a week." A frown suddenly crossed Jennifer's face and she gazed down the street. Could these two problems stem from someone in the circus? She certainly hoped not. Yet, that would seem to be more logical than someone in Oak Grove. What time did Jim say the circus was to leave last night, or had it?

John pulled up in front of Reese's Market and stared in amazement. Jack Reese stood on the sidewalk with Old Ben, Willy, Hank, Gerald, and Sam Cranston. Fruit and vegetables were strewn all over the sidewalk and out into the street. Flowerpots from the window ledges were thrown on the ground, and brown produce bags were scattered everywhere. One of the windows was broken, probably the result of a thrown piece of fruit or vegetable.

"Sheriff, would you look at this mess?" Jack said, more agitated now than he had been on the phone. "Now who would do such a thing?" he asked, running his hand through his thinning hair.

"Is anything missing inside?" John asked as he glanced at the open door and watched Jim walk around the side of the building.

"Not that I can see," Jack said, looking more confused than anything. "They didn't even go inside. I unlocked the door myself when I got here this morning."

"It appears to be just meanness if you ask me," Sam Cranston spoke up, stepping over some splattered tomatoes. "There is no reason for such nonsense," he complained, looking at Old Ben.

John walked through the mess and into the store. Sure enough, a cantaloupe lay on the floor in the middle of the broken glass, confirming his suspicion.

Jim walked in and looked around. "Everything looks okay out back. How about in here? Is anything missing?"

"Jack says no. They didn't even come in," John replied, shaking his head as he turned around and looked at him. "Nothing outside or around back at all?"

"Only some overturned crates," Jim said as he followed his brother outside. Willy was looking at the mess of tomatoes on the ground with a frown on his face.

"Did any of you hear anything?" John asked, looking at the agitation clearly evident in the men's faces.

"I didn't hear a thing," Old Ben said. "I guess if anyone would have heard anything, it would have been me or maybe you, Sam," he said, looking at Samuel Cranston.

"I'm like you, Ben, I didn't hear a thing," Samuel answered. "My lands, you would think I would have heard something."

Willy, Hank, and Gerald all confirmed the fact that they had heard nothing either.

John looked around at the mess. "Well, we are going to have to check with everyone in the next block or so. Maybe someone heard or saw something," he said, looking at Jim. "I'm sorry, Jack. It appears to be nothing more than what you said. It is just vandalism, plain and simple." Irritation crossed John's face as he stepped over some cucumbers. "We'll try to find out who did this."

"What about someone from the circus?" Gerald Williams questioned, looking at the other men. "That's who I would check with first."

"I don't know. They were supposed to leave about midnight last night," John answered, looking at the group of men.

"Well, they could have done it before they left," Sam Cranston commented irritably as he picked up a couple of apples.

John nodded his head, acknowledging the possibility, then raised both hands. "Let's not start jumping to all kinds of conclusions. Jim and I will ride out to the Fairground and see if they are gone, and I'll make some phone calls to see if Chesterville had any problems."

Jim looked at the bewilderment on Jack's face and felt sorry him. He was so meticulous about everything and took great pride in the stocking of his shelves and produce tables.

"We'll let you know if we find anything out, Jack," John said, shaking his head as he looked around again. "What a mess."

"Hand me a broom," Old Ben told Jack. "I'll help you start cleaning this up."

"Let's ride out to the Driscol's and find out what's going on there before we start questioning the neighbors," Jim said, getting in the car. "Poor Jack, I bet this was a shock to him this morning."

Elizabeth sat on the step attempting to comfort her sister when Sheriff Walker and Jim pulled into the drive and up the lane. "Look, Caroline. The Sheriff is here. He will find the thief," she exclaimed, patting her hand reassuringly.

Henry and Trudy Driscol both appeared on the porch when they heard the car in the drive. "Oh, Sheriff, I am so glad you are here. We have been robbed! Robbed, can you believe it? The thief came right up on our porch. Right here where I am standing," Trudy exclaimed as she wiped her forehead with her handkerchief and took a deep, trembly breath. "We sat right here on the porch last night after we came home. He could have been there by the pond watching us the whole time. Oh, dear. What is to become of our town?" She took a seat in one of the wicker chairs and dabbed at her eyes. "You have to do something, Sheriff; both of you," she said, looking anxiously from John to Jim. "This kind of crime cannot go on in Oak Grove. It cannot be tolerated."

"Now, Trudy, calm down," Henry said. "Let's allow the Sheriff to get about his business." He patted her hand and sat in the chair next to her. "Sit down, Sheriff, and you too, Jim."

John took a seat at the table and looked at Henry. "Can you start at the beginning and tell us what happened?" He glanced around the porch and hoped Mrs. Driscol would let her husband do the talking.

"We came home from the circus and sat out here on the porch talking about the evening's activity." Henry looked at his niece. "Caroline took her bracelet off and put it here in this fruit bowl."

John and Jim both glanced at the white, milk glass bowl sitting in the middle of the table. John also took note of a radio and gold clock on a small table between two wicker chairs. Several plants were scattered around the porch and a wicker shelf against the wall closest to the kitchen contained books, magazines, and other various items.

"I didn't want to lose it," Caroline said with tears in her eyes. "It was a birthday present."

Sheriff Walker nodded at her then looked back at Henry.

"Well, this morning she came down to get it and it was gone," Henry said, looking at his niece and hoping she wouldn't start crying again. He couldn't cope with tears. He never could and often wondered why, in heaven's name, he hadn't gotten use to them by now with three females in the house.

"Did you perhaps take it in the house when you went to bed?" Jim asked, looking at the young girl.

"No, I am positive," she answered. "At first, I thought maybe Aunt Trudy or Uncle Henry picked it up and brought it inside. When they said they didn't, I thought maybe Elizabeth did." Tears formed in her eyes and she looked away.

"Sheriff Walker, we have looked everywhere, and the bracelet is not here," Elizabeth said, getting up from the step where she sat next to her sister. She walked over to him, folded her arms across her chest, and tapped her toe impatiently "Someone came up on this porch and stole my sister's bracelet. You need to find out who took it."

"Elizabeth, sit over there," Uncle Henry commanded sternly. He gestured to his niece to sit on the swing, and the thought crossed his mind that she acted like a little vigilante at times. He wished she were a bit more like Caroline or Trudy who were all talk and tears. But no, Elizabeth was ready to jump into action at a moment's notice. He stared at her until she complied with his wishes and then turned back to the Sheriff.

"But he has to understand that someone stole it and. . . ." Elizabeth's voice trailed off and she leaned back in her chair when she saw Uncle Henry's stern look. She could wrap Aunt Trudy around her finger and fool Mary some of the time, but Uncle Henry was a different matter altogether. Elizabeth knew she could only go so far with him.

John glanced away from Jim and looked back at Henry. "Now the bracelet is missing, but we can't be positive yet that it was stolen."

"It was stolen," Elizabeth muttered, refusing to look in her uncle's direction.

John suppressed a grin and continued, "We'll do everything we can to find out what happened to your bracelet," John said gently, looking at Caroline.

Turning to Henry, he shook his head and leaned back in the chair. "We've had another incident last night." He hesitated but knew it would be all over town within the hour so he may as well say something. Glancing at Trudy, he prepared for her reaction. "Reese's Market was vandalized sometime last night."

"Oh, for ever more!" Trudy gasped. "Do you think it is a gang? I've heard of gangs of criminals coming into a town and taking over. What is going to happen to Oak Grove?" she asked, looking at her husband with something close to panic on her face. "It's always been such a nice, peaceful place. Now look what it has become," she exclaimed in anger, "All because of that circus! You mark my words, we will be sorry it ever came to Oak Grove. It could be a cover for criminals, headed up by the big boss."

Henry raised his eyebrows and looked in disbelief at his wife. She evidently had been listening to Captain Midnight with Elizabeth again.

Sheriff Walker leaned forward in his chair. All he needed was Trudy to get hysterical and get the whole town in an uproar. "Now, Mrs. Driscol, I am positive there is not a gang of criminals in Oak Grove. I think what happened last night at Reese's was someone just wanting to cause mischief, and I believe that Caroline's bracelet is going to show up." He hoped he sounded convincing and glanced at Elizabeth, noting the frown on her face as she rolled her eyes in disbelief and sighed loudly.

Jim quickly spoke up. "We've had the same thing happen at our house. You can't find something, you are convinced that it is gone for good, and in a couple of days it shows up."

"Oh, I do hope you are right. Yes. Yes, we've had that happen before too. Henry, do you recollect that time we couldn't find your father's silver letter opener?" she asked and then looked peevishly at the Sheriff. "I sat down to read one afternoon and there it was; right there in my book. I must have used it to mark my page." Trudy sat back in her chair, calming down a bit, and looked at Caroline. "We are going to turn this house upside down until we find your bracelet, dear."

"We are going to walk around the property a bit just to check things out," John said as he and Jim both rose from their chairs. "Hopefully, you will find your bracelet somewhere in the house, Caroline. Henry, will you come with us?"

Stepping from the porch, they headed around the side of the house looking for evidence of anyone's presence. "Henry, did you hear or see anything unusual last night?" John asked as they walked down toward the pond.

"No. Sheriff, everything was just as normal as could be." The Mayor removed his hat and wiped the top of his head with his handkerchief. "I don't know what to think. Someone could have been right down here by the blackberry bushes, and we would have never seen them. The girls used to play hide and seek, and this was one of their favorite hiding places."

The three men stood silent for a moment, looking across the road at the pasture and the forest beyond. None of them were able to make any sense out of what had happened.

"You believe it was stolen, don't you?" Henry asked, looking at the Sheriff.

"I would hope it wasn't, but yes, I think it probably was," John said, glancing at Jim. "I wouldn't say anything to Mrs. Driscol or the girls until we figure out just what is going on."

"No, of course not. Trudy and Caroline get too upset, and Elizabeth, well. . . ." Henry looked at both men and shook his head. "I don't know what to make of it."

"Neither do I, Henry, but we'll see what we can find out," John replied as the three men turned and retraced their steps through the yard to the drive.

"I can't believe this happened. Did they do much damage to Jack's store?" he asked genuinely concerned.

"They broke a window and made a mess of the fruit and vegetables,'" Jim answered as he opened the car door. "Thankfully, he wasn't robbed."

"Well, Henry, we are going to be checking around town. If you would happen to find Caroline's bracelet, let me know." John got in the car and slammed the door. "We will let you know if we find out anything."

Backing down the drive, John looked at his brother. "What do you think?" he asked as he headed toward town.

"I think someone is messing around, but I don't have a clue other than. . . ." He looked at John as they passed the empty Fairground.

"Unless what?" John asked, knowing what he was going to say.

"Maybe it was one of the circus people. There were a lot of young boys working in different areas. And they left Oak Grove late last night," Jim commented, watching his brother nod his head.

"Yep, I was thinking the same thing. If that is the case, I guess we can be thankful nothing worse happened, and it is over and done with."

Mike dropped Leah off at Melba's and headed to Ned's for a haircut. "I think you'll find her foot much better this morning," he chuckled as she got out of the car.

"I hope so," she answered, closing the car door. She watched him drive away, puzzled by his remark.

Walking up the sidewalk, Leah noted the geraniums on the porch. *What a vibrant red color they are*, she thought. Tapping on the door, she heard Melba singing. Leah smiled to herself. Melba had such a beautiful voice. She remembered how shy and withdrawn she had been when she first came to Oak Grove.

She had willingly joined the choir when asked, and at the discovery of such a rare talent, was often asked to sing alone. Melba was like a flower opening in the spring. Her singing released a joy and confidence in her that was beautiful, and she emerged a vibrant, strong, loving Christian woman.

"Leah," Melba said with a bright smile, "what a nice surprise. Come in." She opened the screen and stepped back. "Please, come on back into the kitchen. I was just fixing some iced tea. Would you care for a glass?"

"That sounds nice," Leah replied, following her into the kitchen. Her foot was much better. In fact, it did not appear that anything was wrong with it at all.

Melba's kitchen was a soft green color with white eyelet café curtains adorning the windows. Leah sat her handbag next to her on the floor and took a seat in one of the yellow cushioned chrome chairs. A white tablecloth, with red apples embroidered on the four corners and in the center, covered the table. Green scatter rugs lay in front of the sink, at the back door, and in the doorway leading to the living room.

"Mike is getting his haircut this morning so I thought I would ride along and check to see how your foot is."

"Oh, that," Melba laughed "there was nothing wrong with my foot." She handed Leah a glass of iced tea and answered peevishly, "I just thought it was a good way to get Willy's attention." She took a seat across the table, passed the sugar bowl, and smiled mischievously at her.

Leah burst into laughter. "Why didn't you just strike up a conversation with him instead of going to all that trouble?" she asked, amused.

"I don't know. I haven't been around him that much and really do not know him at all." She stirred the sugar in her glass of tea and laid the teaspoon down on the table. She looked at Leah and confessed, "I find him just a little intimidating for some reason."

Melba gazed through the window a moment and then looked back at Leah. "I guess intimidating is probably not an accurate description. He makes me feel. . . . I don't know," she said softly and then grinned. "Do you know, Leah, that he has black curly hair and very pretty blue eyes?"

Leah smiled at the young girl sitting across from her. "Yes, of course, I knew that. You never noticed before?"

"Well, no. I never paid that much attention. He is always at the garage, and I don't have a car. I have never seen him up close; that is until last night," she said grinning. "He is very handsome."

"Yes, he is," Leah remarked, now understanding her husband's behavior. He knew all along what Melba had been up to.

"Do you know if he has a friend? I mean, does he have a female friend?" Melba asked. "I really don't know anything about him."

"Not that I am aware," Leah answered. "Willy came to Oak Grove, I think, about the age of fourteen. It was before Mike was called to pastor the church. I know that he came one summer to visit his aunt and uncle, and while he was here his mother passed away. I do not know anything about his father, but Willy remained here with the Stantons. I believe they went through some rough times, but he stayed. Then his aunt died, and he and his Uncle William lived alone together."

Leah spoke quietly and watched the emotions cross Melba's face. "His uncle taught him everything he knew about cars, and as he got older, Willy looked after him. Then Pearl Harbor happened and Willy left along with several others. He was wounded terribly and almost lost his leg."

"That explains the limp," Melba said with tears in her eyes.

Leah nodded. "Then shortly after that, his Uncle William died, and he has been alone ever since," Leah said softly, feeling her own eyes moisten.

"Well," Melba said, wiping a tear from her eye, "that explains a lot doesn't it. I would think he would be afraid to love anyone. I mean, he must feel that everyone he loves, dies."

"I think you are probably right, Melba." Leah was impressed with the insight the young girl possessed. "But if I were you, I think I would limp around on that foot in public for the next couple of days. That way, Willy just may feel the need to check on you." Melba looked at Leah and they both laughed.

"You sure have a nice head of hair, Pastor," Ned commented, running his comb through Mike's thick, wavy hair. Mike was not real sure about the compliment since he was the only one in the shop who had much on his head at all. Phillip Driscol, Pete Williams, and Tom Baker, all with a sparse amount, sat in wooden chairs waiting their turn.

The door opened and Clifford Charles, Oak Grove's Dentist, walked in. "Good morning," he said, taking the last empty chair.

"Morning, Cliff," everyone replied at the same time.

He removed his hat and held it in his hand. "Did any of you have anything stolen last night?" he asked with a frown on his face as he looked from one to the other.

Ned paused, holding his scissors in midair. "Stolen? No, why?" he asked, looking at Cliff in surprise.

"We did. Teresa's purse was taken right out of the car last night." He held his hat in his hands, absentmindedly running his fingers around the brim and looked at them with a pained expression on his face.

"Well, I declare; you don't say," Tom said in surprise, glancing around at the other men, then back at Cliff.

"That's right. She tossed it into the front seat when we left the Fairground. I actually sat on it when I got in the car." He stared at the hat in his hand for a minute then glanced up with a perplexed look on his face. "I just left the Sheriff's office, and he said Reese's Market was vandalized last night and the Driscols had some jewelry stolen."

"No," Phillip Driscol said. "Who would do such a thing?"

"Well, I'll swan," Pete commented, staring at Cliff. "Does the Sheriff have any ideas what's going on?"

"If I was a betting man, I would say it was some of those circus people," Tom Baker interjected angrily. "They didn't pull out of here until after midnight last night."

Mike spoke up. "Now, hold on fellas; we can't blame anyone until we know more about what happened." He looked at the confused look on Cliff's face and asked, "Does the Sheriff have any idea who might have done it?"

"Not that I know of," Cliff answered. "I just find it hard to believe something like this has happened. We've never had any trouble before."

"Well, it has to be someone from the circus unless someone in Oak Grove has turned into a thief," Phillip Driscol, commented, sitting back in his chair with a scowl on his face.

The sound of someone running passed through Mike's mind as he watched Ned trim his hair. If it was someone from the circus and they left at midnight, then who did he hear in the woods this morning?

"There you go, Pastor," Ned said, removing the cape from his neck. Picking up a small brush, he swiped the small hairs from the back of Mike's neck and grabbed the broom.

"Thank you, Ned." Mike stood up and dropped fifty cents into the shaving mug on the shelf.

"You're welcome." Ned propped his arm on the end of the broom and stared through the window with a frown on his face. Mike studied him for a moment, knowing he was upset. Ned was one of those people who saw nothing but good in everyone, and for him to think a thief was running loose in Oak Grove was something he couldn't fathom.

"I'm sure everything will be all right. The Sheriff will figure it all out," Mike said, patting him on the shoulder.

Glancing in the mirror, he checked his haircut. "Good job, Ned."

Accusations and concerns about circuses in general filled the shop, and Mike noted the anger on the men's faces as he walked to the door. He paused and winced when he heard a couple of possibilities regarding certain individuals in town. *This could get out of hand*, he thought.

He glanced around the shop at the men. "Fellas, let's not jump to conclusions about anything, OK? It would be a terrible thing to blame an innocent person."

Tom looked at him with a frown on his face. "Well, blame it all, Pastor, someone has to be the villain," he replied then glanced away.

Mike sighed and opened the door. "I am sure everything can be explained. Cliff, I hate to hear about Teresa's purse, but hopefully, the Sheriff will recover it."

"Thank you, Pastor. I hope so too."

Mike stepped outside, walked to the car, and glanced over at the square. He hoped it wasn't anyone from the circus. That would leave a taint on the memory of what had been an enjoyable event. But if it was not someone from the circus, was it someone in town? That would be even worse. Regardless, he needed to talk to the Sheriff and tell him what he had heard this morning in the woods.

Willy glanced up from the tire he was repairing when Mike pulled into the station. Laying the tire down, he walked out to the car. "Good morning, Mike," Willy said. "How much do you need?"

"Fill it up, Willy," Mike said as he got out, leaned against the car, and glanced around the station. Willy kept everything in its proper place, swept clean, and the grass mowed. William Stanton always took pride in the place when he was alive and had passed that on to Willy. *He would be proud*, Mike thought.

"Can you believe what happened to Reese's last night?" Willy asked, pumping the gas.

"I heard about it," Mike replied. "I understand they made quite a mess."

"There was fruit and vegetables thrown everywhere. They even splattered tomatoes on the ground and threw a cantaloupe through the window." Anger flared in his blue eyes and he looked away.

Mike often wondered about the anger in Willy. He knew some of it came from the war, but there was something more. He tried numerous times to reach him but never quite made it and prayed constantly that he could break down the barrier. Mike finally realized he had done as much as he could for the present and accepted the fact that perhaps the Lord planned to use someone else to get through to him.

Melba came to mind, and he glanced at Willy. "I guess you were able to get Melba home all right last night?" he asked, watching his face for any reaction.

"She just twisted her foot. I am sure it will be okay in a couple of days." He placed the nozzle back on the side of the pump and glanced at Mike.

"I suppose you are going to check on her," Mike commented, controlling the grin that threatened. Willy had fallen for one of the oldest female tricks in the world and did not even know it.

"I dropped Leah off at her house this morning while I went to Ned's for a haircut. I guess I better go pick her up."

"Mrs. Daniels sure is a nice lady," Willy commented, screwing the gas cap back on. "How's your oil? Do you want me to check it?"

"I'm kind of fond of her myself," Mike replied as he reached for his wallet. "No, my oil is fine, thanks. Someone probably ought to check on Melba this evening. A twisted foot will swell throughout the day, especially if she is up on it much. I don't know if Leah will be able to get back today or not," Mike said and abruptly changed the subject. "It's fifteen cents a gallon now. Price is going up, isn't it?"

"It is. Texaco raised it a penny a couple of days ago. That will be ninety cents," Willy glanced away, trying to act nonchalant. "I guess Mercy will probably check on Melba. She lives right next door. Here's your change," he said, handing Mike his dime.

"Probably," Mike replied as he opened the car door. "I wouldn't want her to think you rude though. I mean since you had to help her home and know she's injured." Mike closed the door and looked thoughtfully through the windshield "Of course, Melba is such a nice person, she probably wouldn't think anything about it at all if you didn't take the time to check on her. I wouldn't worry too much about it." Mike started the engine. "I'll talk to you later, Willy. Take care of yourself." He drove away, leaving Willy standing next to the gas pump with a confused look on his face.

John and Jim Walker sat in the Sheriff's office discussing the facts as they knew them. Someone deliberately vandalized Reese's Market but did not rob it, a bracelet was taken from the Driscol's back porch, and a purse removed from the front seat of Cliff Charles' car that was sitting in their driveway. No one heard anything out of the ordinary in all of the cases, and there were no clues to be found.

"I would suspect someone from the circus as my first inclination," Jim said, sitting back in the chair with his feet propped up on his brother's desk. "But now I am wondering what Pastor Mike heard in the woods behind the church this morning."

"Hmm," John mumbled, beating the end of a pencil on the desk. "If someone from the circus was the guilty party, they would have been gone by this morning." He tossed the pencil on the desk. "Unless the preacher heard an animal in the woods and it was not a person at all, which would clear that idea up somewhat."

"He could be mistaken, I guess," Jim replied "I don't know. As much time as he spends in the woods hunting and fishing, I tend to think he would recognize the sound of an animal over that of a man running."

"Well, you are probably right about that," John said as he looked across the desk at his brother. "And he didn't see anyone or find anything suspicious, did he?"

Jim sat with his hands behind his head staring out the window. "Just heard someone running. He said he had been leaning against a tree enjoying the morning and figured whoever it was didn't see him." Jim removed his feet from the desk, stood up, and looked out the window. "There's Jen. She had to make a trip to the library so I told her to pick me up. I'm going to go home and have some lunch."

"Do you think it could be any of the kids in town?" John asked, also rising. He grabbed his cap and put it on his head.

"I don't know. I can't imagine who," Jim replied. "Call me later if you find anything Otherwise, I'm going to go home and try to spend the afternoon relaxing. Jen wants me to hang curtain rods. It seems Spiegel had a sale she couldn't pass up. Then I plan to listen to the Cards and Dodgers."

John followed Jim out the door. "Lunch sounds good. I think I'll run over to the café and then talk to some of the neighbors that we didn't get around to this morning. I'll talk to you later this evening," he said, waving at Jennifer as they walked out the door.

"All right, I'll be around the house all day. Call me if you need me."

John watched them drive off and pulled the keys from his pocket. He would check with Mercy and Melba and then ride over to Ron's house. He also needed to run by Cliff Charles' house and check on that situation also. Then he believed he would go home too.

Laura closed the cover of the Nancy Drew book and slid it across her bed. Noelle said The Secret of Shadow Ranch was really good, so she had checked it out at the library. Because of the circus and Caroline's party, today was the first opportunity she had to read it and was frustrated. She had read page seven three times and still didn't know what it said.

Putting her chin in her hands, she stared across the room at Shari's Raggedy Ann doll, hanging halfway off the side of the bed where she tossed it. Jimmy ran upstairs yelling that Dad was going to hang the tire swing in the tree, and she threw it across the room as she ran out.

Poor Caroline, Laura thought Elizabeth called early this morning and gave her the whole story. "I will punch their lights out when I find out who did it," she stated angrily and then said she had to go. "Uncle Henry said I am too sassy, and I am not to use the telephone for the rest of the weekend," she explained hurriedly and hung up.

At lunch, Dad also told them about Reese's Market and Mrs. Charles' purse.

"I would get those people and make them pay," Jimmy said with a mouthful of baloney.

"Jimmy, don't talk with your mouth full," Mom said, giving him a shake of her head.

"Dad, do they have any idea who stole the stuff?" Johnny asked, surprised that someone in town would treat a neighbor that way.

"No, the Sheriff is investigating and trying to come up with a lead of some kind, but everything seems to be a dead end."

Laura finished eating, and after asking to be excused, went to her room to read. She felt bad for Caroline and didn't want to hear any more about it. She knew how pleased she was with the bracelet; besides it was hers. No one had the right to come to your home and take something that didn't belong to him. It just wasn't right.

Laughter drifted in the window and she heard Johnny yell, "Look out, Jimmy! You're going to hit the garage." More laughter followed, and she could hear Dad's deep voice as he laughed and called, "Are you all right, Son?"

She heard Jimmy's muffled "yeah," and Shari's laughter floated through the window.

Laura slid off the bed and walked downstairs, wondering what was causing all the commotion. Passing through the kitchen, she stopped at the cookie jar. It was a brown dog with black ears and had been in their kitchen ever since she could remember. She curiously wondered where it ever came from as she grabbed a couple of cookies then walked out the back door to find Jimmy crawling out of the tire that Dad was supposed to hang in the tree.

"You are going to get hurt," Mom was saying to which no one was paying any attention.

"Get back in, Jimmy," Johnny said. "We'll try it again, and this time don't wiggle around." Holding the tire steady, he waited while Jimmy molded himself inside, and with a shove, the tire and Jimmy rolled across the back lawn over and over. Dad and Mom both laughed, Shari jumped up and down squealing, and Johnny ran alongside the tire with a big grin on his face.

Laura took a bite of cookie and walked down the steps. Jimmy hit the fence and fell out of the tire. He stood up and staggered several steps to the right before falling down. Laura watched her dad lean his head back on the red, metal glider and wipe his eyes as he laughed. Mom laid her head on his shoulder and laughed along with him.

Feeling warm and secure, she sat down on the blanket by the tree and Midnight crawled into her lap. *If someone is so desperate they have to steal, then that is their problem,* she thought to herself. *No one can steal this.*

Shari ran to the fence and grabbed the tire. "I want to try it," she cried, sticking one of her legs inside.

"Wait a minute," Johnny said. "Let's take the tire to the back of the yard first." He grabbed her by the arm, pulled her out, and rolled it towards the back fence.

"Shari, maybe you shouldn't," Mom called and then looked at Laura. "Are you finished reading?" she asked.

"I couldn't get interested," Laura said, leaning back on her arms. "Besides it sounded like you all were having too much fun out here."

Shari crawled inside the tire, fit her body as tightly as she could, and gripped both sides.

"Are you ready?" Johnny asked. "Hold on tight," he yelled and gave the tire a shove. Running along beside it, he laughed at Shari's squeals as the tire continued to roll over and over through the yard. It continued on passed the tree, alongside the garage, and across the driveway before it ran into the honeysuckle bushes and turned over. Shari lay still, not moving. Mike jumped and was across the drive by the time Johnny pulled her from the tire.

"Is she all right, Mike?" Mom asked as she and Laura stood holding onto each other.

Mike picked his youngest daughter up in his arms. Her eyes were closed but she was breathing.

"She probably just fainted," Jimmy said. "That would be just like a girl," he commented, peering up over his dad's arm to take a look.

Mike looked anxiously into Shari's face and gave a sigh of relief as she opened her eyes. "Are you all right, baby?" he asked, hugging her to him.

"Yes, Daddy, but I think I have to throw up." Turning her over, he allowed her to comply with her wish right there beneath the honeysuckle vines.

Chapter 10

Early evening brought relief from the heat of the day. Oak Grove suppers were over, and folks went about their normal routine. Small children got baths, older ones finished dishes, fathers read the paper, and many sought out their porches in hopes of catching a small breeze.

Brenton and Preston sat on the front step trying to come up with an answer to the recent events and decided they were just as confused as their dad.

Brenton broke a twig from the lilac bush and tossed it to the ground. "Everyone thinks it was someone from the circus."

"I know," Preston replied. "Do you think whoever did it is still around here? I heard Dad tell Uncle Jim that Pastor Mike heard someone in the woods this morning."

Brenton shrugged his shoulders. "I don't know. Everyone who came in the drugstore while I was there had a different opinion. Mrs. Charles said she heard that someone tried to rob the bank, but Mr. Williams told her it wasn't so."

"Gee whiz, where did she get that idea?" Preston asked. "Wouldn't that be something?"

"Are you two going to listen to the ball game?" John asked through the front screen. "It is going to start in about five minutes."

He shook his head and walked back to his chair. *Rob the bank? Where in the world did that come from?*

He massaged his temples and rested his head on the back of the chair. The only think he ended up with today was a headache. Perplexed, he closed his eyes and tried to relax. No one in town saw or heard anything out of the ordinary and that was the most puzzling of all. One would think someone would have noticed something.

Brenton and Preston let the screen slam behind them as they came in, jarring his thoughts. He opened one eye and watched them flop down on the couch.

"John, will you put those pajamas on Garrett please?" Ann called from the upstairs hall. Garrett, head wet from his bath, appeared in the doorway carrying a pair of wadded up, red and blue pajamas.

"Come here, buddy," John said, watching him cross the room rubbing his eyes. "Sit up here and let's get these on you." He retrieved the pajamas, slipped the bottoms on, and buttoned the top.

Garrett rubbed his eyes, yawned, and leaned back contentedly on his lap.

John laid his head back again and glanced down at Jordan and Josiah lying in the floor. Jordan's eyes were droopy and Josiah lay on his belly with his chin propped in his hands, staring at several army men positioned in a strategic battle plan. Last night had been a late evening for all of them.

Anne walked into the living room and paused in the doorway. *What a peaceful scene,* she thought and smiled to herself. It was a rarity indeed, in this house, to see one grown man and five boys all sitting quietly and barely moving. If she weren't so tired she would run back upstairs for her new Kodak Brownie and take a picture. Crossing the room, she stepped around Jo and Jordan and sat in the chair next to John, noting the frown on his face.

She knew he was confused and perplexed with the happenings in Oak Grove and didn't have a clue who the culprit was. It seemed everyone in Oak Grove had called today wanting details of what happened, asking if anyone had been arrested, or offering opinions that ranged from one extreme to the other. The last straw was when Mildred Reese called and wanted to know if he was going to organize a posse. John finally told Hazel not to put any more calls through unless it was an emergency, Jim, or Mayor Driscol.

Jennifer called and said they were having the same problem and laughingly said to be sure and thank John for putting a limit on his calls. It seemed that since they couldn't get through to the Sheriff, they were having Hazel ring Jim, and Jennifer said she was about to pull her hair out.

Anne smiled to herself, thinking how tickled they became when Jen told her The First Bank of Chesterville had been hit and a rumor was going around that a crime spree was spreading all over the county.

"Do you want me to get you something to drink or something for your headache?" she asked John quietly.

"No, thanks, hon. I took an Anacin about thirty minutes ago," John replied, opening one eye. "It's easing up a little bit."

The National Anthem came across the Philco and Brenton and Preston settled on opposite ends of the sofa, waiting for the game.

Preston slid down to make himself comfortable and kicked Brenton's feet. "Sorry," he said, pulling his legs up.

Brenton grabbed a sofa pillow and slid onto the floor in front of the radio. Punching the pillow until it met with his approval, he settled on his back ready for the game to begin.

"Cardinals are facing the Dodgers again tonight here at Ebbett's Field." Cardinal Broadcaster, Harry Caray, announced. "Starting pitchers are Howie Pollet for the Cardinals and Rex Barney for the Dodgers."

"What do you think, Dad?" Brenton asked. "Do you think they'll win tonight?"

"They only lost by two last night, 7–5," John answered. "Pollet's pitching tonight. I think we'll beat them." Knowing his youngest son was about asleep, John shifted Garrett to a more comfortable position and commented in a quieter voice, "Although, they did lose last week when Pollet was pitching."

"Musial is up," Preston said with a grin as the roar of the crowd came across the radio. "Listen to the fans."

"He's my favorite player and the best player of all time," Brenton remarked, looking at the ceiling.

Harry Caray continued his commentary on "Stan the Man," while they waited for Rex Barney on the pitcher's mound.

"Gee whiz," Preston complained impatiently, "why don't he just pitch the ball. Musial's going to hit it anyway."

"I hope he knocks it out of the park." Brenton rolled to his side and faced the radio in anticipation. "I wish we could go to a game sometime."

Anne looked at Garrett, sound asleep, and rose from her chair. "Come on, let's go to bed," she said, lifting him from his daddy's lap. John watched her walk to the stairs carrying Garrett on her shoulder, and once again, thought what a good wife and mother Anne was. Laying his head back, he closed his eyes and listened to the rest of the game as the Cardinals proceeded to beat the Dodgers 5–1.

John's eyes opened, and he was instantly alert. Something awakened him, and he lay still, wondering what it was. There it was again! The bell in the bell tower! He reached for the bedside lamp and switched it on.

"What is it, John?" Anne asked as she sat up and watched him slip into his trousers "Is that the bell in the square ringing?" she asked, suddenly wide-awake "What is wrong?"

"I don't know," John said, putting his shirt on, "but I'm going to go find out." Hurriedly he slipped his socks and shoes on.

Anne grabbed her robe and followed him out the bedroom door, a feeling of anxiety creeping up on her.

Brenton and Preston met them in the hall. "Why is the bell ringing?" Preston asked, following his dad down the stairs with Brenton at his heels.

"Dad, what is happening?" Brenton asked.

"I don't know," John replied, grabbing his keys from the table in the hall. "Anne, lock the door behind me," he said, putting his cap on.

"Lock the door?" she asked bewildered. They had not locked a door in the ten years they had lived here. "What on earth for?"

Patting her arm, he smiled reassuringly at her. "Just to make me feel better. I don't think there is probably anything to worry about, but I would feel better if you did. Brenton, you go make sure the back door is locked, and I'll be back as soon as I can."

"Why can't I go with you?" Brenton asked, following John to the door.

"Because I need you to stay here with Mom and the boys. Now do as I say," John replied, looking at him and then Preston. "Both of you" Turning, he walked out the door to the car.

"John, wait up. I'll ride along with you," Pastor Mike called as he jogged across the two empty lots that separated their homes.

The combined fragrance of lilac and honeysuckle floated in the night air as he crossed the field. Lilacs grew in abundance, forming a tall hedge behind a small cottage at the back of the lot that was known as the old Parker place.

Mr. Parker, an old bachelor, died several years ago and with no known kin and no will on record, the house sat empty. Honeysuckle claimed both sides of the property, and several giant oaks offered shade. An enormous weeping willow tree grew right in the middle of the lot and was used as a refuge of sorts by those playing in the field. A hearty abundance of wild flowers sprang up in spite of repeated trampling.

John waved his hand, got in the car, and turned the key in the ignition. He pulled the car lights on just as Mike reached the other side. "What's going on?" he asked, slamming the door.

"I don't know. Let's go find out."

Anne turned the key in the lock and watched them drive away. She looked at the key, and a strange feeling came over her as she stared at it in the palm of her hand. She had locked her door.

"I wonder what is going on," Brenton said, coming from the kitchen "The back door is locked." He looked at her with a confused expression. "We never lock our doors." Stepping between his mom and Preston, they stared through the glass out into the night.

Willy and Ron met on the sidewalk in front of their houses. "Come on," Willy called, heading down the street. He wore a pair of overalls but had not bothered with a shirt or taken time to lace his shoes.

Ron was amazed at his speed. It didn't appear his bad leg hindered him much. Running by the garage and the Cranston Hotel, they made their way to the square and the bell tower, quickly followed by Hank and Young Ben. The four men stared up at the bell. It was no longer ringing, and no one was in sight.

Willy looked around the square. "Now, what is going on around here?" he asked, looking at the others.

Gerald Williams and Eli Smith drove up and jumped out of the car, slamming both doors. "What's wrong?" Eli called as he hurried across the square.

John and Pastor Mike arrived and headed to the tower just as Jim drove up.

The Sheriff looked from one man to the other. "What's the matter? Who rang the bell?" he asked, looking at the group of men.

"Ron and I were the first two here," Willy spoke up. "The bell was ringing when we ran by the garage, but when we got here there was no one in sight. No one."

"What in tarnation is all the commotion about?" Old Ben asked, standing in the dark in his pajamas and bathrobe.

John looked at Jim in confusion. "Did you see anyone run away from the square as you drove up?"

"No, not a soul," Jim replied, staring at Hank and wanting to laugh. He had on a pair of striped pajama bottoms and a plaid shirt.

Michael Madison slammed his car door just as his brother-in-law drove up. "What's happened, Michael?" Alan asked, jumping out of his Oldsmobile. "What's going on?"

"I don't know. Let's find out."

"Did any of you other men see anyone?" John asked, looking from one to the other. Receiving only negative responses and confused expressions, he sighed and walked over to the tower. "I don't know what's happening to this place," he grumbled as he climbed the steps and looked around.

Jim followed, thinking the same as his brother. Standing at the top of the tower, both men looked around. Except for those gathered on the grass below, the place looked quiet and peaceful. Street lamps shed their light on the square, and the night breeze stirred the leaves. The bandstand was empty, shadows from the trees danced across its roof, and honeysuckle lent perfume to the night air. Nothing. There was not a trace of anything out of the ordinary.

"Do you see anything?" Gerald Williams called up to them, making a futile attempt to smooth the left side of his hair back in place. It stuck straight out, and Willy thought it looked like something had sprouted from the side of his head.

"No," John called down, "nothing." Looking at Jim, he shook his head and they climbed back down the steps to the agitated and confused men.

Mayor Driscol drove up and hurried across the square. He wore yellow and green striped pajama bottoms, a blue sport jacket, no shirt, and red slippers. His white straw hat sat crooked on his head, and he toted a double barrel shotgun. "What's the emergency?" he asked, out of breath, "What's the problem?"

"Henry, what in heaven's name are you doing with that thing?" John asked, reaching for the shotgun. "Is it loaded?"

"Well of course it's loaded. What do you expect me to do, throw it at someone?"

John sighed and rolled his eyes. "Take the shells out," he directed, handing it back to him. "We don't need any weapons. The only thing we have to shoot at is each other, and I don't want that started."

Mike, standing behind Willy and Ron, chuckled to himself, wondering if it was the same shotgun Elizabeth was planning to use the day of Caroline's party.

"So what is the problem?" Mayor Driscol snapped. He was miffed and tried to look dignified as he stood there in the garb he had thrown on in such a rush. The only thing that hinted at dignity was his daddy's old shotgun and now that didn't even have any shells in it.

"None that we know of," Eli answered, examining Henry's clothes. "I don't believe you would ever win the best-dressed mayor award, Henry," he laughed.

Mayor Driscol glanced down at his clothes and waved his hand irritably. "I was too worried about what was going on here. I have one hysterical wife who thinks someone is being held hostage, Caroline is crying her eyes out, and Elizabeth wants to take up arms and settle the whole matter. That's the main reason I brought this along," he commented, indicating the shotgun. "I felt more comfortable with the idea of my carrying it than Elizabeth."

John looked at him, easily understanding the last point. "All right, someone had to ring the bell. Let's spread out and search the area. Look for anything that someone may have dropped. Check to see if any of the shrubs or flowers have been trampled. Look for anything."

"Sheriff," Young Ben spoke up. "About eight thirty this evening Melba had Hazel ring me. She and Mercy were playing Canasta in the kitchen when they heard footsteps and a crash on her back porch. By the time I got there, whoever it was had taken off. The only thing I found was a broken flower pot."

Anger rose in Willy, and he unconsciously made a fist with his right hand. How dare someone prowl around a defenseless woman's house, especially Melba's. Recalling how small she was, a protective instinct surfaced, and he felt a sudden need to make sure she was all right. A feeling came over him that a lost opportunity just slipped through his hands, and he didn't quite understand what it was or where it came from.

Jack Charles and Nelson White hurried across the square. "What in heaven's name has happened?" Nelson asked with alarm in his voice as he looked at those gathered.

"No one seems to know," John answered. He looked at the men and then Jim. "You organize a few men and make a quick search. I am going to drive around town and see if there seems to be anyone out and about." John turned to those gathered on the square. "Those of you who are going to stay and look around try not to step on anything. I know it's dark. We'll have to check again in the morning when we can see." He looked up at the bell tower and wondered who and why anyone would want to ring it.

Dr. Miller walked across the square with Ned, "What's going on?" he asked, looking at the group of men.

"Don't rightly know," Old Ben said. "No one knows who rang the bell."

"Okay, Willy, how about you, Ben, Ron, and Hank help me look around," Jim said as he watched his brother and Pastor Mike walk to the squad car. He doubted they would find anything. It was too dark, but they could check anyway.

"I don't much like someone messin' with my bell," Old Ben mumbled as he walked around the side of the bell tower. "Not unless it's an emergency."

Willy's eyes roamed along the ground as he walked toward the bandstand. You couldn't see much. *They might find something in the morning,* he thought, *still it wouldn't hurt to check tonight.* Circling the bandstand, he came around to the front and walked up the steps. He stood quietly and looked back toward the tower, watching the others walk around the square in the dark.

A feeling of being watched washed over him, and he sensed a presence. Not moving, he let his eyes slowly move around the area of the bandstand. His eyes, now accustomed to the dark, sought out the darker shapes of the shrubs and the black areas between the shops as he slowly turned his body in a complete circle. Nothing! Not able to shake the feeling of being watched, Willy slowly walked down the steps and circled the bandstand again.

He debated with himself if he should mention it to the Sheriff and then shook his head. What would he tell him? He suddenly discovered he was psychic and there was an invisible person in the bandstand with him? *"I think not,"* he thought to himself and walked back to join the others.

Samuel Cranston came from the hotel and was talking to Henry Driscol. "I can't figure any of this out," he said. "You say someone was prowling around Melba's house?"

"That's what Young Ben told us. She called and said she heard footsteps and something breaking."

"I didn't see anything. Anyone else?" Ben asked, looking at the others who indicated they hadn't either.

"No, I guess we may as well go home and let the Sheriff and Jim check again tomorrow," Eli said looking at Jim.

"If this don't beat all," Sam Cranston said. "I'm going back to bed. Perhaps we'll find something out tomorrow." He turned toward the hotel. "Ben, are you ready to go? I'll walk with you."

"I reckon. If you're scared, I'll walk you home," Old Ben chuckled. They walked across the square, mumbling to one another as they pondered on the unusual circumstances.

Young Ben fell into step with Hank. "I don't mind telling you, I don't like the idea of someone snooping around our homes." He waved to Willy and Ron who were headed in the opposite direction. "A lot of people are going to be upset. Nothing like this has ever happened. Yes, sir. A lot of people will be worried," he remarked as they crossed the square and headed down Pine Street.

Pastor Mike watched his side of the street, and John watched the other as they drove around. He thought of Melba and Mercy. *Footsteps*, he thought to himself. He had heard footsteps in the woods. *Was it a young person that could move around so quickly?*

John drove passed the square one more time. It was dark and empty. The bell hung silent in the tower.

Mike stood at his study window staring into the woods, a faint smile tugging at the corners of his mouth. All six deacons just left his office: Robert Miller, Elijah Seabaugh, Phillip Driscol, Joshua Hunter, Elisha Cook, and Louis Smith. Normally, one designated deacon met with him every Sunday morning to lend assistance through the coming week and pray for the morning service, but this morning found all of them in his office. The circumstances taking place in Oak Grove the last couple of days appeared to have everyone in a dither.

"Our women folk are frightened, Pastor," Elisha Cook spoke with a worried look on his face. "After the bell ringin' and the incident at Melba's last night, I can understand how they feel," he said, glancing at the other men. "Why Sally made me lock the door last night. Lock my door! I declare; we've lived here all our life and have never locked our house. Never!"

"And I don't mind telling you that I am also worried and wondering who is pulling all of these shenanigans," Joshua Hunter stated irritably "I find myself questioning the actions of some of our own Oak Grove folks," he said in a quieter voice. A look of guilt crossed his face as he glanced around the room at the others and then looked down at the floor.

Phillip Driscol sat forward in his chair and looked around at the rest of the men. "I am concerned about our youngsters. They are either confused or think what's been happening is down right adventuresome," he said, shaking his head. "I am afraid they will get confused about what is proper and what is not. The children in Oak Grove are from good families. Something like this could get them started on the wrong track."

Pastor Mike understood what the men were saying. Leah voiced concern just this morning about locking their door while they were in church. The children voiced anger at the breakfast table, especially Laura over Caroline's bracelet, and the three phone calls he received before breakfast did not help matters.

The men looked at him, wanting answers that he could not give and advice that he did not have. Knowing the only thing that would help, he immediately led them in a season of prayer, seeking that which would calm their hearts. They had spent quite some time praying freely and openly, seeking guidance and comfort in the midst of the confusion. Silence had filled the room for several minutes, then a gradual sense of peace and calmness passed from one man to the next. By the time they left his office, evidence of frustration and confusion was no longer visible in their faces and their attitudes were quite different, altogether. Once again, Mike was humbled and thankful for God's amazing love and guidance.

Still standing at the window, he chuckled to himself. The Lord never ceased to amaze him. The message he was going to preach this morning was not the one he prepared earlier in the week. This morning's sermon had been impressed upon his heart and mind last Tuesday morning during his walk in the woods, and he had not understood the change. Not seeming relevant at the time, it was now precisely what his congregation needed to hear.

The ticking of the clock in the silence of his study caught his ear, and he glanced at his watch, nine o'clock. It was time to head home and gather his family. He began the habit when the children were very small, feeling the need to help Leah get them to church. That small gesture became a habit that he still maintained. The truth of the matter was that he enjoyed walking into church with his wife and children. It always gave him a sense of fulfillment and an awareness of how much God blessed his life.

Walking out his study door, conversation from some of the early folks reached his ear and the bits he picked up were excited and angry. He made his way out the side door and smiled as he glanced up at the cloudless sky, thanking the Lord again for today's message.

Striding down the hill, he walked toward the parsonage across the street. It sat amid several towering oaks and was a comfortable two-story home with a large covered porch. Honeysuckle bushes grew along the side of the driveway while lilacs bordered the empty lot on the north side of the property. The front walk led to the porch and curved around the side of the house to the back door that Mike followed this morning. Taking the steps two at a time, he opened the back door and walked into the kitchen.

"Pastor Mike, your sermon was just what I needed to hear," Sally Wilson said, shaking his hand. "I was starting to place blame on some poor innocent neighbor and I realize now that I was wrong. I need not be so judgmental."

Hank placed his hand under his wife's elbow. "I told her, Pastor. I didn't think it was any of our folks here in town." He glanced at his wife's face and smiled. "We'll not be caught blaming an innocent person, will we, dear?"

"Land sakes, no. I'm going to concentrate on praying for Sheriff Walker," Sally commented. Stepping away, the two made their way down the steps.

Ned and Louise Olson smiled at each other and turned to Mike, "You are right, Pastor," Ned commented. "There is nothing to fear but fear itself. The Lord Almighty has taken care of us all this time. He's not going to quit now over a few minor incidents. I guess we have blown a lot out of proportion."

"My word, Pastor Mike," Louise confessed, looking up at him, "but I let fear get me all worked up last night. I just realized during your sermon that whoever is causing these problems has not attempted to harm anyone, so they can't be too dangerous."

Ned looked at her. "Come on, we better let Miss Mattie get through. The youngsters are out here already waiting for her."

Miss Mattie, Hannah, and Jeremiah made their way slowly out the door. Hannah carried the red and white striped box, and Jeremiah stood patiently behind both women.

Miss Mattie looked into the blue eyes of her pastor. "For a man so young, you have a good ear for what the Lord is telling you," she commented, smiling at him. "When did He impress this message on your mind?" Her clear gray eyes looked directly into his.

Mike smiled at this grand lady standing in front of him. "Actually, Miss Mattie, He had to first tell me the one I prepared was wrong and then He gave me this one. I have to confess, I didn't understand His change, but I have learned from experience that I am wrong too much of the time, and He is right all of the time."

Miss Mattie stared at him for a minute with a tender smile then reached up and gently patted his cheek. She gave him a sweet smile and said quietly, "I pray for you every day, Pastor Mike. Come on, Hannah, let's not keep the children waiting." Turning, she glanced at the candy box then carefully made her way down the steps.

Mike watched Miss Mattie make her way toward the bench beneath the oak and felt a lump in his throat. He needed to tell her just how much he appreciated and loved her.

Leah stood at the bottom of the step, watching and listening to the congregation as they left the church. Their tone and attitude was much calmer than before the service. She silently thanked God for giving Mike the words he shared this morning and felt much better about everything herself. Whatever was going on would soon be explained.

"Leah, thank you so much for helpin' with Mama," Liza Cook said, coming up behind her. "She is actually stayin' in bed and said the church ladies are doin' such a fine job that she doesn't have to worry about a thing." Liza turned as Elizabeth Seabaugh came to stand with them.

"Elijah has gone to the car for some strawberry preserves for you, Leah," Elizabeth said, glancing around for her husband. "I wanted to give them to you Friday when you were at the farm, but I just forgot with all of our visiting and all. Here he comes now."

"Thank you so much, Elizabeth. We all love your preserves, especially Mike," she said, smiling at Eli who walked up to collect his wife.

"I put those preserves on your front porch, Mrs. Daniels," Eli said, removing his hat. "They are mighty good too. Elizabeth and Liza just put them up a couple of weeks ago. You enjoy them," he said, taking his frail wife by the arm. "Come on, let's get you home. I can taste that roast already," he laughed.

"Thank you Eli, you have a good afternoon," Leah said, waving to them as they walked toward the parking lot. Leah sighed contentedly and glanced around the churchyard. Her eyes fell on Miss Mattie on the bench surrounded by children, and the clumps of people chatting together. Looking up into the blue sky, she thought how beautiful the day was. "This is the day the Lord has made; let us rejoice and be glad in it," she whispered, feeling a surge of joy.

"Okay." Brenton said, looking at everyone gathered by the freshly painted gate. "I heard Dad say he needed more eyes and ears to figure this mystery out. "That's what we are going to be, extra eyes and ears."

"You know he's not going to let us get involved in this," Preston said, looking at his brother. "Dad would have a hissy fit if he knew we were going to do something. What are we going to do?"

The note, passed around during Sunday school, said to meet at the cemetery after church if anyone wanted to help catch the thief. Brenton looked at those gathered; Preston, Truman and Simon, Johnny, Larry, Ronald, and Jake.

"We need to check facts first. Everyone go home and write what you know to actually have happened on a piece of paper." Brenton looked at each of the boys. "And think about what you write. If you hear anyone say anything, or if you see anyone do anything that is suspicious in any way, write that down too. Let's meet at the school about eleven o'clock tomorrow," he said with an air of authority. "And don't tell anyone what we are doing, especially the girls."

"Okay, I've got to go," Jake said, looking toward the church. "Mom is waving me to come on."

"All right then, let's go. Don't forget, eleven o'clock at the school," he said as they walked back toward the church.

"Say, that was pretty nice of your dad to mention the fence this morning," Truman said, looking at Johnny. "It does look pretty good, doesn't it?" he said, turning to look at the fence again.

"I think so, if I have to say so myself. We did a pretty good job," Johnny answered.

"Caroline, I am so sorry about your bracelet," Laura told her, wishing she could buy her another one.

"I am too," Caroline said, "but Aunt Trudy just knows we will find it in the house somewhere. We've only looked downstairs, but tomorrow she said we would search upstairs. I know we will find it," she said confidently. Instantly, her confident expression was replaced by one of total dejection as she stared at the church door.

Laura and Noelle followed her gaze, curious as to her sudden change in attitude.

Peter was walking down the steps talking to Paul Wilson with Karen and Terry following close behind. One of them must have said something funny because both boys turned around and laughed. They stood on the sidewalk for a moment talking then looked in their direction.

"I wonder what was so funny?" Elizabeth asked, watching the four step from the sidewalk onto the grass, making way for the other folks.

Caroline lifted one of her brows and turned her back. "I am sure it must be something really hilarious," she stated sarcastically.

Laura and Noelle looked at each other in surprise, wondering at her change in moods. She surely wasn't angry with Karen and Terry. They were her best friends.

"Why don't you just go find out?" Elizabeth asked her sister then rolled her eyes as she looked at Laura and Noelle. "Do you want me to?"

"Don't you dare!" Caroline said, whirling around to face her.

"Well, it just seems to me if you are mad because you don't know what they are laughing about, you should just go over and ask what's so funny," Elizabeth stated, trying to figure out what was so complicated.

"I don't care what they are laughing at. And I am not angry," Caroline retorted, glaring at Elizabeth.

"Well good, cause here they come."

Laura watched Caroline's face turn red and she fidgeted with her handbag. She didn't understand what the problem was either, but she thought Caroline was starting to look like Shari yesterday right before she threw up.

"Did you ever find your bracelet?" Peter asked as he came to stand before her. With both hands in his pockets, he glanced at Paul then back at Caroline.

"No," Caroline said softly, lowering her eyes and dabbing them with the handkerchief she removed from her purse. "Thank you for asking, Peter. It is just so frightening to know a burglar was in your house."

Peter shifted uncomfortably from one foot to the other and ran his fingers through his brown hair. Looking for some clue as to what to say or do, he glanced back at Paul who just shrugged his shoulders.

Laura and Noelle stared at Caroline. What was she talking about? They hadn't heard anything about a burglar in the house, and she just said she knew the bracelet was somewhere inside.

Elizabeth groaned loudly. Caroline was beginning to act more like Aunt Trudy every day. Receiving a threatening look, Elizabeth whirled around, "Let's go talk to Kim and Patricia."

Laura and Noelle hurried to catch up with her. "I am never going to fall in love," Elizabeth exclaimed. "All you do is laugh or cry and you don't want to eat. And if that's not enough, it does something to your mind 'cause I think Caroline has gone crazy."

"Me either," Noelle commented, "It seems very confusing to me."

Margaret Miller laughed and pushed her chair away from the table. "Zachary, are you sure you are not making all of this up?" she asked, gathering her plate and utensils "Ellen, Lynn, if you will hand me the rest of the plates, I will get the pie.

"No, honest, Grandma," Zachary said, scooting back on the catalogues he was sitting on. "Jimmy told me after Sunday school. It was a little green snake. Johnny and Larry White found it right outside the back door. He said Larry said it looked like a Baptist snake so Johnny picked it up and brought it in. He said they could count it as a visitor."

Grandpa Miller leaned back in his chair, slapped his hand on the dining room table, and laughed. "I guess you could call that evangelism of some sort."

Michael smiled at his son who was so caught up in the telling of the tale. "And what did Mrs. Wilson have to say about this Sunday school visitor?" he asked, pitying the poor woman. She taught the girls in the intermediate department, and Hank taught the boys.

"Jimmy said she is real smart. She told Mr. Wilson that she knew it was a boy snake so he should take care of it, and then she gathered the girls from the opening assembly and they all went to class." Zachary looked around the table at all of the laughter.

Ellen, still laughing, rose from the table with a handful of plates and helped Lynn carry the rest to the kitchen. "Mom, your roast was delicious again. I ate way too much. I shouldn't do that," she said, looking at Lynn who rolled her eyes mockingly at her.

"You say that every Sunday and so do I." Lynn stacked the dishes in the sink and grabbed a tray from the cabinet "I'll get the coffee, Ellen. Will you grab the dessert plates? A snake in Sunday school. Can you believe that?" She laughed as she placed the cream and sugar on the tray with the coffee cups.

Ellen giggled, "I would have loved to have seen Sally's face."

Maggie looked with distaste at Zachary. "Did they let the snake go?" she asked wide-eyed, wondering what other Sunday school department it could have visited.

"I don't know for sure," Zachary answered, shrugging his shoulders. "Some said they did, and someone else said they hung it on the wall so they could count it when they took the attendance."

"We never have any fun like that in our class," Abigail complained, looking at her Grandfather.

Alan was still laughing when his mother appeared in the door of the dining room with a confused look on her face. "What's the matter, Mom?" he asked in concern.

"My pie. My cherry pie. It is gone," she said, looking bewildered.

"What do you mean it is gone?" Robert asked his wife. "What did you do with it?"

Margaret looked through the kitchen to the screened in porch and then back to her family seated around the dining room table. "I put it in on the table to cool. It is gone."

Everyone rose at the same time and made their way to the porch. There was no pie in sight.

"Well, I declare," Robert said, looking at his confused wife. "I believe we have a pie thief."

"Ellen glanced at Michael. "Who would steal a pie? Mom is there anything else missing?" she asked, looking around the porch at all the familiar items.

"Not that I can see Land sakes, Robert maybe we should check the rest of the house," she said, hurrying into the kitchen.

Alan walked into the living room. "It doesn't look like anything has been disturbed in here. How about the bedrooms, Dad," he said, following Michael who was already half way up the stairs.

Margaret sat down at the table with a stunned look on her face. "A pie. Now who would take a pie?" she wondered aloud.

"Someone who was hungry, I guess," Abigail said, patting her hand. "Everyone knows you make the best cherry pies in the world, Grandma," she said in a comforting tone, thinking that was the logical answer to the whole problem.

Lynn glanced at Ellen. This indeed was strange, yet funny. They smiled at one another and tried not to laugh.

"Everything else is in place. Nothing has been disturbed," Robert Miller said, coming back into the dining room. "Now, don't that beat all," he commented as he sat down with a puzzled look on his face.

"We can just eat the ice cream without the pie, Grandma. Don't worry," Maggie said. "They didn't take the ice cream too, did they?" Running to the kitchen, she opened the freezer door and sighed with relief. The blue Pevely box was still there. "They didn't get the ice cream," she called back to the dining room.

Sheriff Walker put the telephone back on the receiver, walked into the living room, and looked at his brother then Anne and Jennifer. "That was Dr. Miller. They have had a cherry pie stolen," he said in disbelief.

"A pie?" Anne said. "Is that all?" She looked at her husband and then at Jennifer.

"Apparently so," John answered. "Who in the world would enter a house, take a pie, and not disturb anything else?"

Jim, relaxing back in the chair, shook his head and laughed. "Sounds like someone hungry and pretty harmless. This is getting crazier all the time."

"They actually came in the house and took the pie and nothing else?" Jennifer asked bewildered.

"He said Mrs. Miller put the pie on the back porch to cool when they left for church," John said laughing "When she went to get it—no pie. It was gone."

Brenton and Truman stood in the doorway listening to their parents discuss this latest turn of events. Looking at one another, they both sat on the steps. "I wonder if anyone else has anything missing?" Truman asked, watching Brenton pull a pencil from his pocket. This was one more thing to add to their list of crimes in Oak Grove for the meeting tomorrow.

Willy puttered around the house all morning and realized he was bored to death. Slipping into a clean shirt, he stepped out on the front porch and glanced over at Old Ben's. He was not home. It was Sunday, and Mercy always had him over for dinner. Jack lay down next to him on the front step and looked up at him with gentle brown eyes.

"We are a pitiful pair, aren't we?" Willy said, patting him on the head and receiving a thump of his tail on the porch in gratitude.

Standing up, he looked down at Jack. "Come on. Let's walk over to the square. Maybe we can find something from last night." He strolled slowly down the street with Jack at his heels. Passing the garage, he thought about the tune-up he had scheduled for Clifford Charles tomorrow. That was one of the first things Uncle William taught him. How he missed him.

They had become close those last few years before his death, only having one another to rely on. Willy sighed. He wouldn't get too attached to anyone again.

Passing the Cranston Hotel, he noticed a strange car and wondered who was passing through Oak Grove. The square was empty and no one about *I guess they're resting after Sunday dinner.*

Sunday was the worst day of the week for him. It was a day for families. Walking over to the bench, he sat down and stared at the water fountain. He looked around and thought of the confusion last night. *What a strange thing*, he thought, looking up at the bell tower. Jack sniffed around the bandstand, explored all sides, then came back and sat next to him. Willy looked up into the blue sky, pondering the strange sensation he felt last night. Rising from the bench, he walked over to the bandstand and up the steps. Standing in the same spot, he looked across the square. Honeysuckle floated in the air and birds sang happily. What a peaceful afternoon. He wondered if Melba was okay, and again felt as though he had failed her in some way.

Jack treed a squirrel and sat wagging his tail as he watched it. Willy walked down the steps, crossed the square, and looked over at the café. Always so busy, it was now closed and empty. Nothing was open on Sundays. Passing the bank, he stopped and glanced at the floral arrangements in the window of the florist and then strolled by Edna's dress shop. Miller's drug store also was quiet and he stood and looked at the items in the window. King's Men Cologne. *I wonder what it smells like. I should try something knew,* he thought and then wondered why or where that notion came from. He continued down the sidewalk, Jack at his heels, and passed Reese's Market thinking what a mess it had been and wondered who had done such a thing. The Blacksmith Shop was quiet and closed up. Willy thought of Old Ben in his pajamas and bathrobe last night and smiled to himself. The firehouse sat silent with the doors closed. Sometimes Jim Walker came down on Sunday afternoons and fooled around, but he was not there this afternoon. *He sure is a nice fellow,* Willy thought. *Both of them are nice, Jim and the Sheriff.*

Jack barked and bounded off into a yard. Willy was stunned. He was standing in front of Melba's house. She sat on the porch swing, and Jack sat in front of her receiving a much-appreciated ear scratching.

Willy felt awkward and was aggravated with himself for not paying more attention to where he was walking. He thought about waving and continuing on down the street but found himself rooted to the spot. This was ridiculous. He should wave and call Jack but knew that would be futile. He was enjoying the petting and ear scratching and not about to leave. He would come if Willy commanded, but that seemed a bit extreme if not rude.

"Hi, Willy," Melba called, waving to him. She looked very pretty and relaxed sitting there casually petting Jack, and Willy was, for the moment, taken aback as he looked at her. The long mass of auburn curls was pulled away from her face with a green ribbon that matched her blouse. She wore a pair of khaki-colored slacks and was barefoot.

"Is Jack taking you for a walk?" she asked, smiling at him. Willy watched her push the swing with her foot and found himself smiling back.

Not knowing what else to do, he walked slowly up the sidewalk. "I guess he is," he said, stopping at the bottom step. He looked up at her and thought he had never seen green eyes that color before. Glancing down at Jack, he looked back at her and smiled. "I'm sorry, Jack will stay there as long as you pet him."

"That's okay. I love dogs." She smiled again and continued her petting "I used to have a dog a long time ago. Won't you come up and sit down?" she asked, scooting over to make room for him on the swing.

Willy hesitated and then stepped up on the porch. He walked to the swing, sat down, and watched Jack flop down at his feet and lay his head on his paws.

The same soft fragrance he remembered from Friday night reached him, and he looked out across the yard, remembering how small she felt when he was helping her to the car. He rubbed his chin and glanced at her. "How is your foot?" he asked, looking down at her bare feet.

Melba hesitated for just a brief moment and then replied, "It is just fine. There is nothing wrong with it now." *It is true*, she thought. *There isn't anything wrong with my foot right now.*

She gave him a brilliant smile, and Willy nodded before looking away. He was conscious of his increased heart rate and at the same time aware of a red flag somewhere in his brain. *That smile and those green eyes would snare any man,* he thought. *I need to get out of here.*

"I'm glad your foot is better," Willy commented, glancing at her again. "I was afraid it might swell. It does that if you are up on it too much," he said, quoting Mike and feeling ridiculous as he looked away again.

Melba wondered about his nervousness as she studied him. His black curly hair looked even darker in the daylight and she noted the strong features of his face. He had a very rugged, handsome look about him with lashes that a woman would die for.

"Would you like a glass of lemonade?" she asked, leaning toward him with a questioning look in her eyes. "It is already made. I was going to have one myself," she said, rising from the swing.

He opened his mouth to decline and "yes, that sounds good," slipped out. Willy, momentarily confused by his reaction, found he was unexpectedly pleased to linger a few minutes longer.

He watched her walk to the door and was curious when she paused and looked directly at him. Her lips parted as she started to speak, and then she hesitated, and a slight smile crossed her face. Turning, she disappeared into the house, leaving Willy puzzled.

Realizing he had been holding his breath, he released it and glanced around. Red flowers sat on each side of the steps, and ferns hung from each end of the porch. He noticed a Life Magazine lying on a small table by the window close to the swing and wondered if she had been reading it before he and Jack showed up. A wicker chair sat at the other end of the porch with a table next to it with a small plant on top.

"Here you are, Willy." Melba came through the door carrying two glasses of lemonade. Her foot did appear much better. In fact, she moved very gracefully. She stopped before him and handed him one of the glasses.

"Thank you." He observed her slight form as she settled herself on the swing and was aware that she turned sideways to look at him. "Tell me, what have you and Jack been up to today?" she asked, sipping her lemonade.

Willy stared at the red flowers. "We walked down to the square. It is too nice of a day to stay inside," he commented, realizing what a beautiful day it really was. "I thought maybe I might see something that would give us a clue to what is going on around here." Willy continued to stare at the flowers. Then, as though coming to a conclusion he turned suddenly, laid his arm on the back of the swing, and faced her. He couldn't continue this conversation any longer without looking at her, and he realized that was the very thing he wanted to do.

Melba, conscious of his arm on the back of the swing, nervously sat her glass of lemonade on the table. "Do you have any idea who is causing the problems?" she asked, turning back to him. He was looking directly at her for the first time and she found it unnerving.

"I don't have a clue," Willy replied, taking a drink of the lemonade. He sat the glass on the porch rail and looked back at her. "Were you frightened last night?"

Melba detected a note of tenderness in his voice that she suspected he was not aware of and watched a sudden flare of anger momentarily flash in his eyes then just as quickly disappear.

"No, Mercy was here. I would have been more frightened if I had been alone," she answered, intrigued by the changing emotions that crossed his face. "I am so thankful Ben lives just across the street."

Willy's hand fell to her shoulder and though the grip was gentle it was firm. Melba, taken by surprise at the sudden touch, looked up in wonder and found him staring intently into her eyes. "You call me if you ever need to Melba. I will come anytime." The firmness in his voice and his hand on her shoulder caught her off guard, but she was not frightened and knew instinctively that Willy would be very protective of anyone he loved.

She stared at him for a moment then he self-consciously looked at his hand and removed it from her arm and glanced away. "Thank you, Willy." Melba spoke softly, strangely touched by his actions. "That is good to know. I will." She nervously reached for her lemonade and felt guilty about her foot. She should tell him the truth.

Willy sat back in the swing, surprised at his actions. What did he just do; make himself her official protector? Staring at his glass of lemonade, Willy was suddenly aware that some small part of himself had just been stripped away, leaving him relieved yet puzzled. Old Ben's words echoed somewhere in the back of his mind, "Women want a man to take charge and be their protector."

The slamming of a screen door across the street drew his attention, and he watched Jake run across the yard and pick up his bike. Riding off the sidewalk into the street, he waved and called. "Hi, Melba. Hi, Willy."

Melba and Willy both waved, and Jack raised his head and barked. Melba laughed and leaned down to pet him. "Where did you ever get Jack?"

Willy glanced at the dog and smiled to himself. "When I first came to Oak Grove, my aunt and uncle bought him for me. He was the first thing that ever totally belonged to me. Jack is the first thing that I ever cared about." He looked fondly at the dog, unaware that he just revealed something about himself that he had never shared with anyone.

Jack walked over and placed his head on Willy's knee. Melba watched him lean forward in the swing and rub his ears. *He can't be that complex of a man,* Melba thought. *He has a great capacity for love if he would just allow himself to feel.*

Willy leaned back in the swing and smiled at her as Jack lay back down on the porch. The door across the street slammed again and Carrie ran across the street. "Hi, Melba. Hi, Willy," she called, skipping up the sidewalk. She sat on the top step and started giggling when Jack walked over and lifted his paw.

"He wants to shake hands," Willy told her, watching her take his paw. Jack licked her on the cheek and lay down next to her, relishing the attention he was getting.

"Carrie, would you like a glass of lemonade?" Melba asked, already up and at the door.

"Yes, ma'am, and a sugar cookie if you have one," she requested, fully expecting to get one.

"You got it, and how about you, Willy? Let me get you some fresh lemonade," she said, returning for his glass.

"Yes, ma'am, and a sugar cookie if you have one," he replied, grinning up at her as he handed her his glass. That small comment broke through a barrier of sorts and somehow brought a new sense of ease between them.

Melba laughed and looked down at him. "You've got it."

He watched her walk back into the house, admiring the graceful way she moved and found himself wondering if she had any faults at all. Carrie continued to pet Jack, and from inside Willy heard Melba singing.

It was the one church song he was familiar with, *Amazing Grace.* Someone sang it at his aunt's funeral but he couldn't remember who. He listened to her voice drift through the window. It was beautiful, soft, and clear. Willy stretched his long legs out in front of him, enjoying a feeling that was new; a feeling he did not even recognize as contentment.

Chapter 11

Night fell on Oak Grove, lending coolness from the heat of the day. The full moon shed its light through giant oaks and created dancing shadows on the grass as the night breeze stirred the leaves. Tree frogs and crickets filled the night air, sending their song of tranquillity across porches and into windows. A dog barked from somewhere, and distant voices and laughter drifted from neighboring porches.

Old Ben sat in an old ladder-back chair, playing his accordion, and Willy leaned back in one of the rockers, his long legs stretched out in front of him. Ben sat on the floor, leaning against a pillar of the porch, while Mercy sat in another rocker, tapping her foot in time with the music.

The song Old Ben was playing was familiar to Willy, but he didn't know the name. He knew it was one of Ben's favorites because he played it frequently, and Willy decided it was one that he would always associate with Old Ben.

"What is the name of that song?" he asked when Ben finished.

"The Lily of the Valley," Ben answered, stretching his leg as he moved to a more comfortable position. "It was one of my daddy's favorites."

Old Ben smiled wistfully as he looked at the wisteria vine growing up the pillars of the front porch. The night shadows transformed it into a lacy canopy that stretched up the pillars, arched over the steps, and gently swayed in the night air. "This is another one," he said with a smile and began playing *Turkey in the Straw.*

Recognizing the song immediately, Willy and Ben grinned at each other in the dark. They had bought harmonicas last winter with the idea of learning to play the lively tune but finally gave up. Every time they tried to join Old Ben, one or the other began to laugh, and things went down hill from there. Finally realizing it was a lost cause, they both gave up.

Willy still played occasionally but progressed only enough to play for Jack who usually got up and moved to another room, leaving Willy with serious doubts as to his musical talent.

Mercy glanced at both of them. "What did you two ever do with those harmonicas?" she asked. "You both could have learned to play if you would have been serious about it." She grinned at the memory of one evening when they laughed so hard that all four were wiping tears from their eyes.

"I would be really good by now if Willy would have left me alone," Ben said as he got up from the step with an empty glass in his hand. "Anyone need a fresh glass of tea?"

"No, not me. How about you, Uncle Ben? Willy?" Mercy asked, glancing at both men.

"No thanks, Mercy," Old Ben answered as he stretched his arm and smiled at the bantering flying back and forth across the porch between Ben and Willy. He could find no argument with either; they were both right. Neither one could play. The only thing they produced other than noise was laughter, but as far as he was concerned, laughter was music to anyone's ear so he figured the time was well spent.

"No, I don't care for any either. And you were the one who always started laughing," Willy called after Ben. There was no way he would admit to Ben that he was still trying to learn to play the crazy thing.

Ben walked down the hall and into the kitchen. Setting his glass in the sink, he glanced at a small picture of Uncle Ben and Aunt Carrie on the shelf by the window. They were standing arm in arm beneath the apple tree with Mercy and himself at about the ages of five and nine. Uncle Ben's hand rested on his shoulder, and Mercy was holding onto a corner of Aunt Carrie's apron. They were laughing about something, but he couldn't remember what. It seemed like it was something about worms in the apples. He would have to ask Mercy if she remembered. Ben longed to turn around and see Aunt Carrie standing with a plate of cookies in her hand and that sweet smile she always wore. He really missed her. The thought of Uncle Ben's passing produced a great love in his heart, and a melancholy feeling washed over him as he stood in the kitchen listening to the strains of the accordion drift through the window.

Old Ben was playing another song; a melody that was soft and comforting. Willy watched the fireflies flitter across the yard, and he rested his head on the back of the chair, allowing his mind to drift back to the afternoon. He had been pleasantly surprised with the relaxed feeling he experienced once he made up his mind to enjoy Melba's company. Her enchanting smile and sparkling green eyes danced in front of him, and Willy pondered on the feelings she stirred in him. He could not deny the attraction he felt for her and was puzzled as to why and when he let his guard down. He never had a problem keeping his distance as far as women were concerned, that is, until now.

Willy stared into the night, hearing a screen door slam somewhere down the block, and let his thoughts drift. He should ignore his feelings right now and bury them. She was no different than any other woman. *Now I'm lying,* he argued with himself. *She is different. I don't know why, but she is.* A deep sigh escaped as he thought again of the afternoon and how fascinating her eyes were. She always looked directly at him when she spoke. Willy lifted his head from the back of the chair as a sudden truth dawned on him. It was honesty. That was what he observed in the green depths of her eyes.

"Willy!" Mercy called, shaking him out of his thoughts.

"What? I'm sorry," he said, looking at her; thankful she couldn't see his face in the dark.

"I said, do you think we will have a peaceful night?" Mercy asked again, wondering where in the world his mind had wandered "Or will we be in for another surprise?"

"I hope not," Young Ben said, coming back out onto the porch. He stood and stretched his long arms into the air. "I have to go in early in the morning to check equipment, and I would like to have a good night's sleep."

It was one of many responsibilities he had taken upon himself that no one else took time to do. This attitude, dependability, and dedication had gained him respect and a good position with the Oak Grove Timber Company.

"I'm going to head home. Mercy, are you going too, or do you plan on staying a while?" he asked, looking at his sister.

"No. I'm going too," she answered, rising from her chair. She walked across the porch and leaned down. "Goodnight, Uncle Ben." She kissed him on the cheek and hugged his neck. "I love you."

"I love you too, dear," Ben answered and fondly watched her walk to the swing and straighten the cushion He worried about her and wished she would find a nice young man to take care of her. She stretched herself too thin, watching after everyone in the family.

Old Ben looked at his nephew, standing on the sidewalk patiently waiting for Mercy. How many times through the years had he and Carrie watched Ben stand in that same spot while she collected her doll or whatever toy she carried with her to their house?

Old Ben took a drink of his tea and decided that Ben needed someone too. He wondered about his relationship with Lizzie. She was a sweet girl whose life revolved around the kindergarten class she taught. Mercy told him they were "keeping company" as Ben confessed to her one evening when they were painting Mercy's kitchen. Ben told him they were just friends when he asked about her one day. *What is the matter with these two?* he wondered. Old Ben could almost feel Carrie smiling at him. "When they are ready, the Lord will let them know," she would say and then tease him again about being a matchmaker.

"Good night Willy," Mercy said, patting his shoulder.

"Goodnight, Mercy. Night Ben," Willy replied and watched the two walk down the steps and through the yard.

Jack rose from where he had been laying by Mercy's chair and walked over to Willy. He scratched his ear as he rested his head on his knee. "I guess you are ready to go too," he said, looking at Jack and then thought, *I guess the Preacher was right; I do need to get out more. I'm beginning to talk to Jack too much.*

Willy stood and stretched his injured leg, moving it back and forth. It had a tendency to stiffen up when he sat too long, and tonight was no exception. "Well, Ben I am going to head over to the house," he said, looking affectionately at the old black man. Other than Uncle William, he was the only other person Willy felt a warm attachment to. "Thanks for supper."

Ben always brought Sunday leftovers from Mercy's, and the two shared the supper meal. Mercy had invited him several times for dinner, but he always declined. He was not comfortable with the idea that they all went to church together and then came home for dinner. He didn't feel right just showing up to eat. Willy thought about getting up and going to church a couple of times but never did. What was it that kept him from going? He didn't really know. He just didn't feel like he belonged or that it was necessary.

"Glad to have you eat with me," Old Ben answered as he watched Jack walk down the sidewalk then turn and wait.

Watching Jack follow Willy down the sidewalk and across the street, Ben wondered if anything would develop between Willy and Melba. Shaking his white head, he sighed, and pulled the accordion on his lap and began playing again.

Amazing Grace floated across the night air, and Willy smiled to himself as he walked up the steps. The memory of Melba's clear, sweet voice singing in the kitchen came to mind, accompanied by an unexpected feeling of pleasure.

Leah watched Mike through the mirror as he laid his Bible on the night table and chuckled. She wondered what he found so amusing and turned to look at him.

"What do you find so humorous?" she asked. Laying her hairbrush on the dresser, she crossed the room and lay on the bed.

Mike grinned and yawned. "I was just thinking. There is a pie thief in Oak Grove, and we had a garter snake for a visitor in Sunday school this morning. Whoever said small-town living was boring." He switched the bedside lamp off and lay on his back.

Leah laid her head on his shoulder and snuggled up against his side. "That is not all that happened today."

"What did I miss?" he asked curiously as he kissed her cheek, enjoying the sweet fragrance and the softness of her hair.

"Your message this morning calmed everyone," she said quietly, glancing up at him. His eyes were open and he was looking at the ceiling, rubbing her arm absentmindedly. Leah knew he was thinking about all that happened and she rose up on her elbow and looked at him. "Mike, everyone was really upset and on the verge of blowing everything out of proportion. Things could have turned ugly."

She studied the shadowed pattern of tree branches through the window and sighed as she laid her head back on his shoulder. "I am sorry to say that I had a few thoughts running through my head that should not have been there. Your words were exactly what we all needed to hear."

"I didn't do it, Leah." Mike spoke quietly, turning his head to look at her. "I prepared a totally different sermon. I was walking in the woods the other day when the Lord gave me the message that I preached this morning. I had no idea at the time that all this was going to happen. Isn't He amazing?"

Leah looked at him with tenderness in her eyes. "He always meets our needs, doesn't He?" she said quietly. "He is so good to us."

"Yes, that He truly is," Mike said pulling her close to him. "He never ceases to amaze me."

Mike drifted between sleep and consciousness. Leah was beautiful in her white gown as she walked down the aisle, organ music played, and Jimmy stood at the altar with circus posters in his hand. Mike wondered why he was behind the pulpit and not down in front at the altar waiting for Leah. Johnny and Laura kept moving the piano bench from one place to another, and Shari was ringing bells while she sang *She'll Be Comin Around The Mountain.* The church was empty except for three people in the back row who he had never seen before. Something was wrong with this whole picture.

Aware of Leah lying close to him, he drifted back and forth between sleep and consciousness. Feeling loved and contented, he smiled as the church bells rang again, and then he was drawn fully awake.

Suddenly aware that he was, in fact, hearing a bell ringing, he sat up and shook his head, vowing never to eat late in the evening again. He listened for a minute. There it was again. Someone was ringing the bell in the square.

Leah sat up as he swung his legs off the bed. "Mike, the bell; it is ringing again," she whispered as he turned the lamp on and grabbed his old pair of jeans.

"I know. I wish I knew who it is that is having such a good time driving us all nuts," he grumbled, slipping his shirt over his head and grabbing his shoes.

Leah slid off her side of the bed and reached for her robe. "I wish I knew why," she stated, sharing his frustration. She turned at the knock on their bedroom door. "Dad?" Johnny called from the hall.

"I know. I hear it, Son," Mike said as he opened the door with his shoes in his hand. All four of his children were grouped together in the hall staring at him. "There is nothing to worry about. Johnny, if you want, come with me. The rest of you stay with Mom," he said, looking back at Leah.

"But Dad, why do they keep doing this?" Laura asked, following him down the stairs, more curious than frightened.

Mike sat on the living room chair and slipped his shoes on. "They think they are having fun. That is all." He watched Johnny hurriedly tie his sneakers. "We probably won't be gone long."

Laura, Shari, and Jimmy sat on the steps watching him. "Knock his block off, Dad," Jimmy said, looking at him with a frown on his face.

"I don't think I will need to knock anyone's block off," Mike replied as he looked at Leah standing in the hall with a disturbed look on her face. He rose and walked over to her. Pulling her close, he kissed her on the forehead. "I'll be back shortly. It's okay," he said and then turned and walked out the front door with Johnny close behind.

Sheriff Walker's car was already pulling out of their drive as they crossed the yard. "Someone needs to just hide down at the square and catch whoever is ringing the bell," Johnny commented as he slammed the car door and glanced back at the house. Mom,

Laura, Shari, and Jimmy were looking through the window out into the dark, and it gave him an eerie feeling to be on the outside looking in. Looking at the darkened houses as they drove down the street, he wondered if the stranger moved around at night looking in the windows.

Pulling up to the curb, Johnny saw Brenton and Truman hurriedly open their doors and take off across the square. Following close behind, he saw that several were already gathered, including Willy, Hank, Ben, Ron, and Old Ben.

"It's the same as last night, Sheriff," Willy was saying. "As close as I live, he is already gone by the time I get here."

"He's right," Ron agreed. They lived next door to one another and arrived at the square at the same time both nights. "The bell was ringing when we passed the Blacksmith Shop, but there was not a soul in sight by the time we got here. It beats anything I've ever seen," he said, looking at the other men.

Samuel Cranston and Michael Madison both walked up while Ron was speaking. "I'm beginning to think whoever the prankster is must have wings," Michael commented, nodding his head at Alan and Pastor Clark who walked up behind them.

Sheriff Walker sighed and looked at Jim. "I'll go take a look," Jim offered and began climbing the steps, knowing as well as John that he was not going to find anything.

Jack Reese and Ned hurried across the square looking from one person to the other. "No one?" Ned asked.

"Nothing up here," Jim called down, directing his flashlight around the square.

Truman, Brenton, and Johnny stood together. "It is unbelievable that someone can get up in the tower, ring the bell, and get down that fast and not be seen," Truman whispered to Brenton and Johnny.

John looked around the square in frustration, then up at the bell and the oaks growing next to the tower. *Maybe the culprit was not running away*, he thought to himself. "Jim, shine that light into the trees," he called, looking up at his brother.

Following his train of thought, Jim switched the light on and directed the beam slowly from limb to limb. Nothing.

The Sheriff turned to the three boys. "Can you three be at my office about nine o'clock in the morning?" he asked. "You men, anyone that is able, I would like you to be there too." He looked at the group standing in front of him. "We are going to catch this culprit one way or another."

"I'll take a turn around the square just in case," Jim said. "Come on, Truman."

"I'll take a look too," Willy said, heading in the direction of the bandstand.

"Hold on, Willy. I'll walk along." Ned fell into step with him "I declare, I just don't know what to make of all this. Do you?"

"No, I don't think anyone does. But he's going to slip up sooner or later," Willy commented, glancing around. They approached the bandstand and circled it, looking as well as they could in the dark but did not hear or notice anything. Jack ran ahead, sniffing around the bushes, the flowers, and the latticework then lay down and watched everyone walk around in the dark.

"Not a blamed thing. . . . If this just don't beat everything I ever saw," Ned complained as he walked up the steps and stood in the middle of the bandstand.

Willy followed Ned up the steps, thinking about last night, and leaned against the rail of the bandstand watching several of the men head for their cars. The evening had cooled pleasantly, and he glanced up at the stars, wondering if Melba was alright. Not saying a word, he and Ned stood quietly, watching the others walk around in the dark.

That physical sensation of being watched again crawled up the back of his neck, and he glanced at Ned who was staring straight ahead.

Glancing around nervously, Ned looked at Willy with a strange expression on his face. "Have you ever had a feeling that someone was watching you?" he asked quietly.

"You feel it too?" Willy asked, relieved that he was not crazy after all.

"Only after I came up here in the bandstand," Ned said looking around again. "Come on, let's get out of here. I don't much like this feeling."

"I stood here last night," Willy told him as they walked down the steps, "and the same thing happened then too." Both men walked in silence back to the tower.

"I don't believe in ghosts, but, gosh a mighty, it makes you wonder doesn't it?" Ned commented, watching the Sheriff and Jim talking together by the fountain. "I hope the Sheriff has a good plan to catch whoever it is causing all this commotion. He sounded pretty determined, didn't he?"

"He did." Willy replied, wondering how in the world they were going to catch this guy.

Pastor Mike glanced at the faces of the men gathered in the Sheriff's office. Everyone that had been at the square the last two nights was present with the addition of Elijah Seabaugh, Jacob Cook, and Jeremiah.

"Miss Mattie said she was comin' to town to find out what all this tomfoolery business was about," Jeremiah exclaimed with an almost frightened look in his eye. "And then, o'course, Hannah said she was comin' along too. I told them it was no place for womenfolk, and . . . well . . . I . . . sometime a man just has to put his foot down." Jeremiah held his hat in shaky hands and shook his gray head. "And that's not an easy thing to do with those two, so I just drove off and left them standin' in the yard."

Mike chuckled to himself. He could just imagine the expressions on their faces as Miss Mattie and Hannah stood in the yard and watched Jeremiah drive away. The sudden pity he felt for him lessened some when he noted the stubborn set to his jaw. Perhaps Jeremiah could handle himself much better than folks gave him credit, nevertheless, Mike grinned and wished he could be a fly on the wall when he did go home.

Catching the Sheriff's eye and the expression on his face, Mike figured Jeremiah had done the right thing. Miss Mattie would have arrived, sat down, and tried to take over the whole meeting, coming up with a few ideas of her own.

John looked at Mike with a slight smile, shook his head, and looked around at those gathered.

Brenton, Truman, and Johnny stood in one corner of the office, wide-eyed, with looks of surprise on their faces. They were actually more curious over Jeremiah's nerve to run off with Miss Mattie's car than they were about why they were asked to attend the meeting.

"Well, it is nine-ten. I'm going to go ahead and tell you some of the ideas that I have, and if any of you have any of your own please feel free to share them," Sheriff Walker said as he sat in his chair and tapped the end of a pencil on the desk.

"First, I'll tell you that Mary Smith called this morning. An old hat was taken from her back porch," he said with a bit of humor in his voice. "Now, why anyone would want an old straw hat is beyond me." He looked around the office, taking in the varied expressions on the men's faces. "Mary said she hesitated calling me, but when she arrived for work at the Driscols this morning, Trudy insisted that she do so."

"I encouraged her to call also, Sheriff," Henry spoke up. "I felt anything and everything should be reported. There may be a clue mixed up in it somewhere."

"I agree, Henry," John replied. "Now let's . . ."

The door opened, and Solomon Smith walked in and looked around the office. "I thought I would just come and sit in on the meetin.' One of the ladies from church is with Hope, and she's got her dander up this mornin,' so I thought I would just skedaddle out of there for a while," he said, closing the door. "Sheriff, someone took the mornin' milk right off our porch," he said with an incredulous look on his face. "We didn't hear a sound. He took both bottles. Yes, sir, he took both of them. Now who do you reckon would do that?"

John looked at his brother's grinning face. Jim was finding it more difficult all the time to take any of this seriously, and John had reached the point where he couldn't really fault him. He was beginning to feel the same way, but knew maintaining a proper attitude was necessary in going a long way to prevent hurt feelings and stepped on toes.

"Milk," he stated, staring at a scratch mark on his desk. Sighing, he looked up. "All right, now let's look at the overall situation. Other than the damage at Reese's store, nothing of real significance has been destroyed. Someone was snooping around Melba's place but did nothing more than break a flowerpot. The only robbery of any significance was Teresa Charles' purse and Caroline Driscol's bracelet. Other than that, he has taken a cherry pie, a straw hat, and now Solomon's milk. He did not rob Reese's, which he could have since the window was broken. The Driscols had several things on the porch of more value than the bracelet, which were left untouched. Whoever helped himself to Margaret Miller's cherry pie had access to the whole house but did not take anything else. And as far as the straw hat and milk . . ." John sighed, not even finishing his sentence.

"Are you getting all this down?" Truman whispered to Brenton as he watched him frantically write on the Big Chief tablet in his hand.

Nodding in the affirmative, he continued writing.

"As far as the bell ringing goes, I think it is someone playing with our minds and taunting us," the Sheriff commented. "He does not mean any real harm but thrives on a feeling of importance because he is able to move among us and not be detected."

"So you are saying that you think it is someone in Oak Grove?" Samuel Cranston asked with a surprised look on his face.

"No," John said. "I think he is a stranger to Oak Grove, and we just do not know he is here."

"You said he," Willy commented, "so you don't think it is more that one person?"

"I think if it was more than one they would be easily caught. An individual can hide in the forest, at the mill, anywhere," John replied. "I also think whoever is ringing the bell has to be alone. He is disappearing too fast. More than one person would cause too much commotion."

"I also feel it is an individual," Jim said as he stood against the wall and looked at his brother then the other men. "If it was more than one person, they would be more apt to leave some evidence or make a mistake. So far we have nothing. He has left no clues of any kind."

"It could be a team with just one stealing at a time, couldn't it?" Ron questioned, looking at the other men.

"But where are they hiding out?" Hank asked "No one has seen anyone or noticed anything out of the ordinary."

"What about one of the Blacks?" Ned asked, looking at the Sheriff. Several of the men nodded in agreement. The family lived somewhere way out on the ridge beyond the old Seabaugh Mill. They had several children and stayed to themselves, very seldom ever coming to town. No one seemed to know where they came from or how long they had lived there. In fact, no one other than Pastor Mike could say for sure just where their house was located, and he even became confused once the path ended.

As to the children's education, the county authorities tried numerous times in the past to figure out what to do about the situation, but since the children were delivered at home, there was no official record of their births. One could get shot for showing up at the place, so they had given up any hopes of getting them enrolled in school. The family continued their isolated existence and was never seen except on rare occasions when Mr. Black and one or two of boys came to town for supplies.

"I can't remember the last time any of them were in town," John answered. "They have never caused any trouble in the past. I don't see how we can rightly suspect them," he said, looking at the questioning faces of the men in the office.

"But we've never had a circus in Oak Grove. Maybe that drew them to town," Phillip Driscol commented and glanced at Pastor Mike.

"I would suspect they didn't even know there was a circus here," Old Ben replied as he pulled the pipe out of his overalls. "And if they did, they are so backward they would be scared to death to come near it."

"Still," Samuel Cranston said, "it might not hurt to ride out there and look around a little." He too glanced at Pastor Mike.

"They would not steal anything," Mike said, looking at the Sheriff. "It is not their way of thinking. They may be poor, but they are honest." He glanced around the office at the men. "I can ride out there if you want. It has been a couple of months since I've been there, but I am telling you now, I won't find anything. I know none of them would stoop to this kind of behavior. They may be strange in their ways and hard to know, even frightening at times, but I know them. They are not illiterate, and they work hard for what little they have."

Sheriff Walker looked at Pastor Mike. "You are probably right, Pastor. But I don't know of anyone else that has ever set foot inside their house, and since you are due to pay them a visit I would appreciate it if you did," John said, looking at Mike. "At least we would know for sure."

Mike nodded his head, thinking he would enjoy the trip through the woods. It was about time for a visit anyway.

He had stumbled across the family about three years ago while hunting. Sitting beneath an oak tree close to the creek to rest a bit, he had heard crying not too far away. On investigation, he found a scraggly looking little girl about six years old lying at the foot of a small cliff. A berry pail close by gave evidence of her mission. She was hurt, and her brown eyes were wide with fear. The tear streaked, dirty face melted his heart, and she tried to crawl away from him. Unable to move with her leg twisted at an awkward angle, she stared at him in fear. Finally managing to calm her, he carefully lifted her from the ground and was totally dismayed when she let out a cry and lost consciousness. Not aware of anyone living close by and the desperate need to have her leg cared for, he stood for a moment not knowing what to do. Praying for the Lord's help, he realized to wander any further and get lost would help neither one of them. The only sure thing he knew was the trail back to the car, and he carefully carried her, thankful that she had passed out and was unaware of the pain. Placing her in the back seat, he drove her to Dr. Miller who set her leg.

Sally Black, she told him, was her name. Crying and wanting her mama, Mike set out two days later to take her home, following her directions and the warnings of everyone in Oak Grove regarding the Black family.

He had never been that far up on the ridge and was surprised at the density of the woods. Now he understood why no one could say for sure where the family lived. He drove as far as he could, then started walking. She was easy to carry because of her size, but when the thickened briars and brush hindered each step, he began to question his ability to get her home.

Sally finally looked up at him with an expression very close to exasperation and directed him to an old well-worn path that made the trek much easier. He gave her a weak smile and felt like an idiot for never having found it. Following it for more than an hour, Mike's fear ran from hurting her and doing more damage to her leg to wondering if he would ever find his way back to civilization again. Sally pointed out different plants and herbs as he walked, named the trees, and told him of the roots and berries her mama used. He was amazed at the knowledge the child possessed of the forest and wondered at the patience of the mother who had taught her.

Finally the path ended, and Mike stood dumbfounded wondering which way to go.

Sally grinned, pointed to the right, and told him it was a shortcut. She then yawned and said that the medicine the doctor gave her was making her sleepy. Mike nearly panicked. All he needed was for her to drift off to sleep and he would not know where in the world he was. "Please, Lord," he prayed, "we are both your children. Get us home quickly."

He had not walked more than twenty more yards when he found himself in a clearing, the sound of a gunshot split the air, and a pack of dogs surrounded him. A large log house sat on the side of the hill, and a tall man in a pair of overalls with a shotgun stood on the porch. Mike had been very well aware that the man had not missed his mark and could have shot him if he had wanted.

Several children peeked from windows, doors, and around the sides of the house. A very slender woman ran from the porch and down the hill. Stopping in front of him, her anguished eyes looked her daughter over from head to toe, and she stared at her set leg. Looking up at Mike with tears in her eyes, she led him up to the house.

"Now as far as you three young boys are concerned, I have something for you to do," Sheriff Walker said as he looked at the back of the room at Brenton, Truman, and Johnny. "I would like you to stay after the meeting, and I will explain it to you."

"Yes sir," they all chorused, feeling very important. "Wait till the other guys here about this," Johnny commented under his breath.

"I would like some of us to take up positions in some of the stores where we can have a clear view of the bell tower." John looked around at the merchants gathered in his office. "A couple of you in several places should do it. We will catch this culprit if we have to stay up all night."

"I'm willing to stay up and keep watch," Dr. Miller spoke up as the rest of the men agreed and nodded their approval of the idea.

"Good. If you men will stay here, Jim is going to pick out the key buildings and you can decide who will keep watch in each of them." He looked around at the men. "Whatever you do, don't let anyone know what we are planning."

He stood and looked at the boys. "Now, if you boys will come with me, I'll show you what I have in mind."

The three boys quickly followed the Sheriff outside. "What are we going to do, Dad?" Brenton asked excitedly. He had never been asked to work on a case before.

"I'm beginning to think this person is not escaping across the square," John commented as they walked toward the bell tower.

"Well, where in the world is he going then?" Truman asked, looking at Johnny with a bewildered look on his face.

The Sheriff stopped at the bell tower and looked up. "We've been saying those trees need to be trimmed for the last two years," he murmured, looking at the overhanging limbs spreading over the roof of the bell tower.

Johnny wasn't real interested in trimming trees and wished they would get around to the business of looking for the thief. Truman just shrugged his shoulders when he looked at him, and they waited to see what he would say next.

The Sheriff looked at the boys and pointed to the trees. "Do you see how those limbs are hanging over the bell tower?" he asked, looking at each one. "I want you boys to climb that tree and see if it is possible to get from the tree into the bell tower and back again."

All three grasped the idea at the same time. "Of course, Dad," Brenton exclaimed. "That is probably what he is doing." Truman and Johnny nodded in agreement, and they peered up into the spreading branches of the oak tree.

"First, though, I want you to get up in the tree and see if there is anything that he could have left behind. Look for a scrap of clothing that could have been torn and left on one of the limbs. Look for anything." John glanced around the square at the folks going about their business and hoped they would not draw too much attention.

Brenton grabbed a low branch and scrambled up the tree. Johnny and Truman followed, and John was surprised at how quickly they moved from branch to branch. Perhaps, it was a young person.

"Now do not go any higher than you feel comfortable," he called. "You won't be any help to me if you fall and get hurt."

Several shoppers stopped to watch the boys in the tree, and several folks having coffee in the café looked curiously through the window. Gerald, checking the thermometer outside the drugstore, looked strangely at John then glanced up in the tree. Lifting his hand in greeting, he paused a moment then went back inside. John figured they thought he probably lost his mind, and at this point he didn't much care.

Scrambling around from limb to limb, the boys paid no heed to anything going on below and continued looking around, hoping to find something.

"I don't see anything at all," Truman yelled as he looked up at Johnny who was a couple of branches higher.

"I haven't seen anything either. How about you, Brent?" Johnny glanced down and looked at the roofs of the shops and the people no longer paying any attention. He wondered who and why a person would sit up in a tree and watch people go about their daily chores. He found it unnerving that someone could be sitting up here anytime, watching everything going on and no one would even know it.

"Dad, we don't see anything." Brenton yelled from a height that John was becoming uncomfortable with.

"All right, all three of you get down here," he called, watching them move around in the branches. In a matter of seconds all three were back on the ground.

Truman looked at the Sheriff and shook his head, "I didn't see anything."

"Me either," Johnny said, disappointedly.

"That's okay, boys. I appreciate you looking for me. John turned to Brenton. "Will you climb back up and see how far you can go out on that limb that's hanging right over the tower?"

Brenton looked at his dad and knew what he was thinking. Grabbing the lower branch, he swung himself up into the tree and climbed up several more branches. Looking down, he grinned and waved at those below.

"You are in the right position," John called. "That branch that you have your right hand on; are you able to crawl out on it and drop into the tower?" he asked, thankful that Anne was not here to see this.

"Sure, Dad. That's no problem at all," Brenton answered. He had climbed around and swung in enough trees and vines out on the Seabaugh farm that this was a piece of cake. Carefully leaning over, he took one leap, grabbed the limb with both hands, and swung in the direction of the tower. Throwing his legs in the air, he propelled himself into the tower, grabbed the rope to steady himself, and in the process rang the bell.

Peering over the side of the tower, he looked down and watched a grin spread across his dad's face. Smiling back, Brenton waved at Truman and Johnny and glanced at those on the square who were curious as to why he rang the bell.

"Now, Son," John said, climbing the steps, "Do you think you can get back into the tree?"

Brenton looked back at the limb and felt his heart sink. "I don't think I can reach a part of the limb that is strong enough to hold me," he said in disappointment.

"I don't think you can either," John replied, resting his hand his shoulder. "You did a great job, Brent. It has to be someone taller." "Come on, let's go back down. This answered some of the questions I had."

"Did you need us for anything else, Dad?" Brenton asked, glancing at his watch.

"No, not right now. Thank you, boys, for your help, and don't mention anything about to night, OK?" He turned and walked across the square, wondering how much taller one needed to be to get a firm grip on the limb.

"Come on," Brenton said, "it is ten forty-five. We need to get to the school. The guys will be waiting for us."

Johnny felt in his pocket, hoping he didn't lose the quarter Mom gave him while climbing around in the tree. Assured that it was still there, he looked at Brenton and Truman, "You two go ahead. I have to run over to Reese's and pick up a loaf of bread for lunch. I'll meet you there in just a few minutes."

"Okay," Truman replied, straightening his ball cap. "Try to hurry. We have a lot to talk about," he said, turning to follow Brenton who was half way across the square.

Johnny crossed the street in front of Edna's Dress Shop and passed the drug store. Glancing in the window, he waved at Mr. Williams who was sitting something on the counter in front of either Milly or Molly.

Jack, lying on the bench in the shade between the drugstore and the market, lifted his head and wagged his tail as Johnny approached. If they had no customers, Jack Reese and Gerald Williams could usually be found in the spot that Jack now occupied, talking about everything and nothing.

Johnny stopped in front of the market and looked at the fruits and vegetables stacked in orderly fashion and wondered why anyone would want to throw it all around like they had done. The window was replaced, but *Reese's Market* had as yet to be painted on it.

Opening the door, he entered the store. The smell of garlic baloney and freshly waxed wood reached his nose, and Polly, Reese's parakeet, was doing her usual squawking. The Taystee Bread Man, stacking his loaves on the shelf, paused and smiled as he handed Johnny two loaves of bread.

Mr. Reese, bagging groceries for Ellen Madison, paused as she spoke, "Oh, I'm sorry, Jack. I almost forgot. I need a pound of coffee also." She turned and smiled as Johnny walked up to the counter.

"Hi Mrs. Madison," Johnny said, looking around. "Where is Zachary?"

Ellen laughed. "Actually, he is at your house playing with Jimmy." She took a coin purse from her pocketbook and watched Mr. Reese set the coffee on the counter. "How much do I owe you now?" she asked, watching him push the round, white buttons on the cash register.

"Let's see. Old Dutch Cleanser, Ovaltine, Halo, Ipana, coffee, eggs, and bread," That will be $2.55 cents, Ellen."

"Here you go," she said, handing him three dollars. "I hope you haven't had any more damage to the store."

"No, thank goodness, I haven't," he answered, handing her the change. "Thank you, Ellen." He smiled and slid the bag of groceries across the old wood counter. It was dented and scratched from years of use, but he kept it polished to a bright sheen.

"Tell your mom hello for me, Johnny," she said as she turned to leave.

"Yes Ma'am, I will." Johnny laid the two loaves of bread on the counter and glanced at the clock on the wall above the meat slicer, ten fifty-five.

Mr. Reese smiled at him. "Did you need anything else?" he asked as he dropped the two loaves of bread in a brown paper bag.

"No, sir. That's all Mom said she needed," Johnny replied, lying the quarter on the counter.

"That's twenty two cents then." Mr. Reese picked up the quarter. He waited, knowing that the Daniels' children were always permitted to spend the change.

"Just keep the whole quarter. I'm going to grab some bubble gum," Johnny said as he picked up the brown bag and walked to the candy rack. Reaching into the Dubble Bubble jar, he counted out six. "I have six pieces Mr. Reese," Johnny called as he headed to the door.

Mr. Reese waved his hand in acknowledgment and answered the telephone with the other.

Hurrying from the store, Johnny almost collided with Mrs. White. "Oh, I'm sorry, Mrs. White," he apologized, holding the door for her.

"That's quite all right," she replied, smiling pleasantly at him. "Tell you mother hello for me," she said and entered the store. "Good morning, Jack."

Johnny hurried back down the street, across the square, and around City Hall to the Sheriff's office. Several cars were still parked in front, including his dad's. He grabbed his bike from under the tree and pedaled down Oak Street. Making a right on Hunter, he pedaled the two blocks to Spruce and his house.

"Hey, Shari," Johnny yelled when he saw her sitting on the front porch with Carole. "Will you take this in and give it to Mom?"

"What is it?" she asked as she caught the grocery bag he tossed her.

"Bread. Mom needs it for lunch. Thanks," he called as he rode off through the yard. All he had to do was make a left on Church Street, and he would be at the school.

Oak Grove Elementary consisted of two red brick buildings; one behind the other. A rock wall surrounded the buildings on three sides and a white fence bordered a cornfield on the other. Both two-story buildings were built with arched entrances that formed covered porches on all four sides. The front building contained first through fourth grades, and the back building was used for fifth through eighth grades.

A football field sat directly across the street, and the high school building was located on the opposite end of the field, facing Church Street.

Several boys were already gathered beneath the oak tree in the school yard, and Brenton was in the process of comparing the other boys' notes when Johnny rode up.

"Everyone has pretty much written the same thing," Truman said, looking at Johnny. "I don't see how this has helped at all."

"Well, we needed to check," Brenton said, looking aggravated. "You never know what someone else might have seen or heard."

Johnny sat on the ground next to the others. "So the only other thing we know is that the man is tall."

"How do we know that?" Simon asked, pressing a small, tin cricket with his fingers repeatedly.

Brenton then related to the rest of the boys what he, Truman, and Johnny had just done for his dad.

"Say, why don't we sneak over to the square tonight and watch?" Preston asked. "That would make sense to me. Then we could catch him in the act."

Brenton glanced at Truman and Johnny. His dad was planning just that very thing, but they were not supposed to let anyone know. "We can't tonight, so we will meet here tomorrow at the same time."

"Why can't we meet tonight?" Preston asked, looking curiously at his brother. "The sooner we get started, the sooner we'll find out who it is."

"Because it has to be planned," Brenton replied. "Are we all going to just sneak out after dark, or what? We have to plan it," he said, looking at Truman and Johnny for help of any kind.

"That's right," Truman commented, "we have to do this right, so we don't mess things up. Don't anyone do anything unless you are told."

"I don't see why should we waste another night either," Simon said as he continued clicking the cricket.

"Simon, will you put that thing away," Truman complained, looking at his little brother. He found it in one of his shoes in the closet and had been clicking it for the last two days. He wished he would lose it again.

"Well, gee whiz, excuse me," Simon retorted, giving it a couple more clicks before dropping it in his pocket.

Brenton looked at him. "We might need to use that thing. Who has crickets," he asked, looking around.

Everyone raised his hand. Who didn't have a cricket? "What for?" Preston asked, wondering what he had done with his.

"To signal each other like the Paratroopers did," Brenton replied. "Everyone go home, find them, and also get your Red Rider BB guns ready. We might need them to scare him off. Everyone have one?"

Most of the boys nodded with the exception of Simon, Jake, and Larry.

"Dad's got mine," Simon said with a frown. "I shot a hole in the basement window two weeks ago, and I can't have it for another week."

"I don't have one either," Jake said, "but I've got a sling shot. In fact, I have two. Simon, I'll bring one for you."

"Mom would never let us have one," Larry said, throwing a stick on the ground. "She said I would probably shoot my eye out or someone else's. I don't know what I can do."

"We'll need some lookouts. That will be your job," Truman replied. "What do you think our parents will say when they see us gathering BB guns? Mom will put me through the third degree," he said, "especially since Simon shot the hole in the window."

"We may not need them," Brenton said. "Just get them out and have them ready; just in case. Let's report back here tomorrow at the same time" He stood up. "Remember, not a word; secrecy is very important, and keep your eyes and ears open."

Chapter 12

Mike just finished his favorite meal of stuffed pork chops and was presently enjoying that lazy, contented feeling one gets from overindulging. Lying on the sofa with a pillow propped beneath his head, he stretched his long legs out and closed his eyes. He was not in the habit of taking second helpings, but when it came to Leah's pork chops he had no will power and gave in to temptation with no remorse whatsoever.

Every muscle in his body felt limp, and Mike was faintly aware of the familiar sounds of his family floating around him. Shari's voice drifted through the window as she sang *She'll be Comin Around the Mountain* to the accompaniment of the squeak of the porch swing. Giggling and chatter from the hall bore evidence that Laura was talking with Noelle on the telephone, and Jimmy was searching around in the pantry looking for *a special rag* to clean his BB gun.

"Here, Jimmy. Use this one," Leah's voice came from the kitchen. "Why are you so worried about cleaning it right this minute anyway?"

"Gee, Mom, a man should always keep his weapon in good condition," he replied, in exasperation as though women didn't know anything. "Say, have you seen my cricket?"

Mike heard Leah mumble something about the junk drawer then recognized the sound of Jimmy rummaging through it. "There it is," he exclaimed, slamming the drawer shut. Mike opened one eye as the repeated clicking grew louder when Jimmy ran down the hall, passed the couch, and out the front door.

Closing his eyes, he drifted slowly back to that place of complete contentment. The slamming of the back door jarred him awake, and he knew Johnny was coming back in with the trashcan. The thud from the corner in the kitchen verified it.

"Mom, it is such a swell looking bike," he said in a coaxing voice. "You should just see it. You would know what I mean."

"Yes, I am sure it is," Leah answered in a tone that Mike recognized. She tried to sound casual and pleasant but was never able to hide the firmness in her voice once her mind was made up about something.

"It's a Schwinn. Larry's dad got it on sale at C&G Hardware in Chesterville, and he said that is was really a good buy for a Schwinn."

So that explains his unusual quietness at supper tonight, Mike thought and recalled their conversation from a couple of days ago. Johnny asked when he would be driving to Chesterville, indicating he would like to ride along. "C&G Hardware is having a summer bike sale, and we could stop in and check them out," he had said.

Mike told him they could stop and look, but he didn't think anyone needed a new bike at the present time.

"Oh, Elizabeth Driscol has a new one too, so I guess they are just clearing them out of the store. They said it was a really good sale."

"Umm, your bicycle is broken?" she asked innocently. Mike smiled to himself, *That's one point for Leah.*

"No, of course not, Mom. I've taken good care of it," Johnny answered, his voice trailing off as he realized he just bit his own tail. Quickly he added, "That's why it would be good for Jimmy. He's about too big for the one he's riding now." He sounded very pleased with his comeback, and Mike waited for Leah's response.

That's a point for Johnny, Mike thought to himself and decided he would have to remind his oldest that no means no.

"Well, the bicycle Jimmy is riding is getting a little small. That bicycle belonged to you when you were younger; or did you forget?" Leah asked. Mike knew she turned around and looked him in the eye. She always did when she was getting ready to make a point. "I believe you have had two new bicycles already. Don't you think he deserves a brand new one also?"

There is another point for Leah, Mike thought grinning to himself. *She is doing really well.*

"I know it's a little early, but that's what you could get me for my birthday," Johnny replied, ignoring her last comment. "I was just thinking it would save us some money."

Mike opened his eyes and looked at the ceiling. Johnny was really reaching now.

"A little early?" Leah asked. "This is June. Your birthday is not until November."

"I know, but I can't ride my bike in the snow. Then Christmas will be coming up and you and Dad shouldn't have to worry about it then," he answered, beginning to sound more like the youngest son instead of the oldest.

Silence reigned in the kitchen, then the sound of a chair scraped the floor. *Here it comes*, thought Mike. Leah always likes to take a seat right before the final verdict.

"Johnny, your father and I would love to buy you a bicycle if we had a lot of money, but we do not," she said tenderly. "You have a perfectly good bicycle. When your dad bought it, I thought it was too big for you, but he was wise enough to get the larger size so you would not outgrow it. Your first bike, and Laura's, have both been passed down to Shari and Jimmy," she said patiently. "You both have had brand new bicycles. It is now Shari and Jimmy's turn to get new ones. Do you understand what I am saying?" she asked softly.

Johnny mumbled something Mike could not understand and walked from the kitchen into the hall. Sitting up as he entered the living room, Mike observed the look of defeat on his face. Nodding his head with a frown across his brow, he walked upstairs.

Mike rose from the couch and walked down the hall into the kitchen. Leah was standing at the sink looking out the window. Walking up behind her, he put his arms around her. "Good job, Mom," he whispered in her ear.

"Oh, Mike. I wish we could buy it for him. He is such a good son and never causes us any trouble. But it just wouldn't be fair to Shari and Jimmy." She glanced up at him sadly and laid her head against his chest, welcoming the hug he gave her.

"I know, Hon, you were correct in everything you told him." Mike kissed her on the forehead. "This is one of those growing up times. A child has to learn that they cannot have everything they want."

"Why did he have to come to me? Why couldn't he have asked you?" she asked in frustration as she looked up at him on the verge of tears.

Mike chuckled. "He already approached me with the idea and knew my answer. I guess he thought to persuade you, or at least give it a good try. When we go hunting this fall, he'll be more interested in a shotgun than a bicycle."

"No, Mike. You aren't serious?" Leah asked, looking at him with a mixture of alarm and disbelief.

"Yes, I am. I was thirteen when I got my first gun. He knows all the rules and safety precautions. I started teaching him to respect a weapon the first time we went hunting." Mike looked down into her brown eyes. "He is a responsible son, Leah. I would never buy one for him if I had any doubts. Trust me on this."

"Mike, you know I trust you. It's just . . . he is still my little boy. If you get him a gun, he will seem so grown up. I don't know if I am ready for that yet."

Mike laughed and hugged her to him. "I'm afraid there is nothing you can do about that. Come on, let's sit on the porch. Shari is serenading the neighborhood so we may as well enjoy it too," he said with a grin as he grabbed the dishtowel from her hand and tossed it on the back of a chair.

By the time dusk settled on Oak Grove, the men were at their stations in designated buildings. Mayor Driscol, the Sheriff, and Brenton were at a window in City Hall that overlooked the west end of the square. Dr. Miller and Hank were seated in the hardware store, and Sam Cranston and Willy were in the Cranston Hotel on the east end. Mike Madison and Young Ben were in the bank, and Alan Miller, Eli Smith, and Jim and Truman were in The Chronicle.

"If anyone tries to ring that bell tonight, we'll nab him," Henry Driscol said as he took a seat back away from the window, worried that he would be seen. "I wonder who it is."

"Your guess is as good as mine, Henry," John replied, watching the square. "This may turn out to be a long night."

Brenton was perched on a stool at the window, hoping to catch the first glimpse of whoever it was and wondered how long they would have to wait.

"It's been around midnight both nights, hasn't it?" Henry whispered as though he were afraid he would be heard. He looked at his watch and wondered what time it was but found the room too dark to see anything.

"Pretty close to it, I believe," the Sheriff answered. "We may as well take turns watching."

"How about a cookie?" Hank asked, offering one to Dr. Miller "Sally thought we should have something to tide us over. We might be here a while," he said, munching on the piece he just bit off.

"Don't mind if I do." Dr. Miller helped himself and looked at Hank. "How in the world do you stay so thin as much as you eat?" he asked. It was true, Hank was very thin, in spite of the fact he could eat as much as two men.

"I don't rightly know. I guess I take after my pop. He was always on the lean side," he replied, watching the square. "Say, how about I keep watch for about thirty minutes and then we'll trade. If not, I'm going to fall asleep sitting here staring at the dark."

"That's fine with me. Taking turns is a good idea," Dr. Miller said as he sat back in the chair and bit into the gingersnap. "I brought a thermos of coffee if you would like a cup," he said, motioning to the thermos on the counter.

"I brought one too." Hank looked through the window at the bell tower. *Why do I stay so thin?* he wondered. Sally, with all of her dieting, stayed on the plump side. "I can just take one look at what you are eating and gain weight," she was always telling him.

"It's a good thing those street lamps come on, or this would be useless. We wouldn't be able to see a thing."

"That's for sure," Dr. Miller replied. "I wonder who the Sheriff really suspects is doing all this. He acted like he had an idea, didn't he?" he asked, watching Hank stare out the window.

"I suspect he has an idea too," Hank replied. "I sure will be glad to find out who it is."

"I don't see how we can miss him," Young Ben said, looking out the window of the Oak Grove Bank. "We can see the whole square from here."

Michael sat in one of the swivel chairs that he pulled to the window and commented, "If he shows up."

"What makes you think he won't?" Ben asked, turning to look at him with a puzzled look on his face. "He has the last two nights, and I don't think anyone knows we are here except our families." *And Lizzie*, Ben thought to himself, *but she can be trusted not to say anything*.

Ben chuckled to himself. Uncle Ben and Mercy were trying their best to discover what was going on between them, and out of sheer meanness he refused to admit to anything.

"I don't know, just a feeling I have." Michael propped his feet on Marion's desk. "He strikes at random with no pattern to anything he does. I wouldn't be at all surprised if he outsmarted us tonight."

"He just might," Ben answered as he turned back to the window. They also decided to take turns watching the square, and Ben presently sat on a chair next to the window looking out into the shadows. The flag gently moved as a small breeze stirred the leaves, the benches sat empty, and the bandstand, usually full of children, was vacant. Everything appeared peaceful and quiet. *Who would want to disturb this?* he thought in bewilderment as he considered Michael's words.

"You are right. There is no pattern to anything he does, is there?"

Willy glanced around the parlor of the Cranston Hotel. This was a pretty nice place. He sat on a love seat in front of a window that afforded him a good view of the square and glanced at the gauzy, white curtains that concealed his presence from anyone who might pass by. Across the room, two wing back chairs sat by the fireplace. Bookcases, on both sides, were filled with several volumes, pictures, and various collectibles the Cranstons had gathered from their yearly venture back east. A piano was against the wall to his right, and an overstuffed blue chair sat next to a reading table in front of the window on his left. Several ferns and plants sat around the room on the floor or small tables, giving the room a cozy, comfortable feeling.

Relaxing on the love seat, Willy watched the square. Light filtered in from a small table lamp in the foyer, temporarily obscured by Mrs. Cranston who stood in the doorway.

"Can I get you something, Willy?" she asked. A cup of tea? Coffee? Are you hungry?" she asked pleasantly.

Willy looked at the plump little woman who was such a kind little lady. With her snow-white hair pulled back in a bun and her rosy cheeks, she was, to Willy's way of thinking, a picture of the perfect grandmother. "I don't believe so. Thank you, Ma'am," he said, glancing back out at the square.

"You just let me know if you do," she replied, regarding him for a moment. *That handsome young man needs a sweetheart,* she thought as she walked down the hall humming to herself.

Willy wondered what the others were doing. This was going to be a long night. Somewhere in the house he heard a clock chime the nine o'clock hour.

"I was just upstairs looking out of the window," Samuel Cranston said, entering the room with a cup of coffee in his hand. "The men are concealing themselves well. I couldn't see anybody through the windows. Would you like a cup of coffee, Willy?"

"No thanks. I'll get one later." He looked across the square at the bandstand and thought about the strange feeling of being watched. "What if we don't catch him?" he asked, turning to look at Samuel.

"What do you mean? Land sakes, of course we will catch him. As soon as he hits the square, we'll grab him," he said, taking a seat in one of the wingback chairs.

"I don't know. He's pretty fast. He managed to disappear rapidly the last two nights," Willy commented, wondering how he managed to do so.

"Well, I believe we will find out tonight," Samuel said. "Yes, sir, as soon as he hits the square, we will have him.

Willy was not so sure.

Alan, Eli, Jim, and Truman sat in The Chronicle. "So you and the Sheriff think this fellow is pretty tall?" Alan asked, looking at Jim sitting at the table where Brenton and Truman folded newspapers.

"I'm not positive. The boys were able to get from the tree to the bell tower but not back," Jim answered. "John said it would take someone pretty tall to reach one of the limbs strong enough to pull himself back into the tree."

"If that is, in fact, what he is doing," Eli commented, glancing at Jim and Alan.

"Well, you are right there. We don't know for sure if that is the case." Jim shifted on his stool and watched Truman stare out the window.

"I wonder how old this person is?" Alan asked. "He can't be too old as quickly as he gets around."

"I know the preacher said it is not one of the Blacks," Eli commented, "but they live out in the woods and probably are pretty skillful at getting from place to place without being seen."

"John doesn't seem to think they are involved, and Pastor Mike would swear to it if he had to," Jim answered. "Hopefully, tonight we'll find out who is causing all the commotion."

Propped comfortably on the bed, the children listened intently to Mike's discussion of trusting God when you didn't understand what was happening in your life. This nightly sharing of God's love and direction in their daily lives stemmed from Leah's habit of bringing the children into their room for bedtime stories when they were very small. Through the years it developed into a very precious time they all enjoyed.

Tonight was one they lingered over. Speculation on the recent happenings in Oak Grove was the topic of conversation. Johnny and Laura were more curious about what was stolen than who the thief was. Shari was convinced that it was a hobo that really liked Oak Grove and didn't want to leave, and Jimmy thought that when he was caught, he should be put in stocks on the square like they use to do in olden times.

Mike glanced at Leah and smiled. They all learned very early if they could carry on a conversation long enough, it would prolong bedtime, and Mike and Leah agreed between themselves that ten minutes of tarrying was long enough. Glancing at the clock, Mike punched the pillow with his fist and leaned back against the head of the bed. "All right," he yawned, "all of you, out of here. I have an early morning tomorrow."

Laura looked at the stern look on her dad's face and giggled. His laughing eyes always gave him away, and she leaned back and grabbed her pillow. Giving it a swing, she threw it in his face and jumped from the bed.

"Oh yeah?" Mike yelled as he sent the pillow sailing across the room, hitting her in the back. Jimmy jumped up and began bouncing on the bed, and Shari squealed as she scrambled to the floor and retrieved the pillow. Flinging it at her dad, she missed and smacked Jimmy in the face, knocking him off balance. Mike caught him by the arm, pulled him down, and slid him to the floor in one swift motion.

"No jumping on the bed," he commanded. The tone of his voice was serious, and Jimmy sat on the floor with a surprised look on his face, wondering how he so quickly ended up on his bottom. He stared at his dad with wide brown eyes and found the pillow tossed in his face.

Laughter followed Laura and Shari as they left the room. "Night, Mom," they both called back.

"Goodnight, girls," Leah called after them. "I'll be there in just a minute."

Jimmy sat where he landed and leaned against the wall. "I can't wait to see who they catch tonight. You should have gone, Dad." He looked up at him questioningly and asked, "Why didn't you?"

"Because I'm scheduled for tomorrow night," Mike answered. Jimmy leaned against the bed with his chin resting in his hands. Mike placed his hand on his back and looked at him, thinking how much he favored Leah. It was almost incredible. Shari and Jimmy both looked like her and were often thought to be twins by those getting acquainted for the first time.

"You mean they might not catch him?" Jimmy asked with a surprised look on his face.

"I hope so, but there is no guarantee they will. So, some of us are scheduled for tomorrow evening." Mike adjusted the pillow behind his back and held out his arms for a hug.

"Come on, Jimmy. It is time for bed," Leah reminded him, knowing this could go on for another ten minutes.

"Night, Dad," Johnny said, rising from the other side of the bed. "Night Mom." He kissed Leah on the cheek and walked to the door.

"Oh, Son, I'm going out to the Black's place tomorrow," Mike commented, noticing how tall he was getting. "I would like you to go along."

"Me?" Johnny asked with a surprised look on his face. "Go to the Blacks?" Stories he had heard flew through his mind. "But . . . I . . . well. . . ." he stammered, staring at his dad. Why did he want him to go along?

"Yes, we'll leave here about eight o'clock so get a good night's sleep. It is quite a walk to their place," Mike said, observing the uncertainty in his son's face.

"Walk? Why aren't you going to drive?" he asked with a confused look on his face.

"Well, I'll drive as far as I can, but when the road ends, we'll have to walk a good hour the rest of the way," Mike explained. He wanted to laugh at the expression on Johnny's face. "Goodnight, Son," he said and lay back on the pillow.

Johnny mumbled a goodnight and closed the bedroom door.

Mike chuckled to himself. He would enjoy this trip tomorrow.

Mike and Johnny sat quietly, neither one moving, as they stared in awe at a doe and her fawn about twenty yards away on the opposite side of the creek. Realizing he was holding his breath, Johnny slowly exhaled and continued watching. They were beautiful. Slowly, the doe lowered her head and took a drink. Somewhere a branch cracked and she bounded off followed by the fawn, their white tails in the air.

"Wasn't that something?" Johnny exclaimed excitedly, looking at his dad with wide eyes. "I bet there are a lot of deer up here, don't you?"

"These woods are full of them," Mike answered, taking a drink of water from his canteen. They had walked about forty-five minutes through forest that had become increasingly dense and Mike glanced around, listening intently, knowing the creek was somewhere close. Pushing through some tangled brush, they found themselves not far from the stream and stopped to rest. That's when the doe and her fawn approached They both sat unmoving, not wanting to disturb the scene before them.

Presently they stood in an area flourishing with blackberry bushes. "Taste these, Dad; they are really sweet," Johnny said, popping a couple of juicy berries in his mouth. "We should take some to Mom for a pie."

Mike watched as Johnny reached for another of the juicy berries and grinned slightly when he jerked his hand back. "Ouch!" He looked at his thumb and picked at a thorn. "Why do they have to be so thorny?" he asked, removing the small offending spike.

"You need to take your time." Reaching into the bush, Mike picked a few. He held one up and looked at it thoughtfully before popping it into his mouth, savoring the sweetness of the plump juicy berry, then looked at Johnny. "Think about it, Son. Look at these blackberries." He held one up and examined it. "They are plump, juicy, and sweet.... but you have to watch for the thorns. They can snare you."

He stared at Johnny for a long moment then spoke quietly, "Beware of thorns, Son." He looked up into the trees with a sad expression on his face then looked back at him. "Satan is very cunning. He is also very subtle and when he places thorns in your path, and he will, he makes them appear very appealing."

Johnny watched his dad's face and was not unaware of the look of tenderness he saw "There will be many things in your life that you think you want," Mike continued, "but be careful. Be very careful. Consider its value and its purpose." His dad's voice became so quiet that Johnny strained to hear. "Most of all, determine if it is in accordance with God's Word. You must let that be your guide. If so, then pursue it prayerfully and patiently, letting Him guide you, and He will protect you from the thorns."

Johnny knew what he was telling him was important, and he wanted to ask about the thorns in his life but instead stood silent, watching him.

Father and son looked at each other for a long moment, and the wisdom and love he saw in his dad's eyes touched him somewhere deep inside, relaying a message that words could not express. But for the sound of birds and a squirrel chattering somewhere, the forest was silent, and Johnny knew a photograph of this minute was imprinted in his mind. His dad, standing next to the blackberry bushes surrounded by trees and brush, looking so intently at him would be a picture he would never forget.

A soft smile crossed Mike's face and he turned and headed through the trees. Johnny quickly followed, not wanting to get too far behind. Never in his life had he seen woods this dense before, and he was amazed that his dad knew where he was going.

It can't be too much farther, Johnny thought as he glanced around nervously, thinking of the Black family and the rumors he often heard. They were supposed to be crazy and didn't speak English. Some said they trained wild animals to attack trespassers, and others said that they would just as soon shoot you as look at you. He was pretty certain about that one since Mr. Black shot at his dad the day he took the little girl with the broken leg home.

Deciding to switch his train of thought, Johnny asked, "Why do you think he didn't ring the bell last night?"

Mike had called Sheriff Walker early this morning before they left and found that nothing happened. The mysterious culprit didn't even show up.

"I don't know, Son," Pastor Mike answered, looking carefully ahead. He knew he was walking by instinct now but was sure the Blacks already knew they were close.

Feeling a little guilty, Johnny had to admit he was glad no one was caught and hoped they would catch him tonight while he was on watch. He was glad Dad asked him to go along and wondered if Brenton and Truman had gone last night. That would be so exciting if they did manage to nab him tonight. *Who could it be,* Johnny wondered as he bumped into the back of his dad who had halted abruptly.

Glancing around his dad's shoulder, he saw a young boy about Jimmy's age standing very still in front of them, almost blending in with the brush. Wearing a pair of faded overalls with no shirt, he was thin, very tanned, and barefoot. An old, floppy, straw hat sat atop a mop of sandy colored hair that hung across the forehead of his freckled face, almost covering his eyes. Johnny stared at the boy. He had the most peculiar eyes he had ever seen. They were almost violet.

"Hey, Mike Daniels," the boy said. Raising one hand in greeting and flashing a friendly smile, he then stared curiously at Johnny.

"Hey, Tommy," his dad answered. "This is my son, Johnny." He stepped aside, allowing the two boys to face each other.

"Hey, Johnny Daniels," the boy replied, raising his hand again. Then, unexpectedly, he turned and without another word walked ahead of them through the woods.

Johnny glanced at his dad and received a reassuring smile. "Come on. That's our invitation to the house." They hurried along, following the small boy and his floppy straw hat through the brush.

Much to Johnny's surprise, he suddenly found that they were standing in a clearing surrounded by several barking dogs. One jumped on him, another sniffed around his pant leg, and three more ran in circles around them, barking. An ear-splitting whistle sounded from the porch of a log house that was situated on the side of the ridge. The dogs immediately stopped their barking and ran off to find something of more interest.

A tall man stood on the porch dressed much the same as Tommy but wearing a shirt and boots. Johnny was aware of several children of various ages, appearing from what seemed every direction. Two small children about three and four came from inside the house and stood on each side of the tall man, peering around his legs. A young girl about Laura's age appeared in the doorway. She wore a gray apron over a faded blue dress, and her dark hair hung down her back in one long braid. The boy, Tommy, sat on the step of the porch and was quickly joined by a boy bearing a very strong resemblance. He appeared to be a couple of years older and wore the same kind of hat. Laying a hammer on the porch next to him, he smiled at Mike then stared at Johnny. Two girls about eight and ten emerged from the woods to the right of the house carrying water pails, and a boy about nine dropped down from a tree limb. None of the children wore shoes, Johnny noticed.

"Mike Daniels!" the man on the porch called in a deep booming voice. "Bring yourself up here." It wasn't until then that Johnny realized his dad had not attempted to approach the house.

"Nathaniel." Mike smiled as he walked to the house. "How do I find you and your family this beautiful day?" He stepped up on the porch and shook the man's hand.

"We are as right as rain," Nathaniel answered. He turned and from his towering height looked down at Johnny still standing at the foot of the steps.

"And how are you called?" the man asked, motioning him to come up on the porch.

"Sir?" Johnny questioned, looking at his dad. The children sat on the steps and along the porch and continued to stare at him. He felt as though he was something the circus left behind.

"Your name, Son," Mike prompted him. "He wants to know your name."

"Oh, my name is John," he answered, walking up on the porch. He looked up into the eyes of the man towering above him. They were the same color as Tommy's, and he had the same sandy colored hair.

Johnny stared at him in awe, aware that the man was assessing him in some manner as he looked him over. His chest pounded when the man suddenly looked directly into his eyes and stared. He was very tall, broad shouldered, and had an ominous look about him that left no doubt he expected one to do as he was told.

Suddenly, the man grinned and the change was remarkable. His eyes twinkled and a smile spread across his face, giving him an almost boyish look. He reached out and grabbed Johnny's arm with an iron grip. "Good name; you have a good Holy Bible name," he said, pounding him on the back. Johnny sighed with relief and knew for certain what it meant to be weak in the knees. This would definitely not be a man you would want for an enemy.

A thin woman appeared from the side of the house with two boys. One was about Johnny's age and the other a little older. A smile spread across the woman's face when she recognized Mike, and she unconsciously brushed away a strand of black hair that fell across her brow. The boys, tall for their age, each carried a hoe. They also had the same extraordinary colored eyes and sandy hair as their father.

"Mike Daniels," the woman exclaimed in a soft, smooth voice as she came up on the porch. Her words carried a strange accent, and Johnny wondered what it was. "I am so proud to see you, and who travels with you?" she asked, turning to face Johnny.

He thought he had never seen anyone quite like her. She was very small with a mass of black hair that was braided and wound around her head. Her high cheekbones brought attention to warm, friendly, dark eyes that slanted up at the corners. But it was the bronze tone of her skin that Johnny found most unusual.

"This is my son, Johnny," Pastor Mike answered, removing his hat. "Johnny, this is Nathaniel and Elizabeth Black."

"Oh, I am so proud to know you," she remarked with a smile, touching his arm. "Children, this is Johnny Daniels. He belongs to Mike Daniels," she commented, looking at all of the children gathered on the porch. "Come; let's tell him how you are called."

The girl standing in the door spoke first, using the same soft voice as her mother, "I am called Sarah." She stood very straight with her arms at her sides as though she was ready to defend herself.

The two small ones seated on the step looked up at him. "I am Josie," the little girl said, poking her brother with her elbow.

"And I am Paul." The little boy looked at him shyly and leaned against one of the brown dogs that lay next to him. The rest began stating their names in turn.

A boy leaning against one of the posts raised his hand in greeting like Tommy and said with a grin, "I am called William."

Tommy, sitting next to William, smiled brightly and shoved the straw hat farther back on his head.

"My calling is Claire," a little girl about Jimmy's age said, looking up at him from the bottom step.

A young girl holding Mike's hand smiled up at him shyly, and Johnny knew before she spoke that she was Sally. A bit of mischief shone in her brown eyes and she wore her dark hair in braids "They call me Sally, and I broke my leg," she commented proudly and looked up at Mike with a grin on her face.

"I am called Andrew." A little boy about five years old sat on a split log grinning at him. Johnny grinned back, instantly liking the little guy. *They all have the same smile as their dad,* he thought as he glanced at Mr. Black.

The two boys who appeared from the side of the house with their mother stared at him for a minute, and then the oldest one spoke, "I am called Nathaniel, and this is Joel." He pointed to his brother who merely nodded his head and looked away.

They all had the same sandy colored hair and violet eyes as their father with the exception of the two little ones and Sally who had black hair and dark eyes like their mother. Sarah was a mixture of both parents and had her mother's dark complexion and black hair, but her father's violet eyes.

"Now, come inside. We were just assembling for lunch," Elizabeth Black said as she stepped back and indicated they all go inside.

Johnny glanced at his dad uncertainly, but he was already walking into the house with Mr. Black. The others stared at him, and he realized they were waiting for him to go ahead of them. Johnny smiled and walked toward the door. Sarah stood in the doorway watching him. Her long, black braid hung over her shoulder, and she stared at him a minute. Johnny thought she was kind of pretty for a girl and wondered what Brenton or Truman would think if they knew he thought she was pretty.

Smiling faintly at him, she turned and walked into the house. Johnny followed and they passed through a large room that led to the kitchen.

Sally and Claire, the two girls he saw carrying the pails of water, emptied them into a large, white, enamel pan on a table in front of the window. Sally looked at him and smiled shyly then picked up the two buckets and sat them on the back porch.

Mr. Black and Mike stood at the table by the window washing their hands and talking. Johnny walked over and picked up a piece of something that he guessed was soap and lathered his hands like his dad. It had a strange smell and Johnny wondered what kind it was. They never used this sort of soap at home. A piece of cloth served as a towel, and Johnny dried his hands and stepped away to allow the next person to wash up.

A very long table with wooden benches on each side sat in the middle of the room. Mr. Black took a seat in the chair at one end of the table and his dad sat to his right. "Johnny, you sit right next to your pa," Mrs. Black said, smiling at him. Johnny speculated again about her looks, wondering if she could be part Indian. She donned an apron over her faded green dress, and although it was old, the dress was clean.

Sitting next to his dad, he watched the others wash and dry their hands before taking their places at the table. *Mom would be impressed*, Johnny thought. Jimmy was always being sent back to rewash his hands.

Mrs. Black took her seat lastly at the other end of the table. They bowed their heads and Mr. Black, in his booming voice, gave thanks. "Thank you, God, for Your protection, the food, and our friends. Amen."

Johnny eyed the loaves of homemade bread and felt his mouth water. It had been a long walk this morning, and he was hungry. He did not recognize some of the food on the table but did identify the blackberries he and Dad sampled in the woods. Everything smelled good, and his stomach growled. He looked at the gray tin plates and cups of cold milk, deciding he didn't care what the food was. He was starving.

Now you make sure you take plenty victuals. There is plenty more on the stove," Mrs Black said, passing a bowl of potatoes. Johnny took a portion everything that was passed to him. Mom said it was rude if you didn't. "When you are a guest, you eat what is provided for you," she told them many times.

Johnny looked curiously at the next bowl Joel passed and glanced at his dad who was talking with Mr. Black. It contained something that looked like cooked weeds with scrambled eggs and bacon, and he decided to take only a small portion.

Everything tasted good even if he didn't know what he was eating. He suspected the meat was squirrel. Dad fixed it once, but no one would eat it so they didn't have it again. This tasted good, though. Glancing across the table at Sarah, Johnny wondered if she cooked dinner. She stared back at him for a minute and then lowered her eyes.

He wondered at the silence around the table. None of the children spoke, and the only ones talking were Dad and Mr. Black. Johnny's eyes roamed around the kitchen. The walls were unpainted logs, and the only decoration of any kind was a calendar hanging by the back door. The stove was huge and a box of wood sat next to it. One wall held several shelves containing plates, cups, bowls, and all manner of cooking supplies. A curtain of sorts was pulled to the side, which he guessed was used to conceal the shelves when not in use. The table in front of the window held the pan they used for washing their hands and another wooden bucket that had a water dipper hanging on the side. He was curious as to where the refrigerator was until it dawned on him there was no electricity. A small table at one end of the room held a kerosene lamp and what appeared to be schoolbooks. A ladder to the left of the table extended up into what Johnny supposed was a loft.

Mike proceeded to tell about the circus, gaining the attention of everyone at the table. They were completely enthralled with what he was saying, and Johnny watched the expression on their faces and the wonder in their eyes. It dawned on him that the only outside news they ever got was when his dad came up here. He then launched into the peculiar happenings in Oak Grove.

"Why would someone take something that did not belong to them?" Nathaniel Black asked with a frown on his face. It was the same question that everyone in Oak Grove was asking, but Mr. Black's reaction was incredulous. "How can a body stoop so low?" he questioned with a scowl on his face.

"Nathaniel, I don't understand it either, but there are some folks in this world that do not think the way we do," Mike answered, looking at the big man sitting to his left.

After a while, Mr. Black rose from the table, stood to his towering height, and removed a pipe from the pocket of his overalls. Johnny thought it resembled a corncob and wondered if he made it himself. He produced a small drawstring bag and stuck the pipe down in it. Filling it, he pulled the strings tight and pressed the tobacco down in the pipe with his thumb, all the while looking around the table.

Johnny wondered how tall he was. His dad was six feet and Mr. Black towered above him.

"Come on, Mike Daniels, let's sit on the porch a spell before I have to get back to the field," he said, glancing around the table one more time as if taking into account everyone present.

Mike stood and looked across the table. "Sarah, lunch was delicious as usual. Thank you. Your mother has taught you well."

Sarah's bright smile lit up her face, revealing white, straight teeth and dimples in each cheek. Her eyes grew wide, taking on a brilliant purple hue, and in that transforming moment she looked just like her father. She glanced across the table at Johnny and immediately dropped her eyes in shyness, a red blush staining both cheeks.

"Nathaniel, you busy this young man," Mr. Black said, looking at him and then Johnny. He nodded his head and turned to Mike. "Come on." He put the end of the pipe in his mouth and led the way out of the kitchen.

Johnny watched as each child rose and carried their plate to the table where they had washed their hands. Following their lead, he placed his plate with the others and glanced through the window. Sally and Claire, each with a wooden bucket in their hand, were walking toward the creek with one of the brown dogs trotting alongside.

The other children, evidently responsible for individual chores, immediately returned to what they were doing or began a new task. Sarah glanced shyly at Johnny then took Josie and Paul by the hand. "Come on. It is resting time," she said in the same soft tone her mother used. They both looked behind them and grinned as she led them through a door off the kitchen and down a hallway.

Joel stared at Johnny as he drained his milk and set the tin cup on the table. Without a word or smile, he grabbed an ax from the back porch and walked out the door toward the woods.

"Pay no mind to Joel," Nathaniel commented with just a hint of a smile. "It is my turn to hunt tomorrow. I need to clean my fowling piece; you can watch if you want," he commented over his shoulder as he headed toward the living room.

"Yeah, I would like that." Johnny followed him, wondering just exactly what a fowling piece was.

Walking to the far wall in the living room, they approached a homemade gun rack containing, what Johnny recognized to be, two 20 gauges and two double barreled shotguns. Reaching for the lower one, Nathaniel took it down and led the way back through the kitchen and down the same hall Sarah took Josie and Paul. Two bedrooms were located on each side, and Johnny followed him into the far bedroom at the back of the house.

The room was large and contained three individual beds with a shelf above each bed. Again, there was no paint on the walls, a piece of material hung at the window, and rugs made of some sort of animal skin lay on the floor next to the beds. A small table with a kerosene lamp and chair sat in front of the window, and pegs on the wall contained a few articles of clothing. A large three-drawer bureau sat at the end of the room with a kerosene lamp sitting next to a picture that was leaning against the wall. It was painted on a smooth piece of wood and showed a small, clear stream bubbling over rocks as it cut its way through the middle of a forest. A patch of sunlight reflected off the water, and a few wildflowers grew along the bank. Johnny stared at the painting in amazement. It was very good, and he wondered who painted it.

Nathaniel sat on the bed nearest the door. "Sit there on Joel's bed. He won't care," he said, motioning for him to sit down.

"Are you sure?" Johnny asked, thinking of Joel's behavior. He was the only one who didn't seem friendly.

Nathaniel looked at him in confusion for a minute and then grinned. "Joel won't care. He never converses much." He studied Johnny for a moment and commented, "He thinks you're tolerable, or he would have told you." He looked down the barrel of the gun and asked, "How often do you clean your fowling piece?"

"I don't have a fowling piece," Johnny answered, watching the look of astonishment cross Nathaniel's face.

"You don't have one?" Nathaniel stared at him for a long minute, a questioning look in his eye. "How do you hunt for food?" Picking up a long rod with a small rag attached to the end, he poked it down the barrel and looked back at Johnny, waiting for an answer.

"Well, we don't have to hunt for food. We just go to the store and buy it," he explained, wondering how it would be to rely on yourself for food. "Dad hunts because he enjoys it, and sometimes he brings something home for Mom to cook. But we go mostly because it is fun to be out in the woods." Johnny thought how ridiculous his explanation must sound to Nathaniel. Why would going to the woods be fun when you lived there every day?

Nathaniel stared at him then continued cleaning his fowling piece. "I think I like our way better. I enjoy bringing something home for supper. We take turns; me, Joel, and Pa."

Johnny watched the obvious pride Nathaniel took in caring for the weapon used to provide food for the family. "Dad said when I turn thirteen, I will probably get a 16 gauge," Johnny said, remembering the last time they hunted and he had asked him about it.

"So you have hunted?" Nathaniel asked, looking at him with a little more interest.

"Oh sure, Dad's been taking me since I was nine years old," Johnny said, thinking of the fun they always had and what it was going to be like to have his own gun and hunt by himself like Nathaniel.

"How many years have you had?" Nathaniel asked, closing the barrel of the shotgun "I've had fourteen years last February."

Johnny smiled to himself. They sure had a different way of speaking. "I've had twelve years," he answered in like manner.

"That's the same number Joel is," Nathaniel commented. "I need to put this in its place." He rose from the bed and walked to the door. Johnny followed him down the hall, through the kitchen, and back into the living room. The others were no where in sight and he wondered where they were.

This room was also sparse. A large animal skin lay in front of a huge fireplace at one end of the room. Several chairs and small tables with kerosene lamps were placed around the room, and one large table containing a lamp and a large Bible sat in the middle. Across from the fireplace, a door led into another bedroom. White material hung at the windows and a fiddle hung over a small bed at the other end of the room.

"Who plays the fiddle?" Johnny asked Nathaniel.

"Pa makes music with it and so does Joel. I can't seem to get the hang of it." Nathaniel grinned and looked down at his hands. "Nope, Joel tries to show me, but I can't make music, not like he can. Joel can do anything," he stated with pride. "He plays the fiddle, makes rhymes, and puts pictures on things. Does your Pa play?"

"No, Dad likes to sing, but he doesn't play anything." Johnny looked around the room for more of Joel's paintings but didn't see any. He was surprised at the small amount of *things* in the house. It was bare except for the necessities, and Johnny thought about all of the stuff they had at home.

Nathaniel slipped the shotgun back in the rack and turned to him. "Let's go see what Pa is doing."

A photograph on the mantel caught Johnny's eye. Several Indians wrapped in blankets stood around a fire. "Who are these people?" Johnny asked curiously.

Nathaniel picked the photograph up and looked at it. Pointing at the two that appeared oldest, he said, "They are my grandparents and the rest are aunts and uncles."

The clock on the mantel chimed one o'clock, and Nathaniel put the photograph back. He looked at Johnny, curious as to why he was staring at the photograph, then looked back at the small photo himself. He stared at it for a minute then pointed to a small girl about seven or eight years old. "That's Mom. Her Apache name is Spring Rain, and the chief standing next to her is Geronimo."

Johnny stared in astonishment. Mrs. Black knew the famous Indian chief, Geronimo! He looked at Nathaniel. "Wow, that is something! You should be proud of that. Where was this photograph taken?"

"A place called Fort Sill, Oklahoma," Nathaniel replied. "A lot of them still abide there, but a lot of them are no more." He shrugged his shoulders and looked at the picture again. "I never made any of their acquaintance."

"Wouldn't you like to?" Johnny asked. He couldn't believe it. This was swell.

"I probably never will. Mom gets post from them sometime and always writes words back. She hopes one day to see them again, but I don't know if she ever will." Glancing once again at the photograph, Nathaniel turned and motioned for Johnny to follow.

Johnny couldn't understand Nathaniel's attitude. If he had a relative who knew someone that famous, he would be telling everyone he knew. *Mrs. Black is an Apache,* he thought, glancing once more at the photograph before following Nathaniel through the door. For a reason he could not explain, Johnny felt proud.

Mr. and Mrs. Black and Mike sat on the far end of the porch in chairs fashioned from hickory limbs. "Think on it, Nathaniel," Mike said earnestly. He watched the man and wondered how he would feel if the circumstances were reversed and he found himself in Nathaniel's situation. He looked at Elizabeth's worried face and wished he could relieve her fears in some way.

Nathaniel sighed and stared across the yard into the forest. His face was troubled, and he sat with his hands clasped together.

Mrs. Black stared at her husband with an almost frightened expression and then turned to Mike with a pleading look in her eye.

"I am only thinking of what is best," Mike assured her. He noticed Johnny and Nathaniel standing at the other end of the porch and stood up, knowing it was time to be on their way.

Mr. Black stood along with Mike. "I'll have to study on it. I can't give my word," Nathaniel said quietly. He looked at Mike, searching his face, and knew the only answer he would find would be in his own mind. "It was good of you to visit a spell," he commented abruptly. "I've got to get back to the field."

Mike extended his hand, knowing he had troubled the man but knew there was nothing more he could say. Nathaniel shook his hand and looked at his wife's face.

"I'll be back in a few weeks, my friend." Mike released his hand and walked to Elizabeth, taking her hands in his.

Rising, she looked at Mike with tears in her eyes. "I don't know. . . ." She stared up into the eyes of this kind man she had become so fond of. The confusion in her eyes was evident as she looked at her husband.

"Are you going, Mike Daniels?" Sally asked, appearing in the doorway.

"Yes, Sally, I am," Mike said, bending down to look her in the eye. "Your pa has to get back to work, and Johnny and I have to return home.

Throwing both arms around his neck, she hugged him. "Much obliged for the circus stories and the books," she said, smiling at him.

Johnny noted several books sitting on the porch next to Mrs. Black's chair. He was not aware that his dad brought them. He must have carried them in his pack.

Mike tenderly touched the young girl's cheek. "You are welcome," he said, looking into the brown eyes of the little girl he found by the creek.

"Bye, Johnny Daniels," she said, turning to him as she fondly patted one of the dogs. He was aware that everyone, with the exception of the two small ones napping, seemed to appear at the same time.

"Bye, Sally," Johnny answered, thinking she reminded him of Shari. Following his dad down the steps, they both turned and looked back at the family gathered on the porch. Young Nathaniel raised his hand, and Johnny waved back. Mr. Black rested his hand on Sarah's shoulder, and Joel stood a little behind Mrs. Black, watching them.

"Tommy!" Mr. Black's booming voice rang out. Tommy jumped from the porch, his straw hat flopping and his bare feet flying as he ran toward them. They walked through the yard, followed by the dogs, and passed a flowerbed that Johnny did not notice when they arrived. At the edge of the woods he turned and looked back at the Black family still standing on the porch. Lifting his hand in farewell, he smiled as he watched them wave back then turned to see his dad's back and the floppy straw hat disappearing through the brush. He hoped to come back and get to know this family much better.

Supper was ready when they got home, and there was just enough time to wash up before it was time to sit down and eat. Leah was relating the most recent event in Oak Grove and had everyone at the table laughing.

How different this is from the Black's meal, Johnny thought, remembering how none of the children talked. Dad explained on the way home that a long time ago only adults talked at mealtime, and Mr. Black was probably brought up that way. Johnny was glad it wasn't like that anymore and continued to listen to his mom relate the day's events.

"Milly and Molly were so excited and flustered that Sheriff Walker couldn't understand what they were talking about." Leah laughed and wiped her eyes on her apron. "He was really confused. They did not have their hats on, and he kept calling them by the wrong name, and of course, they kept correcting him."

"I think it's easy to tell them apart," Jimmy remarked, looking around the table at the surprise on everyone's face. Twirling his fork around in his fingers, he stated matter-of-factly, "Milly snorts when she laughs."

Giggling erupted and Mike looked at his son curiously then glanced at Leah who sighed and commanded, "I do not want you commenting about that, young man." Leah glanced at the mirth on Mike's face, raised one of her brows at him, then gave Jimmy a stern look. "That is one of those lady things I spoke to you about. You do not comment on a lady's hat or how a lady laughs."

"I know; but she does. She snorts every time she laughs. That's how I tell them apart. Just watch next time, Mom, you'll see. She snorts."

"You must not talk about Molly snorting," Leah said, looking at him seriously. "I mean it, Jimmy."

"Molly doesn't snort, Mom. She cackles." Jimmy grinned at the others who were laughing and continued, "It's Milly that snorts, she. . . ."

"Jimmy!" Mike's voice cut through the giggling. "What did your mother tell you?" he asked with a stern look on his face.

All traces of humor disappeared from his face, and he glanced down at his plate. Glancing up guiltily, he looked at Mike. "I shouldn't talk about how a lady laughs," he answered quietly.

Feeling a kick on his leg, he glanced at Shari who was busily staring at her plate with a grin on her face. He kicked her back, deciding he would get even with her in his own good time.

Mike continued to look at his youngest son, deciding he definitely would not be invited along on the next trip to the Sweet Shoppe. Noting the frown Jimmy was giving Shari, Mike watched as she innocently buttered a piece of bread, and he wondered what she had done. Knowing Jimmy would pay her back one way or the other, he turned his attention back to Leah.

"How did you happen to be there?"

"I went early to check on Grandma Hope and was passing the Sweet Shoppe when Sheriff Walker drove up." Leah took a drink of tea, set her glass down, and continued with her story. "They both ran out the door, upset and chattering something about their Grandmother Cranston's bed linens. He tried to calm them, but they both insisted on reporting what happened at the same time, and it was impossible to make any sense out of what they were saying." Leah laughed again and sat back in her chair.

"Then they started arguing over whose responsibility it was to take the wash off the line. Both of them thought the other had done it, so the sheets hung outside overnight." Leah shook her head "It was total chaos."

Mike laughed as he imagined John Walker's frame of mind. "How did he get them settled down?" He pushed his plate aside and leaned back in his chair, thoroughly enjoying Leah's bright eyes and her dimples as she laughed and told of the day's adventure.

Resting her elbows on the table, Leah grinned at Mike. "He convinced them to go inside the shop, and he asked me to come along. We managed to get them seated, and the Sheriff told them only one could speak at a time and was finally able to learn what happened."

She absentmindedly scooted Jimmy's glass away from the edge of the table and continued talking, "It seems that Molly accused Milly of not washing all of the sheets because when she took them off the line one was missing. Milly denied it, got mad, and accused Molly of slacking in her duties because it was her turn to do the laundry anyway. It wasn't until they made a thorough search of the house without finding the sheet that they realized someone took it off the line."

"I still think it is a hobo," Shari commented. "He probably likes Oak Grove and is going to stay here and needs it for his bed."

"No, it's not. Good grief; hobos come to the back door and offer to do chores for what they want," Laura replied, looking at her sister. "They always do, and besides that he wouldn't have a bed." She looked thoughtfully for a moment, then commented, "Of course, they do have to sleep on something, and maybe he did need a sheet."

Leah, her eyes wide and curious, looked across the table and asked, "Mike, who would want to steal a bed sheet?"

He shook his head, "Your guess is as good as mine."

"Milly snorts," Jimmy whispered in Shari's ear, and they both giggled.

Mike looked pointedly at both of them until they stopped and got quiet. "Nothing else was taken, I presume?" he asked, looking back at Leah.

"No, not a thing." Taking a sip of her tea, Leah leaned forward and placed her chin in her hands. "I guess you are going to spend the evening at the square trying to catch this *phantom* of Oak Grove?"

"I'm scheduled at the bank with Michael Madison. Johnny is going with me," he commented, looking at his oldest son who had been especially quiet since their return.

"How is the Black family?" Leah asked, glancing at Johnny. She, too, noticed his quietness and wondered about it.

"They are the same. Everyone seems to be doing fine," Mike answered. We arrived just as they were having lunch and, of course, we shared the meal with them. They would have been highly insulted if we had not," he commented, thinking of the family up on the ridge. "Not to say I didn't enjoy it. Elizabeth and Sarah are good cooks."

"You did leave the books and peppermint sticks didn't you?" Leah asked. She began sending books with Mike when he told her that Mrs. Black was educated and taught the children at home. Leah usually included peppermint sticks or candy of some sort, but nothing more. Mike informed her that Mr. Black was very proud and would just send anything else back. He even hesitated the first time she sent candy but relented when he saw the children's faces.

"Mrs. Black is really nice, Mom. They have ten children. I counted them, and they are nothing like everyone says," Johnny commented defensively as he looked at Laura, Shari, and Jimmy. "They are a little different, but they are polite. They really work hard too."

He looked at Leah. "Mom, there is no running water in the house, and they don't even have electricity."

"Yes, I know that. Your father already told me."

"Mrs. Black is an Apache Indian, and when she was little she knew the Indian Chief, Geronimo," Johnny stated with pride.

"A real Indian Chief?" Jimmy asked, with wide, brown eyes.

"Does she look like an Indian princess?" Shari asked. She never met a real princess of any kind, and now Johnny had visited one.

"I don't know if she is a princess or not but she is pretty; I guess. Her skin has sort of a red tint to it, and she is very small. Her hair is real black and she wears it braided and wrapped around her head, and her eyes have the thickest eyelashes you have ever seen." He was suddenly embarrassed by his description and glanced at Laura.

"She sounds very lovely," Leah commented, glancing at Mike. "I can't wait to meet the whole family."

"How do they take a bath if they don't have any water?" Jimmy sat his glass on the table and looked seriously at his dad. "Or don't they?" he asked, smiling. "That wouldn't be so bad."

Johnny also looked at Mike. "What do they do about baths?"

Mike smiled, "They wash up in the kitchen or go to the creek when weather permits."

"Swell, I wish we could do that. But what about when it is winter time?" Jimmy asked, wondering what it would be like to go all winter without a bath.

"They heat water on the stove and bathe in a big tub in the kitchen by the fire." Mike smiled at the astonishment on his children's face. "I did that at my granddaddy's house when I was just a little tike." He smiled at the memory of sitting in the kitchen by the fire in a big, old washtub. Miraculously, there was always a plate of cookies sitting on the table. To this day, he couldn't think of his grandmother without the smell of freshly baked cookies and a bath coming to mind.

"You should see the stove, Mom. It is huge," Johnny commented, looking at Leah and then at the stove in their kitchen. "Dad, how do they keep their milk and butter cold without a refrigerator?"

"Mr. Black built a shed around a spring that's not too far from the house. The cold spring water keeps the spring house cool inside, and that serves as their refrigerator." Mike looked at the expression on his children's faces and continued. "In the summer, they carry water from a creek that runs down the side of the mountain, but they also have a cistern on the back porch that they use when the weather is bad.

"That sounds like fun," Shari said as thoughts flew through her head; playing in the woods, no school, finding small animals, and swimming in the creek. "It sounds like camp," she exclaimed, grinning.

"I think it sounds like a lot of work," Laura commented "What do they do for fun, Dad?"

"Well, they do work hard. In fact, Sarah, who is about your age, and Mrs. Black cook about all day long, some of the boys work in the field with Mr. Black, and some of the others tend to the garden." Mike mused on the question for a few seconds and looked at Leah. "I don't really know what they do for fun. I'm sure they entertain themselves some way because they all seem happy enough."

"Well, I know Mr. Black and Joel both play the fiddle," Johnny offered. "I saw it hanging on the wall in the living room and asked Nathaniel. He also said Joel paints, and I saw one of his pictures. He is really good. I think he could be an artist when he grows up."

Johnny looked directly at Mike. "Nathaniel also said he and Joel have been hunting with their dad since they were seven years old, and they each have their own gun."

He watched his dad's face for a clue that he thought him old enough to own a gun, but he was not paying any attention. He was just looking at his mom, smiling about something.

"What other chores to they have?" Laura asked, thinking she had a pretty easy life and wondered about the girl, Sarah.

"They chop wood for the stove and milk the cow. I know that for sure." Johnny answered. A mental image of Laura or Shari milking a cow came to mind and he laughed.

"What's so funny?" Shari asked looking at him.

"I just can't imagine you guys milking cows."

"And I suppose you think you could?" Laura replied, rolling her eyes at him.

"Sure I could," he retorted though he was not just real sure how easy it would be the first couple of times. "Shari and Jimmy would have to gather eggs probably. That's one of the young kid's chores, I bet."

Leah watched her son's face as he talked about the Black family and knew Mike had been right when he suggested taking him along this time.

"I'm glad we don't have to do all that," Laura exclaimed. "Why do they want to live way up there and work so hard?"

"That's where they are happy right now," Mike commented, looking at Leah. "I don't know how long it will last with the children getting older though."

"Were you able to talk to them about this fall?" Leah asked, suddenly serious.

"Mr. Black wouldn't commit to anything, but he did promise to think about it. I fear I upset Mrs. Black," Mike answered. "We'll continue praying for guidance, Leah. The Lord impressed this idea on both of our hearts, so I am just waiting to see how He works it all out."

Johnny knew whatever they were talking about was the reason for Mrs. Black's tears when he and Nathaniel walked out on the porch. Wondering what was wrong, he was suddenly aware that he cared very much what happened to the Black family.

Laura took the last drink of her milk and set the glass down. "May I be excused?" she asked looking at Mike.

He glanced at her plate and nodded, "Yes, go ahead." Mike watched her carry the plate to the sink and thought about the difference in his children's lives and that of the Black family.

"Me too?" Shari asked, receiving a nod from him. "Laura, it is my turn to wash tonight," she reminded, carrying her plate to the sink. Both preferred washing over drying dishes for some reason, and Shari never failed to announce whose turn it was.

"Fine, but that means it is your turn to sweep the floor."

Shari followed Laura from the kitchen. " Do you want to play jacks before we have to do dishes?"

"May I be excused?" Jimmy asked, wiping his mouth on his napkin. He thought he might just clean his Red Ryder again.

"Yes, you may," Leah answered, smiling at her youngest son and wondering what he was up to. He was being awfully secretive about something.

Johnny listened as his parents discussed the family that now was so real to him. "Do you think you will ever go out there, Mom?" he asked.

"I would like to one day," Leah answered. "When your father thinks it is the right time."

"I do think it is the right time, Leah." Mike rested his elbows on the table and looked across the table at her with a serious expression on his face. "Nathaniel let me know today that he trusts me, but he is hesitant about our way of life. I don't blame him. I would be too if the situation was turned around." He leaned back in his chair and glanced at Johnny before turning back to Leah.

"Elizabeth naturally wants to keep her family near and protected. I think it would set her mind at ease if she knew another mother would be close at hand who loves her children the way she does."

Compassion for Mrs. Black filled Leah's heart and she considered the time when she would have to turn her children loose to face the world. She prayed daily for wisdom to prepare them for that time and sighed, knowing the time would be here before she knew it.

Mike watched the expression on Leah's face. "She needs to meet you, Leah. You are like her in many ways, and it would be good for her to have a friend."

"I would love to meet the whole family," Leah answered with a pleased look on her face. "When?"

Mike laughed. "Soon. We've got to get things settled before school starts," he commented, glancing at the calendar hanging next to the telephone.

Johnny looked at his dad curiously. "Why before school starts?"

Mike sat back in his chair and studied his son for a moment. "I am trying to persuade Mr. and Mrs. Black to allow their children to go to high school."

Johnny stared at him Imagine what a surprise that would be to everyone in Oak Grove.

Mike leaned toward him and began to explain, feeling as though he were speaking to Nathaniel Black all over again. "They need to know the ways of the outside world. The day will come for them to venture out on their own, and they need to be prepared for the future." He glanced at Leah. "Nathaniel admitted today that he knows what I am saying is true, but I suppose he doesn't want to accept the change that is about to come into his life." Mike studied the empty glass sitting in front him. "I explained that since he is fourteen, it is the perfect time to take that step and let him start high school with others his own age.

"Then that would be Nathaniel?" Johnny asked. He couldn't imagine Nathaniel in Oak Grove, but it would be swell.

"I want this information kept at this table for now," Mike said, looking seriously at his son. "I have doubts as to Nathaniel allowing it, and if he does, there will be a lot of adjustments for the boy. We don't need the whole town awaiting his arrival, or certain well-meaning folks will start making plans to help him adjust. I know they mean well, but he doesn't need to feel like he's on exhibition."

"I won't say anything Dad," Johnny said. "I promise."

Leah watched the expression on her son's face He displayed something akin to a protective attitude that pleased her, and he now sat quietly as though he was mulling something over in his mind.

"You know, Mom," Johnny said in a quiet voice, staring at the fork he slowly moved back and forth, "I was just thinking that I have a pretty swell bike." He looked up at Mike and nodded his head slightly as though he just came to a decision. With a sigh of relief and seriousness in his tone, he continued. "My bike is still in really good condition. I think I should just keep it like you said. I don't need a new one."

Tears sprang to Leah's eyes and she reached for his hand. "I am so glad you feel that way, Johnny. I know how badly you wanted a new one, but . . .

"Some kids don't have anything," he interrupted her. "Take the Black Family; I didn't see much of anything in the way of toys or games and yet they all seemed happy I guess I never realized how much I have."

Mike smiled into Leah's eyes and rose from his chair. He walked around the table and placed both hands on his son's shoulders.

Lifting his gaze, Johnny was pleased at the love and pride he saw reflected in his dad's eyes.

"I am proud of you, Son; very proud."

A silent communication passed between father and son in those few seconds. The feel of his dad's strong hands on his shoulders and the love and pride on his face was suddenly the most important thing in the world to him. The image of his dad standing in the woods by the black berry bushes sprang to his mind. He knew he would remember this day for the rest of his life.

Mike stood silent for a moment, looking across the table at Leah, and a slow tender smile touched his lips. Leah returned his smile, wiped a tear from her eye, and rose from the table to hug her son.

Chapter 13

Darkness found Oak Grove settling down for another evening of expectancy. The Sheriff was again in city hall, but tonight Ned Olson and Preston joined him. He looked around the square, wondering if the other men were as aggravated as he was. Hank and Bill Madison, the Postmaster, were in the hardware store, Sam Cranston and Jack Reese were watching from the hotel, and Michael Madison, Pastor Mike and Johnny were at the bank. Jim and Simon, along with Nelson White, joined Alan in The Chronicle.

"If he doesn't show tonight, I suspect he knows we are waiting for him," Sheriff Walker commented, looking out the window.

Preston, listening to his dad and Mr. White, stared out into the darkness. His eyes searched the square, roving from the bandstand, to the water fountain, and back to the bell tower again. He didn't have any idea who or what he was watching for. The light from the street lamps filtered through the trees and created moving shadows across the square, giving the whole place an eerie look.

"How would he know we are waiting for him?" Ned asked. "We've told no one what we are doing, it's dark when we get here, and we all come in the back door." He sounded perplexed. "I don't know, Sheriff. This beats anything I've ever seen. Is it true that Milly and Molly had a sheet stolen?"

"I'm afraid so," John replied absentmindedly as he studied the bell tower. He thought about the confusion this morning in front of The Sweet Shoppe and was thankful Leah Daniels happened by and helped calm them down.

"A sheet! Who or why would anyone take a sheet," Ned exclaimed. "I declare, nothing makes sense."

How was your trip to the Black's place?" Michael Madison asked, swiveling around in his chair.

"The trip was fine. It was just like I expected." Mike looked through the window at the square. "Taking something that does not belong to them would never enter their minds." He looked at Johnny. "Wouldn't you say so, Son?"

"Those people are nothing like what everyone says," Johnny exclaimed. "They are good, decent people. They are just. . . . honest people who live in the hills."

Johnny thought again of Nathaniel's preference for hunting food instead of buying it in a store and wondered what he would think about walking in Reese's Market if he did come to Oak Grove this fall. "They live like they used to in olden times and work really hard. I agree with Dad. They would not take anything they didn't earn themselves."

Johnny realized he was ready to defend them to anybody if need be. Sitting on the desk, he took a drink of his pop and stared through the window, wondering when his mom and dad were going to make the next trip to their home.

Mike smiled to himself in the dark. The trip had been good for his son. For the first time in his life, he glimpsed the world through someone else's eyes and was beginning to realize the more important things in life.

"I hardly thought they had anything to do with this either," Michael replied. "I guess everyone is puzzled, trying to figure out what is going on."

"It won't last long," Pastor Mike chuckled as he looked at him "I don't think this summer will be one we will soon forget. We'll all sit and laugh about it one of these days."

Alan, Nelson White, and Jim and Simon sat in *The Chronicle*. Simon was perched on one of the stools next to the window, anxiously watching the bell tower. Truman was mad because nothing happened last night, and Simon grinned as he thought about it. He was positive the mysterious person was going to show up tonight, and he would be there to catch him.

"Did you check out around the Old Mill?" Alan asked, watching Jim help himself to one of the donuts Nelson brought along from the bakery.

"We sure did, and we didn't see a thing." Jim sat down and looked at Alan. "We checked the woods out by the Timber Company and along the creek. There was no trace of anyone."

"I think it is uncanny that no one has seen anyone or anything unusual." Nelson commented, leaning back in his chair. He propped his feet on the table and let his eyes roam around the dark shadows in the office. "You mark my words, someone knows something."

"I have to agree with you there," Alan said, walking to the coffeepot. "How can a person manage to move around a small town like this and not be seen is beyond me." Pouring a cup of coffee, he took a sip then walked over to the window. "Do you need me to watch a while, Simon?"

"No, I'm okay. I want to be the first one to see him." Simon stared through the window into the dark, wondering when the so-called *phantom* would make his appearance.

Alan glanced at Jim and smiled "He'll make a good detective one of these days." Taking a seat in his office chair, Alan thought back through the years and decided this was the strangest thing he could ever remember happening.

"Someone's coming, Dad!" Simon exclaimed, almost falling off the stool.

Jim, Nelson, and Alan jumped at the same time and looked out the window. Across the square, a lone figure walked slowly in front of the hotel, stopped, and looked up at the bell tower.

"Can you tell who it is?" Nelson whispered as they stared through the window.

"What is he doing? He is just standing there looking at the bell tower!" Simon exclaimed, his heart pounding in his chest.

"Let's just wait and see." Jim strained to see in the dark. There was something vaguely familiar about the man, but the tree branches cast just enough shadows that you couldn't really make out anything other than his form.

"What are we waiting on?" Nelson whispered excitedly. "Somebody needs to grab him."

Jim looked at him with a frown. "What for? It is not a crime to take a walk in the dark. Let's just wait and see what he does."

"I can't see that well, but there's something familiar about the way he's standing," Alan commented quietly.

"I was thinking the same thing." Jim wondered what everyone else was doing and hoped they wouldn't run out and grab him before he made his move.

"Dad, he's getting ready!" Simon exclaimed, placing both hands on the window as he watched him slowly walk around the tower.

"How long are we going to wait?" Nelson asked impatiently.

"Where's he going," Alan wondered aloud as they watched the stranger continue around the bell tower and then slowly make his way across the square. He walked down the sidewalk, passed the hotel, and crossed Spruce Street at the Post Office. Walking into the glow of the street lamp, he dropped a letter in the mailbox and turned around.

"It's Solomon!" Jim and Alan both exclaimed at the same time. Slowly he turned, retraced his steps, and strolled back passed the hotel. Meandering along without a care in the world, he made his way to the corner of Pine Street where he turned left and headed home.

"Good Grief," Alan said. "What in heaven's name is he out mailing letters at this time of night?" He laughed and looked at Jim and Nelson. "We thought we had ourselves a thief, didn't we?"

"Hazel, this is Ellen. Can you ring my brother's house please?" Gripping the telephone with trembling hands and her heart pounding, she stared down the dark hallway.

She had been in bed about to drift off to sleep when the sound of footsteps outside the bedroom window caught her attention. Was it her imagination? She sat up in bed and listened. Someone was definitely there. *Of all nights for Mike to be gone,* she thought in a panic. Quickly making her way across the hall, she glanced in Zachary's room. He was sound asleep.

Hurrying down the hall to the table, she grabbed the telephone with shaking hands and waited for Hazel to come on the line. Perhaps Lynn could see someone from her bedroom. Their back yards joined one another, and Lynn and Alan's bedroom window faced their house *She may not be able to see through the trees,* Ellen thought in dismay.

"Hello?" Lynn said sleepily.

"Lynn, this is Ellen," she whispered as her heart raced. A thump against the side of the house startled her, and she almost dropped the telephone.

"Hello?" Lynn said again.

"Lynn, this is Ellen," she said, not much above a loud whisper. "Can you hear me?"

"Yes, what's wrong?" Lynn asked with alarm in her voice.

"Someone is out back! Can you see him?" she asked, wondering where Zachary put his baseball bat.

"Oh gosh. Hold on a minute," Lynn said worriedly. "I'll check. Wait ten seconds then switch your back porch light on."

Ellen laid the phone on the table and hurried to the kitchen as quietly as she could. Slowing her steps, she made her way to the back door, thankful she had pulled the blind down. Counting to ten, she reached up and flipped the porch light on. The loud pounding of her heart echoed in her ears and she gripped her hands together. In the distance, the eleven o'clock train whistle blew, and the Charles' dog began barking furiously, causing Ellen's heart to race faster than it already was. Cautiously, she put her ear against the door and listened. Nothing! Racing back to the phone, she picked it up.

"Lynn?" There was no reply and Ellen realized she was probably still in her bedroom looking out the window. She carried the telephone as far as the cord would allow and glanced into Zachary's bedroom. Thank goodness, he was still asleep.

"Ellen?" Lynn's voice came over the phone. "Ellen, are you there?"

"Yes. Did you see anyone?" she asked, taking a deep breath.

"No. I didn't see anything at all. Are you sure that is what you heard?" she asked. "What exactly did it sound like?"

Ellen sighed impatiently, "I was almost asleep and I heard someone walking along the side of the house."

"I didn't see anyone at all," Lynn replied as she glanced around her dark living room, wondering what or who was causing the dogs to bark. What if he was trying to look in one of their windows right now? "Something has the dogs stirred up though," she commented in a voice that was not quite so calm.

"Do you want me to ring the bank for Mr. Madison?" Hazel asked. Ellen and Lynn both laughed nervously.

"Bless your heart, Hazel, but I'm glad you're there," Ellen said with relief in her voice.

"In an emergency situation, I make sure I'm available." Hazel assured her. "Now, both of you just relax. I'm going to ring the bank and you can let Mr. Madison know what's going on, so stay on the line."

"I'm going to hang up and look out the window again. If I see anything, I will flip the back porch light off and on," Lynn said, placing the phone in the cradle.

Ellen pulled a side chair from around the corner of their bedroom and positioned it so she could see their back porch through Zachary's window. Listening while Hazel switched the lines over, she took a deep breath and counted the rings. Much to her relief, Michael answered on the third ring. "Hello?"

"Michael," Ellen said, relieved to hear his voice.

"What's wrong, Hon?" he asked with concern, noting the nervousness in her voice.

"Michael, he is here. I heard him outside our bedroom window," Ellen said nervously. "I called Lynn and she checked out back but she didn't see anyone. But I heard footsteps. I heard him walking along the side of the house."

"I don't believe this," Michael said angrily. "I'll be home in just a minute, hon. I need to call Sheriff Walker and let him know what's going on. Are you okay, until I get there?"

"Yes, I am . . . I think," Ellen replied. "Hazel is on the other end of the line so I can talk to her until you get here."

"He's outsmarted us again . . ." Ellen heard Michael telling someone as he was hanging up.

"Are you still there?"

"Yes, Hazel, thank you." Ellen was relieved to hear the familiar voice in her ear and knew she would stay on the line as long as she wanted her to "I wish they would soon catch this prankster."

Ellen sat in the dark listening for more sounds but only heard the Charles' dog and another one barking somewhere down the block. Staring through the dark window, the question of what kind of pajamas Hazel was wearing entered her mind, and she didn't know whether to laugh or cry. Where in heaven's name had that strange thought come from?

"Have you heard anything else?" Hazel asked with a yawn. "I expect he's probably taken off somewhere else by now since you turned your lights on. You did turn a light on, didn't you?"

"Yes, the back porch light is on." Ellen looked down the dark hall. "I guess I may as well turn the light in the living room on. I am wide awake now."

"I expect that's what I would do," Hazel replied. "I would get a glass of warm milk, a book, and make myself comfy. Land sakes, there's no since sitting there scared to death over some rascal running around laughing at all of us. Besides, Mr. Madison will be there shortly."

"Yes, he should be here in just a few minutes. I wonder if any of the other neighbors heard anything," Ellen wondered aloud. "I guess we'll find out in the morning."

Anne Walker awakened and switched on the bedside lamp. She heard John and Preston climb the stairs and then John's voice. "Go on to bed, son." She glanced at the clock, three twenty-five. They finally caught him.

Opening the bedroom door, John looked at Anne sitting up in bed.

She took one look at the expression on his face and knew without asking. "No luck?"

"No. I told the men to go on home." He sat on the edge of the bed and wearily removed his shoes. "I just can't figure it out. It's like he knows what we are thinking and doing." Exasperated, he fell back on the bed and stared at the ceiling. "Here we are watching the square, and he's over at Michael and Ellen Madison's house snooping around."

"Oh, no. I bet Ellen was scared to death," Anne said, glancing anxiously at the window then back at John. "What happened? How did you know he was there?"

"Ellen called Michael. She heard him walking around the side of the house." John yawned and sighed. "She had Lynn look out their window, but she didn't see anyone." John continued to stare at the ceiling. "I drove by the house. Nothing was disturbed except Zachary's basketball. Michael said he put it on the porch when he left tonight, but we found it laying out in the yard. Ellen said she heard a thump, so it was probably him throwing it against the house."

Anne observed the frustration on her husband's face. "It seems like someone playing games, doesn't it? But who and why?" she asked, feeling about as frustrated as John.

He shook his head, "I don't know. Solomon took a late night walk to the mailbox, and we thought we had him for sure until we realized who it was."

Tired and wanting a good night's sleep, John sat up and removed his shirt. He looked at Anne's concerned face and smiled tiredly. "Don't worry, Anne, this can't last forever."

Anne looked into his tired eyes and wished there was something she could do to help but didn't know what it would be. They stared at one another, a look of disbelief frozen on both of their faces. The bell was ringing once again.

"I do not believe this. I do not believe it." John grabbed his shirt from the chair and pulled it back on. "Blame it all, I would like to wring this person's neck when I get my hands on him." Slipping his feet in his shoes, he ran his fingers through his hair and walked around the end of the bed.

"Dad," Brenton called from the other side of the door. "The bell. . . ."

"I know," John said, opening the door. Brenton and Preston both stood in the hall fully dressed. "Well, come on, you may as well ride along." He glanced back at Anne with a sigh. "We'll be right back." They ran down the steps and out the front door.

"Why don't we just sleep in the bell tower?" Preston asked as he jumped in the front seat behind Brenton.

John backed out of the driveway, wondering what it was going to take to catch this guy. Maybe he should take Preston's advice. "Well, we are going to have to do something different that's for sure," John remarked. "But I sure don't know what that something is right now."

Continuing down Spruce, they arrived at the square to find Willy and Young Ben standing next to the bell tower.

Pastor Mike pulled in and parked next to them. "Can you believe this?" he exclaimed, slamming the car door. "I thought he had given up for the night, didn't you?"

"I don't know what to think any more, Pastor," John answered as they walked to the tower. Jim Walker, Truman, and Simon crossed from the other side of the square and joined them.

Standing in silent frustration for a moment, the men just looked at one another. Groaning in aggravation, Sheriff Walker glanced up at the bell, mumbled something unintelligible, and climbed the steps. Reaching the top, he glanced around and looked down at the floor. Lying at his feet was an old straw hat. Bending down, he picked it up, and stared at it in disbelief Shaking his head, he descended the steps and looked at those gathered. Holding the old straw hat out in front of him, he calmly stated, "He brought Mary's hat back."

"Yes sir, Sheriff. That's my hat." Mary said as she looked at the hat he held in his hand. "Where did you find it?"

Sheriff Walker shook his head. "It seems whoever took it decided to return it last night when he came to ring the bell.

"You didn't see who it was?" she asked in amazement.

John handed it to her and shook his head. "No, I am afraid not. It seems he paid a visit at the Madison's last night, too.

"Oh, no. Is everything OK?" Mary asked, tossing the hat on the sofa. She looked at him with concern. "Would you like a cup of coffee or something?"

"No thank you, Mary." John released a tired sigh and reached for the doorknob. "He outsmarts us at every turn."

"Well, Sheriff, I am sure you will catch him," Mary said encouragingly. "Thank you for bringing this old straw hat back to me. It is not very valuable but I wear it everyday."

"That's okay, Mary." John opened the door and walked down the steps. He strolled slowly down the sidewalk, stepped from the curb, and leaned against the patrol car. Glancing up and down the street at the houses, he wondered what in the world was happening to this quiet little town. He closed his eyes for a moment and thought about what he should do differently. *I guess I'll see if Jim has any ideas,* he thought to himself. Thinking about Jack Reese's telephone call early this morning, he wondered what was going on there and decided he better check on that first.

Driving leisurely down Pine Street, he noted the neat little yards with their well-tended flowerbeds. Everything seemed peaceful and ordinary; nothing amiss. John shook his head in bewilderment.

Maybe he would stop by and visit Pastor Mike. His listening ear and wisdom always had a calming effect, and right now he needed that. Pastor Mike seemed to take everything in stride, and John knew it was the result of his faith. He had heard him say many times how the Lord is not surprised at anything because He knows about it before it happens, and since He knows what the end result is going to be, why should I worry about it." His eyes reflected such trust and confidence that one always came away from a visit with him, knowing everything was in God's hands and it would be alright.

Pulling up in front of Reese's Market, John waved at Abigail Cranston, making her way to the Oak Grove Drugstore. Closing the car door, he walked passed the fruits and vegetables stacked neatly on the table and reached for the door.

"Good morning, Sheriff," Mildred Reese said cheerily, smiling at him as she blocked the doorway.

"Good morning, Mildred. You are out early this morning," John answered, hoping he was not going to get the third degree. It was too early in the morning.

"I walked over with Jack this morning to make sure nothing was disturbed. I have some shopping to do and thought I would get an early start." She continued smiling at him, and with all the tact of a cobra patted him on the shoulder.

"Goodness, Sheriff, you look just awful. I know you haven't been getting much rest, but you should really try to take better care of yourself. I've never seen you looking so bad." She leaned toward him and, in a confidential tone, lowered her voice, "Stop by the drugstore and pick up a bottle of Geritol. That will do the trick." She paused and looked at him curiously. "I understand you had another long night," she commented with a questioning look in her eye. She remained in the doorway, and John knew she would not move until he said something.

"I'm afraid so, Mildred," he answered. "Is everything okay at your place?" He continued holding the door and wondered what she would do if he just let it slam in her face. Feeling guilty, John smiled at her.

She was actually a very nice lady, but between her and Trudy Driscol they knew everything that went on in Oak Grove. They habitually traded stories until the end result was nothing like the actual fact, and he learned a long time ago that the smartest thing to do in a conversation with either of them was to let them do the talking.

"Oh, yes. Everything is just fine at our house, thank you," Mildred said. "No problems since the night they made such a mess here at the store. I really thought you would have caught the person responsible for that by now." She put her gloves on, switched her purse to the other arm, and looked up at him with a smile." I understand Ellen Madison heard someone at her house last night," she commented, waiting in eagerness for some tidbit of information.

"Yes, she heard something, but we are not sure what it was," John answered, beginning to get impatient and not about to say any more than he had to.

"Well, I imagine it probably upset her. I do hope you find this vermin who thinks he can take anything he wants from whoever he wants!" she exclaimed, getting all worked up. She rearranged her blue hat in a huff and remarked, "I heard the Clarkson's have out-of-town company. You might want to check on them. You just never know what kind of people they might be."

"Mildred, remember what Pastor Mike said Sunday about accusations," John remarked, wishing she would get out of the way. He glanced up at her head, "That hat is very becoming."

"This old thing? Why thank you, Sheriff," she said beaming. "Yes, you are right about Pastor Mike's sermon. It helped me tremendously. I just hope some of the other folks in town apply it to their lives. My land, some people just don't listen to a thing, do they? Well, I must really be going; I'm meeting Trudy at the drugstore." She patted his arm. "I'll tell Gerald to set a bottle of Geritol out for you. It will make you feel much better." She turned and rapidly headed for her meeting with Trudy.

"Thank you, Mildred," John replied, standing in the open doorway. He watched her hurry passed the bench and disappear into the drugstore A slow smile touched John's face and he walked through the door. "Morning Jack," he called, walking to the soda cooler.

"Morning, Sheriff," Jack answered, hanging up the telephone. It hung on the wall over an old oak table used for boxing grocery orders. "David!" he called. "We have an order for the Cranstons." A string hung from a nail with several clothespins attached, and he clipped the grocery order to one of them.

John walked to the counter. "What did you want to see me about?" he asked as he took a drink of his Coca-Cola. Laying ten cents on the top of the cash register, he wondered what was up now.

"Hi, Sheriff," David said, coming from the back of the store with a broom in his hand.

"Hi, Dave," John answered, glancing from father to son. Jack could never deny this boy. He looked just like him. Both had brown eyes, sandy-colored hair, and noses that were a little on the thin side. David was a couple years older that Brenton and a nice, friendly kid. One usually saw him all over town delivering groceries.

He sat the broom in the corner, retrieved the order from the clothespin, and grabbed an empty box from beneath the table as he read the order.

"I just wanted to let you know that I think someone is helping himself to some of my fruit and vegetables," Jack said, rubbing his chin with his fingers. "He's not making a mess or anything, but I notice when something's missing."

"Are you sure?" John asked, knowing Jack would not be mistaken about that. He took pride in the way he arranged everything on the shelves and the tables outside.

"Oh yes, I'm sure. I don't really mind a few missing pieces if the fellow is hungry. I just wish he would make himself known so we could give him a helping hand." Jack looked down at the floor then glanced up at John. Leaning close with a concerned look on his face, he asked in a quiet voice, "You don't suppose it could be Cooley, do you?"

"Cooley?" John looked at him in surprise. "I wouldn't think so. He's done a lot of things in the past, but I've never known him to steal anything."

Thomas Jefferson Cooley, his wife, and two children lived on the outskirts of town along the creek beyond the school. A friendly, good-hearted man, he primarily worked as the janitor for the Oak Grove Public School. He was also the caretaker for the town square, the fairground, and mowed the grass at the Oak Grove Baptist Church.

Delivering coal during the winter months gave him extra money, and he was often seen doing odd jobs around town all year long.

The wiry little man was only thirty but appeared to be a good ten years older. No one really knew where the family came from; "back east" was about they only thing anyone knew.

He and Alice came to Oak Grove, a young, newly married couple, about twelve years ago and bought the old cabin down by the creek where they remained. Folks in Oak Grove were fond of Cooley and Alice and respected their desire to live quietly and to themselves. Cooley, as everyone called him, never complained about anything, and although not very educated, he was able to repair most anything simply by trial and error.

Alice, wanting to help her husband, always talked about going to work but Cooley refused, saying he would take care of his family and preferred her to stay home to care for Tommy and Betty Jean.

He finally relented one day when Pastor Mike visited and said the church was looking for someone capable and particular enough to keep *The Lord's House* clean. Alice expressed delight in the offer, explaining to *Thomas* that she had plenty of time with both children now in school. Between the two of them, they convinced Cooley that it would work out well for all concerned.

Hearing around town what a good job Alice was doing and how the church never looked so nice, Cooley began attending Sunday services. Mike suspected his attendance was more out of pride than anything, but whatever the reason, he was thankful for his presence.

Cooley's one weakness raised its head about once every couple of months and set him on a binge that usually lasted the whole weekend. One Saturday, finding a comfortable spot in the bandstand, he sang and played his banjo to an ever-increasing crowd of folks. After about four hours, John was in a quandary as to what to do with him when he refused to quit and go home.

"Everyone is enjoyin' it too much fer me to up and quit playin' now," he argued when John tried to take him home. Not wanting to cause any more commotion than necessary, he managed to convince *the audience* to disperse and talked Cooley into playing in the office so both, he and Jim, could listen to his music in comfort.

Weaving their way across the square, they finally got him settled on a cot in one of the cells. Thinking he would surely quit any minute, John and Jim found themselves stuck with listening to his off key singing until they thought they were going to lose their minds. Deciding to take him home to preserve their own sanity, he suddenly got quiet and they realized he was sound asleep.

Pastor Mike, after getting a tearful phone call from Alice, arrived to get him out of jail and take him home. Cooley, sitting in the open cell drinking a cup of coffee, confessed to Mike, "when the urge hits and the juice gets a grip on me, it just won't turn loose."

Holding his head in his hands, he admitted how sinful he was and sheepishly promised Pastor Mike not to embarrass him or the church folks anymore by coming to *Sunday Meetin,'* as he called it.

Unaware of the kind of man he was dealing with, he watched in shock as Pastor Mike turned around and yelled at Sheriff Walker. "Call the Deacons and tell them to get someone to preach for me Sunday. I'll not be there. I'm a sinner too, and I don't want to embarrass anybody." He slammed the cell door and sat down on the cot next to Cooley. "If sinners are not welcome in church, then all of us might just as well stay locked up in jail or the prisons of our own choosing," he proclaimed in his loudest preaching voice.

Cooley stared at Pastor Mike and didn't move for a good ten minutes. The Sheriff wasn't sure what to do or who to call, and Jim sat in the chair with his feet propped up on the desk, his hands behind his head, watching in amusement. Mike leaned back against the wall, tried to identify the odor of fruit that produced the juice Cooley had consumed, and wished he could see the look on Leah's face when she found out he was in jail.

Cooley studied the floor for a few minutes and then walked to the cell door with a look of wonderment on his face. "Now don't that just knock your hat in the creek," he exclaimed, looking at John. "I guess you better open this door and let us out. I expect it's better for us sinners to be in church than sitting here in this jail cell."

Cooley's binges slacked off considerably after that, and there was even a rumor around town that he had given it up altogether. Whatever happened, he now seemed more confident and content with life and even began coming to *Sunday night meetin's.*

Sheriff Walker looked at Jack with a doubtful expression. "Now do you really think Cooley would steal anything? Doesn't he have a running grocery bill?"

Jack looked guilty. "Yes, and he always pays it every month. I don't know what I was thinking. That's the bad thing about all this, John. I don't know what to think anymore."

"I don't either. It's about to drive me nuts. Nothing else is missing?"

"No, not a thing," Jack answered. "Like I said, if someone is hungry I don't mind them taking something. It's not that much. I just thought you ought to know. It might help you catch him."

"I appreciate you telling me, Jack. I'll see what I can do about it," John said, looking at the kind grocer. "Although he is not taking much, it is still stealing, and you should not have to put up with it." John almost told him that maybe he ought to bring the produce in at night but knew that would fall on deaf ears. Jack always left it outside and would continue to do so unless something drastic happened.

"Good morning, Mary," Jack called as Mary Smith came in the door, carrying a sack of produce.

"Good morning, Jack," she said, smiling as she placed the bag on the counter. "I have five roast'n ears, a head of lettuce, and three tomatoes. Morning to you again, Sheriff." She flipped her straw hat with a finger and grinned.

He looked at the hat and laughed. "If I would have known you needed to come to the store, I would have given you a ride."

"No, that's okay. This is my daily exercise," she assured him. "That's how I noticed this old hat missing. I always wear it in the sun or when I'm walking.

"Well, I'm glad you have it back. Hopefully we will find everything else also." Placing the pop bottle on the counter, John waved to David who was busily boxing the grocery items. "Alright, Jack. I'll get back with you later. Have a good day Mary," he said, walking toward the door.

"You too, Sheriff," Mary called. "Jack, I need two pounds of ground beef."

John stood outside the grocery store gazing at the tables of fruit and vegetables then glanced around the square. Whistling, he walked to the patrol car, got in, and drove off.

Willy walked out of the garage. "Morning, Sheriff. What can I do for you?" he asked, wiping his hand on a rag from his back pocket.

"Fill it up, Willy. Is everything okay around here?" John asked, looking around the station William Stanton left to him when he passed on. Willy, just like his Uncle William, took a great deal of pride in keeping the place clean and everything in its proper place.

"Hi, Sheriff," Simon yelled as he and Preston rode up on their bikes. "We need to air up our tires, Willy."

Propping his bike against the side of the garage, Preston walked over to the car and stepped up on the running board. "Dad, can I have a nickel?" he asked, jumping back and forth from the running board to the ground. "I'll pay you back when I get home, I just forgot to bring it with me."

John reached in his pocket and produced the request amount. "It's a little early for a candy bar, isn't it?" he asked, looking through the window at his son.

The cardinal ball cap sat crooked on his reddish blonde head and the freckles on his nose were more pronounced from the summer sun. His light brown eyes with just a hint of green were full of mischief, and a grin spread across his face. "Thanks, Dad I need it for later." Taking the nickel, he made one last jump from the running board and headed for Simon and the air hose. "Aren't you finished yet?"

"Do it like I showed you or you will bust the tire," Willy called and then turned to look at John while he filled the gas tank "I believe our friend paid me a visit last night."

"What do you mean?" John looked around curiously then back at Willy.

Removing his cap, Willy wiped his forehead then set it back on his head and looked at John with a slight grin.

"When I came to open the garage this morning, I noticed a couple of tires that were against the side of the garage had been rolled almost to the street." Shaking his head, he chuckled as he put the nozzle back on the side of the pump and replaced the gas cap. "I tell you, Sheriff, this is getting more comical every day."

"I'm afraid I have to agree with you, Willy," John said. "Is anything missing?"

"No, nothing," Willy said, watching Simon and Preston carefully air their bicycle tires.

"Blame it all, it is one more piece to a puzzle that I can't put together," John said, shaking his head and reaching for his wallet "How much do I owe you, Willy?"

"It'll be one dollar and twenty cents, Sheriff," Willy answered, suddenly preoccupied with something across the square.

John handed him the money and followed his gaze but didn't see anything but Melba standing in front of her shop talking to Mary Madison.

Mary's husband, Thomas, was one of the co-owners of the Oak Grove Timber Company. They were nice people but not too sociable. Other than that, John didn't see anything of interest. Turning back to Willy, he found him busily cleaning the windshield. "Thank you, Willy. Don't let those two blow the tires off their bicycles." He laughed and nodded his head at Simon and Preston.

"They should be okay. I showed them how to do it. Have you come up with any clues or leads?" Willy asked as the Sheriff started the engine.

"Not, really. Just an idea that is forming in my head, and I'm not sure about that. Let me know if there is anything else out of place," John called as he drove away.

Willy waved and nodded his head. Looking back across the square, he saw Mrs. Madison going into the bank. Melba stood in front of the salon looking in his direction. She looked very trim, her hair was pulled back away from her face, and he could see that she was smiling as she lifted her hand and waved. Willy felt his heart quicken, returned the wave, and reluctantly watched her go back into the salon.

No more than a few weeks ago, the playground at Oak Grove Elementary School abounded with children's laughter and excitement as they enjoyed the last days of school. But today, with summer vacation in full swing, the jungle gym, slide, and teeter-totters sat idle, looking forlorn. An occasional breeze gently moved the swings lazily back and forth, and Johnny had a sudden thought that the whole place looked somewhat lonely and wondered what it would be like to go inside and walk down the silent, empty halls.

"Well, where is everyone?" Truman asked as he leaned against the oak tree and looked down the street. "What time do you think it is?"

"It has to be after eleven," Brenton commented as he studied the paper he held in his hand. He had spent all evening compiling one long list of everyone's notes and couldn't find any pattern to it at all.

The familiar clicking of cardboard against bicycle spokes caught Johnny's attention, and he looked up to see Jake pedaling down the street. "Here comes Jake," he commented, waving at him.

Turning loose of the handlebars, Jake waved both arms in the air and coasted the rest of the way down the street. Small for his age, he made up for it in spunk and was never known to back down from a dare of any kind. Once Jake got an idea in his head, he never gave up and had an uncanny ability to talk everyone else into agreeing with him even if they thought it a lost cause.

Last summer they managed to hack their way through the brush behind the cemetery and found an old tumbled down log cabin that no one knew existed. Only about fifteen feet square, they decided it was just big enough for a clubhouse. The roof had holes, the door was gone, and every animal in the forest left evidence of occupancy. Discovering a gaping hole on one side, they were absolutely certain it was the result of cannon fire during the civil war, and thrilled with their marvelous find, Jake concluded that it was an historical site, and they set out to *fix it up.*

It took only two days of clearing the area around the cabin before they decided to forget the whole thing. But Jake, with enthusiasm and determination, convinced them they would all be famous one day for restoring it, and until then it would be their secret clubhouse.

For the next several weeks they hauled scrap lumber, tar paper, pieces of tin, paint, and anything else they could get their hands on to repair the place. They cleared brush, repaired a broken step, and hammered and nailed. Using pieces of tin weighted down by boards and rocks, they covered the holes in the roof and rigged an old chicken house door they found to slide back and forth to keep the animals out. All the while Jake kept coming up with more ideas to the point of carrying logs and using pieces of lumber to fashion some semblance of tables and chairs. Unable to acquire enough paint of one color, the walls were a variety of black, brown, white, and red.

Finally, realizing they had done all they could, they decided that all in all it looked pretty good. It might never be considered a genuine historical site, Jake admitted, but he pointed out all they had done to it, and they ended up electing him the first official president of the club.

"Larry and Ronald are right behind me," Jake announced, laying his bike on the grass. Removing his ball cap, he wiped his forehead and hung the cap on his handlebars. "Man, it is hot, today. Where's Simon and Preston?" he asked, looking around.

"They are together somewhere," Brenton answered. "I don't see why they can't be on time. Preston's never on time for anything."

Leaning against the tree, Johnny looked across the football field and couldn't imagine Nathaniel attending Oak Grove High School. What would he think walking into the three-story building for the first time? He didn't have any doubt the kids would like him after they got to know him, but he had never been away from his family and all that he was use to. This would be a whole different world for him. Johnny suddenly wondered where would he live? He would have to ask Dad about that.

"Do you, Johnny?" Jake asked, wondering what he was thinking about.

"What?"

"Do you think the Cards will beat the Phillies tonight?"

Breaking a twig in half, he tossed it in the grass. "I don't know. I can't believe they lost last night. They should have won."

"I can't either," Jake replied, "and Beazley was pitching too."

"Yeah but Oscar Judd pitched for the Phillies," Brenton commented. "That's what did it."

"Here they come," Truman said, watching Larry and Ronald ride down the street with Simon and Preston about a block behind.

"Finally," Brenton said, glancing at the list he held in his hand. "Where have you guys been?" he asked as Larry and Ronald dropped their bikes on the ground.

"I had to help Mom. At the last minute about four customers walked in," Larry said, producing a white sack of donut holes. "Here I brought these."

Truman caught the sack Larry tossed him and opened it, popping one in his mouth.

Simon and Preston rode through the gate and dropped their bikes on the grass. "Guess what," Simon said, flopping down on the grass. "The *Phantom* was at Willy's last night."

Preston dropped down next to him and caught the sack Truman tossed him "We stopped to air up our tires, and Willy told Dad that someone took a couple of tires that were leaning against the side of the garage and rolled them down to the street."

"Did they steal anything?" Truman asked, motioning for Brenton to add it to the list.

"I'm getting it," he said, writing rapidly.

"Nope. Willy said they didn't take anything," Simon answered, tying his shoe. "He said they just moved the tires around. I think Willy figures it is a kid having fun."

"My dad said the same thing," Ronald commented, unconsciously rubbing his fingers on his lucky rabbit's foot. "But I don't know who it would be. We know everyone in Oak Grove."

"Maybe it's someone visiting that we don't know about," Larry offered.

"That is a possibility," Brenton commented thoughtfully. "Someone who is visiting from Chesterville maybe and is bored. If we could just catch him in the act . . ."

"How are we going to do that?" Preston asked. "Dad and the other men have been watching for the last two nights, and he didn't come around."

Truman closed his pocketknife and looked at the boys. "Do you know what? I think whoever it is knows the plans, and I think the person he is getting the information from does not even know it. Any one of us could go home and talk about what is going on. If we had company, we wouldn't even know we were giving him information."

"You're right, Truman" Brenton said, tapping his pencil on the ground. "We need to do something and not let ANYONE know what we plan to do."

"Yeah, but what is the something?" Simon asked, reaching for the donut sack.

"Well, the first thing we need to do is to find out if anyone is visiting in town. I think we ought to hop on our bikes this afternoon and check everywhere. Truman and I can check in town." Brenton said, folding his notes and sticking them in his back pocket.

"If we do find someone, we can form a stakeout and follow him," Larry said excitedly.

"Yeah, I found my cricket and I bought a whole new pack of BBs," Ronald exclaimed, looking at the others. "We ought to at least be able to scare him off."

The whistle at the firehouse sounded its long blast, signaling the noon hour. It had been installed when the new firehouse was built, and Oak Grove adjusted in no time to the twelve o'clock whistle each day. Mothers found that it fit their daily routine and expected their children home for lunch within a matter of minutes.

Simon stood and rolled up his pant leg. "Preston, Jake, and I can check the houses out toward the Driscols and the Seabaughs."

"Then, Ronald and Larry, you check the other side of town. Go all the way down to Cooley's house. That should cover about everywhere," Brenton said, picking up his bike. "And don't anyone say a word to anybody."

"Whatever you do, don't act suspicious," Truman said, looking at them. He stood and picked up his bike. "Just act natural and friendly to whoever you talk to."

"OK, I'll see you after lunch," Jake said, getting on his bicycle. "Preston, call me after you eat and let me know where and when to meet."

"Come on, Simon. I'll race you home," Truman called over his shoulder.

Within a few seconds, the oak tree in the schoolyard showed no trace of boys or bicycles. A silent, lonely figure sat hidden in the cornfield beyond the playground and peered out in confusion, wondering where the boys went in such a hurry.

Chapter 14

Simon, Preston, and Jake pedaled up the long lane leading up to the Seabaugh Farm. Their home was a favorite place for the children of Oak Grove. Mr. and Mrs. Seabaugh never had any children of their own, therefore welcomed any and all who appeared at their door, which was quite frequently.

Mrs. Seabaugh was a short, plump, white haired, little lady with gray eyes that mirrored a great love for those around her. She had been in ill health for as long as anyone could remember and spent most of her time quilting, crocheting, knitting, and tatting. The girls of Oak Grove found her infinitely patient as she instructed them with whichever project she happened to be working on, and they often sought her help on gifts for Mother's Day, Christmas, and birthdays. A bright smile and sense of humor accompanied her patience, and with the added delight of cake, cookies, or whatever Liza happened to be baking that day, they found it to be one of their favorite places to visit.

The children, likewise, also loved Mr. Seabaugh. He was a tall, muscular man with a face tanned from years of work in the fields. He was the best storyteller that was ever born; so the townsfolk or anyone whoever listened to him spin one of his tales said. He often picked up his fiddle or harmonica and added a little extra emphasis to one of his stories to the delight of those listening. When not in the field, one could always find him on the porch sitting in his rocker with a chunk of wood and his pocketknife, magically carving a figure of some sort. Today, the boys found the porch empty when they pedaled up the lane.

Putting the kickstand down, Preston looked across the yard toward the garage. Yellow daisies bordered a flagstone walk that led from the garage to the back door, and he noted that the car and truck were both visible through the open door. "They are here somewhere," he commented.

Mr. Seabaugh and Jacob are probably out in the field," Simon said, sitting down on the step.

"Well we can talk to Mrs. Seabaugh or Liza." Jake walked to the steps of the porch and stood still. "It's awfully quiet. Do you suppose she's taking a nap?"

Walking quietly up onto the porch, the three stood at the screen listening. All was quiet except for the loud ticking of the clock on the mantel. "I think she's probably sleeping," Jake whispered. "Come on, let's find Liza."

Jumping from the top step, he turned and grinned. Liza always rebuked them if she was around to witness it. "Lawsy me, that step is too high! You're gonna break a leg sure as anythin'," she continually told them.

Simon and Preston looked across the yard for any sight of her then jumped at the same time and followed Jake around the side of the porch.

"Well good afternoon, boys," Liza remarked, smiling at them as she stood next to the snowball bushes at the side of the house. She held a basket of fresh cut flowers in her hand, gathered from the small flowerbed that grew between the two homes.

"I was just gatherin' a bouquet for my table," she commented, holding the basket out. "What are you boys doin' out here today?"

"Hi, Liza," Preston said. "We were going to visit with Mrs. Seabaugh for a little bit, but it was so quiet we guessed she was sleeping."

Liza sat the basket of flowers on the picnic table. "Well, you guessed right. Miss Elizabeth naps about this time every day." Looking at the three boys, she smiled to herself, wondering what they were up to. "Maybe I can help you with somethin?"

"We were just out riding around and thought we would go for a swim at the old mill," Simon answered, sitting on top of the picnic table. Glancing at Jake, he widened his eyes, hinting for him to say something.

Mr. Seabaugh's family had built Seabaugh Mill along the creek years ago, and out of habit, the children always stopped to let them know they would be at the creek. More often than not, they received something to munch on or were allowed to ride the tractor if Mr. Seabaugh happened to be headed to the field, which was reason in itself to stop.

"If you have any out of town company, they are welcome to come along," Jake commented, rather proud of himself as he glanced at Preston and Simon.

Liza suppressed a smile and reached up to remove her straw hat. They couldn't be more obvious if they tried.

"That's mighty nice of you boys. I am sure my out-of-town company would love to take a dip today. It certainly is warm enough for it." Wiping her brow with the end of her apron, she sat on the bench. "But we don't have any company."

"You don't?" Preston asked disappointedly. "Well, we were just checking. But if you ever do, we will be glad to swim with them."

"We sure will. You just let us know when they get here." Simon slid from the picnic table and looked at the basket of flowers. "They sure are pretty, Liza." The three stood awkwardly for a minute, glancing at one another.

"We don't have any company, but I believe I do have some ginger snaps. Would that interest you at all?" she asked, smiling fondly at the boys.

"That sounds really good to me." Preston grinned as he looked at Simon and Jake.

"Come along then." Liza gathered the basket of flowers and walked across the yard with the three boys trailing behind. A delicious aroma that smelled an awful lot like apple pie greeted them as they entered the back door, and they looked at one another, wishing it was done.

Liza walked to the sink and filled a vase with water. "You boys sit down while I put theses flowers in some water." She motioned toward the table, and they took a seat while she removed the flowers from her basket. Placing her blooms in the water, she pondered what was going on as she sat the arrangement in the middle of the table. Just about an hour ago, she had gone through the same procedure with some of the older boys and wondered what they were up to.

Reaching into the cabinet, she produced four glasses. "How about some lemonade?" she asked, retrieving a pitcher from the refrigerator. "Preston, grab the cookie jar will you?"

He lifted the cookie jar and carefully sat it in the middle of the table. Liza told them one day that it belonged to her mother, and it was very special to her. A wooden lid with a worn, red knob fit snugly on top of the round glass cookie jar, revealing fresh baked gingersnaps.

"What are you three up to?" Liza asked, pouring lemonade in the glasses. Handing one to each of the boys, she poured a glass for herself and sat down in one of the chairs, watching them gulp the cold lemonade.

"This hits the spot, Liza. Thanks." Preston eyes strayed to the cookie jar, and he wondered how long it was going to take her to offer them one.

"Yeah, it sure does," Simon remarked, looking at the other two. They watched her remove the wooden lid, tear three pieces of waxed paper and place four cookies in the center of each. Pulling the edges up around the cookies, she twisted the ends.

"How's that?" she asked, pushing the cookies in front of each of them. "Now, what's goin' on? You can't fool me." She looked directly at Jake, waiting for an answer. He seriously studied the vase of flowers as though he was looking at them for the first time in his life and swung his feet nervously beneath the table.

I might as well tell her the truth, he thought. They hadn't fooled her at all and here she had been nice and given them cookies. Why did she have to be so smart and know everything? Liza, he thought, was worse than his mom was when it came to stuff like that. Jake glanced across the table at Preston and then back at Liza who was waiting for his answer.

"Well, Liza, you know all about the trouble in town. No one, not even the Sheriff, can catch the person who is stealing everything." The words tumbled out Jake's mouth between bites of cookie. "Since no one thinks it is anyone that lives here, we kind of thought maybe it is someone visiting Oak Grove. We are riding around checking to see if anyone has any company, that's all." He twisted the end of his waxed paper and glanced at Simon and Preston.

Liza looked at the three boys, staring at her with wide eyes. "I guess that is an idea, and I know you are just tryin' to help, but just because someone may be visitin' Oak Grove doesn't make that person a thief." She took a drink of lemonade and sat it down. "Pastor Mike said we should not blame anyone until we find out who is guilty." Liza looked at the three and smiled. "You wouldn't want to hurt an innocent person's feelin's, would you?"

"Oh, no, ma'am." Preston shook his head. He remembered the time he was blamed for breaking a candy dish in the Dime Store. He was standing in the aisle looking at the bins of candy while he waited for his mom when it fell on the floor. Everyone turned and looked at him and Mrs. Reese, who worked there at the time, told him to be more careful. He was trying to explain that it was not his fault when another one hit the floor. It seemed that someone stacked too many together and they were sliding off the shelf.

"Well, you see? I think if you happen to come across someone visitin' Oak Grove, it would be a good idea to make him or her feel welcome." Liza observed the guilt on their faces and smiled as she patted Simon's hand. "I know you are just tryin' to help, but why don't you just go swim and have fun. Let the Sheriff and Jim Walker worry about it."

"I guess you're right, Liza. Well, I guess we'll go on up and swim," Jake commented, relieved she didn't give them a good talking to. She was pretty good at that when she wanted to be.

"That pie sure smells good," Preston said, glancing at the oven, wishing it was done. "Well, guys, let's go. Thanks for the cookies and lemonade, Liza."

"You're welcome. Have fun," she replied, watching them grab their cookies and head for door.

"Tell Mr. and Mrs. Seabaugh hi for us," Jacob said as he walked out the door.

"I sure will." She followed them to the door and stepped out on the porch. Watching the boys cross the yard, she shook her head and thought again of the recent happenings in Oak Grove and also wondered who was responsible. Raising her hand, she waved to them as they pedaled down the lane.

Glancing at her watch, she spoke to herself, "I guess I better check my apple pie and take a piece over to Elizabeth." Glancing toward the larger home, she figured if she wasn't already awake, she would be shortly.

She stood on the porch and watched the boys pedal the half mile down the lane and turn up Old Mill Road. Liza smiled and walked back into the kitchen, wondering what it would be like to jump in the creek once again. None of the boys showed any evidence of having swim trunks but, of course, thinking back on her childhood she remembered her own brothers taking a dip in the creek wearing only their under garments.

The pie was done. Liza could tell by the smell. Grabbing a couple of potholders, she walked to the oven and removed the pie. Setting it in the window over the sink to cool, she walked to a small table by the window that overlooked the pasture and turned the fan on. "It's mighty hot today," she said to herself as she stood in front of the fan, welcoming the air it blew around. Gazing out over the pasture, she thought back to the days when she and her friends would run up to the old millpond to cool off. Chuckling, she wondered what the boys would think if she showed up unexpectedly and jumped in the creek with them. She figured they would think she probably lost her mind.

Simon, Preston, and Jake pedaled their bikes up Old Mill Road. One had to get a good run on it to make it up the steep incline that led into the woods. Towering oaks and cedar trees lined both sides of the road, and the branches at times grew together forming a canopy of sorts.

At the top of the hill the road curved to the right and continued farther up into the woods where it forked to the left, leading to the Oak Grove Timber Company. The boys stayed to the right and followed the road as it wound its way farther up the ridge to the old Seabaugh Mill. As they rounded a bend in the road the sound of laughter and splashing reached their ears.

"Truman and the guys are here," Simon yelled back at Jake and Preston. The three rode across the stone bridge that crossed the creek and followed the road around the front and along the side of the old mill.

The old building sat at the edge of the creek, its paint weathered to a faded red. *Seabaugh Mill,* once painted in bold white, was now bleached by the sun and barely readable. The wheel, sitting idle in the water, gave testimony of its use in the past. Farmers came from outlying areas and neighboring communities not only to grind their corn and wheat but also to visit with friends and neighbors and catch up on the latest news.

Nestled at the edge of the creek amid the oak trees, it created a serene atmosphere and would have been a delight to many a photographer if they had known of its whereabouts. Blackberries grew in the woods on the north side of the creek, myriads of violets waved their heads, wild honeysuckle grew around the mill, and daisies scattered themselves throughout the area.

The mill, one time bustling with activity, now was used for swimming during the summer and ice-skating in the winter if snow and ice didn't make the trek up the hill too treacherous.

"What are you doing out here?" Johnny yelled, floating in a black rubber inner tube. He watched the three boys drop their bikes in the grass and remove their shoes.

"The same thing you are! What do you think?" Jake called back, already shedding his jeans, adding them to the pile on the grass. Wading slowly out into the creek, he braced himself with each step. The spring fed creek flowed from a source somewhere farther up on the ridge and was always cold. He stood for a minute, then took a deep breath and dove into the water. After the first initial shock, it felt good after the long, hot ride.

Brenton sat on the dock shivering and watched Jake splash in the water. Mr. Seabaugh built the dock several years ago for the children and occasionally came up himself and fished off the end of it.

Truman waded along the bank trying to catch a turtle that eluded him and finally gave up. His legs getting numb from the cold water, he climbed up on the dock and sat down next to Brenton.

Preston and Simon both hit the water about the same time. "Wow, it's cold!" Preston yelled as his feet hit the water. The creek at the old mill pooled into a fairly large pond then narrowed as the water flowed downstream snaking its way by the Oak Grove Timber Company, around the outskirts of town, and through the woods beyond the Baptist Church where it meandered off into the woods.

Simon swam out a short distance and floated on his back, looking up into the trees above his head. Rolling over, he swam back to the dock and waited as Johnny tossed the inner tube on top.

Heaving himself up out of the water, Johnny sat on the edge of the dock dangling his feet and grabbed Simon's arm, pulling him out of the water. Moving around to the other side, he watched the turtle surface then disappear beneath them.

"Did you find out anything?" Brenton asked as Simon sat down. "Did you check all the houses?"

"No one has any company," Jake said, peering over the end of the dock. "Somebody help me up." Laying both arms on top of the boards, he looked at the boys and waited for one of them to help him. Thinking it too much trouble to swim to the bank and too small to pull himself out of the water onto the dock, he usually hung there until someone helped him.

Brenton jumped up, walked to the edge, and held his hand down to him. "Come on."

Jake grabbed his hand, placed one foot on the edge of the dock, and Brenton gave a tug, pulling him up out of the water. "Gee willikers, Jake, you're all wet," he laughed and released his grip, letting him slide back into the water with a splash.

Standing on the edge of the dock laughing, Brenton waited for him to surface, instantly aware that he should not have turned his back. The shove came from behind, and he heard Preston's laughter as he hit the water. Bobbing to the surface, he looked at Jake, and they both grinned. Swimming to the bank, they crawled out and yelling at the top of their lungs ran across the dock.

Truman knew from past experience that revenge could involve any of them and took matters into his own hands by jumping into the creek. He laughed with glee as he broke the surface and watched Preston and Johnny hit the water; arms and legs flailing in the air. He, at least, deprived Jake and Brenton the satisfaction of throwing him in the creek and laughed as he looked at them standing on the dock. Feeling a hand grasp his ankle, his laughter turned to sputtering as he found himself jerked beneath the surface.

With Jake and Brenton hitting the water again, a merciless bout of dunking and splashing occurred until Johnny yelled, "enough!" and swam to the edge of the creek. Climbing out of the water, he plopped down on the dock and lay on his back, breathless and shivering from the cold water.

One by one the rest followed until they all lay stretched out on their backs on the warm dock.

The sun was just moving beyond the treetops, and they lay quietly listening to the water lap lazily against the small fishing boat tied to the side of the dock.

"I wonder what we should do now?" Preston asked as he looked up into the trees and watched a squirrel run out on a branch and stare down at him curiously."

"I don't know," Simon answered, lying on his stomach with his chin in his hands. "I don't think anybody knows."

"Dad said he had an idea but wouldn't say what it was." Brenton sat up and dangled his feet over the side. "He is really aggravated that he can't figure out who is stealing all this stuff."

"I'd like to knock his block off. And I would too, if I knew who it was." Preston, with a determined set to his jaw, rolled over on his back to dry the front of his underwear. A warm breeze floated across the dock, and the sound of a distant woodpecker's tapping drifted through the woods.

Simon sat up and joined Brenton on the side of the dock. "Willy said that almost everyone who comes in the station has a tale to tell."

"Yeah, but it may not all be true." Johnny commented as he sat up. "Laura couldn't find her roller skates yesterday and just knew someone stole them. She found out later that Shari was using them over at Maggie's." He stood up and looked at the cool water. He would have to bring Nathaniel up here if he comes to Oak Grove. *He would like it here*, Johnny thought.

"The clubhouse!" Brenton exclaimed suddenly, looking at all of them. "No one has checked there."

"Of course. That would be a perfect place for someone to hide," Truman agreed slapping his hand on his leg. "Very few people even know it is there."

"Then let's go. Let's go check to see if he's been staying there," Johnny said, looking back and forth at the rest. "Why didn't we think of this before?"

A train whistle blew in the distance and Truman jumped up "Gee whiz, Brenton. That's the three o'clock train. We have to go." Leaping from the dock to the creek bank, both boys dug through the pile of jeans that were thrown in a heap in the grass.

"Tomorrow morning. Let's meet tomorrow and ride out there," Brenton said, hurriedly pulling his jeans on. "Ten o'clock; we'll meet at the school again."

"Let's bring our BB guns," Preston added. "We might need it."

"See you tomorrow," Truman yelled, pulling his shirt over his head and getting on his bike. "Simon, you better get home."

"I will," Simon yelled back then looked at Preston and Jake. "We better make sure we bring our crickets too. We might need to use them."

"Yeah, we better be prepared," Jake agreed, as he watched the three older boys pedal around the side of the mill and cross the bridge. A movement in the water caught his eye, and he watched the turtle that Truman tried to catch surface, look around, and slowly climb out of the water.

Jake looked at Simon with a frown. "My underwear is still wet, and I'm going to be itching," he said, holding his jeans in one hand and scratching his backside with the other.

Preston sat on the grass and rolled his pant leg up. He didn't want to get it caught in the chain again like he did a couple of weeks ago. He still had scratch marks on his elbows.

Simon pulled his jeans on and watched Jake dance around trying to dry his underwear. "That's not going to help. Just put your pants on. They'll dry on the ride home," he said, picking his bike up from the ground.

In a matter of minutes they were dressed, crossing the bridge, and pedaling down the road toward home.

The water at the millpond, now still and undisturbed, shimmered as the last rays of sun fell behind the trees. A lone figure peered from the window of the mill and searched the dock and creek for any sign of activity. The splashing and laughter that filled the air just a few minutes ago was now but a memory, and the millpond was quiet and peaceful. It was once again a place where he would not be disturbed.

Simon pushed the swing back and forth with his toe and thumbed through the Marvel Comic Book he had traded Preston yesterday. Neither words nor pictures registered in his head. He laid *The Case of the Joker's Crime Circus* on the swing and looked down the street for a glimpse of Truman.

Things were fine up until a few minutes ago. Swimming at the millpond was fun, Mom was fixing his favorite supper, and tonight's episode of Captain Midnight was one none of the guys wanted to miss; then he opened the back door.

"Don't plan on going anywhere after supper. Your Father called and said he wanted to talk to you and Truman," she said when he walked into the kitchen. He asked what Dad wanted, but she said she didn't know and continued frying chicken. Mom didn't look angry, *but maybe she's covering up,* Simon thought and headed to the front porch so he could warn Truman. Pondering on the matter for a few minutes, he decided he wasn't guilty of anything except shooting a hole in the basement window two weeks ago. Truman must have done something, and now they were in for one of Dad's lectures.

Delivering the last newspaper, Truman rode into the yard and dropped his bike on the grass. Sport sat up, barked, and lay back down wagging his tail. He watched Truman walk towards him and lifted his head, tilting it sideways while he scratched his ears.

"What did you do to get us in trouble?" Simon looked at his brother accusingly and glanced toward the screen door.

"I didn't do anything. What makes you think we are in trouble?" Truman asked, glancing at the comic book lying next to Simon.

"Because Mom said for us to not make any plans after supper. Dad wants to talk to both of us."

"So? That doesn't mean anything, unless you did something you weren't supposed to," Truman said, wondering what Simon had done this time.

"I didn't do anything."

"Neither did I," Truman retorted, grabbing the comic book "Where did you get this Batman comic?"

"Preston traded me for *Alfred, Private Detective*."

Jim pulled into the drive, noticing the boys on the porch, and smiled to himself. *I can't wait to see their faces when I tell them,* he thought to himself. He removed the key from the ignition, opened the door, and was greeted by Sport who was excitedly wagging his tail. Reaching down, he patted his head and watched him run ahead to the back door.

"Hi, Hon," he said, kissing Jennifer on the cheek. "Supper smells good."

"How was today?" she asked, wiping her hands on her apron. "Did anyone else have anything stolen?" She looked at him curiously and sat a platter of fried chicken on the table.

"We thought so for a while," Jim replied, grabbing a drumstick. "Mrs. Cranston called this afternoon and said Sam's wallet was missing." He looked at the confusion on her face and grinned as he took a bite of chicken and leaned against the kitchen cabinet. "They found it. Sam paid the Watkins Man, and it seems they got to talking about the baseball game and he put it on the foyer table instead of his pocket."

"Well I am glad it was not stolen," Jennifer said with relief as she spooned mashed potatoes into a bowl and watched him finish the drumstick. "Supper is ready for the rest of us since you've already started," she laughed. "Tell the boys to wash up, will you?"

Jim walked down the hall to the front door. "Time for supper, guys. Come on in and wash your hands."

Closing the comic book, Truman laid it on the swing, and walked to the door. "I guess we'll soon find out what he wants."

Jennifer was looking at Jim with a confused look on her face when the boys came to the table. "Isn't that kind of a strange idea?" she asked, taking her seat.

"Not when you stop to think about everything that has happened." Jim looked at both boys as they sat down. "It looks like you two have been up to the mill pond," he commented, looking from one to the other.

Truman could never understand how his parents knew when they went swimming. Never for a moment did he stop to consider the evidence of sun on his nose or the telltale sign of creek water in his hair. "We got hot and rode up to the Old Mill to cool off."

"We stopped at the Seabaugh farm to let them know we would be there," Simon commented, thinking that sounded pretty responsible and might impress him He sure didn't have *the look* he usually wore when they were in trouble.

After raising their brows questioningly, at each other a couple of times, they finally relaxed, figuring whatever it was, Dad wasn't mad. In fact, he appeared to be in a very good mood. Simon pushed his plate back. "May I be excused?"

"Not just yet. I want to ask you something," Jim said, looking at both of them. Simon rolled his eyes toward Truman and took a deep breath. *Here it comes*, he thought.

"Your Uncle John and I need your help tonight." Jim also pushed his plate back and accepted the cup of coffee Jennifer sat in front of him. Taking a sip, he asked, "Do you think you are up to camping out on the square tonight?"

Truman's eyes widened as he looked at his dad and then at Simon. "Yeah, that would be swell," he said, grinning.

"Boy howdy, yes!" Simon exclaimed. "But what for? Is anyone else going to be there?"

Jim smiled at the excitement in their eyes. "There sure will be: most of your friends, your Uncle John, Willy, Ben, and Eli Cook." He looked at Jennifer, smiled, and looked back at Truman and Simon. "Finish your supper and we'll head down to the square about dark." Jim smiled mysteriously. "We're going to catch the phantom tonight."

Leah and Mike stood on the front porch and watched the Sheriff drive off with Johnny and Jimmy.

"It seems to me boys get to do everything," Shari commented with a frown on her face. I don't see why we couldn't go along."

"I think this is strictly a man's job tonight." Mike grinned at Leah and chuckled, "If nothing else they will have a good time."

Both boys hurriedly scurried through the house grabbing quilts, flashlights, and pillows when the Sheriff appeared at the door saying he needed to borrow Johnny and Jimmy for the evening.

Leah heard the murmured conversation on the porch between Mike and the Sheriff and was curious as to what was going on.

"Now wouldn't that be something." The rich timbre of Mike's laughter drifted through the front window, and Leah smiled. Whatever it was, it couldn't be too serious; not when they were laughing about it.

"What are we going to do, Sheriff?" Jimmy asked, dragging his pillow through the yard. Climbing into the back seat, he wondered if they were being deputized and was proud that he was asked to come along. Usually, when Brenton, Preston, and Johnny did anything he was considered too little, but tonight was different. Jordan and Zachary were even going along, and they were just little kids.

"I'll tell you when we get to the square," Sheriff Walker replied, hoping against hope that his instinct was correct on this. If not, he was going to feel like an idiot.

By the time they reached the square, dusk was settling on Oak Grove, and the street lamps were just coming on. Jim Walker pulled up behind them, and Truman and Simon jumped out of the car with their pillows and blankets. "What do you think is going on?" Simon asked, falling into step with Preston and Jimmy.

"I think the Sheriff is forming a posse," Jimmy stated, looking at several that were already gathering at the bandstand.

"I'm not sure about that," Preston replied, "but I know it has something to do with catching the thief." Preston dropped his pillow and blanket on the grass and sat down next to Jake.

"What are we doing here?" Jake asked. His brown eyes were wide with curiosity, and he was hoping Preston would know what was going on. "Dad wouldn't tell me anything."

"I don't know," Preston said, turning his flashlight off and on to make sure it worked. After supper Dad came upstairs and told all of us to get our stuff together because we were going to camp out tonight."

Willy and Young Ben, walking across the square toward them, seemed to be in deep conversation about something. Willy carried a tow sack slung across his shoulder, and Simon wondered what he had in it. He had the distinct feeling that something really important was about to happen.

Glancing around the square, Simon noted the dark windows of the now closed and locked shops. The absence of familiar neighbors, busily coming and going from one store to the next, seemed very strange. It was almost dark, and he watched the fireflies flittering back and forth, then looked up at the moon, barely visible in the trees. The street lamps cast just enough glow to create shadows around the honeysuckles and cause dark, black places between buildings. He suddenly wasn't too sure catching *the phantom* was going to be all that fun.

There's nothing to be scared of, he thought as he noted Jordan, Josiah, and Zachary sitting on the bottom step of the bandstand playing *Rock, Paper, Scissors*. Brenton, Truman, and Johnny were looking through something in a bushel basket, and he wondered what was in it.

Standing in the bandstand, looking at the boys with their pillows and quilts, Sheriff Walker knew he was not going to get any sleep. He wondered where the older boys were when a shrill whistle sounded from the direction of the Cranston Hotel. Peter waved his arms, and John noted that David was carrying his guitar.

He watched their approach, glad that everyone who was supposed to be here was present. Not knowing how to explain his idea without ruining the plan, he stood quietly for a moment and then came to the conclusion that telling only as much as necessary would probably be best.

"Well, boys, thank you for helping me tonight. I guess you are wondering what this is all about," he said, looking at the curious expressions on their faces and marveling how a group of boys could get so quiet. He smiled slightly and looked at them seriously. "I think the person we are trying to catch is not from Oak Grove." Glancing at his brother and the rest of the men standing along the back of the bandstand, John glanced at the flier he held in his hand, folded it, and stuck it in his shirt pocket.

"He is considered a missing person, not a criminal. They just want him found, safe and sound, and back home where he belongs. He has to be hungry, and we need to let him know we are here to help."

The boys listened quietly, trying to sort things out. One thing they did know for sure; they had been correct. He was not someone from Oak Grove.

Jim stood in the back staring at City Hall, Willy was studying the floor, and Ben and Eli were talking quietly to each other. The Sheriff had filled the men in on his plan this afternoon and received the same reaction from all of them. When asked if they knew of a better idea, they all said no and agreed to go along with him.

"Boys, your purpose tonight is to let him know we are friendly. I am told he is very shy." John looked at the confused expressions and hoped they would cooperate like he expected. "He's been hanging around for a few days now, and he may recognize some of you. Being lonely and hungry, I am hoping he might decide to wander over and join us. So let's have fun and see what happens."

"Where are you going to be, Dad?" Jordan asked, looking up at him with his pillow in his arms. "Are you going to camp with us?"

"Yes, I am," John answered, "but I am going to sit up in the bell tower and see if maybe I might spot him. Eli and Jim will be here in the bandstand, and Ben and Willy are going to sit over on the bench by Reese's Market."

He looked at the men and knew they had doubts that he would even show up, but John figured it was worth a try. "Did you bring everything you need?" Receiving affirmative nods from the four men, he turned once again to the boys.

"Okay, fellows, get out there on the square and have a good time. If he does come over, be nice and friendly to him."

Preston looked at Simon and Jake. "I wonder who he is. Dad said he was shy."

"I bet it's one of the Black's," Simon answered, throwing his blanket on the ground. "Everyone says they are backwards. That means *shy*; not the way they walk," he explained, remembering when he was confused about it He use to think that if someone was considered to be backwards, they didn't know how to walk forward until Old Ben explained it to him one day when they were sitting on the bench by the fountain

"But why would one of the Blacks come here in the first place, and why wouldn't he just go back home? Jake asked. "That doesn't even make sense."

Everyone says they are mean and live by themselves because they don't like people." Preston rolled his blanket out and sat down to remove his shoes and socks. "I don't think it is one of them either."

Quilts and pillows soon lay spread in a circle between the bandstand and the bell tower as the boys began making themselves comfortable. Peter and David found themselves surrounded by the younger boys and grinned at each other.

"What do you think the Sheriff meant about him recognizing some of us?" Johnny asked Truman who sat cross-legged on his quilt. "How would he know who we are unless he's been really good at following us around. And if that's the case, why didn't we see him?"

"I don't know. It sounds like he ran away from home, doesn't it?" Truman asked, looking around the square. "That would explain why he doesn't want to be seen. Evidently, he doesn't want to go home." Truman glanced at the bushel basket his dad was carrying.

"Here you go, boys. This is for all of you," he commented, placing it in the middle of the group. It contained a wide assortment of fruit and snacks. "Help yourself."

"I wish we knew who we were watching for," Josiah said, catching a box of Cracker Jacks someone threw in his direction.

John Walker sat in the bell tower and looked across the now dark square, trying to distinguish the shapes of those scattered about, but the quarter moon did not shed enough light to see clearly. Glancing at the small area next to Reese's Market, he could barely make out the forms of Ben and Willy sitting on the bench. Glancing at the bandstand, he could see no one but knew Jim and Eli were sitting on a couple of chairs toward the back. Gazing down at the middle of the square, he saw the group of boys clumped together like one big lump of coal in the night. Squinting his eyes, he wondered why they were so quiet and vaguely made out the taller shapes in the middle as Peter and David. One of them was gesturing with his hands, and John caught a few words drifting up to him "midnight—werewolf—death." He chuckled to himself, *what an opportunity to scare the wits out of the boys*. A few minutes later laughter erupted, and several boys jumped on the storyteller.

The night air felt good on John's face after the heat of the day. He settled in a wooden folding chair and propped his feet on one of the railings. Most of the boys brought flashlights, and rays of light flashed back and forth in the trees, across the bandstand, the water fountain, and into the store windows.

Approximately an hour passed, and John stood up to stretch. He stared at the stores, trying to see through the dark shadows beyond the buildings, and wondered if this whole idea was going to work. He was at a dead end and didn't know what else to do. Unconsciously he felt for the flyer in his pocket and wondered about it. He had received it from the Chesterville Police Department three days ago, laid it on his desk, and forgot about it. He came across it yesterday while clearing his desk, and the present plan came suddenly this morning when he ran into Mildred Reese coming out of the market. He was fairly certain the picture on the flier was the one they were looking for.

Laughter rose from the square, and the boys scattered in all directions. Someone was shining their flashlight, attempting to follow the shouts of the other boys. Flashlight tag. John grinned and continued to watch.

"It's you, Truman! I got you!" Jake yelled, switching his flashlight off. The boys scattered again, calling his name from all directions Truman ran across the square, flashing his light back and forth, and jumped behind the snowball bush next to the bell tower. The beam of light fell on Josiah. "Gotcha!" He laughed and took off around the other side.

Willy and Ben sat on the bench laughing as they watched the boys scurry around the square, hide behind the bandstand, on the other side of the bell tower, and in the honeysuckle bushes.

"If nothing else happens tonight, they are at least having a good time," Ben said, stretching his legs out in front of him. The two men sat in amused silence for a few minutes. "Do you think he will show tonight?" Ben asked.

"Well, the Sheriff seems to think if they can get his attention, he might be curious enough to come around unless he is too scared." Willy stood up and stretched his long frame. His injured leg had a tendency to stiffen when he sat too long. "I don't know. Everything he has done has been unpredictable."

The boys, giving up on flashlight tag, settled down on their quilts, and John wondered what they were doing as he strained his eyes to see if he could spot Jordan. He had not planned on bringing him since Zachary was spending the night, but when they both looked at him with such pitiful expressions, he didn't have the heart to leave them behind. The eleven o'clock train whistle sounded in the distance, and he settled back in the chair, wondering what Jim and Eli were doing to stay awake.

Down on the square, the boys sat quietly and listened to David strum his guitar. "How did you learn to play?" Brenton asked, rolling over on his stomach.

"I taught myself." He concentrated on tuning one of the strings and then continued, "I just started messing around with it when my uncle gave it to me and learned to pick out a few songs."

Spreading his quilt between Jimmy and Preston, Josiah grabbed his pillow, dragging it across Preston's face. It took a few seconds and a dirty look from his brother before he finally settled into a comfortable position and stared up at the stars. The summer breeze carried the strains of David's guitar, and the music of tree frogs and crickets began to lull him to sleep. He rolled to his side and faced Jimmy. "This is fun," he said quietly.

"Yeah." Jimmy yawned and rolled on his side, finding it hard to stay awake.

Preston, Simon, and Jake lay on their backs looking up at the stars. "Where is Ursa Major?" Preston asked, putting his hands behind his head.

"Where's what?" Simon looked at him curiously. "What is Ursa Major?"

"The Big Dipper," Preston said quietly. "Brenton said it is Ursa Major and the Little Dipper is Ursa Minor."

"There's the Big Dipper," Jake remarked, pointing to the night sky. "And there is the Little Dipper."

"I see it," Simon yawned. "There's the North Star. Right over there." Rolling onto his stomach, he gathered the pillow beneath his head "I wish whoever is suppose to come would get here. Look, they're already asleep," he whispered, pointing to Jordan and Zachary.

The clock at City Hall chimed the midnight hour and most of the boys silently counted the chimes. The large clock with its Roman numerals hung on the front of City Hall, and most folks in Oak Grove paid little attention to it during the day.

During the evening and night hours, the chimes had a different affect altogether. The familiar sound, heard in the darkness while sitting on the front porch or lying in bed, filled one with a sense of peace and reminded them that all was well.

"Don't fall asleep or you might miss him," Preston said as he sat up and glanced at the bell tower. "It is dark out here. The moon isn't very bright tonight, is it?" He looked toward the bandstand but couldn't see Uncle Jim or Eli. Willy and Ben were, he guessed, sitting on the bench by the oak tree. Lying back, he looked up at the stars again. David and Peter were talking about girls.

"Is Caroline your girl?" David asked.

Brenton, Truman, and Johnny became quiet so they could listen to the conversation. Lying on their backs, not saying a word, they were curious as to see what they might hear.

"I don't know. She sure is pretty, and she's nice too." The tone of Peter's voice sounded like he was confused or trying to hide something.

Brenton rolled over and grinned at Johnny and Truman.

"Of course, she's pretty and nice," David persisted. "But do you like her? Is she your girl? I think she likes you."

"I don't know about that. Do you really think she likes me?" Peter asked, and then he was quiet for a moment "Dave?" He hesitated and then asked, "Why are you asking? Do you like her?"

"As a friend, I do." David answered as he continued to play. He stopped for a moment and then murmured, "I think Terry Charles is cute. I like her but. . . ." he lowered his voice and they couldn't make out what he was saying.

"Have you ever liked a girl?" Truman asked Brenton and Johnny quietly, suddenly curious about love and girls.

"Not me. I have two sisters, and they sure are mysterious at times; especially Laura," Johnny commented. "Dad told me one day that it will get worse before it gets better, and I might as well accept it. I'm not real sure what he meant by that."

Truman continued to look at the stars. "I heard Dad say one day that you can't live with them and you can't live without them. So what are you suppose to do?"

"Well it seems awfully confusing to me. I mean Peter and David can't figure it out and they are a lot older than us," Brenton said as he slipped his shoes off. "I guess some of them are kind of nice to look at, but they can't do much of anything."

Preston lay on his side, his eyes closing with a will of their own as he listened to the murmuring of the older boys. Opening one eye, he glanced at Simon. He was asleep. His heavy eyelids closed again and he drifted off.

How long he had been asleep, Preston did not know. Josiah pushed his brother's arm. "Go back to sleep," Preston mumbled. A few seconds later he felt Josiah's touch a second time. Preston, still half-asleep, rolled to his back. "I said go to sleep," he murmured again. Josiah shook his arm a third time and Preston sat up. "What do you want?" he asked, turning to look at him. His eyes widened in surprise, as he looked full into the face of a hairy monster. He was dreaming. That was it. The creature reached out and touched him on the shoulder again. "Help! Somebody, help!" Preston shouted, jumping to his feet.

The creature, startled by Preston's shout, took a big leap and landed on Truman's back. Rolling to his side, Truman jumped up, yelled, and he and the furry animal jumped from blanket to blanket like they had choreographed the steps.

Sheriff Walker jumped at Preston's shout and looked down at the melee below. Boys were running in all directions, shouting and swinging pillows. Some managed to find their flashlights and were shining them randomly while they waved their arms. One of the flashlight beams fell on something furry in the middle of the scramble, and then the light flew in another direction. John watched as one of the boys shined their light on the animal and began chasing it across the square Everyone was shouting and in a state of total confusion. Willy and Ben jumped and were running across the square with Jim and Eli coming from the opposite direction.

"Willy, can you get him?" Jim yelled, running behind the boys. "Don't let him get away!"

Eli caught up with Jim and the boys at the bell tower. The animal was right in front of them and Eli made a quick dash to the left, thinking to head him off. Ben, anticipating the same move, came from the right. Both men, seeing their opportunity, threw the nets they carried. The small creature jumped quickly away, and the nets fell on Simon, Zachary, and Josiah.

"What are you doing? " Simon yelled, trying to stand up. The net held him to the ground as Zachary and Josiah rolled, twisted, and tried to jerk the net off. All three tugged, yelled, and kicked until they were hopelessly tangled in the mess.

"Get us out of here," Zachary shouted, unable to move. Josiah's foot was pressed against his chest and Simon was lying on his arm.

"Everyone lay still!" Josiah shouted. "Someone will have to cut this thing. I can't move."

The three boys lay hopelessly tangled in the net and watched the pandemonium around them. Willy was shouting at Ben to "go to your right," lights flashed in all directions, Eli was swinging a quilt, and it sounded like Jordan was crying. The three boys watched in amazement as the animal make a quick ascent into the oak tree by the bell tower.

The Sheriff had anticipated this move but was still taken by surprise when the animal swung from a branch into the tower and grabbed the rope. The ringing of the bell jarred him senseless as he dove for the animal, trying not to crack his head on the bell

"I'm down here," Jim yelled as he started up the steps. "Do you have him, John?" The ringing of the bell continued amid the scuffling in the tower. Flashlights were aimed at the bell, boys were yelling, and Simon, Zachary, and Josiah were shouting their complaints, trying to free themselves once again from the nets.

"Hold on!" Eli shouted as he knelt down beside the boys. "Are you all OK? The net is not around anyone's neck is it?" he asked, anxiously trying to see them.

"We're OK, we just can't move," Zachary answered as he watched Eli grab the nets in his hands, trying to separate them.

Willy and Ben watched as the animal jumped from the steps of the bell tower into the middle of the boys grouped together at the bottom of the steps. Scattering in all directions, the small animal took the opportunity to scamper off across the square.

Eli stopped trying to free the boys, realizing it was useless in the dark. "I'll need some light to get you free. Just sit and watch." He sat on the ground next to them, looked around the square, and burst into laughter.

It was a scene of sheer bedlam. Boys and men ran in all directions, and a small animal scampered toward the bandstand. Flashlights, still shining, lay on the grass where they had been dropped, Simon, Zachary, and Josiah were still hopelessly tangled in the nets, and Sheriff Walker was walking around in a daze holding his ears. Automobiles were beginning to arrive at the square, and Old Ben, Ron, and The Cranstons walked up in their nightclothes.

Eli could do nothing but laugh. This was the funniest thing he had ever seen. He glanced over at the three boys tangled in the nets and laid back in the grass, laughing hopelessly.

The wild chase around the square lasted another few minutes, and the monkey made another mad dash for the bandstand, disappearing through a piece of loose latticework at the bottom. Crowding around, the boys chattered in excitement, tried to see through the lattice with their flashlights, and argued over how big the animal was and who had seen him first.

Eli, still chuckling, followed Simon, Zachary, and Josiah across the square, relieved that they were no longer tangled in the nets. With Mrs. Cranston holding a flashlight in each hand and Sam and Old Ben's help, they finally managed to untangle the nets and free them. Once loose, they took off across the square toward the bandstand as fast as they could go.

"Circle the bandstand," John shouted loudly. The ringing in his ears persisted and everything else seemed muffled. Jim was saying something, but all John could see was his mouth moving.

"Here," the Sheriff yelled again, pointing to a portion that was pulled loose. "This is where he has been hiding."

Several men who responded to the bell ringing gathered around, wondering what had happened and why Sheriff Walker was shouting. With all of the boys talking at once, it was nearly impossible to get the particulars of what was going on.

"Let's all get quiet," Jim shouted above the chattering, shouts of excitement, and laughter. Resting his hand on his brother's shoulder, he shook his head. "We are not all deaf. Quit yelling."

"What did you say?" John asked, putting his hand to his ear.

Jim laughed at the perplexed expression on his brother's face then turned to the others. "Everyone stay where you are. Does anyone see any other place where the lattice work is loose?"

Willy stared at the bandstand and a slow smile spread across his face. It was the very spot he had been standing when he felt he was being watched, and now he knew the reason. He was either standing right on top of the culprit, or the culprit was watching him from above.

Sheriff Walker circled the bandstand, still trying to shake the sound of the bell from his head. "Whatever you do, don't anyone let this monkey escape." He stared at the loosened latticework, still not sure he was thinking clearly. The silence caught his attention, and he looked up at Mayor Driscol, Hank, and Gerald Williams who were staring at him with dumbfound expressions on their faces.

Alan and Mike Madison were talking to Eli and Pastor Mike, laughing over the whole situation, and Nelson White and Ron were headed back across the square.

"Now what do we do with him?" Ben asked. "We've go him cornered, but we can't stand out here all night guarding him, and I don't know about you, but I don't think I want to crawl under there and pull him out."

The clock at City Hall struck one, and John glanced at all the men and boys gathered around. The absurdity of the whole situation hit him full force, and he began to chuckle. Sitting on the bottom step, he laughed until he had to wipe his eyes with the back of his hand. In a few minutes his head finally cleared, and he listened to the retelling of events of the last thirty minutes. Eli and Ben were explaining to Simon, Zachary, and Josiah how and why they ended up in the nets, Preston was retelling his encounter with the animal and how he thought it had been Josiah, and every other boy was giving his version of what happened. No one seemed able to comprehend that a monkey was the cause of so much commotion and confusion. John knew, by morning, the tales would be even more colorful.

But for now, he was going to have to decide how to get the monkey from beneath the bandstand and figure out what to do with him when he did. Leaning back on the step, he watched those with flashlights shine them through the latticework.

Mayor Driscol, a look of wonder on his face, stood in front of the bandstand where the Sheriff was sitting and let his eyes roam around the square, finally coming to rest on those peeking through the lattice work. Hooking his thumbs in his suspenders, he looked at Sheriff Walker with a look of total disbelief. "I declare, who would have ever thought. . . ." He shook his head, opened his mouth to say something then closed it again. Looking up at the night sky, he sighed and then commented, "I'm going home and going to bed. I'll see you in the morning."

John watched him walk across the square and decided that would be the best thing for everyone. "Listen up," he called, standing up. "Look at me. This chimp needs to calm down before we attempt to get him out. All of you go back to the middle of the square." He looked at Jim who was already motioning and urging the boys to head back.

"Okay." John ran his fingers through his hair and looked down at Jordan and Zachary. "Is there any fruit left in the basket or has it all been trampled? Go see what you can find."

Willy looked at him. "I think I'll stay right here. After what he's put us through, I don't want him to escape."

John shook his head and smiled. "Then I'll go with the boys and quiet them down. Jim, if you and Willy will stay here and make sure he doesn't get out, I'm going to encourage the rest to go on home."

"What are you going to do now, Sheriff?" Mrs. Cranston asked, pulling her robe close around her. She adjusted the hair net over her white curls and stared at the loosened latticework. "Land sakes, I can't believe a monkey caused all this confusion. What are you going to do with him?"

"We'll get him out one way or the other." John replied, walking along with the Cranstons and Old Ben across the square. The other men, talking and laughing, headed back to their cars.

"I guess you know what kind of tales will be circulating around town by morning, don't you?" Pastor Mike laughed, falling into step with them.

"Oh they will be quite colorful, I'm sure." John replied.

"I would offer to take some of the boys home, but I don't think you could tear them away from here tonight," Mike commented.

Sorting through quilts and pillows, the boys were still laughing and chattering excitedly, and Mike knew this was one night none of them would ever forget. "I guess I'll head home too. You were right, John. You did a good job."

"Thanks, Pastor. I'll see you tomorrow." John sat on one of the quilts and watched him leave, thankful the mystery was solved.

"Here, Dad. Here are a couple of bananas that were not smashed," Jordan said, sitting on the quilt next to his father. "That's all I could find."

"I found this half eaten apple and a smashed Moon Pie," Zachary commented, holding them out to Sheriff."

"That's fine, boys. That should do it." John glanced around, leaned back on his elbows, and gave a sigh, "Now all we need is an animal trainer," he murmured, gazing up at the stars. He was suddenly very tired.

"What about Jimmy?" Josiah asked. "He's really good with animals."

"Yes, Dad, he really is," Brenton commented as he and Johnny walked up behind him. "Animals, for some reason aren't afraid of Jimmy. When we are out at the Seabaughs, they all come to him."

"Remember the day he came out of the barn carrying that little chick?" Johnny asked, looking at Brenton. He laughed and spoke to the Sheriff, "He was carrying a little chick in his hands, another one on his shoulder, and one was sitting on the top of his head."

John looked curiously at the boys and sat quietly thinking. "Where is Jimmy?" he asked, glancing around in the dark.

"That might be him over at the bandstand talking to Willy," David answered, pointing to a small figure about Jimmy's size. The street lamp on the corner cast just enough light to outline the two. David sat down on the blanket with his guitar clutched tightly in his hands, relieved that it had not been stepped on. In fact, he was thinking it was a miracle someone had not trampled it with everyone running in all directions.

"Jimmy would be just about the right size to squeeze through the lattice work," Brenton said.

"Let me think a minute," John said, standing up. "I'll be right back. You boys try to stay quiet for a while so we don't scare this chimp any more than he already is." Walking toward the bandstand carrying the two bananas, a smashed Moon Pie, and a half-eaten apple, John wondered if tonight could get any crazier.

"What do you think, brother?" Jim asked at his approach. "Willy and I were just thinking that if we could get him out, Willy has a cage we could put him in."

"It's plenty big. Uncle William used it to keep pups in. Aunt Lydia didn't want them running loose in the house, and she didn't have the heart to leave them out in the cold so he bought it somewhere." Willy glanced at the Sheriff. "I can walk over to the house and get it if you want. It's sitting right there in the garage."

"That sounds good. I would appreciate it, if you don't mind to fetch it, Willy." He looked down at Pastor Mike's youngest son, sitting on the ground next to the bandstand.

"No, I don't mind. It is no problem. I'll go get it now," Willy said and strode off across the square.

"I understand you like animals," Sheriff Walker said, kneeling on his right leg with his left elbow resting on the other as he looked at Jimmy. "Is that correct?"

"Yes, I do," Jimmy answered. "Dad says I have a way with them." He looked up into the Sheriff's face. "I don't know why. They just like me."

John glanced at Jim, "Well then, Jimmy, would you want to give this banana to him?" John wondered if he should do this or not. What if the monkey went crazy or something?

"First, let me look under the bandstand with my flashlight and see what he's doing, and then I'll let you give him the banana."

"Swell, I can do that," Jimmy answered, taking the banana the Sheriff handed him.

John looked at his brother's questioning face. "I figure if we can get this monkey to trust one of us he may just come out a little easier than if we tried to drag him out." John glanced at Jimmy again. "All the boys say Jimmy has a way with animals so I thought we might just let him give it a try."

John dropped to his hands and knees with his flashlight. Pulling the loose trellis back, he turned the light on, shining it around. "Where in the world . . . ? Good grief! You should see the stuff he has stashed away in here, "John remarked chuckling. "There is no doubt now who our thief is. Oh, there you are," he said as the light fell on the chimp, sitting quietly against the wall staring at him.

"I can do it. There's no problem," Jimmy said almost pleadingly as he crawled on his hands and knees next to the Sheriff.

"All right then, come on. Have a look," John said, allowing him enough room to crawl next to him and peek inside. "Hi, monkey," Jimmy said in a quiet voice "Are you scared?"

The animal turned his head and looked the other way, ignoring him. "That's okay, here is a banana. I bet you're hungry." Jimmy spoke quietly while he peeled the banana and held it out to him. Looking at it for a minute, the chimp glanced back at Jimmy then turned his head in a sulking manner.

Tossing it gently toward him, Jimmy said coaxingly, "You eat that, and I'll give you some more."

Backing out away from the loose trellis, Jimmy looked up at the Sheriff. "I bet he's thirsty too. We need to get him some water."

"I have the cup from my thermos. Let me fill it at the water fountain," Jim said, walking up the steps. He brought the thermos of coffee to help him stay awake and now thought what a foolish notion that had been What ever made him think it would be a quiet enough night that one could fall asleep. Now where was it? It was right next to his chair when everything broke loose. Glancing around in the dark, he saw its dark shape across the floor.

Jimmy sat on the ground with his back up against the loosened latticework. "He got it," he said, smiling in the dark at the Sheriff.

"How do you know?" John asked, wishing Willy would hurry up with the cage. Jimmy sat with his ear against the lattice, listening.

"I heard him move, and then he smacked his lips." Jimmy grinned again. "I wonder what his name is and where he came from?"

"His name is Jasper, and he belongs to the American Circus Company," John replied, reaching for the flier in his pocket.

"How do you know that?" Jimmy asked as he took the piece of folded paper and looked at it. Shining his flashlight, Sheriff Walker motioned for him to read it. Jimmy unfolded the flier and looked at it. The name Jasper was written above the picture of a monkey with information listed below:

Missing Chimp
Last seen in the Chesterville area
$500 REWARD
Please contact Cletus Morton
American Circus Company
Yellowstone 8–4222

Jimmy glanced up at the sheriff. "So this is Jasper?" he asked. "How could they just forget him?"

Sheriff Walker sat next to him on the quilt. "I don't know, Jimmy. I guess he just got away and no one was aware of it. I don't even know why they thought it was Chesterville instead of Oak Grove. I guess when we return Jasper we'll find the answers to our questions."

Jimmy handed the flyer back to him, crawled back through the loosened piece of lattice and flashed the light around. "Hey, Jasper. I see you ate the banana. Do you want some more?" Jimmy held the second half of the banana out to him and watched as he stared at it, then turned his face away again.

"That's okay. I'll lay it right here for you. I guess you are pretty mad because they forgot you, huh? Well, we will call Mr. Morton to come and get you."

At the mention of Mr. Morton, the chimp looked at him. "I'll be back," Jimmy told Jasper and backed out of the bandstand, pushing the lattice back in place.

"Here it is," Willy said, placing the big, square cage he carried on the ground. "This should be plenty big for him for a day or two."

"Willy, do you know his name is Jasper?" Jimmy asked as he stood up and examined the cage. "He probably won't like that."

"Yes, I know his name is Jasper. Sheriff Walker showed me the flier this afternoon," he answered, checking the door of the cage to make sure it worked properly. "We are going to have to figure out how we can get Jasper in this thing without him running off."

"That won't be hard," Jimmy answered as he sat down next to the loose lattice again. "Jasper, are you okay?" he asked, listening intently.

"How about a cup of water for Jasper," Jim said, returning from the drinking fountain. Glancing at John and Willy he asked, "How's it going?"

He handed the cup of water to Jimmy and watched as he loosened the lattice and crawled back in.

"He's doing really well," John answered. "This is the third time he's gone under, and he's had no problem with the chimp. This time Jimmy scooted far enough beneath the bandstand that only his feet remained visible.

"Come on, Jasper, I know you are thirsty." Scooting the rest of the way in, he sat against the side of the latticework and held the cup of water out to him. Sitting the flashlight on the ground with the beam shining upward, it allowed just enough light so the two could see each other. The chimp stared at him and then glanced at the cup of water Jimmy placed on the ground. He slowly walked over to the cup, picked it up, and carried it back to his side of the bandstand. Looking at Jimmy for a minute, he lifted the cup, drank all of the water, and rolled the cup across the ground to him.

"Are you all right?" Sheriff Walker asked quietly, not wanting to scare the chimp and wondered how long this was going to take.

"I'm okay, but we need more food. I'm hungry too," Jimmy said through the lattice. "Can you get us something to eat?"

The familiar chimes at City Hall marked five o'clock. The last couple of hours had been quiet, and Jimmy remained under the bandstand with Jasper.

John, Jim, Ben, Eli, and Willy sat on the ground talking quietly amongst themselves. Worn out, the rest of the boys had fallen asleep; the night cradling them in slumber.

The gray of the eastern sky was just turning to a light shade of pink, and waking birds chirped and flitted from tree to tree.

"The preacher was right on top of things with his sermon last week, wasn't he?" Ben commented quietly, more to himself than the others.

John moved a little, trying to get some feeling back in his left leg. "He sure was. There was no doubt in his mind that the thief wasn't anyone in town. Did you notice that?"

"I did," Jim answered. "He was positive about it too."

Ben watched pink and yellow streaks spread across the sky and thought about the conversation he had with his uncle a couple of days ago. "He told Uncle Ben that he had prepared another sermon, and God told him to change it. Isn't that something; to be so in tune with God the way he is?" Not saying anything for he moment, he then commented quietly, "I want to be more like that."

"I guess we all do," Eli murmured, rubbing his eyes and yawning.

The men sat quietly for a few minutes, watching daylight chase the night away. John spoke softly, "I feel close to God a lot, but Pastor Mike is. . . . well, you can see God reflected in him."

"Wouldn't the world be a better place if we were all like that?" Jim asked wonderingly. "I wonder why we aren't? "

"He told me one time that when God called him to preach, he didn't feel worthy or have enough confidence to answer the call," Eli commented, as he recalled their conversation. "He said the Lord dealt with him for several months before he realized God didn't call him to do it on his own. All he had to do was trust and follow Him, and he said once that truth was established in his mind and heart, his life has never been the same."

No one said anything for a few seconds then John said softly, "He's a fine Pastor. He really cares about us."

"He cares about everyone," Ben replied, then chuckled. "Remember the time he locked himself up in jail with Cooley?"

Jim laughed and stretched his legs out. "I don't know of another Pastor that would do something like that. It did some good too. Cooley attends pretty regular now, doesn't he?"

"He sure does, and I don't think he touches the stuff anymore either." Eli answered, looking across the square at the boys scattered at random as they slept peacefully on the ground.

Willy sat quietly, listening to the men talk and pondered on the idea of how one heard God speak. He watched the sun rise above the trees and thought about a supreme being up there somewhere; but where was He, who was He, and how did one get to know Him?

Willy's thoughts drifted from Pastor Mike to Old Ben, Mercy, his Uncle William, and Melba. They all had something that Willy couldn't quite put his finger on; something that eluded him for one reason or another. What was it?

The thought of Melba lingered in his mind. She was so pretty. Willy smiled to himself as he thought of the night at the circus when she turned her ankle. *She felt so fragile, but she's not*, Willy thought. Melba has an inner strength. It is reflected in her eyes; in her whole being. *Where does that come from*? he wondered.

"I think I'll check on those two," John whispered as he stooped down and peered through one of the holes in the lattice. Smiling to himself, he thought of what the boys told him and how true it was. Jimmy does have a way with animals. He was sound asleep, lying half on his side against the latticework. Jasper, deciding sometime in the last couple of hours that Jimmy was a friend, had moved closer to him and also slept.

That picture would be worth a thousand words, John thought as he turned the flashlight off and sat next to Ben. "They are both asleep," he chuckled. "Like a couple of old buddies."

Willy, still holding the collar and leash he grabbed from the garage, handed it to John. "If you think he can get this around his neck, we won't have to worry about losing him while we move him to the cage."

"I don't know. I guess it is worth a try. Jimmy said he wouldn't like the cage," John remarked as he looked at the collar and leash. "He's going to have to use it, though, until Mr. Morton comes for him."

By six o'clock the sun had climbed into the sky, and most of the boys were stirring around, making their way back over to the bandstand. Pastor Mike, arriving at the square, parked his car and stepped out just as Melvin drove slowly by in his white milk truck and parked in front of the Cranston Cafe. The familiar red circle with the words, *Dairy Fresh Milk*, shone brightly in the morning sun, and Mike waved at him as he slid the door open and stepped out. Wearing his usual dark, blue shirt and trousers, he straightened his cap, grabbed two trays of milk and headed to the Café with his delivery. Mike knew he would head for Reese's Market next then make his way down Pine Street and finish his deliveries for the day.

"Hey, Dad." Johnny called as he noticed his dad standing next to the car.

Mike waved back and headed across the square, noting the exhausted men sitting on the ground by the bandstand. Smiling to himself, he felt a stirring of compassion, knowing none of them would be worth a whole lot for the next couple of days.

"You'll never guess what happened!" Johnny exclaimed, joined by several other boys who began relating their version of the tale all at the same time.

Pastor Mike chuckled as he sorted through the information he was able to glean from the excited voices. The animal imprisoned beneath the bandstand was either a six-foot monster or a small chimp, he found it questionable that Sheriff Walker fell out of the bell tower, and he was amazed that there was a million-dollar reward for the animal.

From the precise description of the peril they were in, he did find it believable that Zachary, Josiah, and Simon actually were caught in a net, and he listened and laughed as they excitedly retold the whole incident.

"It sounds to me like you had quite an exciting night. I am proud of you guys. You captured the thief," he commented, looking around the crowd. "Johnny, where is your brother?" he asked as his eyes roamed the square.

"Oh, he's underneath the bandstand with Jasper," Jordan announced. "He's been there all night."

Pastor Mike looked across the square and laughed again. John, Jim, Willy, Eli, and Ben still sat on the ground under the oak tree looking like they had no plans to get up anytime soon.

"What's the matter, can't you fellows take it any more?" he laughed as he walked up to them. "I understand you have my youngest son locked up with a wild animal."

Rising slowly to their feet and grinning tiredly, the men stretched and moved around. Willy absent-mindedly rubbed his injured leg and yawned. "He at least got some sleep," he said tiredly.

"I've never seen anything like it. That boy does have a way with animals, doesn't he?" Jim commented, checking his thermos "Man, I would like a fresh cup of coffee."

"Hey, Dad, is that you?" Jimmy called from beneath the bandstand.

"Yes, Son It's me. Are you okay?" Mike asked. Picking up the collar and leash lying on the ground, he looked at it and told him, "I think you probably ought to try putting this on him if he will let you." Pulling the corner of the lattice back, he handed it to him, noting the big smudge of dirt on his cheek and imagined how dirty he must be.

"Okay, just a minute."

Mike rested on one knee, waiting for his son to emerge, while the rest of the men and boys gathered in anticipation of seeing Jasper for the first time in the daylight.

Slowly the lattice moved outward, and Mike stepped back. For a few minutes nothing happened and everyone crowded together, staring at the opening. Jimmy's dark head appeared and he looked up and grinned.

"Hi guys," he said as he crawled through the opening of the loose lattice. "I want you to meet my friend, Jasper." Grinning broadly, he stood up and tugged on the leash. Out from beneath the bandstand Jasper emerged, not looking nearly as frightening as he had in the dark. Sitting quietly next to Jimmy, he looked around at those gathered then glanced back up at him.

"It's okay, we're all your friends," Jimmy said, looking at him. Much to everyone's astonishment Jasper reached up, took Jimmy's hand, then put forth his best grin and shook his head. Laughter and cheering erupted, and the boys dropped down on the grass to pet and get a better look at him.

A familiar voice called from across the square. "Is anyone hungry?" All eyes turned to Mercy, waving from the door of the Cranston Café. "Breakfast is ready and Mr. Cranston said it is on him today."

"That sounds good," Jim Walker commented. "Come on, boys, I've worked up an appetite; how about you?" Several took off for the café, whooping and hollering, while others tarried to get a closer look at Jasper.

"I don't know about you, but a nice hot cup of coffee would sure hit the spot for me," Willy said. Tousling Jimmy's hair, he smiled and looked at the small culprit that had been the cause of all the confusion in town. "Way to go Jimmy! You did a great job with Jasper."

"Thanks, Willy. Sheriff, you better look under the bandstand. Jasper has collected a bunch of stuff." Jimmy looked at his dad, his dark eyes innocently defending the chimp. "He didn't really steal anything. He was playing and didn't realize what he was doing."

"That's okay," Sheriff Walker replied. "I saw it last night. We'll gather everything up and return it to the owners."

Ben grinned at Jimmy. "You sure know how to handle animals. I think you might turn out to be quite a veterinarian one of these days."

Jimmy wrinkled his nose and replied, "I don't think so; I don't like them and I only eat vegetables because Mom makes me."

A burst of laughter filled the air and Jimmy looked questioningly at his dad. "You're thinking of vegetarian, son." Pastor Mike laughed as he hugged his son close to him. "A veterinarian is an animal doctor."

"Well then, that wouldn't be so bad," Jimmy commented, looking down at Jasper then at the cage. "Can he come with us?"

"I don't see why not," Sheriff Walker answered. "After all, he's the reason we are getting a free breakfast. Come on, let's go eat."

The men walked across the square, allowing the rest of the boys and Jimmy and Jasper to lead the way.

Inside, the café was a hub of activity, noise, chatter, and laughter. Louise and Mercy were both placing platters of eggs, bacon, ham, biscuits, and pancakes on the tables. The tale of last night's escapade was getting longer and more colorful with each telling, and soon the café was a den of excitement and laughter as Jasper was given a seat in one of the booths next to the window. Once again in the spotlight, he entertained the customers with some of his best chattering and misbehavior.

The merchants, opening their shops early, gathered in the café to see the now famous Jasper. Much laughter and joking accompanied the tales of last night's escapade all to the tune of "Shoo Fly Pie and Apple Pan Dowdy" that blared from the jukebox.

Jim Walker made himself at home behind the counter and poured several cups of coffee, pushing one toward Old Ben and Pastor Mike.

"Thank you," Mike said loudly over the noise "Do they pay you more here than at the firehouse, Jim?" he laughed, noting the white linen towel tucked into the front of his belt.

Jim sat the cream and sugar on the counter and glanced around the café at all of the commotion. "They couldn't pay me enough to have this job."

Mercy made a quick dash around one of the tables, heading for the kitchen. "Jim, the boys need milk. Get it for them, and Pastor Mike, you grab the syrup and butter for the pancakes please," she called over her shoulder as she disappeared through the kitchen door.

Jim looked at the swinging door then back at Pastor Mike. "I guess we are both hired." Pushing the lid of the cooler aside, he loaded his arms with milk cartons and stacked them on trays Mike found beneath the counter. Grabbing one for himself, Mike loaded it with butter and syrup and headed to the tables.

"Over here, Dad," Johnny called, waving at him from across the room.

"Mr. Walker, I need some milk," Jake yelled waving both arms. "Some syrup too."

Making his way from table to table, Mike was reminded of the chickens he use to feed when he was a boy. They would cluck, flap their wings, peck at one another, and run around in circles until he scattered the chicken feed.

He grinned as he watched the boys reach for syrup, toss biscuits across the table, chatter with their mouth full and poke one another while they stabbed a whole pancake and ate it from the end of their fork. *Their mothers would be proud*, Mike though with a chuckle. Every table manner known to a mother was being ignored, and no one cared in the least.

Outside, the now empty square was quiet, and last night's adventure was told only by the evidence left behind—blankets and pillows still lay strewn about, and shoes, socks, and various articles of clothing were scattered everywhere on the grass. Discarded flashlights lay where they were dropped, and the bushel basket that held fruit and snacks was turned on its side, empty of its contents. The lattice on the bandstand that had been Jasper's hiding place for the last several days hung loose, telling a story in itself. Sunshine and blue sky had replaced the night, and a gentle breeze stirred the fragrance of honeysuckle. The fountain bubbled up, spraying a mist in the fresh morning breeze, birds sang cheerily in the tree branches, and the clock at City Hall chimed the 7:00 o'clock hour, heralding the beginning of a new day. The mystery of the last few days was solved, and the sleepy little town of Oak Grove had written another chapter in the hearts and minds of those who would one day look back and remember that summer so long ago.

EPILOGUE

Fourth of July was one of Miss Mattie's favorite holidays. It had been her custom for the last twenty years to invite all of Oak Grove to her home, and this year was no different. The fact that the mystery involving Jasper was solved only added to the excitement of the day. Sitting in a wicker chair on her front porch, her eyes sparkled with tears of joy, and a deep contentment filled her soul. Pastor Mike and Leah sat on the wicker love seat to her right, and Old Ben rocked in companionable silence on her left next to Reverend and Mrs. Clark. Good friends and neighbors rested comfortably on blankets, benches, and wooden folding chairs scattered on the porch and across the lawn.

Today commenced early with Hannah in the kitchen throwing orders to Jeremiah and hurrying him along. She was quickly wearing a path from the back porch to the kitchen as she ran back and forth double-checking everything he did.

Stomping through the kitchen with a scowl on his face, he shook his head and muttered to himself as he passed Miss Mattie. She sat at the kitchen table calmly drinking a cup of tea, amused at the two, as she watched Hannah flit back and forth and Jeremiah getting more exasperated by the minute.

It was the same every 4th of July. Hannah always got herself worked up trying to get things ready way too early, in spite of the fact that several of the townsfolk always came out in plenty of time to help with the preparations. Up at daylight, she hauled Jeremiah out of bed, fixed breakfast, and sent him out to take care of the horses early so he could get back and help her.

Mattie suspected Jeremiah took the opportunity to collect his thoughts because he always carried a big mug of coffee and headed in the direction of the creek rather than the barn.

"We've been doin' this how many years, Miss Mattie. Don't you think by now she would get the idea that I know what I'm suppose to do?" he grumbled, coming back into the kitchen. "The ice cream freezer! She doesn't even have the recipe made up yet, and you would think she's ready to crank the handle."

"Just go and get it, Jeremiah, and be done with it. Think how good the ice cream will taste later today." Mattie chuckled as she watched him jerk open the large pantry door and disappear inside, muttering to himself.

Years ago, at her insistence, Daniel built the pantry to accommodate everything needed in the kitchen and dining room. One could walk into it and find anything within arm's reach, thanks to Hannah's organizational skills.

Jeremiah emerged from the pantry with two wooden ice cream freezers in his arms "Yes, ma'am, it sure is worth the fuss. I don't think anyone has a better recipe than Hannah does. But blame it all, if she can't find my last nerve sometime and step all over it." Setting them on the table, he opened his mouth to say something, closed it, and sat down across from her.

"Jeremiah, have a cup of tea with me," Miss Mattie said in a calm voice, reaching for the teapot.

"I'll be dogged; I believe I just will," he remarked with a hint of rebellion in his voice. "First let me get the rock salt. I just as well, before she starts fussin' about that." Shaking his head again, he rose and disappeared into the pantry.

By eight o'clock, Cooley arrived, greeted Miss Mattie, and chased Jeremiah down. Never attending the celebration for years, he had a change of heart after the episode when he and *the Preacher* found themselves locked up in jail together. Besides, now that Alice was the *official church cleaning lady*, he felt it his responsibility to contribute to the 4th of July celebration.

Somewhere along the line, Cooley assigned himself the task of getting the food tables assembled. Taking the job very seriously, he showed up at 8:00 on the dot. By 8:30 he was in the barn pulling the required number of saw horses out on the lawn, heeding Hannah's orders of where to place them. Assuring her he remembered from last year, he would suggest *she go on back to what she was doin' and let him worry about it.* Jeremiah found it best to stay out of the line of fire while Miss Mattie watched in amusement as Cooley carried the boards down from the loft, cleaned them up, and placed them across the saw horses, ignoring Hannah's continuous checking that he was doing it to her satisfaction.

Cooley and Hannah had argued that first year he showed up to help and every year thereafter. He insisted the boards be nailed to the saw horses, and Hannah, just as insistent, said it wasn't necessary and there was no time for it.

"A fine 4th of July this will turn out to be when one of them younguns runs by and dumps all the food on the ground," he had argued, leaning deliberately on one of the boards, causing it to fall on the ground.

Hannah, wishing she had a rolling pin in her hand to use against the side of his head, gave in, fearing this just might be the year something like that would happen, and she would never hear the end of it.

Not wanting to admit he could possibly be right, she glared at him. "You did that on purpose, Cooley I said there's no need for it, but I'm not in the mood to listen to your babblin,' so you just go right on and do what you want," she had retorted, leaving him with a satisfied smile on his face.

From that day on, they had a mutual respect for one another. Cooley was aware that Hannah relented when she didn't have to, and Hannah, grudgingly had to admit he was one of the few people that ever talked her into changing her mind about anything.

Hannah now stood on the porch, satisfied with the tables, and watched Cooley drive off down the lane on his way home to get Alice and the children. Others were arriving to help, and Miss Mattie joined her on the porch to greet them.

Laughing and anticipating the day's event, the folks made their way into the house, ready to get things underway. Freshly laundered tablecloths were spread over the makeshift tables, and plates, cups, silverware, and glasses were carried out. Men carried washtubs from the basement to the shade of the oak trees, and others toted fat, oblong watermelons and placed them in tubs of ice.

Ginger and Peaches, saddled earlier by Jeremiah, were in the near pasture in readiness for the children. Horseshoe stakes were hammered into the ground, the crochet set placed on the west lawn, and the badminton net strung on the east lawn.

Friends and neighbors began arriving about noon and, as usual, parked in the west pasture. Children raced for Ginger and Peaches, and men helped their wives carry bowls of every kind of vegetable, desert, and meat one could imagine.

Tall cakes, cookies, and warm pies were given extra care and placed on the desert table with Elizabeth Seabaugh's popular, huge, blackberry cobbler sitting in the center. Pitchers of iced tea and wooden ice cream freezers, covered with newspapers and kitchen towels, containing every flavor imaginable were carried into the kitchen.

Heaping platters of golden fried chicken sat on the meat table along with sliced hickory-smoked ham, carved roast beef, chicken and dumplings, and barbecue ribs. Pots of green beans and new potatoes, baked beans, mashed potatoes, corn on the cob, and fresh peas were placed with the other vegetables.

Another table held a variety of slaws, potato salads, fresh sliced tomatoes, cucumbers and onions, pickled beets, relishes, and Jell-O salads that would make anyone's mouth water.

Loaves of homemade bread, biscuits, corn bread, and rolls sat on a smaller table with the plates and flatware.

The sound of ringing horseshoes against iron pegs soon filled the air, and children's laughter drifted from the near pasture and while they chased one another around the yard. The buzz of friendly laughter and chatter filled the house, spilling out onto the porch and lawn.

The younger folks, involved in a lively game of badminton, teased Terry Charles unmercifully about her lack of coordination. David Reese's eager instruction on the proper way to hold the racquet didn't do much to help the game, but it did increase Terry's interest in the sport a great deal and caused a lot of giggling and whispering.

The mallet striking the crochet ball came to one's ear, accompanied by an ongoing, albeit, good-natured argument. Mercy, Melba, and Lizzie were taking the brunt of ridicule as Saul, Willy, and Ben taunted them as to their questionable talent for hitting the ball in the right direction.

Everywhere one listened, the tale of Jasper was told and laughed about. Caroline Driscol proudly wore her bracelet. "It is just beautiful," she said, showing it to Miss Mattie. "Laura Daniels gave it to me as a birthday gift, and I was so upset when it turned up missing. Jasper took it," she said laughing. "Aunt Trudy cleaned it for me. See how pretty it looks. I just love it."

By four o'clock, excited shouts and cheering were heard from the far field as the blue and red softball teams found themselves tied six to six in an all out battle for the 4th of July championship. Pastor Mike and Leah sat with several other parents and younger children in the shade of the oak trees, watching the game in amusement. The rivalry increased with each inning and finally culminated in a seven to six victory for the blue team when Johnny hit a home run over the fence.

Sheriff and Anne Walker were sitting on the porch visiting with Grandma Hope and Mrs. Seabaugh when Jim appeared at the front screen. "Hey, John, grab Willy and Ben. You won't believe the fireworks this year. Let's go ahead and bring them up out of the basement."

Miss Mattie always provided an over abundance of fireworks, ordered at random from a catalogue, and never knew what she was getting. "I just order what sounds interesting or pretty," she commented one year after an explosion shook the windows in the house and almost deafened everyone present. Since then, they found it wise to check the fireworks ahead of time so they would know what they were dealing with. Miss Mattie insisted they shoot all of them for fear of burning the house down if she had to store them, thus providing a fireworks display that was a sight to behold.

The sun dipped below the distant ridge and dusk crept across the hills. Miss Mattie listened to the excitement in the children's voices and watched them find places on quilts spread out on the front lawn.

Sheriff Walker, Jim, Willy, and Ben carried the fireworks away from the house down close to the road. Empty bowls and platters, washed and dried, were carried to the cars, and Ginger and Peaches were free of their saddles. The sack races, horseshoe tournament, and washer games were over, and the badminton and crochet sets were put away.

Finally, the highlight that everyone, young and old, waited for was at hand. Anticipation shone on each face as dusk faded into night.

Mike and Ellen sat on the east end of the porch with Alan, Lynn, and their parents. "Did you notice Willy and Melba came together today?" Lynn asked Ellen, looking pleased.

"Yes, I did," Ellen glanced around looking for a glimpse of the two that appeared to have thoroughly enjoyed one another's company all day. "Wouldn't that be wonderful if something developed between them." Ellen remarked, grinning at Lynn and her mother.

"They certainly make a handsome couple." Margaret Miller smiled in agreement then noted her husband's grinning face. "What are you smiling at?"

"If it was up to you three, you would have them married off in a week."

Alan laughed and looked at Michael. "What are you going to wear to the wedding?"

"Oh, I definitely have to get something new. I simply don't have a thing to wear." Michael looked sideways at Ellen and laughed.

Trudy Driscol's voice carried across the porch. "Mr. Morton was so pleased to get Jasper back. And he was good on his word. The city council thought the $500 reward should be used for the school. Not for the building of course, but for children that perhaps might need some assistance with their education." She wiped her forehead with her handkerchief and continued, "I think it is a splendid idea, if I have to say so myself. Henry asked what I thought about it, and I assured him that I thought it was an excellent idea. You know that not all children are as fortunate as others are. Why, I remember one year, about six years or so ago, I can't say for sure, but there was a child that I will not name, that really did need some things and several of the good people in Oak Grove took it upon themselves to . . ."

A loud boom ended Trudy's conversation as a myriad of stars filled the sky. Melba sat on the swing at the far end of the porch waiting for Willy to join her. She had been pleasantly surprised Sunday afternoon when he and Jack walked by her house. Inviting him in, they spent the afternoon listening to the Cardinals/Pirates game and then went for a walk on the square. On returning home, Melba asked him to stay for cake and coffee, and they shared an enjoyable evening laughing and talking. Willy seemed eager to learn all about her life, but to Melba's disappointment was not as willing to share much of his.

She walked with him to the edge of the porch as he was leaving and watched him walk down the steps. Willy paused and turned around. Looking at her intently for a long moment, he didn't say a word, and Melba was aware of her rapid pulse. For heaven's sake, he was doing nothing but looking at her. He stood with his hands in his pockets and she watched a slow smile touch his lips. Casually placing one foot on the bottom step, he asked if she would care to accompany him to Miss Mattie's on the Fourth of July.

She now watched him walk up the lawn towards the house. He wore a pair of khaki trousers and a blue shirt that turned his eyes such a striking color that she found herself staring at them when he arrived to pick her up. She again was astonished that she had lived in Oak Grove all this time and never realized how handsome he was. Leaning around to open the car door, she caught a scent of his cologne, and though she was not familiar with it, she thought it suited him well. Melba was acutely aware of his nearness in the car and realized she was like a schoolgirl on her first date. Out of sheer nervousness, she started laughing and wondered what in the world was coming over her.

He glanced at her in surprise. "What's so funny?" he asked with a grin on his face.

A dark curl fell on his forehead and she had an impulse to brush it back, but she just looked at him and laughed again. "Willy, I am so nervous, and I don't know why."

He grinned and glanced at her hand lying between them on the seat. Reaching over, he covered it with his and chuckled, "I guess that makes two of us. I thought you would tell me you were going with Mercy today." He put his hand back on the steering wheel and they both laughed.

The fireworks display was about to begin and the children presently were happily waving sparklers in the air. Melba smiled as she noticed Caroline Driscol and Peter

Williams sitting on a quilt holding hands while Terry Charles and David Reese sat on the quilt next to them.

Willy walked passed those on the porch, paused to say something to Pastor Mike and then made his way to the porch swing. Smiling at her, he sat down and slid his arm along the back of the swing. Melba was conscious of his hand resting lightly on her shoulder and a warm feeling spread through her.

"I guess that loud boom was the signal that the display is about to begin?" she inquired as she looked up at him, catching the scent of his cologne again.

"It was. You won't believe all the fireworks Miss Mattie has provided. It will take close to an hour to shoot them all." Willy stretched his legs out in front of him in a manner that Melba already recognized as a resting position, and she wondered if it was because of his injured leg.

"Good, I love fireworks," she answered as a shower of stars filled the sky. The night sky soon became a panorama of color and noise, much to the delight of everyone. Rockets climbed into the night sky, fountains lit up the lawn, and loud whining noises rose in the sky and burst into a kaleidoscope of color. All eyes were turned to the sky while everyone relaxed in chairs, and many lay back on their quilts, watching in awe and wonder.

Another loud whistling noise permeated the air as a rocket rose high into the air and exploded into red, white, and blue stars that rained down like a summer shower. "Oh, how beautiful," Melba whispered. She turned and looked at Willy, realizing he had been staring at her. Her heart beat rapidly, and for a long moment they gazed into each other's eyes, aware of something new and different in each other. Willy's gaze fell to her lips, and Melba felt the pressure of his hand on her shoulder, pulling her to him. He glanced up into her eyes again, and a terrific explosion rent the skies. Startled, Melba jerked in surprise, laid her hand on his chest, and stared up into the sky with wide eyes. She looked back at him, noting her hand still resting on his chest and withdrew it. Willy, grinned at her, captured her hand, and didn't turn it loose. Without a second thought, Melba very comfortably laid her head on his shoulder and enjoyed the warm hug and chuckle that came from deep in his chest. As far as Willy was concerned, he could think of no other place he would rather be than where he was at the present time.

Pastor Mike leaned over to speak to Leah when his gaze rested on the two nestled comfortably on the porch swing. Leah glanced up into her husband's smiling face and her eyes followed the direction of his gaze. She smiled at him, "Maybe you could let Willy give you a few lessons," she taunted.

Pastor Mike slipped his arm around Leah and kissed her on the temple. "Whatever you say, wife, whatever you say."

"I believe this is the best fireworks display we've ever had," Old Ben commented as he watched another explosion light up the sky.

"Ben, you say that every Fourth of July," Mattie laughed, looking at her old friend, "and we've seen quite a few."

"Yes, we sure have, but I don't say that every year. Do I?" Old Ben questioned, looking at her in surprise.

"I reckon you do, Ben," Hannah replied, overhearing their conversation. "Every year, as long as I can remember, you say, *this is the best fireworks display we've ever had.*"

"You don't say. Well, I declare; this year they really do seem prettier," he commented more to himself than to anyone. He didn't remember saying that every year.

Miss Mattie laughed as she patted his old hand resting lightly on the arm of his chair. He had been such a dear friend all these years. "We are just old, Ben. Everything looks prettier to us."

"I don't know if I can agree with that. I looked in the mirror this mornin,'" he said seriously and then chuckled as he glanced at Miss Mattie. "I think the fireworks somehow just seem more special this summer," he said as he watched the night sky light up again.

Mattie sat lost in thought, her head resting on the back of her chair. The hot July air had cooled, and the fragrance of honeysuckle mingled with sulfur from the fireworks drifted back and forth on the night air. Soft voices murmuring in the dark, and the laughter and squeals of delight reached her ears. The night sky again burst forth in color and lit up the lawn, revealing familiar and dear faces turned to the sky. How she loved these people and this time in her life. This summer brought something different to their town, tested their faith in one another, and left them with a special memory. "Maybe you are right, my old friend," she said looking at Ben. "Everything about this summer has been special."

Old Ben looked around, his eyes scanning the ridges painted black against the night sky. The full moon created dancing patterns on the grass as the breeze rustled the leaves on the trees, and the near pasture, bright in the moonlight, spread away over the hill. His gaze shifted to Willy and Melba, and a smile spread across his face. He glanced around looking for Mercy and found her sitting on the edge of the porch with Saul who had his arm around her shoulder. Ben arrived with Lizzie, and they were sitting on a blanket with several small children. He smiled to himself as he looked again at the night sky. He could see God's hand at work and felt as though Carrie was smiling at him.

"Yes," Old Ben replied very softly, "it has been special You know, Miss Mattie, I think this will be a summer we will remember—a summer we will long remember."

July 4, 1946

Tate Publishing & *Enterprises*

Tate Publishing is committed to excellence in the publishing industry. Our staff of highly trained professionals, including editors, graphic designers, and marketing personnel, work together to produce the very finest books available. The company reflects the philosophy established by the founders, based on Psalms 68:11,

"THE LORD GAVE THE WORD AND GREAT WAS THE COMPANY OF THOSE WHO PUBLISHED IT."

If you would like further information, please call
1.888.361.9473
or visit our website
www.tatepublishing.com

Tate Publishing & *Enterprises*, LLC
127 E. Trade Center Terrace
Mustang, Oklahoma 73064 USA